I0769260

The *Sisterhood* of *Whispers*

By
Grace Siplon St. Lawrence

Inkling Books

Book cover by Lucy Kagan. Illustrations by Grace Siplon St. Lawrence. Editing and formatting by Heather Ryder.

Inkling Books, LLC
Raleigh, North Carolina
www.inklingbookspublishing.com

Ordering Information:
For details, visit www.greenveilvolumes.org.

Print ISBN: 979-8-9916764-3-4

Second Edition

Dedication

To Emma and Susan: the women who make me better.

The Schools of Magic

School of the Earth:

- ❖ Herbalism: The domestic tier of the School of the Earth. The manipulation of the earth's organically occurring magic.
- ❖ Naturalism: The intermediate tier of the School of the Earth. The manipulation of the forces of nature.
- ❖ Evocation: The advanced tier of the School of the Earth. The harnessing of the forces of nature within and around the caster.

School of the Void:

- ❖ Enchantment: The domestic tier of the School of the Void. The endowment of void magic into non-living things.
- ❖ Horology: The intermediate tier of the School of the Void. The manipulation of time.
- ❖ Conjuration: The advanced tier of the School of the Void. The manipulation of the forces of the void.

School of the Mind:

- ❖ Empathy: The domestic tier of the School of the Mind. The sensing and manipulation of emotion.
- ❖ Divination: The intermediate tier of the School of the Mind. The reading of thoughts and future events.
- ❖ Illusion: The advanced tier of the School of the Mind. The alteration of perception.

High Sorcery:

- ❖ The mastery of all three schools of magic.

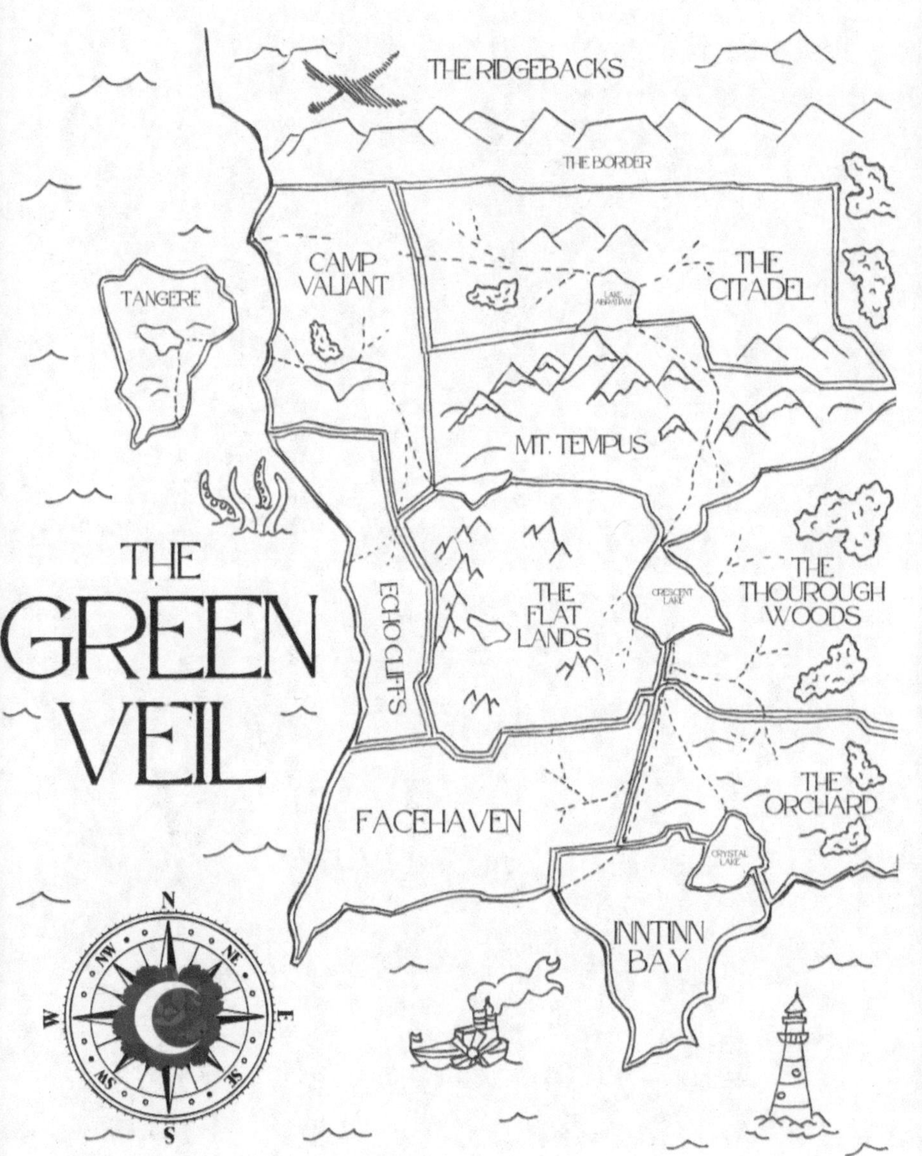

THE RIDGEBACKS
THE BORDER
TANGERE
CAMP VALIANT
LAKE ABRAHAM
THE CITADEL
MT. TEMPUS
THE
GREEN
VEIL
ECHO CLIFFS
THE FLAT LANDS
CRESCENT LAKE
THE THOUROUGH WOODS
FACEHAVEN
THE ORCHARD
CRYSTAL LAKE
INNTINN BAY
N
NW NE
W E
SW SE
S

PROLOGUE:
THE WITCH'S PLEA

Maybe two minutes, if I'm lucky.

This was the only thought in her mind as the wide-eyed witch burst into the attic, the door slamming behind her with such force that it seemed to shake the bones of the little house. Scrambling forward in her haste, she threw herself to the floor in the far-left corner of the cluttered room. With a pang, she felt the scraping of the ragged wood against the flesh of her knees and inhaled sharply. The room smelled of dust and brass, filled with unwanted furnishings they had discarded there over the years. Her husband had often suggested they sell the pieces.

"A bedframe here, an oil lamp there, could bring in a decent price," he had said.

She'd merely smiled and responded, *"Things have a habit of finding their way back to me. Might as well give the lamp a shorter journey."*

She ran her fingers down the groove of the first floorboard and counted one, two, three, four from the wall. With one sharp thwack, she brought a tight fist down on the right side of the fourth board, sending the length of wood and a cloud of sawdust bursting up. It clattered with a hollow pitch as it rocked across the floor, eventually settling in the center of the room. Reaching down into the exposed hiding place, her fingers caught hold of a cool, smooth object that sent a familiar jolt of electric power up her arm. In one motion, she pulled the leather-bound book out from the floor and laid it flat. A piece of moonlight caught the silver symbol etched into its cover: a crescent moon set over a blooming flower.

Flipping through the pages with nimble fingers, she tried to steady herself with a slow, shallow breath, her constrictive girdle keeping her from taking a deep one.

"I sure won't miss these things," she mumbled to herself, "wherever I'm going." If she could have brought herself to crack a smile then, she would have, but what came next lay too heavily on her chest for such things.

For Protection. She stopped on this page. The paper was stiff, not yet softened with age. Her fingertip shuddered along its surface while she traced her own handwriting. Regret crept in, yellow and sluggish, slowing her frantic mind. Why hadn't she committed this book to memory? Why had she warded it against duplication? Why could she never manage to plan past her next breakfast? All she had given up to scribble down these incantations, and now she would leave them here to turn to dust and rot.

"Why shouldn't you take them?" the dark voice in the crawlspace of her mind whispered. *"They're yours, after all."* She thought of the countless days spent huddled over these pages, whispering these magics to life. Suddenly, her hands gripped the book tight, and the dark little voice beckoned.

"You can leave."

In the blink of a luxurious eyelash, she could have been gone, far away and too powerful to be tracked. And yet she remained still, blinking. She couldn't run, couldn't vanish—she could only sit and listen to her own ragged breath. She was anchored to this place still. She felt the weight even now. A little girl slept just across the lake, safe in a warm bed; her own creation, eight years old. Her daughter grew each day to look more and more like the man who had once asked her to dance. That little girl may be safe from what was coming for her mother that night, but would she be safe in the years to come? Could the danger ever return?

"She won't have you… So leave her this." The softer, maternal voice that spoke now was impossible to ignore, the primal instincts of motherhood clashing with her drive for survival. Her grip loosened once more and she began to speak.

"I call upon the Earth, still warm beneath my feet."

Somewhere below, the front door rattled with the force of powerful hands knocking. Her whole body grew taut in anticipation, and even her own pride could not stop it from shaking. Neverthe-less, the witch pressed on.

"I call upon the Void, still breathing its shadow deep."

Below her, the front door gave way to a masterful blast of white fire, and the men entered the home, shouting commands with militaristic power. She rushed and stumbled over her next words like a stream gushing over rocks. With each phrase, the forces pushed against her, unwilling to yield their strength. The witch went on, now bellowing her words with forced confidence.

"I call upon the Mind, that our precious secrets keep."

The rising sound of hurried footsteps was drowned out by the growing tempest that circled the woman and her book. Her eyes sunk deeper in her skull, and her pearlescent skin glowed with moonlight and the faint green hue of a witch's will. She felt her airways constrict and her chest tighten, pressuring her to stop now, take it all back. Pulling from her core something she had not yet discovered, she cried,

"Rise to her aid—Earth, Veil, and Mind I do entreat!"

Two men clamored through the doorframe, one with his bow drawn, the other's hands still crackling with the embers of white flame. The first stopped abruptly as he took in the room before him. The other clumsily stumbled into him with a grunt, singeing his partner's coat. Before the pair was an empty attic, lit only by moonlight, with every floorboard in its place. One may have never known the witch had been there at all if it wasn't for the pattern burned into the boards: a crescent moon set over a blooming flower.

Chapter One: The Witch's Walk

It was my eighteenth year, and I, Hildegarde Birch, decided that I no longer enjoyed apples. After years spent hurrying through the orchards on my way to academy, baking apple pies in my domestic studies classroom and being gifted polished granny smiths by friends—or those who wanted to be more than friends—I'd had just about enough. To me, their texture had always been that of sodden tree bark, and they tasted of unripe winter plums. The only thing I'd ever been fond of was their smell. One deep breath in and the crisp, sticky scent conjured up memories of lazy harvest mornings spent lounging in the fallen leaves, trudging through the village with a basket too full for my little arms to carry, or my mother's kitchen on a cold night's suppertime.

"I won't be bringing home any apples today," I announced to a robin resting on a nearby branch. "I don't care what Auntie Irenee wants."

The little bird cocked its head with disapproval. Ignoring the silent scolding, I pivoted on my heel, swinging my heavy basket to give me momentum as I continued down the pebble path to the lavender field. I was in a funny sort of mood, and the robin didn't deserve to deal with me that way. Auntie Irenee had banished me from the kitchen, which seemed foolish considering how hopeless of a cook she was. Instead of assisting with the Harvest meal, I was to gather a bushel of apples, which I would not be doing.

"If you want to send me out to forage, I won't complain," I said, speaking for my own amusement as I shuffled down the path, scattering pebbles with the tips of my shoes. "But I'll be foraging for my *own* purposes, thank you very much."

I regretted not wearing my cloak. The light chill brushed my bare arms, leaving goosebumps in its tracks. On my way down the path, I went out of my way to crack a dry leaf under my heel when the spirit moved me. Harvest time in our village of the Orchard was a sight to see. Every tree was lit up in shades of amber and scarlet, boasting their perfectly ripe fruits. The flowers displayed their most brilliant blooms, knowing they would be the last of the year. The air was thick with finality as each living thing prepared for its rest. I had seen even my fellow academy students taking moments to deeply breathe this same air, all of us huddled over textbooks and preparing for final examinations.

As I passed an orchard keeper's shed, I caught a glance of myself in a dusty windowpane. Though I couldn't call my features typical, I'd never seen myself as unattractive. Sometimes I thought of myself as just unusual enough to be intriguing. I was shorter than most of my classmates, standing only slightly higher than I had as a child. I was also plumper than the other girls, but I had never minded that, despite how often my mother had told me to. My skin had the round tightness of a well-grown tomato, but in a shade more resembling that of an acorn—I'd always felt at home in it.

Though my features were mostly soft and round, my nose cut out at a severe angle and ended in a sharp point, just like my mother's. I had never much liked my nose. Many admired the deep umber color of my hair, though, which I could never quite keep contained in the two braids that I let fall over both of my shoulders. I wondered if I would always be this size or if I could possibly sprout up like a beanstalk when I became old and gray.

I knew that line of thinking was illogical at my age, but in my defense, anything was possible in our magical land of the Green Veil.

After forgoing the apples, I could now focus on the remaining items on the list of herbs I had set out to gather that day. Though not helpful for my growth, they might help settle the nerves of my poor aunt. I may have been put out by

Irenee's behavior that day, but I was not unsympathetic to her frustration. The old woman was without a doubt busying herself over the stove, faced with making the coming holiday merry and bright. She always stressed over making it just as it had been before the two of us were alone.

The scent of lavender filled my nose as I reached the flower field, and I fumbled in my dress pocket for my recipe. On a scrap of paper, I had scrawled a short list of ingredients on my way out the door. Last was *3 sprigs of lavender, picked fresh.* Or was that an *8*? My handwriting had always been lousy.

On my way in, I dropped three copper coins in the wooden box that hung off the fence of the field. People trusted each other here. The Orchard had always been known as the best territory to raise a family in the Green Veil. No one was inclined to mistrust a village full of herbalists, housewives, and shopkeepers, and nor should they. This was a place with no underbelly, no secrets lurking in dark alleys. I had grown up like all children of the Orchard—happy and wild. There was a lifetime supply of trees to climb, rivers as clear as glass, and thick vines hanging over the riverbanks just waiting to be swung from. There were miles of open fields where imaginations could get blissfully lost. My love of this green place was rivaled only by my love of the people within it.

The waves of lavender rippled in the breeze, sending their aroma to embrace me as I made my way through the stalks. I used two hands to raise up my heavy basket a bit, not wanting to damage the plants as I walked through them. I felt their soft fingers brush against my knees as I waded to the center of the field where I always collected my sprigs. The crop was no better at the center than at the edge, but I enjoyed this little tradition. In the middle, I could look out at the world around me and see it not as a girl, but as a proud sprig of lavender. When you are lavender, there are no questions to answer or plans to lay—just fields full of floral family. And, of course, I knew Rae enjoyed me smelling of them, but that was just a bonus.

A thick gust of air swept through the field, sending the flowers and my poorly contained hair stretching west. We called these winds the gales. They marked the changing of the season. As a girl, when the gales blew in, I would run out into the fields and let the winds tell me where to go, like a little boat at sea.

My mother would run after me and call, "Careful, Hildegarde! The winds will blow you away from me!" Not slowing down, I would call back to her between excited shrieks, "They will blow me home!"

Lavender can calm almost any worried mind. That's what made it so useful for an herbalist. I decided to take eight sprigs, just to be safe. As I made my way out of the flowers and back up the hill, I could hardly remember what had made me cross before, and the tainted memories of my mother loosened their grip. I always made these fields my last stop so I might return home better than when I had left it.

My arm was not feeling as tranquil as my mind, though. It was growing heavier the more I added to it, but I suspected the moss-covered stone to be the true culprit. It was much larger than I would have liked, but this particular brew called for the moss of a settled stone. If my perfunctory herbalism lecturer, Mr. Fennel, was to be believed, a "settled stone" was to be found in the shade, at the base of a healthy tree, and sunk at least one inch into the earth.

"Hildy!" a silhouette from down the path called. I squinted to try and make the figure out in the fading light. By the time I recognized her, she had nearly run me over.

"Do you remember when we need to turn in our horology final? I've completely lost my lecture book," the breathless girl asked, pushing a strand of red hair out of her face.

"Well hello to you, Copper. And it's due on the last day of lecture, but he said it's optional. I don't think Mr. Spindell thinks too highly of our class," I answered, rolling my right shoulder back to relieve some of the discomfort from my basket. The girl who stood across from me bobbed with energy, unable to keep her weight on one leg for long. Copper Penning, named aptly for her signature hair color, was a good friend of mine, but not someone I thought of as being my best friend. She was a fantastic acquaintance to everyone she met. There was not a soul in the Orchard who disliked her, and, likewise, not a person who could call her their closest friend. It seemed her nature to be unanchored in every way possible, always moving and bouncing around.

"I think you're right. We should show him, though—make a proper time loop or something," Copper suggested, gesticulating with her pale, freckled hands. "Are you on your way home? I could walk with you. I'm heading to Lisel's for supper. She's as dull as a tack, but her mother is an excellent cook."

"Sure. I'd love the company if you don't mind," I offered, wondering if walking a block with this young woman would completely counteract the calming effect of the lavender fields. But I had no reason to be rude. I had known Copper for a great many years, and she was never anything but cheerful and well-meaning.

"I don't mind at all. Let me take that for you." Without so much as a grunt of recognition, she took hold of the basket's handle and hitched it over her shoulder, though she did let out a small sound in reaction to the unexpected weight. "Leave it to Hildegarde Birch to lug rocks around without breaking a sweat." She laughed her signature giggle as we started walking, which sounded equal parts frog and happy baby. I couldn't help but smile.

It was obvious why no one could dislike her. She might annoy you, but in the same breath she would do something inexplicably thoughtful. Perhaps if she could steady her energy, she might make a powerful empath.

"As much as I'd love to prove Mr. Spindell wrong, I'll be lucky if I can even get the gears to turn in my pocket watch," I confessed, turning the subject back.

"You're the one with a horologist for an aunt. Irenee built my father a time chamber to speed up our kitchen stove in less than ten minutes! I'm sure she could offer a few nuggets of wisdom," Copper huffed. She had adjusted her hold on the basket three times now in the few minutes we'd been walking.

"She's too busy. I'd just end up feeling bad for pulling her away from her work." I swung my arm around in wide circles as I spoke, relieving my sore shoulder.

"You worry too much," she said firmly. She had settled on holding the basket in her left hand now. Being a good deal taller than me, the basket knocked against her knee as it swung with her steps. "Make sure you save a shot of this calming brew for yourself."

It shouldn't have surprised me that Copper could identify my brew from seeing only half of the raw ingredients. She had always been an excellent student. She had to, if she wanted to live up to the potential of her brother, Arnold. He was just one year older than his sister and a complete savant. He may not have been too popular with the girls of the academy, but he certainly was with the lecturers.

Every year she had to follow on the coattails of her brother's genius. The only thing she ever consistently beat him at was originality.

"How is Arnie? Rae and I haven't seen your brother in a while," I asked, curious. I had thought of Arnie as one of my dearest friends, but at the start of his senior year last year, he had become something of a recluse.

"You and me both. Some people have lives, friends, maybe even a date or two, but not my brother. He's got his books and his applications to fuss over. He says that the Academy of High Sorcery isn't interested in wizards who waste their lives on outings and foolishness. I say they aren't interested in lame shut-ins who can't speak to a girl to save the kingdom. I doubt even an illusionist could get through to him. Maybe I can take another crack at it if he pulls himself away from his scribblings long enough to come to Harvest dinner tomorrow. Not that it will be much of an occasion with Dad doing the cooking, though."

Her voice slowed as she finished her sentence. It had been two years since Ruth Penning had passed on. A sleeping sickness from the coast had spread across the southern territories, and she had always been of a fragile constitution.

It was hardly uncommon to have lost a family member, however, even in the Orchard. Fighting along the northern border had scraped on for years, even after the conclusion of the

Great War. Every flare-up and skirmish claimed more fathers and brothers of the Green Veil, but to lose a mother was a rarity, even to an illness. The Penning siblings and I were not so different in our losses—just as it was unusual to lose a mother, it was doubly unusual to have no parents at all.

"If your family's meal falls through, you could all come over to our home for Harvest," I offered, hardly thinking the plan through. Auntie Irenee would surely have a fit with such a last-minute addition, but I had been missing Arnie and liked the idea of having Copper around for a laugh.

"I would accept in a heartbeat, but I'm sure Dad and Arnie will give some line about not wanting to impose or some other self-sacrificing phrase."

"You won't be imposing! We're having Raemond and Maegon over too. A larger group would only make it a more proper celebration. Besides, it's Harvest. The whole point is to share the wealth." We had stopped now, having reached the gate to my front garden.

"Well, I'm on board, And I bet with some nudging, Arnie will come around. He wouldn't want to miss the chance to see you and Rae in the same place. The three of you used to be joined at the hips. It was a bit frightening, actually." Copper handed off the basket with a grunt and offered her hand. "You've got yourself a deal."

I shook her hand with mock seriousness. "Dinner starts at dusk tomorrow."

She nodded and started walking energetically backward, still facing me with a big grin. "I'll bring a pie! It'll be bad! But it'll be pie!" she called, her figure shrinking as she made her way down the road.

"Tell Lisel I say hello!"

"Oh yes, good—we'll have something to talk about now!"

I chuckled and opened the gate. With the tiresome basket in hand, I made my way through the overgrown garden, toward the earthy, stone home glowing amber in the low, gray light.

The kitchen was a war zone. Scattered across the sprawling table were disemboweled pumpkins, the shards of a broken pot, and a once-proud mortar and pestle now stained with what looked like desiccated poppy seeds. In the midst of the chaos swirled Irenee Thorne, a large witch with an equally large presence. Her wisps of gray hair peeped out from her velvet cap, frizzed by the heat of the room. She wore a ruffled cream apron that did not suit her, covering her more standard style of a satin blue suit, which was now quite wrinkled from the frenzy of activity.

"Does it usually take a full day to pick six apples, Hildegarde? Or did you trip and fall into one of my time locks?" she snapped. I could practically see her steaming. Or perhaps that was the plum sauce boiling behind her. Irenee towered over me, both in stature and in authority. She shared the same angular bones as her sister, with a jaw that could cut down a small tree. When she grew angry, the lines around her eyes folded in on themselves, causing her to age at least a decade. She might have been quite frightening at that moment if it hadn't been for the collapsed cocoa cake she held in front of her with two flamboyant oven mitts.

"Um, about the apples…" I started with a grimace, setting the basket down on the one exposed corners of the kitchen table. Irenee glanced down at its conspicuous contents.

"I will pin you to the roof by your toes!" she cried, dropping the pathetic cake onto the wood planks of the counter with a thud. I could hear sizzling where the scorching pan met the wood. "I've just sent this cake to the dark abyss of the Void, and now there are no apples for me to make a simple tart!"

Irenee spat the words at me, oblivious to my growing amusement. "Why would you sabotage our only chance at dessert?" She leaned over the table, her eyes shooting daggers at me.

"Copper is bringing a pie," I said quickly, bracing myself.

"And why would Copper Penning do a thing like that?" Irenee asked slowly, inching closer to my face. "Does she owe you a debt?"

"She does now. I invited the Penning family to our Harvest dinner."

A baking tray flew across the room along with two oven mitts after being flipped by Irenee's broad hands. I reactively shielded myself from the shower of charred appetizers that flew from the tray as it made its way through the air. A clang rang through the room as the metal sheet hit the floor, followed soon by my own roaring laughter, which I was no longer able to contain. Irenee shot a bristling look at me before turning on her heel and storming out of the kitchen.

"Oh come on, Auntie. The more the merrier," I called after her as she stomped down the hallway.

"You are my curse!" Irenee yelled, ending the conversation by pointedly slamming her study door. I laughed once more at my aunt's desperate attempts to shock me. This was not an unusual kind of interaction in our home. Irenee Thorne was perpetually cross about something, whether it be the rain, a stubborn drawer, or the preparation of a large meal. Her fuse was as short as one could be, and at any moment she might burst.

I was an unlikely match for her. Where another might find her temper off-putting, I found a way to make a game of it. I had always enjoyed a dash of the dramatic. We could quarrel until the beams of the home split, but beneath all the bluster was an enduring love, which was a most fortunate occurrence since we were all we had left to call family.

CHAPTER TWO: THE WITCH'S SACRIFICE

I busied myself with cleaning up the kitchen. It was tedious work, but not daunting. The enchantment a local vendor had placed on our kitchen sink would not wear off for another week, so I needed only to place the dishes within it to wash them. The only bother was that I could not seem to find the enchanted dish towel to dry them. Had I used it after brewing that energy tonic the previous week? I couldn't recall, but either way, it certainly hadn't been left in my room.

As I sorted through the deep cupboard under the sink, I smelled something burning. I bustled over to the stove where I found the plum sauce boiling over. This pot was in a time chamber to warm it quicker, but I couldn't reverse it without my aunt. The only solution was to pour the sauce into something else and let the empty pot keep warming on its own. Careful not to burn my hands, I filled up a sauce boat decorated with painted flowers. For all my aunt's fumbling, the sauce smelled delicious.

My belly lurched, reminding me that I hadn't eaten since breakfast. Thankfully, I had left a bowl of crawfish stew from yesterday's lunch in the icebox. It was the same recipe that had put me at the top of my class in domestic studies my junior year. I had always been drawn to cozier applications of earth magic, which lent themselves to cooking and brewing. I loved the meditative process of chopping, stirring, and repeating that went into my brews. Nothing was left to chance: follow the instructions, keep your composure, and all will come out just right.

The enchanted pot proved useful in quickly heating my dinner. I sat down at the now mostly clean kitchen table with my warm bowl of stew and a hunk of spiced bread. On my first bite, I heard the crashing of waves on a pebble beach. The stew had been seasoned with poppy root and sea salt, a concoction of my own making. When the two ingredients are steamed for just the right amount of time in a sturdy iron pot, they create a subtle memory drug. Mixed in with the crawfish, the taster was likely to experience memories of the ocean.

I breathed in the spray of the sea. Somewhere in the distance, I could hear Uncle Maxx shouting for me to join him in the water. I felt linen cloth on my bare legs and the sun freckling my shoulders. I could hear the sound of Irenee's humming being carried along the breeze.

With the last spoonful of soup, I was back in the kitchen. Irenee was not humming anymore, and Uncle Maxx was long gone.

I spent the rest of the evening mixing up the stress relief brew. The recipe had only called for three sprigs of lavender after all, but I was glad for having extra. The lavender fields would wither as soon as the frost came, and I could preserve the remaining five sprigs with one of my aunt's time locks. Each sprig had to be twisted between your palms until the stem was bare. Next, I soaked the settled stone in oil to lift the moss off undamaged. It was a good thing I had not scraped it off initially, not wanting to lug the thing home.

I juiced eleven butter berries with a handheld press next. While doing this busy work, I had set a pot of chamomile tea to steep. The recipe called for a kettle at least fifteen years old, which wasn't difficult to find in our home. Aunt Irenee had never thrown away a perfectly good kitchen utensil in her life, or a usable rag, or a fine piece of scrap paper. I slowly poured the pot of tea into the cast iron pot with the rest of the ingredients. The steam that rose from the brew smelled like a set of warm, clean sheets on a cold night.

The final instruction read: *Add to the simmering potion one deep breath. Serve warm.* No further instructions. I settled on being as literal as possible. I inhaled slowly through my nose, held my breath while positioning my face just over the pot, and exhaled with a sigh into the mixture. The color changed from the yellow of chamomile to a shimmering lilac.

I ladled two scoops into a teacup, and after locating the matching saucer, I made my way to Irenee's study. I knocked lightly with the knuckle of my right pointer finger, balancing the cup and saucer in the other hand.

"Auntie Irenee? I made you some tea," I called in my most sing-song tone.

A heavy pause. "Well bring it in then. Before it gets cold."

I entered slowly, not wanting to spill my expertly brewed potion. The aging woman was seated at her dark wood desk, hunched over a set of intricate golden gears that she was fashioning into a mantle clock. She did not look up from her work to greet me. I couldn't tell if this was a conscious slight or just a product of her deep concentration.

"And what will this tea do to me? Turn me into a head of cabbage?" Irenee said snidely, still focused on her work.

"No, I haven't found that recipe yet," I tossed back, coming to stand near her desk. I was careful not to get close enough to disturb her delicate work.

"Never give up on a dream, Hildegarde. Lesson number one."

"I'll just leave the tea for you. I can see you're busy." I scanned the desk for an empty space, but every patch was buried beneath open books and metal instruments.

"No need. Just give me one moment…" Her voice trailed off as she tightened a final, impossibly small screw. She set her instruments down and fell back in her chair with satisfaction. "Give it here," she said, motioning for the cup. I handed it to her with both hands.

Irenee put her sharp nose right to the brim of the cup, closed her eyes, and took a whiff. "Reading a good book on a sunny day," she exhaled with a smile. "Well done."

I could never predict another person's reaction to my concoctions. I really needed to start writing them down to compare. My favorite yet had been Raemond's reaction to a giggling tonic. To him, it smelled of an old man's flatulence. Not a particularly pleasant scent, but funny nonetheless.

"What's this going to be?" I asked, motioning to the clock.

"If all goes well, it will count down to the next major rainfall and chime an hour before any unexpected showers." Irenee had now taken a few sips and was already growing more pleasant.

"That sounds more like divination to me," I remarked. I didn't want to doubt my aunt's capabilities, but I was skeptical. Horology and divination were entirely different studies of magic, and they were both at tiers that required a special license from their respective academies.

"When one has a firm grip on time, there is always an element of divination to it. The primary difference is that I *myself* cannot predict the future, but my clock can," Irenee explained, inching further down in the large chair as she relaxed.

"That's incredible. I can't imagine doing something like that," I said softly. I looked down at my shoes, which had some fresh scuffs from my day's journey.

"And I cannot imagine brewing a tea that could make a crotchety old bat like me feel peaceful," she offered with a warm smile. "I can't even bake a flapjack without flying off the handle."

"We can fix it tomorrow before dinner," I said confidently, shifting to lean on my aunt's side of the desk. "We have time."

"What would I do without you?" Irenee said, now smiling. She placed her hand over mine.

"I thought I was your curse."

"You should know not to listen to me."

"I do," I said, laughing softly. Irenee's smile faded as her gaze became thoughtful. She pressed her thin lips together and took a shaky breath in through the nose.

"It's been five years since we lost your uncle." she said, gazing at the old sign that hung above the office doorway. *Mister Thorne's Trinket Trove*—her late husband's enchantment boutique. "I still don't know how to do this on my own." I could see her eyes were misting over, but she was too stubborn to let a tear fall.

"You don't have to," I said, tightening my grip on her hand. "You've got me."

"When your mother was here—" Irenee started, but I stopped her sharply.

"She made her choice." I didn't want to hear about how much better our lives were before my mother left me.

"There is still so much that you do not understand, my girl," Irenee said, returning my squeeze.

"I understand enough," I said, not making any attempt to hide my bitterness.

We remained silent for a long moment. I knew if I asked her to elaborate, she would have, but I didn't want to know. I knew that my mother would have given hundreds of excuses for leaving, but they wouldn't change anything. All that mattered was that I had grown up without a mother, and she made that choice for me.

"I'm sorry I forgot the apples," I finally said, bringing the tension to a close.

"That's all right. I'm tired of them anyway."

The next morning was a flurry of activity. After the disaster of the previous evening, we had to work especially hard to pull together the dinner for seven. When working as a team, we functioned rather well. Irenee could speed up bake times with the controlled time chamber she had fashioned in the oven, and I could focus on all the preparation. Not only was I a confident cook, but when the opportunity arose, I was bold enough to experiment with adding a pinch of dried lemongrass, or maybe pepper flakes, to infuse a dish with a sense of memory. If my hypothesis was accurate, the minced meat pies should remind the guests of childhood play, and the plum sauce should make every joke a tad funnier.

"Rust my gears," Irenee cried out, midway through preparing the yeast rolls, "I've lost my mother's breadbasket!"

"That's all right," I said as I hurried to her side, sensing an impending tantrum. "We can use my herb basket to hold the rolls."

"No, that won't do!" Irenee began to wring her hands. "We always use her basket on Harvest. It's a tradition."

"Did you take it out of the house?"

"Why would I do that?" I saw her frustration building.

"Well then, it must be here somewhere," I said, using my most dulcet and assured tone, rather like the one I used to calm a horse. "How about I check the attic while you finish the rolls?"

"Okay," Irenee said, taking a deep breath. "It's the woven one, with a fig leaf pattern on it."

"I remember what it looks like," I called back, already bounding up the steep stairs. The house stood three stories tall, but you wouldn't be able to tell from looking at it. The ground floor was sunk a bit into the earth, and the ceilings were very low. So low, in fact, that Irenee couldn't really navigate through a few of the doorways with her tall frame. The third floor contained only one room—an attic barely wide enough for two people to lie across.

I, however, had no trouble maneuvering through this small space. I had always felt quite comfortable in the attic. There was something about its ancientry that made me feel settled. It was an archive of sorts for the Birch family. All of my father's old books sat proudly on some dusty shelves, and beneath the window there was a chest full of Maxx's old clothes with a lid never properly closed; tucked in the back right corner was my little crib, painted to match a robin's egg. A taped-up box sat inside it, left there by Irenee after she and Maxx had moved in and had never gotten to unpacking it, even after ten years.

Nostalgia got the better of me. I pulled out a wooden crate from under an old bed frame and began rifling through it, discovering a handful of letters from a distant cousin recently tossed in there, a doll with pink porcelain cheeks, and a small quilt that smelt of moths. As I lifted the quilt, a frame was revealed at the bottom of the crate, and I locked eyes with my father. My mind grew quiet as I lifted the brass frame up to the subdued light.

He looked noble in his striped suit, and his smile was as warm as ever. Standing beside him was my mother in a flowing cream dress. The photo had been taken on their wedding day, as their dress and obvious joy showed. The new Mrs. Birch stood just slightly taller than her husband. I huffed with amusement as I remembered how he would beg her to wear flats for the sake of his pride. My father's dark brown arm was wrapped tightly around the small of his bride's back. I had always loved the rich color of my father's skin. I'd wanted so much to match him, but my mother's milky complexion had left me somewhere between the two.

Baldwin and Maude Birch, a handsome couple if there ever was one. No matter the soft and loving look of my mother in the photo, I could not help the anger that swelled in my throat.

Her disappearance had cost me more than just a mother. After a divination spell to find her had moved him to search in Tangere, my father had died in a freak storm sailing the island. Naturalism and evocation had been used to monitor and alter the weather of the Green Veil for generations, so such storms were very rare, but when harsh weather managed to creep through the cracks, the results were catastrophic.

They looked so happy in the shiny frame. Of course, they had always looked happy to me. Up until the end.

I returned the photo to the crate and set it back into place. Harvest was a hard time for me. Memories of better days were in every aroma and tradition. I didn't need to add to my melancholy with pointless reminiscing. I scanned the attic, this time looking with my original purpose, and quickly spotted the breadbasket perched on top of a broken grandfather clock. I started toward the clock, but in my haste, the front of my shoe caught itself under the large woven rug that lived at the center of the room, and I began to fall forward with full force. As my momentum propelled me forward, the rug pulled my trapped foot to the side, making my body tilt to the right. I landed softly in a pile of dusty linen sheets that we saved for guests.

I had always been exceedingly lucky when it came to physical harm. Ever since I was a child, danger seemed to miss me by an inch. When lightning had struck Crystal Lake the previous summer, I had only just stepped out of the water. When the boy working next to me in my herbalism course had added a wrath pepper to his energy brew, causing the pot to violently explode, every shard missed me.

This pattern had not gone unnoticed. After several such occurrences, our principal had gotten to calling me "Blessed Birch." I'd hated that nickname. He had given it to me only two months after Uncle Maxx's death, and it felt more like mockery than endearment.

But, nevertheless, I was glad to have landed in the sheets as opposed to flat on my face. I stood up, careful not to lose my footing on the upturned rug. It was then that something caught my eye. Part of a dark, curved marking on the floor now peaked out from beneath it. Curious, I kicked the rug again, making it roll over on itself. The symbol now fully revealed, I placed it immediately. Burned into the floorboards was a crescent moon set over a blooming flower—it was the emblem of high sorcery.

Everyone in the Green Veil was capable of some magic. It was a guarantee at birth. But the study of sorcery was overwhelming, with many facets and considerations. Divination required skills that evocation didn't, and vice versa. That was why witches and wizards were asked to study only one school of magic. Irenee had chosen horology after Maxx died, and I expected to continue my study of herbalism throughout my life in the Orchard. Our academic system was all very neat and orderly: everyone had their domestic roles or their school of study, with wives and mothers being expected to do some simple studying in one of the lower tiers of magic before having a home to care for. But to study high sorcery was to bear it all.

It could take a lifetime of focus to just be capable of *holding* such power without it destroying you. To excel in it was almost impossible. Currently, there were only two living high sorcerers in all of the Green Veil, and they both served as councilors to the king. Yet, somehow, the symbol was here in our attic.

An invisible force called to me. Without thought or reason, I knelt down and reached out with an unsteady hand. As my fingertips hovered above the burned grooves, I felt a subtle heat radiating from them. After a moment of hesitation, I let my pointer finger fall to touch the scorched wood. There was a flash of brilliant white light.

Panicked footsteps echoed through the room, which was drenched in the pale moonlight. My hair began to whip into my face as a warm gust of wind circled the room. Dazedly looking around the attic, feeling somehow outside time, I heard an incantation in the old language. I turned toward the center of the room to see a thin witch crouched on the floor. The silver dress was wrapped tightly around the spindly woman as she sat in the eye of the indoor storm. I took a sharp breath of recognition.

"Mother?"

The burning on my fingertip grew painful and I was forced to withdraw, falling back against the boards of the attic, newly restored to daylight. A bird chirped outside the open window. I sat up so quickly that the room momentarily fell out of focus. Blinking rapidly to clear my vision, I stared at the place where my mother had been, now empty save for the scorched symbol. A throbbing in my finger prompted me to look at the damage done. Across the second fingertip on my right hand was a raised mark, pink and swollen, matching the curve of the line I had just touched.

"Hildy!" Irenee shouted from two stories down, "Have you found it yet?"

I took one last look at the ominous symbol before kicking the rug back into place, careful not to make contact again.

"I found it!" I called back, my voice squeaking conspicuously. "Be right down!" I hurried over to the clock and grabbed the basket. With it in hand, I bounded down the two flights of stairs, landing heavily on each step.

"You looked flushed," Irenee said, looking up from the duck she had been glazing to see me standing before her, huffing.

"I must be out of shape," I suggested, glad the sudden burst of physical activity made a suitable cover for my rattled nerves.

The rest of the meal preparation spanned to late afternoon. The time passed with a tension that Irenee thankfully did not perceive. The old witch fussed over lightly burned dishes and repeated on a loop that she was "never any good at this sort of thing."

Her general lack of patience and calm had made it quite a surprise when she decided to pursue horology. Study of time was tedious and deeply intellectual. Introductory lessons included things like sitting in front of a melting ice block for hours, memorizing each phase to replicate later. Horologists were often mocked for moving too slowly, never willing to jump to a conclusion if they felt it under-researched. Irenee had the opposite mentality.

For her, there were never enough hours in the day, so she used her manipulation of time to speed up the daily motions. But no matter how much laundry she could dry in a matter of minutes, she could never regain the thirty-four years she had given to her marriage instead of her magic.

The laws had always made sense to me. Irenee had explained many times what the Tri-Generation War had taken from the Green Veil. Both of her parents were sent off to fight on the border when she was only a girl. My mother, Maude, wasn't even three years old when their parents had been killed in the earthquake an enemy naturalist had unleashed on the front lines. My aunt and mother were members of what became known as the Orphan Generation.

The Green Veil may have won the war, but the last twenty years of combat were the bloodiest the kingdom had ever seen. By the time the fighting was done and the white flag was raised, almost every child had lost at least one parent. There were no celebrations, no military parades, just a year of mourning as the people buried their dead. The kingdom was victorious but crippled. In our history classes, we were intoned with the decisions that had been made to end that age of death and despair. There were still enemies at the border, factions of radicals who would not surrender, but the people of the Green Veil were not anxious to step back onto any battlefield.

A new king had been crowned—a mere boy of twelve. He too was a member of the Orphan Generation. After gathering the most skilled divination witches and wizards, a plan was made. To ensure that no child would be left orphaned, and to facilitate the repopulation of the kingdom, the witches of the Green Veil were asked to make a sacrifice. Any witch who wished to have a family would not be eligible to study any intermediate or high tier of magic. They would not be called to the border or serve on any political council. They would study lower fields of magic that served their children and spouses: herbalism, enchantment, and empathy.

The women who chose this path were praised by their communities for ushering in an age of hope and a return to family values. Women who still wished to study higher tiers of magic could do so, but upon entering their school of study, they were to swear an oath to never marry or bear children. I always wondered if this deterrent for women was intended as a law for societal efficiency or as a punishment.

Either way, this tradition had endured and was a fact of life for me and all of the other Green Veil women. Irenee had chosen Maxx over magic when she was eighteen, but sadly, it had turned out the two could not conceive a child. Instead, she raised her little sister, my mother, to be the ambitious vixen she would become.

Despite the lack of children, Irenee was only eligible to study horology once Maxx passed away. Herbalist techniques had not yet found a cure for the deteriorating organ disease he had contracted. A widow's right to subsequently dedicate herself to a study was an amendment added to boost the educational system. The government saw no harm in childless, old widows pursuing higher education. Some of my classmates said this was because the women were too old to reach a level of mastery. It could take a student of time fifty years to be truly great, and she had thirty years left at best. We all knew it was unlikely that she would ever become more than a time tailor. I had heard a lifetime of her opinions on the matter, but no amount of groaning was going to change a law that had stood for decades, nor was it going to expand the lifetime still available to her.

Irenee was clearly never meant to be an empath. The perception of moods and concealed thoughts was never her strong suit, which meant she hardly noticed my silence over the hours we spent cooking the rest of the evening. It was a miracle that I didn't ruin every dish I touched. I could not tear my mind away from the symbol burned into the attic floorboards.

Why hadn't I just asked Irenee about it when I'd come down the stairs? Perhaps she had never even seen it. It might be just as big a surprise to her as it was to me. But if she did know about it, then she had made a conscious choice to hide it from me, even covering it up with that rug. Who was to say Irenee would even tell me the truth if I asked her point-blank?

As I sprinkled thyme into her hearty minced meat filling, the thought occurred to me to slip a bit of honesty brew into Irenee's nightly cup of tea. Then I would know the truth, one way or another. But the idea of violating my aunt's trust left a slimy feeling in my stomach. It was one thing to give her a calming draught, but it was another altogether to steal something from her mind without her knowledge. Maybe the mark had nothing to do with any member of my family. Our cottage was old and must have housed many other families over the years. Or perhaps it had been a practical joke at the hands of a mischievous child with a fire charm. Of course, none of this could explain away the vision of my mother now seared into my memory.

"Blast this damned chamber!" Irenee slammed the oven door suddenly. "It keeps changing time signatures on me and now it's gone and burnt the beans." She dropped the dish straight into the sink and swirled around to look over her calculation book.

"We don't need beans," I piped up, speaking for the first time in hours. "We have plenty of dishes already." We both looked over the counter full of steaming plates of food. Following a small nod, Irenee raised her right hand over the oven. Her long fingers each tensed and curved at precise angles, like tree branches come to life.

Once each of the five was in their place, Irenee whispered, "*Tempus reditus.*" The time chamber placed on the oven was lifted, and the whole room seemed to slow. Time shifts changed the air around them, so it took a moment to readjust to a neutral environment.

In the moment of quiet stillness, I made the decision not to ask Irenee about what I had

seen. There was no point in bringing up unpleasantness on the evening of Harvest. Plus, I feared
she already knew the answer. That symbol very well
could be the reason why there were so few family
seats at the Harvest table tonight.

Chapter Three: The Witch's Harvest

The kitchen smelled thickly of biscuits and clove when the Wimples arrived for the Harvest feast. Raemond Wimple and his little sister, Maegon, entered as they always did—with comfort and familiarity. Maegon fluttered through the door and ran straight for me, throwing her arms around my waist as soon as the distance allowed it. Her head of chopped black hair came up to just under my chin. Barely twelve years old, she was one of the few in my social circle who I could truly tower over. Raemond lingered at the entry, smiling as his sister and I embraced.

I looked over the bouncing little girl's head to take in the sight of him, leaning against the doorframe with folded arms. His light smirk left a dimple in his olive-toned cheek that made my heart ache. He wore a loose, cream button-up with the sleeves rolled up past his elbows. The thin fabric was a bit wrinkled where it tucked into his dark slacks, which had also been folded up at the hems. It was rare to see Rae in any attire that one might call formal, but he maintained his signature edge with a pair of dark leather boots, a carved silver belt buckle, and the single, defined black curl that hung down in the center of his forehead, sectioned out from the rest of his shiny, straight hair which ended in a jagged line just above his shoulders.

Raemond Wimple was the sun of my life, and everything else just circled around him. We had known each other for most of our lives, blossoming from childhood companions to poorly concealed crushes to eventually the love-crazed caricatures we grew into. For years, it was just a waiting game to see when the two of us would finally go steady. It took entirely too long for Rae to confess his feelings to me; he made me squirm in my self-consciousness for years. When he finally did, it was on an afternoon swimming at Crystal Lake. The heat in the Orchard was so unbearable that day—the result of poor weather control—that our secondary academy was forced to close until the temperature went down. Rae, Arnie, and I had taken refuge from the merciless heat in the cool waters of Crystal Lake, along with everyone else that day.

All those years, while Rae and I had been falling deeper into mutual infatuation, Arnold Penning had been at our side, an unwitting witness to the love story of his two best friends. Under the midday sun, we three lay side by side on the dock that floated in the middle of the lake, catching our breath after a race from the shore. Rae had won, as always, and I was busy worrying about Arnie's pale skin. As we baked in the sun, I swore I could see new spots popping up on the boy's already freckled chest. Rae began teasing us about our pitiful performances in the race, and Arnie hurled unrelated insults back at him. One of the jeers was so ridiculous that we broke out in a fit of laughter that did not subside for several minutes. I can't remember what was said or who said it, but it sent us howling.

When we did quiet down, Rae turned to me and confessed his feelings with a simple, "I love you." A concoction of joy and shock bubbled up in my gut as I studied his face, trying to discern if he was making a joke. I let impulse take control, and my question was answered when I laid a kiss on him that he returned with enthusiasm. That was the moment everything changed—we could no longer hide behind childhood. In one instant, the future came rushing in, and I was offered a choice: love, or everything else.

It had been two years since we had lain out on the dock with nothing to lose. Since then, our lives had barreled toward the future. Rae spent every moment he wasn't with me training in evocation, a high-tier magic that focused on replicating the natural elements. He was readying himself for his eventual military conscription.

The Wimple family boasted a proud line of military men, dating back to the beginning of the Tri-Generation War. Raemond's decision to enlist was more an eventuality than a choice. Similarly, after that day on the dock, I knew what my life would look like—Rae and I would get a home of our own, one we filled with laughter and love as we started our family. So, I busied myself with herbalism, training for the day I might be preparing calming brews for children of my own. And for Arnie, he gave himself over to the all-consuming studies of high magic. As the bond between me and Rae had grown, I admit that Arnie faded into the backdrop. Maybe the distance was to do with his dedication to his academy applications—he was a year above Rae and me. Or maybe it had been motivated by the grief of losing his mother. But either way, it now felt like he was miles away, even though he lived just down the street.

"Raemond and Maegon," Irenee exclaimed, descending the stairs in a deep blue silk wrap dress. "You both look a picture." Maegon finally released me and dashed over to Irenee to give her a quick hug.

"Now, I just love this," Irenee said, motioning to Mae's matching ensemble. She looked like a little pumpkin with her burnt orange button-up and fluffy skirt. Her mini green cape really brought the eccentric look together.

"Not me," Mae said with a frown as she fussed with the high collar of her cape. "Not like I had a choice, anyway. Mom bought it for me before she left with Dad for the Citadel." She looked as if she had been sucking on a particular sour candy as she said this.

"If you can keep it between us," Irenee said quietly, crouching down to eye level with Mae while remaining exceedingly elegant. "I have a few mink collars upstairs in my wardrobe that would pair seamlessly with that shade of orange, and may add a certain level of maturity to your *ensemble*." Irenee's voice twinkled conspiratorially.

"Auntie…" I started, begrudgingly turning to square up with the tall witch, but she did not break eye contact with Mae.

"You may have to endure a side glance or two from the *earthier* amongst us, but that is a small price to pay for glamour," Irenee said, speaking pointedly to only the little girl, who was thoroughly convinced.

"I don't mind the looks!" Maegon was already bounding up the stairs with youthful vigor. "Thank you, Irenee!" she called back, almost an afterthought. Irenee swept back up to a standing position, chuckling to herself. Rae made his way to her and smoothly kissed her on the cheek. She had to bend a touch at the waist to receive it, but Rae was able to recover his dignity with some playful, flirtatious comments. I rolled my eyes at the spectacle.

One may have found it odd for a young couple so in love to wait so long to greet one another, but it was not at all uncommon for Rae and me. We shared one fault: we got bored quickly and easily. To ensure that this quirk never affected our relationship, we had developed a series of games and tactics to keep each other on our toes. Once at an academy formal, I had pretended not to know Rae and challenged him to win my heart all over again. At the last Lammas celebration—a holiday that marked the coming of winter with the giving of sentimental trinkets—Rae had purposely gifted me a gaudy floral necklace that smelled heavily of sugar roses, something he was sure I would hate. He planned to reveal later in the night that he had purchased the services of an illusionist, and so it was really a simple gold locket that held the memory of our first kiss. Much to his chagrin, I had seen right through the illusion and loved the gift on sight. We concluded the peddler had made some error in the charm, but Raemond made sure I still knew the whole planned charade.

Our little games changed daily, and we had both developed a talent for recognizing them in an instant. On this day, I quickly deciphered that today's challenge would be to refuse to speak first, and I was committed to winning this round.

I busied myself with plating the various dishes of our feast while Irenee and Rae chatted away about Mr. and Mrs. Wimple's trip to the Citadel. They had been invited to the capital to celebrate Harvest at the King's Feast. Rae's father was being honored that year for his work as sheriff in the Orchard. After some discussion, Sheriff Wimple had decided it prudent to attend the celebration without his children. He had told Raemond that Maegon was much too young to understand the etiquette of the court, and so Raemond should stay to take care of his sister and focus on his final examinations.

I did not have to preoccupy myself for long. There was a timid knock on the front door that I wasn't certain I had actually heard. I put down the rosemary I was about to sprinkle over a dish, wiped my hands, and took a few steps toward the door. As I got closer, I could hear muffled voices just outside.

"We can just go in," a soft female voice said.

"That would be rude," a more anxious man responded in a harsh whisper.

"This is the Birch house, not the royal compound."

"Well, excuse me if I choose not to behave like a mannerless—"

I opened the door on the Penning siblings. Copper beamed at me, reveling in the discomfort of her older brother. Arnie looked back at me with the stiffness of a wooden figurine.

"We, uh, weren't sure if we should knock or not," he said, his voice lower than I remembered. I was struck by the painful reality of our withered friendship. We had not actually spoken in almost a year, and here he was, feeling like practically a stranger.

"Either is fine—" I began, forcing my tone to sound normal and relaxed.

"Bring the smelling salts!" Rae boomed from behind me as he made a beeline for Arnie. "You've emerged at last."

He pulled him into an embrace, clapping him twice on the back. I stepped aside to allow Copper enough room to enter. She scurried in after me, promptly setting down the pies she held in order to grab hold of both of my hands.

Her face lit up as she looked me up and down. "You look so beautiful I could just pummel you!"

"Thank you, I think," I said, smiling back at the odd girl. "You look great too." She did look beautiful, in a way only she could. She wore an eggplant blouse tucked into a gray, striped full skirt. The real eye-catcher of the outfit was an emerald green snakeskin belt cinched tightly at her waist. The same snakeskin was also featured on her heeled boots.

I couldn't imagine how ridiculous I would have looked in an outfit as eye-catching as that one. I had opted for a white and red checkered dress, which buttoned up to the neck. The only flashy part of the ensemble was the red pumps that matched my dress and lips.

"And look at this guy," Rae said, motioning to Arnie, still clasping his shoulder with his other hand. "He belongs at the King's Feast in this get-up." Arnie was as overdressed as Irenee in his three-piece suit. He wore an uncharacteristically decorative cravat that I couldn't help but smile at— a smile I stifled quickly as Arnie's cheeks lit up scarlet.

"Where's your father? Is he joining us?" I asked Copper, swiftly changing the subject.

"No," she answered just as swiftly. "He has a headache."

A lie. I didn't need to be an empath to see that, but I didn't push. The Pennings had enough on their minds tonight, and I could only assume the absence of their mother was weighing heavily on them all. I knew the feeling.

"Well, I feel very old," Irenee said, breaking the palpable silence. "It's a good thing I've aged so gracefully or I might feel silly spending my Harvest with a hoard of overly perky adolescents." The tension eased immediately, and even Arnie managed a laugh.

Maegon returned with a snow weasel wrapped around her neck, its little head resting on her left shoulder. Irenee applauded her choice while the rest of us tried to hide our amusement, all except Raemond, who proceeded to be a ventriloquist for the late creature all night, lamenting its early demise for the sake of accessorization.

It was a group effort to transport the Harvest feast to the table set up in the garden. After several round trips and a few minor burns, the many plates, sauce boats, and baskets covered the cream tablecloth with barely enough room for the place settings. The scene looked quite picturesque against the setting sun that lit up the sky with fiery tones. Irenee had hauled her gramophone outside and set it up on an adjacent tree stump. She selected an album of swinging brass band songs that rang through the yard. Even the shrubs seemed to sway to the soul-filled rhythm.

I took one final trip to the kitchen to put Copper's pies in the oven so they would stay warm until dessert. I turned back to the door and found Raemond standing there, leaning just as he had when he first arrived.

"You do look beautiful tonight." He broke the competitive silence with a soft smile, forfeiting our little game.

"Have you been here this whole time?" I teased, slowly strolling toward him. "I hadn't even noticed." Raemond closed the distance between us, snaking his arm around my waist.

"You couldn't ignore me if you tried," he said as he leaned in to kiss me. I couldn't help but giggle against his lips as I wrapped my arms around his neck, putting the game to rest. Raemond pulled away, exhaling slowly.

"Happy Harvest, Hildegarde."

"Happy Harvest, Raemond."

The scent of butter and spices floated around the Harvest table as Irenee carved and served up hearty helpings of braised duck. Each of us helped ourselves to a generous ladle of plum sauce, which fulfilled its intended purpose in enhancing the night's humor. When Raemond pointed to the remaining duck carcass and asked his sister if she would perhaps like to wear that in her hair so the weasel would have some company, Copper nearly fell off her chair laughing. This may have been aided by the fact that she had yet to find the bottom of her cup of elderflower wine, but I took pride in the reaction all the same.

Even Maegon was given a nip of wine, which seemed to grow her confidence amongst the older group of young men and women, which was hardly unearned. The whole table was left thrilled after she sent a small band of golden fairies waltzing across the table, a perfected illusion that was seriously impressive for her age.

In all of my tampering with the herbs in each dish, I had been careful not to include any concoction that might stir up painful family memories for anyone at the table. Irenee had lost her sister and husband, the Pennings were without their mother, and I had enough grief in me to last a lifetime. Better to stay in the moment than to get lost staring backward.

The feast went by at a trotting pace, dish after dish: buttered biscuits, minced meat pies, braised duck, rosemary-ginger pudding, pumpkin soup with a crust of poppy bread, cheesy potatoes with a honey glaze, and a finishing pot of mint tea to soothe the stomach before dessert. Even with this remedy, though, we needed a respite before the final course.

"I think I'll take a brisk walk down to the lake, if anyone would like to join me," Irenee said, groaning a bit as she stood. "The willow wisps are always out on the night of Harvest." Mae shot up like a groundhog, unaffected by the gargantuan meal she had just devoured.

"I want to see the wisps! I never get there in time." The energetic girl had already reached Irenee at the head of the table.

"Then we'd better hop to it," Irenee said, coaxing her along. The two set off down the path, Mae chattering away at Irenee's side. The rest of us sat for a moment in the silence that accompanied full bellies. The sky had grown dark, and the table was now illuminated by a string of jars that hung over our heads, each containing the yellow warmth of a glowing firefly. Arnie was the first to stir, straightening up to pour himself another cup of tea.

"Are you all ready?" he asked the group nonchalantly. "In one week, you'll all be done with the academy. No more safety net after that." The question hung between us, passed around in shared glances.

"I know I am," Rae countered, bravado in his tone as he boasted, "I've only been training to be a King's Man since I was thirteen. I'm more than ready to get out on that field." He draped his arm along the back of my chair, giving my shoulder a quick squeeze.

"So you're really going?" Arnie asked, leaning forward as he pressed his weight against the table.

"A year at Camp Valiant? Living in tents with thousands of other dirty boys?" There was a challenging sting to his tone.

"And girls," Copper piped up from her slumped position. "Some girls go to Camp Valiant," she said, giving her brother a pointed glare.

"That's true," Rae interjected. "To be fair, they sleep in separate tents, but I understand your sentiment."

"Maybe you should go with him, Copper," I chimed in. "If anyone could knock Rae off his high horse, it would be you," I said as I raised my cup in recognition of the smug girl.

"And why don't *you* go?" Arnie said suddenly, turning things on me. "Evocation is just two steps up from herbalism in the school of earth, and you've already mastered that." He motioned to the demolished meal that sat in front of them. I felt Rae's arm tense behind me, reacting to Arnie's probing tone.

"Very funny," I said, giving him a dismissive wave. I preferred to resort to self-deprecation if it could diffuse a situation. "Channeling the power of the earth into my bare hands is a far cry from adding a few ground herbs to sticky pudding." I feigned a chuckle, looking away from the table.

"Don't start with that," Copper cut in. "You're brilliant, Hildy—that can translate to *anything you want*." She punctuated the end of this affirmation by whacking her brother on the arm a few times. I noticed he was unable to hide a small wince.

"That's very sweet of you, Copper," I said, feeling a warm wave of gratitude for my friend, "But I'm really happy staying here. I like what I do, and I want to keep doing it. Besides, if I went off and studied evocation or maybe even naturalism, Rae and I wouldn't be able to, um, you know…" I trailed off as my cheeks rose in temperature. It was implied every day that Raemond and I would someday get married, but we had never said it aloud. I shot a glance at Rae to try to signal that I hadn't meant to say that as a given fact, but he was one step ahead of me. He took my hand and held it in both of his, then brought my fingers up to his lips and kissed them. He knew how to soothe me in an instant. Copper looked on with an affectionate smile, but Arnie was visibly uncomfortable.

"Well…" Copper began, drawing out the word to herald a big, impending announcement, "I'll be off to Facehaven if they'll have me." She spoke with the crisp surety of someone who had thought through every detail of the plan repeatedly for a long time. "I'll study enchantment, meet some new people, and keep my options open."

"In case some poor sucker actually offers to marry you?" Arnie said with a guffaw. The smirk on his face vanished as he clumsily dodged the biscuit she threw at him. We all knew it was a good plan, though. Enchantment was considered a domestic tier of magic—the lower tier. She could still travel to other cities and experience new things without losing her chance at a family in her future.

"At least I won't be bunking with Dad, begging the stiffs at the Citadel to let me in," Copper snapped, hurling a sharp insult at her brother. She shifted to the very edge of her seat and pulled her shoulders forward into a somewhat pitiful posture. "Please, Your Majesty," she said in her best Arnie voice, "I'll be a real swell high sorcerer, I swear. I'll study hard and take a vow of celibacy, just for the hell of it!"

This sent Rae into a fit of unrestrained laughter, and it was Arnie who threw the biscuit this time. He didn't miss, the fluffy dough making a soft thunk off Rae's forehead. Laughter started bubbling out of me, and eventually both Penning siblings were able to crack a smile. Losing myself in the camaraderie of the moment—and also suddenly feeling a desperate need to unburden myself—I made a choice.

"I found something in my attic this morning. Something weird," I blurted. All eyes fixed on me, my abruptness catching even myself off guard. Perhaps it was the growing sense of security in the friendship at the table, or maybe it was the nostalgia of the friendship I'd also lost at the table. Either way, I wanted these people to see the sigil. Maybe they could help me understand it.

With great anticipation, I led them up the narrow stairs to the attic. It was pitch black. Rae uttered "*Feu nunc,*" and the solo flint bulb that hung in the center of the room flickered on from the simple fire evocation, casting a circle of warm light.

"What are we supposed to be looking at?" Arnie asked, scanning the space with great interest. I had placed the carpet back over the sigil, so to everyone else, the attic looked perfectly commonplace.

"If I show you what I found," I started, just now considering the consequences of my choice, "you can never tell a soul. Not Irenee, not Maegon. No one can know." I met the eyes of each of them to convey the gravity of what I was asking, and each silently nodded in return. With this assurance, I approached the rug and silently unveiled the symbol.

Arnie's reaction to the image was instantaneous—he crouched beside the pattern and scrutinized the scorch marks. The other two didn't move, but Copper's mouth dropped open like a trout. Rae's pose remained neutral, but I could see the obvious tension on his brow.

"I found it this morning," I said, breaking the brief silence. "When I touched it, it burned me." I held out my right pointer finger as proof.

Arnie exhaled, still gazing at the marks as he reached out to touch its edge. Upon contact, he inhaled sharply and recoiled almost instantly. "If it's still burning like this, that means whatever this spell did, it's still in effect," he explained, armed with years of studying the intricacies of spellcasting. "This would have been a powerful spell… More powerful than anyone in the Orchard could have managed. It's continuing by recasting itself over and over."

"Did you see anything when you touched it?" I tested, impatient for some reassurance.

"No," Arnie answered, looking at me quizzically. "Burned like a horsefly bite, though."

"A crescent moon, a carnation, and a north star center," Copper said slowly, her eyes darting between me and her brother. "That's high sorcery."

"But why?" Rae asked, finally speaking up. "Why would a high sorcerer have been in your attic?"

"It was my mother," I said in a small voice. Arnie stopped examining the symbol, Copper's head jerked toward me, and Rae froze. "I saw her, or a vision of her, when I touched it. She looked exactly the way I remember her—beautiful and... completely terrifying."

"I thought your mother was banished for illegal conjuring," Copper stammered.

"She was. I mean, that's what she was charged with, but when I saw that vision or something from the past, everything just clicked." I had the undivided attention of the whole room. "I remember starting to fall off my bike once, and she caught me with a gust of wind—that's evocation. She could finish cooking a three-course meal in minutes—that must have been with horology. And she always knew what I was thinking. Not just in a motherly way, but word for word—definitely empathy. If she was able to perform feats from every school of magic—earth, void, and mind…" I trailed off then, the trepidation in the room spiking. "What else could that mean?" I motioned timidly to the sigil.

"I believe you," Arnie offered softly.

"You do?" I asked, genuinely taken aback by his immediate support. He raised his eyes to meet mine.

"I do," he said, giving me the smile—albeit a small one—that I desperately needed at that moment.

"I do too," Copper said assertively, jumping in on the coattails of her brother. "It all makes sense. You're good at everything, so it must run in the family."

"Rae?" I asked, turning to my boyfriend. He was now sitting in a wooden chair against the wall; he was hunched, with his weight on his knees and his hands tightly clasped.

After a long pause, he looked up at me with somber eyes and said, "I'm sorry, Hildy. I'm so sorry about your mother." I realized at once what he meant. Raemond had always had a wide enough gaze to see the big picture in front of him. If it was true that my mother had practiced illegal acts of high sorcery, she would never be able to return to the Green Veil—not with her life.

CHAPTER FOUR:
THE WITCH'S ANSWER

Academy graduations were not lengthy or emotional affairs. They consisted of the principal reading the names of those who passed their final examinations, a short speech from the mayor about the responsibility of using magic, and the symbolic turning of the pins. Nevertheless, I couldn't help feeling sentimental as the string quartet began to play. The instruments had been enchanted to amplify their volume so that the melody would not be carried away on the wind. Graduations in the Orchard were always held outside on the banks of Crystal Lake. I had attended the ceremony every year that I could remember, watching friends and mentors pass on to new adventures, but now I was the one moving forward.

Through the sound of violins, Principal Lupine instructed the graduates to "witness the turning of the pins." I looked down as my stone in the center of the academy crest pinned to my robe faded from green to red, symbolizing my freshly earned independence. I had to crane my neck over my right shoulder to catch Rae's eye. Birch and Wimple were about as far apart alphabetically as possible, so he stood a great distance away. Regardless, I found his gaze in an instant, and he beamed back at me with pride. That smile could have melted all the snow off Mount Tempus.

"Now you embark on the path before you, armed with the wisdom of your elders," Principal Lupine continued. "Choose your path wisely, always carrying within you the values of Orchard Academy —honesty, balance, and purity. Congratulations and best wishes."

The crowd erupted into celebration. Graduates embraced any student in sight, parents applauded their children, and underclassmen who had come to observe called out the names of their friends. I heard Irenee wolf-whistle from her back-row seat. As was the custom, we then all sent our ceremonial flat caps flying. There was a gasp of wonder as the flock of caps reached their zenith and suddenly burst into white carnation petals. Through the shower of carnations, I saw Copper running at me full speed. Her embrace would have sent me flying backward if her own tight grasp hadn't prevented any movement at all. Holding me in more of a vice grip than a hug, she shouted in my ear, "We're free!"

Within an hour, the graduates had transformed the shore of Crystal Lake into our own private festival. Several young wizards had built a towering bonfire where they were now roasting sausages and goose patties. Many of Rae's fellow Camp Valiant recruits had gotten a pickup game of "ugly rugby" going, an unnecessarily aggressive sport specific to the region. A large group of witches had gathered beside the game to cheer on their friends and boyfriends, their taunts and words of encouragement made even more inspired by the large bottle of apple liquor making its way through the group. Copper headed up a small band of hopeful enchantment students in their scheme to amplify an old gramophone to ten times its intended volume. When they eventually succeeded, the beach boomed with the kind of raucous music parents called "noise." As soon as a particularly swinging guitar solo came on, Copper pulled me out to dance with her group of friends. When I was finally able to pry myself away from her grasp under the pretense of needing another drink, I found Raemond by the fire.

"What's the game today, Ms. Birch?" Rae asked, taking hold of my hand and spinning me to the beat of the still blasting gramophone. I stumbled a bit, having now finished several mugs of ale on an empty stomach.

"No games, Wimple. Not today," I giggled as I tumbled forward into his waiting arms and planted a kiss on the laughing boy.

"Let's get some food in you," Raemond said as he smiled down at me while I continued to sway a little. We took a seat on a log next to the fire, and I happily devoured the goose patty Rae had lovingly prepared. We all looked on as the sun set over Crystal Lake. I couldn't help but feel a queer kind of finality as the sun set on the final day of our childhood.

Copper and Arnie found us nestled together as the fire slowly crackled down to embers, the original builders now far too sauced to be trusted with open flames. Copper precariously carried three tankards of hot cider that she methodically passed off to me and Rae. Arnie had his own steaming mug in one hand and a half-eaten sausage wrap in the other.

"Arnie!" Rae cried, perking up at the sight of his estranged pal. "Two social gatherings in a week? There must be something in the air."

I jabbed Rae's rib cage with my elbow. I knew he didn't mean any harm in teasing Arnie—that was the way things had always been with us. But, all things considered, I felt as though we needed to work back up to that level of familiarity. Rae glanced at me with a look that said, "It's all right, I know what I'm doing."

"I went home to get him," Copper said as she grabbed hold of her brother's arm and pulled him down beside her, almost spilling his hot cider in the process. "He had to experience at least *one* proper party before giving his soul over to 'a lifetime of diligent study.'" She affected the persona of a pompously dignified intellectual as she finished her sentence. "You all remember his graduating class? They just didn't have our stamina. Everyone was home and in their beds by dusk. That's no way to send a young man into the world."

"I concur," I said and raised my mug to Arnie, hoping to let him in on the joke.

"Here, here," he returned the gesture.

"To the Orchard!" Rae cried, thrusting his tankard up with pride. A few random students nearby also gave some hearty cheers.

"To getting the hell out of the Orchard!" Copper added before taking a hearty swig.

The rest of us followed suit. I could only take a modest gulp due to the drink's temperature, but Rae did not seem to have this problem. We looked on with awe as he downed the entirety of the mug's steaming contents. A few onlookers applauded when he emerged with a gasp for air. I laughed and leaned into him, and he wrapped his arm around me to shelter me from the chill. Off in the distance, the gramophone now played a soulful ballad. A group of drunken couples gave some hoots and hollers as they took a dip in the frigid lake.

Rae stoked the fire back to life, and Copper and Arnie began recounting a sidesplitting story of their quest to liberate all of the apothecary's dung beetles when they were children.

Surrounded by the celebration and laughter of those I had known all my life, I was hit by a sudden sense of loneliness. I had loved my time at the secondary academy. Looking around at my fellow students, I knew each of their names and shared a fond memory with every last one. In the coming weeks, they would all scatter in the wind, setting off to study new schools of magic. This year's graduating class was small—roughly fifty students total—and to the best of my knowledge, barely a third of them were staying in the Orchard. All of them were witches planning to start a family, just like me. I did not envy those going off to the far reaches of the county. The Orchard was home to me. I could not imagine having a life anywhere else. I only wished the familiar faces would be staying closer to me. As the melancholy crept over me like a cloud, I felt Rae turn to look at me. He slid his hand down from my shoulder to my hand and stood.

"Let's take a walk," he offered with a small nod of his head, motioning away from the party. I accepted, grateful for his perceptiveness, and we set off on the path that ran alongside the lake, hand in hand.

"You're leaving tomorrow," I said, breaking the silence. It was not a question—I'd known the date of his departure for weeks now, but it was a topic that we had shied away from up till now.

"I have to," Rae said, watching our feet as he spoke. "Arriving in time for early training will set me apart from the rest. I already have my father's shadow looming over me, so I need all the help I can get." He tightened his grip on my hand. "It would be foolish not to go."

Rae waited for a response from me that did not come. I didn't want to risk ruining the makeup Irenee had so skillfully applied with my tears. "It's only a year, and then I'll be back. We can handle a year. We'll write every day, I'll be back for holidays, and it will all fly by," he said in a chipper voice that I could tell was forced.

I took a deep breath, pushing myself to ask the question that had been weighing on me ever since Raemond had announced his acceptance to the camp. "But it won't be just this year, will it? If all goes the way you want it to, you'll be a King's Man. Then he can send you wherever he wants, and he'll call you up to the border whenever—"

"That's the whole point, Hildegarde," Rae said, cutting me off. "Do you think I relish the idea of being a good little soldier? Taking orders all day? Does that sound like me to you?" He had stopped in the center of the path. "The point is to keep this place safe, to keep my family safe." He took both of my hands tightly in his. "To keep *you* safe." His gaze was glued to mine. "I'll go to the border. I'll go where the king sends me, and then I'll come home. Here. To you. Every time."

Rae's sudden surge of passion floated between us like static energy. I buzzed with the desire to seal the distance and melt into his arms, but I remained still with the anticipation of the question to come. Rae, who was known for keeping a cool exterior, started to show his nervousness in his hands trembling.

"Hildegarde Birch…" Rae began, just above a whisper, "If you will wait for me, and if you find that you still want me in one year's time…" Here he paused to smile at his own self-deprecation. "There is nothing I would like more than to come home to you…" I drew in a sharp breath through my nose as he finished, "every day for the rest of my life." I let my breath out as I held back the tears that were already welling up.

"Raemond Wimple," I said shakily, "you've got yourself a deal." I had barely gotten the words out before Rae took me in his arms, lifting me off my feet. We both laughed as he swung me in a full circle. When my feet touched the ground once more, Raemond pulled my face to his, sealing the arrangement properly. "I was hoping you would get down on one knee, but I'll take what I can get," I said, teasing him through the enormous smile overtaking my face.

"Oh, shut up," Raemond huffed, then drew me back in for another kiss, silencing any further jokes. From the distant beach, the small crowd around the bonfire let out an assortment of whoops and hollers. There was no way to tell if they had deciphered Raemond's proposal from watching the exchange or if they were just at the diminished state of now cheering for any act of physical affection. Either way, I no longer felt the melancholy of being alone in a crowd.

I sank gratefully into my bed, the coils squeaking under my weight. My feet sighed with relief as I kicked off my heeled sandals. They hit the wall with two hollow thuds. I knew that loosening my girdle would maximize my comfort significantly, but that would require sitting up, which I was in no mood to do. I hated waist cinchers. They were dreadfully uncomfortable, and the boning left red lines pressed into my skin. With the formality of graduation, though, I had felt a need to heighten my appearance somewhat.

My mother had worn a girdle every day of my life. Maude Birch was a woman who dripped with glamour. Her beauty was almost scary, with every desirable trait accentuated so far beyond the norm that I remembered her seeming practically inhuman sometimes. Each of her limbs was long and thin, almost spider-like. She had to alter the waistline of every article of clothing she purchased in order for the fabric to hug her dangerously small body. Yet she still had worn those girdles every single day, satisfied only with perfection. Imagining my mother hiding from the Green Veil authorities in some dank cave in the wilderness, I still could only picture her with her waist cinched and hair done. Though it was far more likely that she had illusioned a whole new life for herself. Perhaps she had even found a new family.

I inhaled deeply and smelled the bonfire smoke thick in my hair. The night's events had left me reeling. Rae had proposed! Well, he had almost proposed. He had not asked the question exactly, and no ring was presented, but I was glad for that. I didn't want to spend the first year of our official engagement so far apart. This way, everything was unofficially officially settled. Raemond would go off and make a name for himself at Camp Valiant, I would have a year to study herbalism in the Orchard, and then the two of us would begin our life together. All the questions and fears that had been swirling around my mind could be put to bed. I had made my choice, and now I could rest. Just as I began to drift off to sleep, there was a gentle knock at my bedroom door.

"Is anyone alive in there?" Auntie Irenee cooed, cracking the door open.

"Barely," I grunted, forcing myself into a seated position as the pesky girdle jammed itself into my ribcage. Irenee let herself in. She was carrying two parcels, one in each hand.

"I remember my graduation night," Irenee wistfully began, taking a seat on the end of the bed. "Maxx and I went skinny dipping in Crystal Lake, and I was wheezing for a week. I kept trying to make myself herbal remedies, which of course I had no skill in, so I ended up dying my hair violet."

"Too much iris in the brew?" I asked. I had seen this result in a few of my classmates' potions before.

"Yes, but the color suited me. I ended up keeping it for three months," Irenee said with a smirk. Then she abruptly offered me the smaller of the two parcels. This one was wrapped in a deep blue paper with small silver moons printed across them and a thick black ribbon tied around it in a bow. "Happy graduation, Hildegarde."

I took the little package and smiled at my dear aunt. I unwrapped the paper, careful not to tear it, and revealed a green velvet box that opened with a click. Inside was a golden wristwatch with a thin leather band.

"Irenee, it's gorgeous..." I held it up to catch the light of the flint bulb on my bedside table. At the end of one of the hands, there was a little sun, and a moon tipped the other. Along the perimeter of the watch face, characters of the old language had been etched into the gold.

"Until we meet again," Irenee chimed, as if she had just read my mind. "There's the normal time at the center, but see the dials in the bottom there?" I looked closely to see three small numbers, each reading zero. "When we are apart, that will tell you how long it will be until we see each other. It's very accurate—it can count down to the second. But if that's too indulgent, I can remove it."

"No, don't!" I blurted, cutting her short. "I love it, Irenee. It's so perfect. Thank you." I lunged at her and held her in a tight embrace. She reciprocated, albeit very stiffly.

"Now, if you go off on a wild adventure or go study at some faraway school, you'll have the assurance that it isn't goodbye." Irenee was clearly holding back tears as she let me go.

"Luckily, I don't think we'll ever have that problem. I'll never be more than an acre away," I said while clasping the watch to my left wrist.

"Right, while you're studying herbalism. But if you go off to the Thorough Woods to learn naturalism, it may be of some use."

I chuckled, unsure whether she was kidding or not. "Why would I study naturalism?" I asked, deciding to test the waters.

"Of course, there's nothing wrong with herbalism, but you're already so good at it. I figured you'd want to challenge yourself at some point, and naturalism would be the obvious next tier of study," Irenee said, looking as if we had discussed this many times before.

"I can't study naturalism," I said, locking eyes with her. "I'm getting married."

Tension enveloped the room. Irenee withdrew her hand, which had been resting on my knee. "You're what?" she asked coldly.

"He asked me tonight," I said, figuring I didn't need to clarify.

"Raemond Wimple asked for your hand in marriage the day before he leaves for a year?" It was more an accusation than a proper question.

"He didn't ask me outright. It was more of a promise." We sat in tense silence before I pressed on, "It isn't like you didn't see this coming. You knew we were moving toward this. You know how much I love him."

"Love away," she said, waving her hands dismissively. "But you don't have to rush into a commitment that you can't take back." She seized my hand in hers. "Give yourself time to study herbalism or enchantment. Study empathy for all I care. They're low tier studies, and practicing them won't bar you from having a family one day. If you still want him after some time apart, take him then. At least you'll have seen some of the world." She brought one hand up to pinch the bridge of her nose. "You're still a child in so many ways!"

"A child?" I ripped my hand away. "I'm no more a child than you! You, with your tantrums and fits. I don't need your scolding. You don't need to play mother. I've been motherless for ten years, and I turned out just fine." I was on my feet now, looking down at my aunt.

"Be as cruel as you like, but you won't enrage me out of my opinion. I have always acted in your best interest, just as I am doing now." Irenee stood up to meet me, now towering over my slight stature.

"How could marrying the man I love not be in my best interest?"

"Because it's a trap, Hildegarde. You know I loved your Uncle Maxx, but I had to lose him to see the truth. They marry us off to keep us weak. Your mother knew that, and they chased her out of the country for it!" Irenee's voice started to rise, each word meant to bite.

"My mother was an egomaniac who chose power over her own family! Over me!" My face had suddenly become hot and wet with tears.

"Maude was never chasing power, and she never chose magic over you. Everything she did, she did to protect you," Irenee said in what felt like a placating tone.

"Then where is she?!" I screamed. "She could do a hell of a better job if she were still here. I may never see the world or study high sorcery, but I will be a good mother, and I will *never* leave my child alone in this world. That's more than she ever did."

"Hildegarde, there is so much you still don't know." Irenee tried to take both of my shaking hands, but I withdrew them before she had the chance. She pressed on with desperate compassion, saying, "Had it been my place, I would have told you the truth long ago, but now the truth has tangled itself up in all these silent years. I wouldn't know where to begin. But you have to understand that your mother loved you with all her power."

"The only proof I have of that is your word," I spat.

"You have this," Irenee said, reaching to grab the second parcel off the desk where she had set it and dropping it on the bed. It bounced once before its weight settled into the plush center of the mattress. It was a sizable rectangle wrapped in weathered parchment and tied with a single string of twine.

"What is this?" I asked, nonplussed at what Irenee might be offering me.

"It's a gift…" Irenee said, her electric eyes meeting mine, "from your mother."

I sat back down on the bed and gingerly lifted the tattered present. As I set it in my lap, it felt warm, almost alive. With unsure hands, I untied the twine and plunged a fingernail into the fold of the paper. It ripped with a dry crinkling, exposing a patch of soft, black leather. The room, which had been mild and temperate, began to rise in temperature as I uncovered more of the book. Irenee's loose hair began to sway in the light current of the circling air, which seemed to emanate from the silver sigil on the cover of the now fully exposed book. I lifted my bewildered eyes to meet Irenee's, whose were now brimming with tears. She sat back down at my side and laid a slender hand on the book.

"She risked her life to create these magics," she said, her fingers circling the embedded crescent moon. "They were the source of her greatest power, but she left them behind. On the night the watchmen came for her, she took the time to hide this here before fleeing. She left it for you."

"You can't know that," I said shakily. "She could have left it here to protect her secrets, to keep others from having them."

"Open the book, Hildegarde."

There on the first brittle page was my mother's elegant handwriting with all its flourishes and crisp lines. There was one simple sentence in the center of the page. It read:

To my Hildegarde. May the winds blow you back to me.

Chapter Five: The Witch's Tale

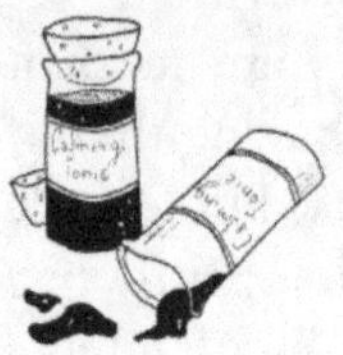

My hair frizzed in the steam that covered the platform. An anxious young man bumped my shoulder as he hurried onto the train, his face streaked with tears from bidding farewell to someone dear. Rae and I were standing face-to-face in pained silence. Rae wore a long traveling coat and had a hefty duffle thrown over his shoulder. He had said his goodbyes to his family at their home before he left with me at dawn for the station. I was certain I must have looked as exhausted as I felt. I had not slept for even a moment the night before. The weight of unanswered questions sat heavily on my chest, a menacing creature that was too unnerving for rest. And yet, I had not unburdened myself by telling Raemond any of it. In fact, we had walked all the way without a word.

"Hildy," he said, gingerly taking my limp hand, "I know last night was a whirlwind, and if you've changed your mind, I would underst—"

"No!" I said, springing back to life. "I haven't changed my mind about anything. I love you." I leaned into him as he exhaled his tension. "I just had a rough night."

"What happened?" he asked, his brow furrowed.

"I just…" I trailed off. He was leaving in a matter of moments to begin the most stressful academy in all of the Green Veil. There was nothing he could do to help me now, and it would only make him feel guilty for leaving. "…couldn't sleep," I finished. It wasn't an outright lie, just a fraction of the story.

He pulled me in close for a tight hug. "I meant what I said." I could feel the heat of his breath against my neck as he spoke. "I want to come home to you." Then I felt something cold and round pressed into my palm. "I want to marry you."

I looked down into my clammy hand and saw a small silver band with one delicate moonstone.

"It's really happening," I exclaimed, my voice catching in my throat. I didn't have time to catch that breath again before Raemond pulled me back into a soft kiss. Later, I would wish my mind had not been elsewhere for that kiss. I would savor it in my moments alone, as I should have when it came. But in that instant, I was elsewhere, and before I knew it, so was he, leaving only a ring in my hand.

Since Harvest, the air had grown colder each day, and I now wore a green woolen coat to keep off the chill. As I trudged along the path back home, wiping away some tears that kept stubbornly falling, I spied a bush of lemon-nettles just off the road. Knowing it to be a key ingredient in a salve for a busy or distracted mind, I hurried over to collect it. With my head buried deep in the shrub, I did not see or hear the girl approaching me from behind.

"Whatcha doing?" The voice came in loud and impish in my left ear. I swatted the air as I spun on my heel, coming face to face with Copper.

"Dammit, Copper," I cried, pressing a hand to my chest, "You are a menace." She, of course, was folded over in laughter at my frightened jump. Through the sharp breaths I took to regain my composure, I released a bit of bubbling laughter. Copper gathered me into her long arms and swayed with me side to side, still chuckling.

"I'm sorry, sweet thing," she said into my ear, holding me tight. "I can never resist." She released me from her captive embrace after a playful squeeze. "What are you doing up so early? I figured you'd be sleeping until dusk after the night you had." Copper eyed my face closely—likely taking note of the bags that hung heavily from my eyes, now red and puffy.

"I saw Raemond off at the station," I said, looking down at my boots. "He was on the first train out."

She took me in her arms again, holding me more steadily this time. I appreciated the warm affection and sank into it.

"He's going to be okay," she breathed into my ear, catching me off guard. In all our talks about the future, I had hardly considered the risk Rae was taking. There was still conflict at the border, and knowing him, I was certain Raemond would volunteer to be on the front lines if asked. As if having read my mind, Copper stepped back to look me dead in the eyes.

"He isn't just strong." She held my shoulders as she said, "He's smart. He'll be the boy to beat the moment he arrives. Everyone says so." I appreciated the sentiment, but it failed to calm my nerves.

"Did you ever consider going to Camp Valiant?" I asked, my distracted thoughts prompting a convenient change in topic. She had always been fearless and quick to show her skills. If any girl could have matched up to the rough and tumble boys of the camp, it would have been her.

"I'm not good with authority," she said with a smirk, dancing the line between humility and self-deprecation. "I'll be happier shut up in a Facehaven workshop. I'm better with wood and wire than with people," she said, giving a vague gesture toward her ears.

It was only then that I noticed Copper's earrings. From each of her lobes dangled a golden swallow, both flapping their wings in perfect time with her breathing. No doubt she had made the birds herself and also used a rune of her own imagining. I could see her future so clearly: she would go to the Academy of Enchantment and spend her days tinkering away over her fantastic creations as her fellow workers bustled around her. Perhaps she would marry if a man came around who could keep up with the frantic pace at which she lived, but either way, she would be happy, busy, and self-assured in her actions.

Yesterday, I had felt the same way about my own path, but now everything felt coated in fog. I could see the way still, but only with some strain.

"Copper…" I said quietly, then stopped to scan the road before us. We were alone, only the early morning haze our witness. I whispered, "It was my mother who made the mark in the attic. Irenee confirmed it last night. She practiced high sorcery, and Irenee has known all this time."

Copper nodded slowly, her lips pressed tightly together. Softly, she responded, "You *really* had quite a night last night." My eyes flitted down to the ring I had absentmindedly slipped on the middle finger of my left hand instead of my ring finger.

"She didn't only practice it," I said, my voice shaky. "She was a master. A spell-maker." Her eyes widened as she took a clumsy step back from me. She scanned the surrounding terrain for potential witnesses and likewise found nothing but trees and sky.

Nevertheless, she clasped me tightly by the hand and said abruptly, "Come with me."

She hurriedly led me off the road and over some rolling hills that ran adjacent to the path. As we scurried down the slope, she hissed, "I may have the impulse control of a toddler, but even *I* wouldn't say something like that on the main road." We stumbled over a patch of rough earth before settling into the soft moss of a willow grove. Wisps of ghostly blooms hung about, masking us from any onlookers.

Her expression was dead serious, angry even, as she stared at me. "Blast, Copper," I huffed as I snatched my hand back, bewildered by her uncharacteristic sobriety. "There was no one else on the road. No one could have been listening."

She took a single, decisive step toward me, holding my gaze. In a low voice, she whispered, "Someone is *always* listening when you talk of such things." This caught my attention, and a shiver ran down my body. Copper may have been prone to hyperbole, but not to paranoia. I could not disregard the earnestness in her eyes as she pressed on. "Mama used to warn me about speaking out of turn. When I was little, I thought she was just like all the other mothers, getting on us about etiquette and pointless customs. But before she died, she told me to be careful… deadly careful. She told me that a girl has to be twice as innocent as any man to be seen half as lawful."

"Because it's a trap, Hildegarde." Irenee's warning from the night before rang in my ears, and I suddenly became sharply aware of the metal band around my finger.

"There's more to tell..." I croaked, my throat having gone very dry. "She wrote a spellbook, at least three hundred pages, and she left it for me."

Copper took in a sharp gasp as she slapped her hands over her mouth. She began to speak before she had lowered them, "Oh, Hildegarde," she said in a muffled cry, "What are you going to do?"

"I have no idea... Do nothing? That's all I can do. I'll lock it up somewhere and let it gather dust."

"If anyone finds it in your home, you will be in a heap of danger, and so will Irenee. Unlicensed high sorcery is more punishable than murder." Her warning caused terror to spike in my chest, and I spun away to take a deep breath, my hands laced in my thick hair.

"Then I'll destroy it. I'll burn it in our hearth fire tonight—"

"Don't you dare!" Copper cried out, ignoring her own advice about discretion. "Do you understand what it takes to create a book like that? There's a reason high sorcery is nearly impossible to practice. The smallest flaw can kill the caster in an instant. Not to mention its worth. I can't tell you what Arnie would do to get his hands on something like that."

"You think *Arnie* would risk his life for a book? I wouldn't exactly describe him as a rebel," I snapped, my volume spiking in return.

"No one *should*, but three rejections from the Citadel will make even the most pathetic souls desperate enough to commit crazy acts."

I paused. "Three rejections?" I had only heard of the first, which had come just after his graduation.

"He received the third letter last night. I told him to wait after the first time, but he just had to apply again at the mid-year term. So, he's made a fool of himself before the council three times in one year. Do you think they'll ever accept him now?" Copper said, her face bitter. This was a misfortune she definitely did not revel in.

"How is he?" I asked, my fear and anger at this complicated situation moving aside for my growing pity. All Arnie had ever wanted was to study at the Citadel. Though I could imagine him thriving in any of the high-tiered studies, I knew they would never bring him satisfaction. It would be the best or nothing for that boy.

"He's a puddle of a man. He opened the letter with Dad and I at the table, but as soon as he read it, he ran off to his room. I don't think he wanted us to see him cry. He was so sure he had been accepted that he'd even brought home a bottle of sparkling blackberry wine to celebrate. Now it's sitting on the shelf, probably doomed to just gather dust."

When she spoke again, she suddenly took me by the hands. "My brother is weeping himself dry for the wisdom he'll never receive. I live each day in fear that I will never be granted an opportunity to pursue my true ambitions. And here you are, holding more power than anyone within this pathetic little territory, prepared to throw it all away."

I certainly had thought of all the danger that book held; the thoughts had kept me tossing all through the night. But it was its potential I had not considered. Had my mother left it for me to use? I had no lofty ambitions like the Pennings, but could I lock that book in the cupboard and still live the life I had planned for myself? Would I be able to ignore the power that lay within, or would I give in to its call, as my mother likely had before me?

But I could never cast those magics. I'd been told horror stories in my youth of unworthy sorcerers who'd bled out through their eyes and ears or tore themselves into a dozen pieces with spells above their capabilities. I saw myself dead on the floor after casting my mother's most elementary spell. What good would those pages do then?

Copper's hair glowed like embers in the rising sun, and the rays beaming in changed the willow buds from looming ghosts to flickers of gentle light. The world around me was gloomy no longer, the promise of a fresh day rising with the dawn. And yet I still felt a sharp chill deep in my bones. I could not leave these questions un-answered, not if I wanted to reclaim the inner peace I had possessed only one day before.

"Copper, I have to go," I said, securing my satchel back over my shoulder and starting toward the road.

"Wait, Hildy," she called, "Please know that what I said, I only meant out of love for you."

"I know that, Copper, and thank you."

A heavy thud rang through our house as the front door hit the wall. Irenee's coffee jumped from her mug as she jolted up in shock. I stood in the doorway, my left arm still extended with the force it took to throw the thick wooden door open.

"Hildegarde Birch!" Irenee shouted without looking at me, absorbed with trying to shake the droplets of coffee off her silk robe. "This dressing gown is from the Citadel."

"Oh, put some tonic on it. You don't need to be a naturalist to remove a stain," I dismissed, ad-vancing through the door and making for the ice-box.

"Would you close the door? I'll catch my death in this chill," Irenee grumbled, pulling her robe tightly around herself. Without a word, I dropped a bottle of tonic on the kitchen counter in front of her before turning back to push the door shut with my foot. With my dramatic entrance over, I turned on my heel to face Irenee.

"What in the name of necromancy is wrong with you, girl?" Irenee chided as she forcefully dabbed the coffee spatters with tonic.

"I want to know everything," I announced with my newfound certainty. "I need to know how this all happened to us."

Irenee gawked at me for a moment, dropping the rag to her lap. Taking a moment to compose herself, she then motioned with a graceful hand to the stool beside her. "Have a seat, love." I did so, sitting upright in anticipation.

Before continuing, Irenee set her hand on my knee. "I assume it is your mother that you want to know everything about?"

"If everything I've learned in the past few days is true," I said, looking down at my hands, "I didn't know her at all. I should know who she was, at the very least." I looked up at Irenee, who nodded softly before beginning.

"Your mother was a true talent, not unlike yourself. I could see it from the start. As you know, I was the one to raise your mother for the most part. I was already a woman when our parents died, and Maxx and I had a home of our own. Maude was a great blessing for our lives— as you have been—since we could never have children of our own. But even then, I was never truly a mother to her. I let her do as she pleased. I wasn't built of maternal stock, which you have seen well enough. I had no clue how to best steer her course, so I never tried. She was as wild and free as the first gusts of Harvest. Since children can practice any school of magic without punishment, she dabbled in them all. I was sure she would go off to study a higher tier of magic and live the life I never could. We were thrilled beyond words when she was accepted into the Academy of Illusion. Maxx and I threw her a party that this town would never forget."

"Mother was going to study in the Flat Lands?" My eyes widened picturing it: a young Maude's hair loose and blowing chaotically in a desert storm. If there was one wonder in the Green Veil I had ever dreamed of seeing, it was the eerie mysticism of the oasis where the Academy of Illusion stood.

"She was," Irenee said, her eyes distant with the mists of nostalgia draped over her. "I could not have been prouder. We put her on that train without a single tear shed. It was Baldwin who couldn't take it." Irenee looked like she had just bitten into something horribly bitter. "He had fallen in love with her. He knew who she was and what she wanted, and yet that didn't stop him from chasing after her. The day she boarded the train, he caught a ride with an empath caravan to meet her at her stop in Facehaven. He brought her home that same night." Irenee clenched her fists on her knees. "I will never know what Baldwin said to her in that city to change the entire course of her life. She never explained it to any of us, and two weeks later, she was married next to the lake in the very same place we had just celebrated her send-off. I would have wept for her, but she looked so happy. By springtime, you had come along, and it looked as though Maude was okay with settling into a domestic life."

I thought of my mother's smile in the wedding photo I had seen in the attic. If I had heard this story as a younger girl, it would have seemed terribly romantic, but now, I could not ignore a sinister nagging in my gut. Irenee went on.

"At first, she was so busy with you, she hardly had the time to think of magic. When you were a baby, your father was studying divination in Inntinn Bay. Your mother stayed behind for the support Maxx and I gave her with you, but for those first two years, we hardly saw Baldwin. He was free to pursue his highest ambitions while your mother was left to raise you. He achieved those ambitions, as you know. He went on to serve as one of the Orchard's chief Foreseers and was even called upon to serve on a commission for the king."

I recalled all the happy moments with my father and realized just how many of them were of the joy I had felt when he came home with some new toy, the happiness outweighing all the tears shed at his frequent absences. Irenee pressed on.

"Once you were older and slightly less work, I noticed Maude becoming increasingly more restless. She set out to master all the lower-tier magics through independent study—not technically illegal, since they can be practiced without a license, but highly uncommon for a housewife. It took her less than a year. You were hardly speaking full sentences, and she had mastered enchantment, empathy, and herbalism. So she started combining them. She enchanted your favorite stuffed toy, a little green goose, with an empathy charm. Whenever you felt stress or fear, it would waddle over to your arms. I told her she had to be careful. She didn't have the training to protect herself from the toll that too much magic can take on a witch.

Sadly, I was right. The more she lost control of the casting, the more she lost control of reality. It got to the point where we would find her wandering the streets barefoot in the snow, looking for willow wisps or dancing naked on the roof. She would burst through our door in the dead of the night, you cradled in her arms and rave about how she was being watched by the clocks. Your father was afraid for her and brought home a powerful calming tonic from an herbal healer in the Citadel. For your sake, she started taking it each morning. Only it didn't make her calm—it made her numb. For a year, she lived like the walking dead, never casting an enchantment, never brewing a potion, staying out of everyone's minds. It was the worst thing I'd ever seen. The life had been drained from my sister. Her cheeks lost their color, she shrank down in size, and even her voice turned quiet."

"I don't remember any of this," I exhaled through dry lips.

"You wouldn't," Irenee said, sweeping a tear away from her soft cheek. "You weren't even five then, and we did our very best to shield you from the worst of it. But Maxx and I reached our breaking points with the herbs and tranquilizers. We came to your home when your father was out of town and drained every vial of that foul stuff into the lavatory, where it belonged. It wasn't easy getting her back. For days, she cried for her medicine and broke down into cold sweats. Maxx couldn't bear to watch, so he took you to our house to wait out the storm. But it was all worth it. Maude found herself again somehow. She started corresponding with other mothers from different territories, and they gave each other strength. So much strength, in fact, she found a new focus in her life and was able to master higher tiers of magic."

"But how? How could she practice illusion or evocation without detection?" This was the question that had been holding possession over my mind. Empathy, enchantment, and herbalism were viewed as non-threatening by the Wizard Council and therefore remain unregulated, but any second or third-tier activity required a license that wives were prohibited from earning. The Wizard Council employed watchmen to seek out violators and bring them to a very harsh justice.

"That's what I asked her the first time I saw her clear the clouds from the sky," Irenee said, actually smiling at the memory. "She simply told me that she had friends in her corner. She must have spoken honestly because she went undetected for another three years. Those years were the best in my life. Maude was content, you were happy, Baldwin seemed to be a good husband and father, Maxx had just opened his shop, and I had the privilege of basking in the joy of my family."

Irenee's eyes suddenly turned flinty. "But that all changed in a single night. Like a bad memory, your mother came bursting through our door with you once again. Only this time she was of sound mind—terrified—but herself. She told me she had to go away, that things had escalated quicker than she had planned, and she could no longer keep us safe from her actions. She told Maxx and me that we could only trust the people in that room. I mentioned your father, as he was not with us because the king had called him to the Citadel for council, but she remained firm on that point.

"That was when she told me about the book and where to find it, when the time came. She told me to protect you, gave you a kiss, and was gone. The next morning, the Wizard Council issued a warrant for her arrest. I never saw my sister again," Irenee finished in a quavering voice. She sniffled and wiped more tears away. "For years I've been trying to piece together each memory, to make some sense of that last night, and I keep coming back to the same moment—the night of Maude's wedding, when I was helping her to change from her long ivory wedding dress into her party dress for the reception. I couldn't help asking why she

had given up her education for Baldwin. For the
first time since she had returned home to us, her
mask of joy cracked, and without looking away
from her own reflection in the mirror, she said,
'Women are born with the strength to sacrifice.'
That was all she ever said on that. Whatever that
sacrifice was for… she paid dearly for it."

Chapter Six: The Witch's Parting

Irenee and I had not spoken a word in the time it took my aunt to brew a pot of black tea and pour us both cups. I cradled the warm, delicate saucer in my hands, unmoving as I remained lost in the pattern of my breathing. Irenee sipped from her cup rhythmically and watched my face, waiting for me to respond.

"The letters…" I managed, my brain finally producing a clear question. "The ones that she wrote to other wives—do you know where the responses are?"

"No, and I've looked," Irenee said. "But if they were of any significance, your mother likely would have destroyed them. If not, then perhaps she merely threw them away." We both looked down into our teacups, unsure of what to say next. Suddenly, Irenee sat upright, eyes wide.

"There is something else!" She clinked her cup down as she hastily stood. "I'm getting daft with age. I had almost forgotten." Her sentences were faint as she was already starting down the hall into her study. I wasted no time following. As I approached the room, I heard the rustle of papers and muttering.

"Here it is," the old witch cried in triumph as I rounded the corner. She stood behind her desk with its large drawer open. In her hand, she clasped an unmarked envelope with a black wax seal.

"This came to our house by messenger a few days after your mother's disappearance." She held the letter out to me, and I gingerly took it, thumbing it gently. "The seal won't break or come off, and the paper won't rip. I have to assume it was sent by a talented enchanter."

I noticed a dark stain dried on the seal. Giving it a closer inspection, I asked, "Is that blood?"

"It's mine," Irenee admitted as she sat in her great chair, closing the drawer. "Maxx used to sell blood seals in his shop. They only open with the blood of the intended recipient. I thought mine might open it since Maude and I are sisters, but I was wrong."

"So you think I could open it?" I inferred.

"You are of Maude's body. You grew inside her. Never underestimate that power—it's nature's greatest magic." She quietly offered me a small blade from her desk. I took it, noting that it was, ironically, a letter opener. Without hesitation, I pushed the knife against the tip of my thumb. Wincing at the sting, I then set the knife down on the desk where I had laid the letter. I had to squeeze my thumb with two fingers to get a bead of scarlet blood to form, then I brushed my thumb over the seal. We both hunched over the letter in anticipation. As soon as the blood touched the seal, it began to melt away as if the blood itself was molten. I ripped the letter open, taking care to avoid the hot wax, which was already hardening again on the paper. Inside, there were only a few lines of ungraceful text. I strained to make it out, but I read aloud as I deciphered.

> *My Dear Friend,*
>
> *I am moved by your plight and your cause to free the women of the Veil. I deeply wish that I could come to your aid, but I must confess myself unable. I have to put my own children ahead of the Sisterhood. My affection toward you is vast, and so is my pain in this cowardice. I can only hope my previous words of counsel were of some significance. Forgive me. You are stronger than I. Be well, sister.*
>
> *Your Unworthy Friend,*
> *Lacey Neddles*

"She must have been one of Maude's fellow mothers," Irenee said, her eyebrows scrunched in thought as she speculated. "An enchanter, judging by the blood seal."

"What cause is she referring to?" I was reeling from the cornucopia of new information I had received in the past hour.

"Your guess is as good as mine. You'd have to ask Lacey." The thought left Irenee's lips as a small joke, but as soon as it was said, we both stared at each other, recognizing the potential.

"If she is an enchanter, she could still be in Facehaven," I said, my thoughts buzzing with the rush of deduction as I leaned forward on the desk.

"Or at the very least would have studied there," Irenee mumbled, leaning forward with equal interest. "They keep records of former students on file, so someone there should know where she ended up. During my time with Maxx at the Academy of Enchantment, I made friends with many students who went on to become professors, so I have some connections there."

"If Mother was part of some secret organization, someone in it must know what she did to get arrested," I mused. "They may even know where she fled to."

"And Lacey could be the gateway to those women."

"We have to find her."

"*You* have to find her," Irenee said with crisp certainty.

"Me?" I was instantly taken aback, "No way. If I'm going to do this, I need you with me."

"This is your path, Hildy, not mine," Irenee said, her eyes cold and piercing as she stared at me. "She may be my sister, but the answers to your mother's story will impact you and all your life ahead of you. Rae is off becoming the person he will be, but you, Hildy, you've seen nothing of the world beyond the Orchard. You need to go and find some truth out there, without me pestering you. There could be a lot of risk in finding this information, but I think it's about time you understand some of the dangers facing you in this world. And I know you've got a good head on your shoulders." She folded up the letter carefully, then held it out to me as an offering. "Follow this path where it takes you, and if you come out of all this content to be an Orchard housewife, you will have my unconditional blessing."

It was a challenge; Irenee was testing my resolve. I saw the bait dangling in front of me and resented the setup. Did she truly believe a road trip could change how I felt about Raemond? About my future?

"I'll be heading into a city I've never set foot in, completely without you," I pressed, wondering if she would back down from her suggestion.

"It will be a big new adventure," Irenee replied with a twinkling smile.

"And how will you judge my every decision with me so far away?" I asked, poking the sleeping bear because I felt more comfortable with an argument than the gravity of Irenee's suggestion.

"I suppose I'll have to take a break," she said breezily, not budging in her resolve. I was feeling bewildered and unmoored at this sudden shove to leave the nest.

"But I can't go there all alone," I confessed, peering up at her timidly.

"Well, of course not," she agreed. "And it says a great deal about your character for you to admit that. So seek help along the way. Accept the support of friends and the kindness of strangers, on the rare occasion you find them. You can't do it all by yourself, but you *can* do it without me."

"I'm not my mother. I'm no great caster," I said as my voice caught in my throat. My chest felt tight as I fought back a warm surge of panicked tears. "I'm just a kitchen witch."

"Oh, Hildy," Irenee said tenderly, shaking her head. "I only wish that someday you can come to see the power in that." She looked at me with misty eyes.

"I'm not shipping off to war, Auntie," I responded, now confused why she was looking at me sentimentally. "Facehaven is only a few hours away, so why make this such a big deal that I *have* to do it alone?" Irenee sighed and pursed her lips.

"A few hours can feel like a lifetime, Hildegarde."

Caught between curiosity and stubbornness, I took a deep breath, realizing the truth in my own words. This wasn't me going off to war— it was just going to visit an academy in the neighboring city. What was the big fuss?

I took a steadying breath, then raised my chin and said, "Fine. I'll go find Lacey Neddles, I'll follow the trail, and when it runs dry in a few days, I'll be right back here where I belong." Irenee bowed her head soberly, agreeing to the terms.

We started travel preparations at once. The rest of the day was spent huddled over maps and lists prepared by Irenee. We decided it would be easiest for me to travel to Facehaven by train. If anyone were to ask, I would have the plausible deniability of touring the facility as a potential student. I found it unlikely that anyone would think to question a young witch traveling to a low-tier school, but Irenee stressed airing on the side of caution at every turn. With that in mind, she equipped me with a list of Facehaven enchanters who could be trusted. Some of them had been schoolmates of Irenee's, others had done dealings with Maxx's shop. The list was short but certainly valuable.

Next, we set upon my wardrobe to select a few versatile outfits, a task that should have been rather quick. However, Irenee kept second-guessing each article of clothing I selected, and eventually I left her to finish the job on her own. With her preoccupied with my personal styling, I prepared a few simple brews that I thought might prove useful: my go-to stress relief brew, a mild honesty tonic, and a rather theatrical potion that could cause a large explosion when exposed to a flame. I could not imagine a real-life scenario that would require such a thing, but it was reassuring to have something that felt protective. I gathered as many dried herbs and vials of extract as I could justify, attempting to be prepared for all possible potion needs that might arise. Lastly, I remembered that I still had leftover Drops of Familiarity, more affectionately known as Fast-Friends Candies, from a school project. I packed the last handful of these along with the potions and ingredients in the sturdy wooden brew box Irenee had given me for my last birthday.

With the packing complete, we sat down for a dinner of soup and bread. Irenee couldn't stop gushing about the people I would meet and the things I would see on my travels. She flipped between encouragement and caution, warning me to be wary of soldiers and watchmen, recommending a few scenic stops to make on my way back, telling me not to draw attention to myself, and making a list of items and fabrics she would not mind receiving as souvenirs.

I tried to listen to her, but my mind was skipping like a rock over a frozen lake. All I wanted was to retire to bed and take a few silent moments for myself. When I finally did so, I found my baby blue suitcase neatly packed and sitting on my quilt. Beside it was its matching accessory case, my brew box, an outfit laid out to be worn the following morning, and one other bag I did not immediately recognize. It was a plain leather satchel with a bronze clasp. I took it in my hands, and its worn-in brown tone faded to forest green. At once, I recognized it as my mother's shoulder bag. It had been enchanted to match seamlessly with the wearer's outfit. On my mother's shoulder, it had typically been brilliant red or polished silver, but on me, it suffered a more understated palette. With whatever it had inside, the bag was notably heavy. I went to open it and remembered the last of the bag's tricks—it only opened with a kiss on the clasp. Maude had certainly had her own way of doing things. With a quick peck, the clasp sprang open to reveal the sole inhabitant: my mother's spellbook.

I slept terribly, filled with both childlike anticipation and foreboding fear; it was like I was watching an incoming thunderstorm. Though the night air that crept through my cracked window was cold and dry, my brow was thick with sweat. The narrow bed frame creaked and shifted with my tossing weight, and just as I found some peace and began to doze off, a rude grunt from the beams of the old home woke me again.

Abandoning any hope of rest, I sat up. The room was so full of moonlight that I could navigate it with no other light. Without a clear reason, I reached down to the pile of luggage strewn on the floor next to me and pulled up the satchel, which now turned a red plaid to match my pajama set. I kissed the clasp and removed the heavy book with care. Opening the cover with a shiver, I began gingerly turning the brittle pages. The same pulsing hum emanated from the open pages as before, but the sensation was less intense. I did not know what I was looking for. Perhaps I just wanted to see my mother's graceful penmanship. I stopped on a page with a small drawing of a hand beside the title. The tendons on the hand were pronounced with tension, and the title read "*Bannir fjende.*" I racked my rudimentary knowledge of the old language for some translation of the phrase but could conjure nothing. The remaining text on the page was likewise unintelligible. Still captivated by the artistry, though, I stroked the lettering with my pointer finger. Suddenly, the haze of sleep began to wash over me at last. My eyelids grew heavy, my breathing slowed, and I fell back against the goose feather pillows.

The hot wind slapped against the girl's cheeks, sharp with the fragments of sand it carried. The sun hung low in the sky, which seemed to stretch out endlessly against the flat horizon. In all directions, the red, cracked ground surrounded her without respite. Somewhere in the distance, a storm approached. A rumble of thunder shook the dry ground. Suddenly, a wailing cry pierced the eerie calm with anguish. A woman lay against the hot earth, crumpled in on herself. Her naked flesh was just as dusty and dry as the terrain that surrounded her. Matted, jet black hair concealed her face, but even so, one could tell she was sobbing from the way her chest violently seized. The girl made her way toward the woman, filled deep with sympathy, but she stopped in her tracks at the sight of the thick, dark liquid pooling around her. The girl scanned the woman's deflated body and saw it was the pitiful woman's own blood streaming down her bony legs.

I woke with a start to the song of a swallow perched just outside my window. I had slept with the book cradled in my arms, leaving red indents on my skin. As I scanned the pile of luggage in the fresh morning light, the grotesque image of the wailing woman tumbled further back into my subconscious until I could hardly recall the haunting dream. I dressed quietly in the outfit my aunt had laid out for me: a pair of burgundy slacks, a knit sweater of light cream wool, and a pair of suitable brown boots. Feeling the nip in the air, I finished off my traveling ensemble with an excessively long scarf and my well-used green cape. My mother's satchel faded to a red umber leather to match my trousers. Of course, I also put on Irenee's watch and Rae's locket, two important remnants of home.

Irenee and I had said our farewells at dinner the night before. I was meant to be on the first train early that morning. It was the safest way to travel while maintaining a low profile. Irenee had not cried or given a drawn-out goodbye. She had merely said, "Be extraordinary, and be yourself." I did not see how I could be those two things at the same time, but I had still nodded and embraced her, knowing she meant well. Instead of pursuing greatness, I wished only for the strength to depart, which I needed desperately as I stood at my front gate, unable to move. The train was leaving in twenty minutes, and if I did not begin walking now, I would not be on it.

The morning mist curled around my ankles, heavy with a foreboding that seemed to seep into my bones. I turned around, trying to etch every detail of home into my memory—each stone, each wooden panel, each crack—unsure of when I'd see it again. It likely wasn't long though, maybe a week, or just a few days. This didn't need to be a long trip. One week and then I could come back to wait for Raemond. I repeated the timeframe like a prayer, willing it to strengthen me as I said goodbye to the rickety old house. This house—where I was born, where Maxx had died, where Raemond had walked me home so many nights—was my heart and soul. Yet somehow, I found the strength to turn away, leaving it behind in the morning mist. Maybe I was stronger than I gave myself credit for.

The Orchard was quiet as I made my way down the stone streets. The occasional crunch of a dry leaf under my boot punctuated the stillness, though I stepped on them only when they were directly in my path. A few cottages glowed softly, mothers stirring early to prepare breakfasts. The scent of sweet biscuits drifted from a chimney, momentarily tempting me to stop and ask for one. But I pressed on, my hunger repressed as I walked through the thickening fog. As I rounded the final corner toward the station, a voice behind me cut through the stillness.

"Hildy!"

I didn't need to see the person to recognize the voice. Copper Penning was bounding toward me, suitcase in hand, and her gangly brother Arnie was trailing behind.

"Did we miss it?" Copper called as she skidded to a halt at my side.

"We've got six minutes," Arnie replied, pointing to the clock tower. "The bell hasn't tolled yet. You'd know if we'd missed it." His tone was laced with his usual condescension and grumpiness.

"I couldn't hear anything over your huffing and puffing," she shot back, snatching his rucksack and swinging it over her shoulder. "This boy's seriously out of shape," she directed at me.

"What are you two doing here?" I demanded, my eyes darting to the clock and back to the Penning siblings.

"Aunt Irenee sent me a note last night," Copper said cheerfully, oblivious—or indifferent—to the edge in my voice. "She said you were headed to Facehaven and thought I might like to come along, seeing as I'll be moving there next season."

"And Arnie?" I asked, uneasy about how much Irenee might have revealed.

"He had nothing better to do," Copper answered for him. "Maybe he'll find his calling in enchantment."

"Don't even joke about that," he muttered. He was clearly in a foul mood, possibly from the early hour, his recent rejection, or both.

"So, you're coming along to..." I trailed off, not sure what I could safely say out loud.

"To help you," Copper said, clasping my shoulder. "To find whatever it is you're looking for." Irenee's words surfaced in my mind: *"You can't do it all by yourself."* This was her parting gift, I realized.

"If we're going, we'd better get on with it," Arnie grumbled, snatching back his rucksack and hefting my suitcase as he started for the train. Copper leaned close, her breath warm in my ear.

"He doesn't know," she whispered, nodding toward her brother, "but I'm in. Whatever you're up to, I'm along for the ride." I pulled back, meeting her gleaming, mischievous grin. Despite myself, I smiled back, letting a flicker of excitement momentarily displace my trepidation.

"Though, if you want to fill my brother in on everything, I know we can trust him," she said, looking at me more solemnly. I felt my heartrate spike at the idea of sharing this new and overwhelming burden with my friends. Likely noticing my hesitation, she quickly followed up with, "I'm also perfectly happy keeping him in the dark."

"Step lively, ladies," Arnie called from the platform as the train's whistle sounded. "Adventure awaits, or whatever."

Copper grabbed my hand, and without any more time for me to dwell in my fears, we dashed to the train as it began to groan forward. Laughing like children, we scrambled aboard,

Copper hauling me up after her. Arnie had retreated inside and was waving us into the cabin. But I held up a hand, gripping the railing tightly and turning to face the horizon.

The sun's first streaks stretched across Crystal Lake, speckling the trees with fiery reds and golds. I caught a glimpse of smoke curling from the chimney of my cottage—no doubt Irenee boiling water for her morning coffee.

Arnie poked his head out the car door. "Come inside—it's freezing out here."

"I've never left before," I said softly, feeling the tears pricking the corners of my eyes. "What am I without this place?"

"You're you," he replied flatly. "Only someplace else."

I glanced at the watch Irenee had given me. The three tiny dials at the bottom read: *342 days, 8 hours, 22 seconds*. Nearly a year until I'd return. The weight of that realization hollowed me out. An intrusive voice whispered to jump, to escape the future stretching out before me. But my feet stayed rooted. My knuckles whitened as I clung to the railing, the tracks blurring beneath us as the train picked up speed. I looked out at the Orchard's trees, their branches swaying westward in the season's final gusts.

They will blow me home, I assured myself.

CHAPTER SEVEN: THE WITCH'S FILES

There were no private cabins on the trains that left the Orchard. Even if you were a wealthy merchant or a mother with young children, your options were the same as everyone else. But at this early hour, the train was almost empty; the train car Copper, Arnie, and I had entered was ours alone.

The watch's reading still had me rattled. My mind raced through possible explanations. Irenee had made a mistake. She was playing some elaborate joke. Or maybe she'd set the clock to track the wrong person, and it was actually the station attendant who wouldn't be around for another year. I forced my posture to relax, convincing myself not to believe what I'd seen.

Arnie stood by one of the center poles, staring out at the blurred scenery rushing past. Copper, already settled on a bench, pulled a paper sack from her bag. The smell hit me before I saw what was inside—juniper berry scones. My stomach growled, and I all but pounced on her offer to have one.

"So, Hildegarde," Arnie said as he swung lazily around the pole to face me, his voice cutting through my buttery, sweet scone haze. "Seen any good high sorcery lately?" Copper's shoe smacked against his shin before I could respond.

"What?" he yelped, glaring at her. "I'm just making conversation."

"Well, don't," she snapped, narrowing her eyes.

"It's fine, Copper," I said, resting a hand on her shoulder. I turned to him, my gaze level as I said seriously, "I shouldn't have shown you the mark. I know better now. It's only caused unnecessary danger and concern."

"No," Arnie said as he dropped onto the bench across from us, his tone equally serious now. "I think a sigil of high sorcery burned into your attic floor causes *necessary* concern."

"Shhh," Copper hissed, swatting at him as her eyes darted around.

"Copper, you're so paranoid," he chuckled, his tone full of mockery. "No one is listening to us, no matter what ghost stories Mom told you."

"They are not ghost stories," she shot back, her voice rising before she caught herself. She lowered it again, speaking deliberately. "You wouldn't understand—you're a boy."

"What does that have to do with anything?" Arnie said as he threw his hands up, his face now derisive. I couldn't help but raise an eyebrow. Had he always been this arrogant and dismissive?

"Everything," I said quietly, gripping my mother's satchel with both hands. The weight of the words silenced him, and he leaned back, a flicker of guilt crossing his face as he stared at the bag.

Copper, always quick to steer a sputtering conversation, seized the opportunity. "How's Raemond?" she asked brightly, passing Arnie the last scone without looking at him.

"I haven't heard from him yet," I admitted, realizing with a pang that, in the whirlwind of yesterday's events, I'd forgotten to miss him. "It'll probably take him a few days to settle in."

"How will he know how to reach you? Did you tell him about this impromptu vacation?" Arnie asked as he picked at the scone, his cheekiness returning.

"Irenee will tell him where I am, I guess." It struck me that I hadn't made arrangements for my aunt to explain my sudden departure, but I trusted her to manage it. But then those ominous numbers on the watch replayed in my mind, casting doubt over all my assumptions.

"Besides," Copper interjected, sensing my unease, "he'll be learning light and wind evocation soon, so he can use those for a calling charm. That's how the generals communicate with the border forces without getting intercepted."

I gave her a grateful smile. She really had a knack for giving the right reassurances when people needed it most. I really needed to thank

Irenee for sending her along. Copper's moral support already felt like a lifeline. Arnie, on the other hand, was a mixed bag.

As we sat there together, I crafted explanations in my mind, testing out ideas that might make him understand how I was involved in high sorcery without revealing the full truth. The best excuse I had so far was that I'd been secretly recruited by the watchmen to track illegal high sorcerers for the king. But something told me he'd never buy it.

Years ago, I would have trusted Arnie with my life. But the man he'd pushed himself to become now felt like a stranger. Who knew what he'd be willing to do to achieve his ambitions, especially as he became more desperate.

Copper was different. Despite the newness of our deepening friendship, I trusted her instinctively. With a jolt, it hit me that in all the secrets I'd dared to share with her, I'd somehow left out a crucial one.

"Oh, I almost forgot to mention," I said, breaking the silence and trying my best to sound casual, "Raemond and I are engaged."

Copper jolted upright so quickly she nearly slid off the bench. "You are?" she shrieked, her voice a mix of awe and glee. "When? How?"

I felt heat rising in my cheeks as I thought of Rae, a whole world away. "He sort of asked me twice," I admitted with a shy smile. "Once at the graduation party and then properly at the train station."

She clutched her hand over her heart, looking utterly enchanted. "That's so romantic," she breathed.

Arnie, of course, flattened the energy of the moment. "So where's the ring?"

I slipped the band off my middle finger and held it out for him to see, feeling a quiet satisfaction at the chance to put him in his place. "It's too big to fit on the proper finger," I explained, displaying my comically small hands before he could make some sarcastic remark.

"Well, I can fix that," Copper offered, reaching for the ring. "That's just a simple shrinking enchantment—"

"No!" The word burst out of me before I could stop it. I pulled the ring back, rubbing it as I tried to smooth over my alarm. "I was actually thinking I'd wear it on my necklace… for safekeeping," I added, shooting her a knowing look. "You know, until everything is sorted out."

She caught my meaning and gave a subtle nod, sinking back into her seat without another word. I unclasped the delicate locket from around my neck and slipped the ring onto its chain. Relief washed over me as I fastened it around my neck, glad to have my fingers free. But even as I settled the locket against my chest, I couldn't shake Irenee's voice in my head. *"It's a trap."*

The rest of the journey passed in slow, measured hours—about five in total. Arnie buried himself in a thick book about the origins of the Festival of Time, barely glancing up. After Copper exhausted every question imaginable about my engagement to Rae, she dozed off, her head tipped against the window.

But sleep wouldn't come to me. I stayed glued to the window, watching the landscape shift as the train sped toward Facehaven. The orchards and rolling hills of home gave way to open plains, and my heart leaped a little at the sight of a golden field of wheat. The cabin filled with warm yellow light as the stalks blurred past the windows, so different from the lavender fields of home.

When the train emerged from the field, the city's skyline came into view, cutting sharply against the horizon. I knew that Facehaven wasn't as towering as the Citadel's palaces and spires, but its buildings stood higher than anything I'd ever seen. Steep gable roofs reached toward the sky like jagged peaks, and the midday sun bounced off the plaster walls, making the whole city gleam like a beacon.

I marveled at the stark contrast to the Orchard. My home was built of sturdy stone and earth, simple and functional, while Facehaven was built for elegance. Its plaster walls and dark wood exteriors exuded refinement. Flags in vivid hues rippled in the breeze while window boxes brimmed with sunflowers.

The city wasn't just a place, it was a promise— a gateway to something larger than the life I'd known. I clutched my mother's satchel, watching as the train pulled closer to the vibrant buildings.

"Something to see, right?" Copper murmured, leaning over to share the angle of my view at the window.

"It really is," I replied, an excited grin spreading across my face.

"Interesting historical fact," Arnie interrupted, popping up from behind his book, "The original architecture of Facehaven was heavily masonry-based and resembled the Orchard, but then King Abraham issued a nationwide beautification decree, requiring every territory to develop its own unique design. That's when they introduced their signature wood-and-plaster aesthetic."

"Riveting," Copper deadpanned. "I truly hope you keep those mouthwatering historical tidbits coming."

I stifled a laugh. "I thought it was interesting," I said as the train slowed to a stop at the main station.

Before the brakes had fully engaged, Copper was on her feet. As we stepped onto the platform, I was struck by the energy of the crowd. Commuters bustled around us like a swarm of impeccably dressed ants. Facehaven's reputation for fashion was no exaggeration—its citizens treated clothing and accessories as an art form.

Copper's swallow earrings, as charming as they were, suddenly seemed modest compared to the flamboyant creations parading past us. A grand-looking gentlewoman walked by wearing a hat crowned with a massive silk butterfly, its wings flapping gently on their own. At her side, a gentleman sported a snakeskin cravat complete with a face and flicking tongue.

"I want one of those," Arnie muttered, admiring the serpentine neckpiece.

"I'll make you one," Copper said over the hum of the crowd, "but *only* if you behave yourself." I couldn't help but laugh, grabbing her arm in excitement as we finally spilled out of the station and onto the city street.

Facehaven unfolded around me like a dream. The buildings loomed tall and impressive, their steep gables and plaster facades bright in the afternoon sun. Shiny buggies zipped by on the cobbled roads, their engines rumbling like low thunder.

On the sidewalks, groups of children in colorful outfits pressed their faces to ornate shop windows, marveling at the wares inside. Women strolled arm in arm, chatting animatedly about the latest accessories and trending décor. Men sauntered by in sharp suits, their polished shoes clicking rhythmically against the stone.

As the academy bell tolled in the distance, a gaggle of students darted past us, clutching books to their chests and laughing as they rushed toward the school gates. Copper followed them with her eyes, a wistful smile on her lips.

I watched them too, a spike of envy curling in my chest. Their joy was so obvious, so uncomplicated, as if they'd found their true place in the world.

Arnie insisted on finding lodging before we did any sightseeing, eager to set down his suitcase and change out of his wrinkled travel slacks. Copper found us a place a stone's throw from the train station called the Iron Pot Inn. I paid for a single night with some of the traveling money Aunt Irenee had given me. She had gifted me nearly sixty gold, which had seemed like an excessive amount at first, but staring again at the numbers on my watch, I now understood just how quickly it could vanish.

Once we got to our room, Arnie made Copper and me look out the window while he changed into a fresh pair of corduroy pants that made him look at least twice his age. Copper was perfectly happy in the fitted purple dungarees she'd been wearing all day, though she did pull on a light coat with a floral pattern that slowly bloomed and wilted, no doubt meant to show off her enchantment prowess. Me? I made no adjustments. I suppose it was a rebellion of sorts against my glamorous mother and aunt. I've never been one for vanity.

"Where to first?" Copper asked once Arnie was dressed and ready.

I had already given it some thought on the train ride, and I'd decided the best first step would be to head to the Academy of Enchantment and track down Dennis Daymont, a bookkeeper Irenee had befriended while there. He was one of the names on her list, and there was a good chance he had Lacey Neddles' address in his collection of school documents.

"Didn't you want to tour the academy first?" I prompted Copper, trying to keep Arnie oblivious of our true objective. She nodded eagerly. I knew she would go along with whatever I said, but this was also something she'd love to do anyway.

"I did," she replied, her head bobbing. "Very much."

It was no lie. She was practically bursting to see the place where she would spend the next four years of her life. It was lucky, really, that Copper was already accepted there. No one would question our motives with her being an incoming student.

The Academy of Enchantment was just around the corner from the inn, and its bell tower made it easy to locate. It was the highest point in the city, and it was tucked away from the busy streets behind a large iron fence. As we passed through the gates, we were greeted by a lush garden filled with chrysanthemums and towering oak trees. The campus was full of life—some students picnicked on the grass, others tossed a ball around, and some sat beneath trees, engrossed in their books. Copper was practically glowing as she took it all in, and I couldn't help but compare this famous institution to the herbalism school back home. The sheer size was enough to set the two apart, but there was also the energy.

At the herbalism school, students worked mostly from home and only came in for lectures or to have their brews evaluated. No one lingered on campus for the sake of the campus itself. Here, though, there was something electric in the air, something that made it clear this was a place of possibility, of growth.

Arnie held his head up, admiring the building's elaborate design. It stood at nine stories tall, though the bell tower at the center must have been at least eleven stories. The white walls gleamed in the sunlight, contrasting beautifully with the dark brown wood that framed the structure. I wondered if those extra beams were what allowed the buildings to stand so tall, but then figured that a lot of it was likely decorative, looking too elaborate to be structural. Ivy crept up the first two stories, covering a few of the large iron windows.

The school stretched along the block, divided into sections by sharp peaks in the shingled roof. It almost looked like an entire block of individual buildings had been squeezed together. Despite the length of the structure, the main entrance was clear, with an arched doorway that stretched up as high as the ivy. The two doors were open, and students and professors were pouring in and out.

As we neared the doors, Copper trotted ahead, giddy with excitement. She slipped inside without hesitation, and I hurried to follow, partly because I wanted to get to work, but also because her excitement was infectious.

As soon as I stepped inside, I was hit with a wall of sound. The workshop was enormous—larger than I had imagined. It took up the entire length of the first floor, and the ceiling was a full two stories high. Witches and wizards were buzzing around, each with their own worktables, and scattered between them were stations full of materials and machinery.

There were all kinds of inventions—cunning little toys, household appliances, extravagant clothing, and one student even had a whole automobile in progress. Professors wandered the room, offering advice or simply admiring the work. The air smelled of wood shavings and pine needles, and I couldn't help but notice Copper taking a deep breath, her eyes closing in contentment. She looked like she had just come home after a long journey.

"May I help you?" A cheerful voice chimed from the front desk, just a few steps beyond the entryway. The nameplate at the end of her desk read *Mrs. Mavis Herring*.

"Yes," I answered from Copper's shoulder, breaking our quiet moment of awe. "My friend here," I motioned to Copper, "was recently admitted for next season and was hoping to get a tour." I pushed myself to match the receptionist's chipper demeanor.

"Of course she can," Mrs. Herring cried, beaming and gesturing for us to approach her desk. "What's your full name, young lady?"

"Copper Louisa Penning, ma'am," she replied, finally breaking out of her reverie.

"Lovely name," she said, her smile unwavering. She muttered to herself, "Penning, Penning, Penning," as she flipped through the pages of a large reference book. "There you are!"

She stopped and dropped her finger on a spot in the book. "I'm going to make a note that you came for a visit. Your future professors always see that as a good mark." She winked at Copper before scribbling something next to her name.

"Miss Penning exhibits a real can-do attitude and a smile that could soften a horsefly," Arnie whispered in Copper's ear. She jabbed him in the rib with her elbow, trying to hide her amusement and stay composed.

"I'll call you our best tour guide," Mrs. Herring said, putting her pen down and ringing a little golden bell that hung on the wall behind her.

"I was wondering if you knew whether Dennis Daymont was working today?" I interjected, excited to start my own research.

"Dennis is always working," Mrs. Herring replied with a light laugh.

"Do you think I could pop in and say hi while they're on their tour?" I asked, trying to sound casual. "He's a family friend."

"Sure thing! Dennis never gets visitors." She directed her beaming smile at me now, touching her hand to her heart. "Bookkeeping is downstairs on the right. Just take that flight of stairs behind me." She pointed back to the towering spiral staircase at the center of the room.

"Thank you so much," I said, mustering a huge smile before turning to Copper and Arnie. "Have fun on your tour!"

"Say hi to Dennis for me," Mrs. Herring called as I made my way to the stairs. I gripped the strap of my satchel tightly. It had been hard to decide whether bringing the book along was more dangerous than leaving it in the room unattended. My shoulder ached from the weight, but my instincts said it was the right choice. Still, there was a nagging sense that someone was watching me as I descended into the dimly lit basement.

The hallway glowed with a sickly green light from the few bulbs hanging along it. I turned right, just as Mrs. Herring had instructed. The hallway was long, stretching on until it ended at a single door. I felt safe in assuming it would lead to bookkeeping. The only sound was the echo of my shoes as I walked toward it. Seeing the modest wooden design made me think that all the grandeur of the academy had been reserved for the public areas.

The department was just as dim as the hallway, but the light inside was warmer and more inviting. The room stretched so far back that I couldn't see the end of it. The walls were lined with books and files, and narrow doorways further divided the space into sections I couldn't see into. It reminded me of the home of a well-read packrat, cluttered but cozy.

"Hello?" I called meekly, my voice swallowed by the sea of shelves. "Mr. Daymont?" After an uncomfortable span of silence, I raised my voice a little more. "Mr. Daymont!"

"I'm in obituaries," a dry little voice squeaked from somewhere in the stacks. I stepped forward cautiously.

"Where's that?" I called, unsure where to go.

"Forward," came the simple instruction. I felt silly for asking, as forward was really the only direction in the department. After passing through sections marked *Disciplinary Records*, *Employment Files*, and *Materials Expenses*, I arrived at a sign reading *Obituaries*.

An old man crouched over a crate of newspaper clippings, shakily filing them one by one.

"How may I be of assistance?" he asked without looking up from his task, his voice warbling.

"Are you Mr. Dennis Daymont?" I asked, scanning him quickly. He was shorter than I was, though I figured his crouched posture might be overemphasizing that. His clothes, each a different shade of brown or beige, hung off him like they'd been made for someone much larger.

"I am, if memory serves," he chuckled, a wheezy sound that didn't sound particularly healthy. He held a scrap of newsprint close to his face, straining to read it.

"I'm looking for some contact information on a student from here," I said, inching closer. He seemed old enough that hearing problems were pretty likely.

"Bully for you," he muttered, finishing with the clipping and filing it away in a large parchment folder within the crate. I couldn't tell if he was irritated or just bemused by my demand.

"My aunt sent me," I said finally, deciding to use my better hook. "Do you recall Irenee Thorne?" At the mention of her name, Mr. Daymont finally turned and looked up at me quickly, his knees creaking.

"Irenee Thorne?" His voice was full of affection, as if speaking about a long-lost relative. "How is she?"

Now that he was facing me, I could take in his features more clearly. He wore spectacles so thick they looked like they could give you vision into space. His bright blue irises filled the lenses completely, and attached to the outer corners were additional, smaller lenses, each poised to be rotated into place for easy use.

"She's well," I said, offering him a smile. "She's a horologist now."

"Of course she is," Mr. Daymont replied without hesitation. "She was the best of them. The very best of our stock." He stood up and came closer to me, abandoning the remaining news clippings on the floor. "Let me get a better look at you."

He moved so quickly that I barely had time to step back as one of the larger side lenses clicked down over his right eye. He craned his neck to study me with great detail.

"Name," he demanded.

"Hildegarde Birch," I responded quickly, stepping back as he continued his inspection.

"Well, Hildegarde Birch," he said, still not removing his eyes from my face, "There isn't much of a resemblance, is there?" He clicked a green lens into place over his left eye. "But there is something in the brow."

I stood still, unsure of how to respond. Suddenly, the lenses fluttered back into place, and he stepped back, settling into a more polite stance of observation. "Which records are you interested in?"

"I'm trying to get in touch with a former student who went here. For… some research I'm doing," I said, rattled from his intense scrutiny but still managing to remember the partially true story I'd crafted. "Perhaps I could get any contact information she left?"

Mr. Daymont nodded, then scurried over to the center of the room, where he stepped onto a rectangular foot rug I hadn't noticed before.

"Hop on," he instructed, motioning for me to stand behind him.

"Oh… okay," I replied, gingerly stepping up onto the rug. He clapped his hands twice, then extended them in front of him. I spotted a glimmer of something shiny catching the light at the far end of the room. In a moment, the object became clear—an ornate brass handle connected to a long chain was shooting toward us. Mr. Daymont caught it with ease.

"To alumni personal files," he declared with a flourish, and with that, we were yanked forward. The rug pulled us along with surprising speed. I grabbed his shoulder to steady myself as we glided smoothly over the floor. We came to a stop just a few steps from the back wall. I stumbled slightly at the abrupt loss of velocity, catching my breath before stepping off the rug. Mr. Daymont released the brass handle, and it slithered back into place against the wall.

"Name," he asked again, spectacles now intent on the file boxes as he shuffled swiftly down the row.

"Neddles," I said, trying to keep up. "Lacey Neddles."

"And here are the N's," he said, smiling at the convenience of it all. He followed a line of boxes with his finger and stopped at one labeled *NEA-NEJ*. He pulled it out with a grunt and balanced it against his chest. I offered out my hands, but he dismissed me with a shake of his head.

"*Tabula dehors.*"

A plank of wood shot out from the book-case, cutting the space between us with a magically sturdy shelf. He calmly set the box down on the new surface and began rifling through the files.

"Here we are," he said, lifting out a manila folder. I stepped forward and reached for it, but he swatted my hand away.

"For official eyes only, young lady." As he looked through the folder, he said, "I can only share information that students have permitted to be made publicly accessible." His many lenses shifted into place as he flipped through several pages.

"Interesting," he murmured, peering closely at one of the documents.

"What is it?" I asked, feeling a sense of un-ease settling in.

"Only a contact address was provided, and it just says 'Cloaked door within the Riverview district.' Very interesting…" He trailed off as his eyes flicked over the document again.

"What does that mean?" I asked, my stom-ach tightening.

"To be frank, it means Mrs. Neddles did not wish to be found by anyone who didn't know her. Riverview is a neighborhood on the east side of the city, a five-block radius around Rusty's Brew House, if I recall correctly. It seems like she lives *somewhere* in that area, but likely isn't fond of visitors." He flipped back through the pages like he was sifting through a puzzle. "I wonder where her tax documents are sent. She could get into some trouble with that."

"Is there any other address? Any other means of contacting her?" I asked, my voice thinner than I meant it to be.

"I'm afraid not." He closed the file with a decisive snap.

The sharp edge of defeat cutting into me, I muttered, "Thank you for your time, Mr. Daymont," and took a step back, ready to leave.

"Wait just a moment," he said, holding up a hand. "There's something on you."

I froze. "What is it?" I asked, glancing down around me, expecting to find something crawling on my arm or clinging to my coat. But there was nothing.

"I'm not sure," he replied, his glasses clicking and whirring as an assortment of lenses slid into place. "Perhaps a curse."

My heart sank. "A curse?" I asked, lamenting. The past few days had been complicated enough.

Mr. Daymont tilted his head, his gaze narrowing through the maze of lenses on his spectacles. "No, not a curse," he corrected, his tone thoughtful. "But there's certainly something powerful on you, girl."

I instinctively reached up to hold the strap of my satchel, fingers digging into the worn leather. My pulse quickened, but I willed myself to stay calm. He couldn't know about the spellbook—I was sure of it. Besides, his focus remained on my face, not the bag.

His lenses clicked again, retracting one by one until his glasses returned to their original shape. He straightened, almost nonchalant. "You should get that looked at," he said, as if it were a perfectly normal piece of advice.

"All right… I, uh, I will," I said.

"Off you pop," he said with a wave toward the entrance. "Happy hunting."

"Thank you, Mr. Daymont," I replied, my voice steadier even though my nerves hummed. He was now intent on returning the file to its box and the box to its place on the shelf, seemingly uninterested in further conversation.

I thought about asking to use the rug-and-handle contraption for the trip back but decided against it. It wasn't worth the hassle—or interrupting him again. Besides, the walk would give me time to think.

Finding Lacey Neddles was going to be harder than I'd expected. Riverview was the logical first step, but what then? What was I supposed to do, walk around asking strangers if they'd seen a hidden door? The idea was laughable. Risky, too. Discretion was still key. Maybe divination could help me locate the cloaked entrance, but I didn't have the faintest clue how to do that, and likely neither did Copper.

"There's certainly something powerful on you, girl."

The words rolled around in my mind like a storm cloud. I told myself not to dwell on them. Mr. Daymont was just a peculiar, eccentric old man, likely harmless. But what if he was right? What if there *was* something wrong with me?

For days now, I'd been uncovering pieces of my past, truths I hadn't even known to question. But I hadn't stopped to think about what those revelations might have done to *me*. The weight on my shoulders was heavier than just the spellbook now, and I shivered as I walked.

I made my way back up the dim corridor, each step echoing in the stillness like a question I couldn't answer.

Chapter Eight: The Witch's Door

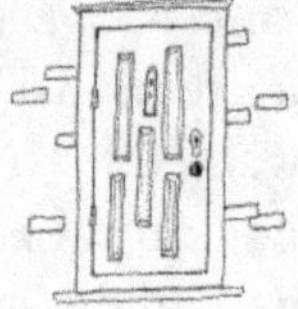

I stared at a bead of condensation trailing down the side of my ale glass, trying to tune out Copper, who was now on her ninth minute of describing her tour of the academy. Across from me, Arnie sat forward in his chair, absent-mindedly running a finger along the rim of his glass, which he had barely touched.

"And all the materials are *free*," Copper exclaimed, repeating that point for at least the second time. She was literally bouncing in her seat. "Anything you want to make, they *want* you to make it." She picked up her second mug of cider and drained the last of it. For a moment, there was blissful silence.

The background noise of Rusty's Brew House filled the gap—laughter, clinking glasses, and the jaunty pub band playing in the back corner. I gathered that this was a popular place for students; I watched young witches and wizards close to my age milling about the billiards tables, dancing next to the stage, and filling the tables with empty glasses of cheap drinks. The quality wasn't great, but no one here seemed to care. On another night, I might have enjoyed myself too, but tonight I had too much on my plate—too many questions and no clear answers. Getting to Riverview without raising Arnie's suspicions had been easy enough. Now, though, I had no idea how to proceed while keeping him unaware.

"Can we order now?" he snapped as Copper opened her mouth to continue speaking.

"I haven't even looked at the food yet," she replied, pulling a tattered menu toward herself.

"That's because you haven't stopped talking since we sat down," Arnie groaned, slumping back in his seat.

"It'll only take me a minute," she said coolly, though she still hadn't looked at the menu yet.

"I'm starving," he grumbled, resting his forehead against the table.

"I told you to pack snacks," she said, flipping through the menu.

"If we stop talking," I cut in before Arnie could explode, "she'll choose faster."

Copper smirked, and he let out a sigh of defeat. "Done." She slapped the menu down. "I'll have the bacon melt on spiced rye."

"Oh, that sounds good," I said, my stomach growling at the thought. "I'll have the same."

"So I guess I'm ordering for both of you?" Arnie asked as he got to his feet.

"Thank you, Arnie," Copper said, giving him a genuine smile.

"I've got it," I offered, digging into the pouch of my satchel for money.

"Don't worry about it," he said, waving me off, and he practically skipped toward the bar.

"That was nice of him," I grumbled.

"Had to happen sometime," Copper replied with a grin before leaning forward across the table. Her voice dropped to a whisper. "So what happened? What were you looking for in bookkeeping?"

I stole a quick glance to make sure Arnie was still in line to order, then leaned in and rushed through my explanation. "My mother was in contact with some women before she disappeared—I think they were working on something together, but I don't know what. An enchanter named Lacey Neddles had mailed her a letter with a vague apology that arrived after my mom went into exile. Since she was an enchanter, we figured she went here, and Irenee was friends with the man in bookkeeping. I was trying to find information to contact her."

"Did you?"

"No. All she left was a vague note about living here in this neighborhood behind a cloaked door. Nothing else."

"An entrance cloaking?" Her eyes lit up. "I've always wanted to learn that."

"Any idea how to find one?" I asked, hopeful.

"Not really," she admitted. "If it's sloppy work, you might catch inconsistencies—lighting glitches, flashes of reality breaking through—but that's only with amateurs."

"Something tells me Lacey isn't an amateur," I said, sinking back into my chair with a sigh.

Copper scooted around to the chair next to me and lowered her voice. "Real quick—is that…" she trailed off, nodding at my satchel.

I nodded. "But you can't tell Arnie." I peered out of the corner of my eye and saw that he was now at the front of the line.

"We're going to have to tell him *something*," Copper whispered. "He's not an idiot."

I finally voiced a question that had been bothering me. "Why did you bring him? You *knew* it would make things difficult."

She hesitated, then said, "He's talented, Hildy. He can and will help, if you'd trust him just a little."

"I don't know…" Memories of Irenee, Rae, and my mother flared in my mind. If Arnie decided to report me, they'd all be at risk. I wanted to believe he was still the boy I trusted, but these stakes felt all too high.

"You've got to decide quickly," Copper said, motioning—not subtly—to Arnie heading back with three plates.

"That was fast," she remarked as he set the food down and slid back into his chair.

"Enchanted kitchen," Arnie said with a grunt before digging into his pork pie.

I followed suit, taking a bite of my sandwich as I mulled over Copper's words. Arnie *was* talented, and if anyone had a shot at finding Lacey, it was him. But my trust wasn't coming as easily anymore, not after everything.

"Arnie—" I started, but I stopped short as a hooded figure entered the tavern, much taller than the rest of the young crowd and moving extremely surreptitiously. They slid in front of a group playing darts, and nobody reacted to them. One of the players threw a dart that missed the hooded figure's head by mere inches, the thrower not hesitating and the hooded figure not flinching.

"What?" Arnie asked through a mouthful of onion rings.

"Do you see that person in the hood?" I said, pointing subtly with my finger. Both he and Copper turned to look, their eyes casting about.

"Who?" Copper asked, confused.

"I don't see any hoods," Arnie added.

"They're by the case of alcohol at the bar," I said. The person wrapped their arms around the crate of bottles.

"I see the case..." Copper started. "Oh, that was weird."

"I saw it too," Arnie said to Copper.

"It? Did you see *the person*?" I pressed.

"No," Copper said in bemusement, "but the case just vanished."

"It's a glamour," I breathed as the figure slipped toward the exit. Instinct driving purpose through me, I jumped to my feet and started moving forward. "I'll be right back."

"Wait!" Copper cried, dropping her sandwich back on the plate. "I'm coming too."

Arnie groaned. "We just started eating!"

"Then don't come," Copper snapped, throwing on her coat as she hurried after me. I was already out the door, everything in me screaming that I needed to keep this figure in sight. Behind me, I could hear Arnie calling Copper's name, but soon enough I sensed him catch up, his footsteps heavy with reluctance.

"What are you two doing?" he demanded after I pulled him behind a brick wall.

"Quiet," I hissed. The hooded figure was just ahead, turning left at the next block. We followed carefully, weaving through Riverview's streets until the figure ducked into an alley about five minutes from the pub. I peered around the corner, holding my breath as they bent down to turn a spigot on the wall of what smelled like a bakery.

The beams of the building groaned and shifted, revealing a small, brown door etched into the plaster. The person unlocked it with a thick brass key while balancing the crate on their knee with practiced ease, slipped inside, and disappeared as the wall reformed behind them.

"Okay, that I saw," Arnie admitted, staring at the wall in amazement.

"That was a cloaked door," I whispered with excitement, "*and* we're in Riverview. I'd say fate just smiled on us." Without waiting for input, I left our shadowed spot and headed to the spigot on the wall.

"What are you going to do?" Copper whispered, already at my elbow. I turned the spigot as I'd seen the figure do, and I watched the door reappear before us, my heart swelling with an indescribable emotion.

"I'm going to knock," I said, deciding to believe my frantic heartbeats were pounding with confidence. I lifted my fist, bringing it down sharply against the door in several quick raps. "Lacey? I know who you are, and I really need to talk to you," I said to the door, my voice low and steady.

Almost immediately, I heard metal on the other side of the door shifting, then the unmistakable click of a deadbolt sliding out of place. I stepped back just in time as the door swung open with surprising force, revealing a little witch who darted out into the alleyway like a hound released from a cage. She didn't say a word, but her glare was fierce, and she pressed a finger to her lips in a command for silence.

But I couldn't help myself. The words slipped out before I could stop them: "Maude Birch."

Her finger dropped, and I saw her eyes flicker from anger to something else. Recognition? Disappointment?

"She was my mother," I said, pushing through the silence that followed, hoping she would understand. For a long moment, Lacey didn't move. Her eyes were fixed on me, her arms hanging limp at her sides, and then, without a word, she gave a subtle nod toward the entrance. I didn't hesitate. I stepped inside, Lacey's intensity increasing the sensation of weight on my shoulders with each passing second. The others followed and we all silently filed into the cramped little room.

It was small, barely big enough to hold more than the essentials, yet everything in it was deliberate. An icebox, a wood-burning stove, shelves filled with books, a single bed, and a square table in the center. The rest was filled with materials I recognized from my mother's world: enchanted trinkets, half-finished potions, and torn pages from old books.

There were empty bottles piled near the door, and my eyes lingered on the new crate of brandy sitting atop the icebox. Was Lacey staking out here? Where was her family? She had mentioned her own children in the note, but I didn't see any signs of family life here.

Lacey heaved the door shut behind us, locking it up tight with a deadbolt and a heavy metal bar; the scraping metal caused tension to settle over the room.

"Were you followed? Were you seen?" Lacey whispered, speaking for the first time while her face was pressed to the silver peephole.

"No," I whispered back.

"You're sure?"

"As sure as I can be," I stammered.

Then we were suddenly face-to-face, and she was wrapping me in a warm embrace, her grip tight. "Hildegarde Birch!" she exclaimed, as though she had just found a long-lost child. I stiffened at first, but there was something so familiar in the way she behaved that I couldn't help but let my guard down just a little. She pulled back, examining me with a sort of awe. "How beautiful you are," she said, her hands resting on my face as if trying to memorize me. I wanted to smile, to thank her, but something about being inspected by a stranger, no matter how kind, made me uneasy.

"Lacey Neddles?" I asked again, needing to be sure, even though I already knew.

"The very same," she replied, her voice filled with a strange mixture of pride and sorrow. "I'm surprised your mother told you about me."

"She didn't," I admitted, feeling a strange pang of guilt. I reached into my bag and pulled out the letter I'd found earlier. "I found this."

The moment her eyes landed on the seal, she gasped. She held the letter to her chest as if it were something sacred, and I watched as tears welled up in her eyes. "It didn't arrive in time," she gasped out, as if the weight of those words was enough to crush her.

I nodded, not sure what to say. She clearly hadn't had the chance to apologize for whatever she thought she had done wrong, but I needed her to know there was no point in dwelling on that now. There was too much at stake.

"That's just as well," she muttered, dropping onto one of the rickety chairs, her face falling. "She never had to see my cowardice."

I shook my head. "Everyone disappointed my mother," I said quietly, sitting beside her. "Especially me."

Her gaze softened, but then she looked away, appearing to gather her thoughts. "No, you're wrong," she then said with a quiet intensity. She stood up and took a few steps across the room to retrieve something.

She turned to show me a stack of letters she had pulled from a small chest. "She sent me fifty-eight letters," she said, holding them like treasures, "and *each one* was about you—how proud she was of you and how eager you were to learn. She told us about your first potion—that healing tonic for sore muscles. You made it for the old cat that came to your doorstep for milk." She smiled wistfully, like she had been there. "Maude was so proud. We all were."

"We?" I asked, sitting up straighter. This was the kind of information I needed. Lacey faltered for a second, her eyes clouding over with regret. She shook her head, like she was trying to stop herself from saying too much. "Excuse me," she muttered, turning away and moving toward the stove. "You don't want to hear me prattle on about the good old days."

"Actually, Mrs. Neddles," Copper interjected, "We came here precisely to hear you prattle on about the old days." Lacey glanced at the three of us, and her eyes lingered on Arnie a bit longer, her expression tense. I could see the hesitation in her eyes.

"What did your mother tell you?" she asked softly.

"Nothing," I answered honestly, settling back into my seat with a shrug. There was no point in pretending otherwise

She studied me for a moment, then she said even more softly, "I doubt you were privy to the full extent of Maude's powers, then."

I leaned forward, determination building up inside me. "I think I know just enough," I said before pulling the bag up to kiss the clasp, then reaching in to bring out the thick spellbook. It somehow felt even heavier now that it was in the open.

Lacey froze, her eyes widening in alarm. Her expression shifted to one of reprimand as she said, "Hildegarde, having that with you is not only foolish but extremely dangerous." Her voice was low and urgent. "You should have left that cursed thing hidden where it was."

"Well, it's not going back under the floorboards now," I said, meeting her glare. "And I need your help."

Arnie's voice, shriller than usual, cut through the tension. "Are you telling me that you've been carrying around a high sorcery spellbook and didn't tell us?!"

"I knew," Copper said, not helping the situation at all. I frowned at her, but she just shrugged.

Arnie groaned, his eyes wide with anger and some fear. "Great! So we've been carrying around illegal cargo this whole time, and no one cared to tell me?"

I was about to tell him to calm down, but Lacey cut me off. "The danger is more than just legal— it's life-threatening. Do you realize what danger you've put yourself in?" Lacey said, her voice panicked and exasperated. Her gaze was transfixed on the book. Before I could respond, a shrill call echoed through the room, and I instinctively clutched the book to my chest. The noise was deafening. Arnie and Copper both winced as they covered their ears. I heard Lacey's voice crack as she muttered a command, and the bird's cry ceased.

"Someone else has found the door," she said grimly. "We don't have much time." I was frozen, my heart racing, but I forced myself to focus.

"Who? Who found us?" I demanded, though a small voice in me said I already knew the answer.

"It doesn't matter who," she replied, her eyes darting to the door, then back to me. "Put that blasted thing away," she snapped. I stuffed it back into my bag. "Now hurry here," Lacey barked, emanating urgency as she moved to the back wall and grabbed the edge of a short bookshelf. The bookshelf swung open, revealing a narrow passageway.

"You must go. Now!" she urged, motioning for us to enter. At first, I didn't hesitate, but then something stopped me.

"Wait! Do you know where my mother went? Or where she was trying to go?"

Lacey hesitated, her eyes flickering with uncertainty as she chewed her bottom lip. "Far away, I'd imagine," she said at last, almost as if she were trying to convince herself.

"Who would know where?" I pressed, unwilling to leave without more answers.

Lacey took a deep breath, wavering, then finally nodded and said, "Haute." She clasped my hands tightly. "Haute Brood. He was the only one of us with the influence to help her."

"Where is he?" I squeaked, my mind spinning with hope and fear and confusion.

"The Citadel—he's an empath in the king's service."

I gaped at her. "The king's service?" I repeated, my heart pounding in disbelief. But Lacey was already ushering us into the passage, physically shoving our shoulders to make us move faster.

"Don't take the train. It's the first place they'll look," she warned. "And trust no one else."

With that, her figure disappeared as the darkness swallowed us whole. I thought I caught a small sob right before the hidden door clicked shut, the sounds of the world beyond fading into an unnatural silence. As we all stood there for a moment, shoulders pressed together and panting nervously, I knew that whatever was coming next would upend everything.

Chapter Nine: The Witch's Stones

Arnie practically exploded through the door, sending it slamming against the wall with a crash that made the entire Iron Pot Inn shudder. The force of it startled me, but I was determined to keep my composure. I walked in after him and leaned against the back wall beside the window, folding my arms as I watched him start pacing furiously. His face was red, and he kept rubbing at his jaw as though he were trying to erase the thoughts tumbling out of his mouth.

"I keep to myself, follow the rules, don't make waves, and for what?" he muttered, eyes frenzied. "To get dragged into a government conspiracy?"

He wasn't even really talking to us. It was more like he was trying to exorcise whatever demons had chased him through the storm drain exit from Lacey's hideout. Copper and I exchanged a look as she took a seat on one of the creaky beds, but we stayed silent, letting him burn through his fuel.

"Why did I come along?" he asked the air, then laughed bitterly. "Oh yeah, to relax. Take my mind off high sorcery. Great job, Arnie. Now look at you." He stopped pacing, a sardonic grin on his face. "Maybe I'll make it to the Citadel after all… in handcuffs!" His high-pitched laughter faded into uneven breaths, and I could see him fraying at the edges.

"Okay, time to interrupt," Copper said from her spot at the edge of one of the beds, holding up a single finger like she was in a classroom. "We should be devising some sort of plan right about now."

Her tone was light, casual even, and Arnie spun toward her in wild disbelief. "Well golly, Copper," he exclaimed, throwing his hands into the air like a deranged magician. "You might just be on to something." He leaned in close, resting his hands on his knees, his grin sharp and humorless. "If we just put our brains together, there's nothing us kids can't solve. Not even being wanted criminals for carrying an illegal instrument of high sorcery!"

He straightened, turning his accusatory energy toward me. "What's the punishment for illegal high sorcery again? Oh right. Death."

Unfazed, she cut in, "None of us has used the book. We can't be charged with illegal acts of high sorcery when we haven't done any."

He let out a cackle, throwing his arms wide. "We don't know how they'll punish this, Copper. It's never happened before. Only the king's high sorcerers have ever written new spells—you know that's the law."

"This isn't helpful," I finally said, my voice quiet but firm. I gazed at the still street below, wanting its calm to somehow seep into me. "It's done and the choice made, so now we have to figure out some way to move forward."

"Choice?" Arnie shouted louder than was wise, and I turned to him with a warning glare, but his frustration boiled over. "I don't remember being offered any choice! My sister dragged me to a Hildegarde pity-party because you were sad and alone without your boyfriend, and now I'm a wanted man."

"If you think this pity party was for Hildy," Copper said, reclining back onto the mattress with a casual air that only infuriated her brother more, "then you're thicker than I make fun of you for being. And you aren't a wanted man—we don't even know if the people at Lacey's door were after us."

Arnie huffed, returning to his pacing. "All I know is that until tonight, I'd never snuck into an academy for information, never spoke with people potentially part of some crazy cult, and never fled through a secret tunnel. Then Hildegarde pulls that book out of her bag, and suddenly we're on the run."

"Then just go," I said, my voice slicing through the room. Arnie froze, his wide eyes locking onto mine as if I'd slapped him. I held his gaze head-on, my words deliberate. "Go on home to your desk and your books and spend the rest of your life fighting to prove you're something other than ordinary. Meanwhile, Copper and I will take this illegal book along the trail my mother left and maybe, just maybe, do something extraordinary."

He stood there, his mouth opening and closing like a fish out of water. I didn't waver. I motioned toward the door with a flick of my hand. "If you leave now, you might catch the last train." The room was silent except for the sound of his ragged breathing.

From her perch on the bed, Copper broke the silence with a voice rich with approval and admiration. "Hildegarde, I couldn't have said it better myself." She stood, her movements confident as she approached her dumbstruck brother. Her hand landed on his back with an actually tender pat.

"Arnie, you're stuck," she said with the kind of direct honesty only a sister could deliver. "You've been stuck for a year. And now fate's handed you a chance to do something exciting, something that might actually dislodge you from this pathetic rut, and you're going to turn your nose up at it?" She turned her attention to me, nodding toward the satchel slung over my shoulder. "May I?"

I hesitated for a moment before raising the bag up. Her intent was clear, and though this book had brought nothing but trouble, I trusted her. I knew it was hard-earned, but it still surprised me how naturally it came. I kissed the clasp and handed it over.

Copper slid it from the bag as though it were something sacred. The air in the room shifted, that familiar unease settling over us like a shroud. It happened every time the book came out, its presence a tangible, weighty thing.

"What are you doing?" Arnie's voice cracked, his expression pinched with fear as she extended the book toward him.

"All I'm asking," she said softly, her thumbs stroking the worn cover, "is for you to hold it." Her voice held no mockery, no taunt—only sincerity. She gazed at the book reverently, like it was a miracle she could scarcely believe existed in her hands. "It's more than just dangerous cargo. This… this is power, Arnie. The kind of glorious magic you've dreamed of your entire life. Right here. You may never get a chance like this again."

Her words landed with the precision of someone who knew her audience well. Arnie reached for the book, not out of pride, but belief. As she transferred its weight to him, something shifted. His red hair caught a faint breeze that seemed to come from nowhere, and his freckled complexion glowed like he'd just returned from a sunlit meadow. His breath hitched, sharp and fast, before settling back into a more deliberate rhythm.

I looked at her uncertainly, but she was watching her brother, intent and confident. His eyes had closed, and an eerie calm seemed to flow through him. For a moment, it was as though he and the book existed in a world apart from ours.

Finally, his eyes opened, and he spoke with quiet conviction. "If we went to the Citadel," he began, his words deliberate, "how would we get there?"

I let out a sigh of relief so profound I felt it in my bones. Meeting his gaze, I allowed myself the faintest of triumphant smiles. "Carefully," I said.

The next step in our plan came courtesy of Copper's sharp memory and keen eye. She'd seen a flyer at Rusty's, pinned on a chaotically overstuffed bulletin board, that advertised an empath market down by the river with a traveling caravan preparing to leave for Inntinn Bay that night. If we could join their journey as far as the southern coast, we could take a boat north after that, avoiding the trains entirely. Arnie had grumbled about the time it would add to our trip—a three-week trek instead of a two-day ride—but I reminded him this was precisely the kind of travel the watchmen wouldn't think to monitor.

Now, as we made our way toward the market, he trudged along, weighed down by three suitcases and a layer of mud that clung just as thickly to his boots as the riverside path. "I think we would've had time to go back for our things *after* speaking to the caravan leader," he huffed, sweat shining on his forehead.

"Best to be prepared," Copper replied breezily, skipping ahead with an energy that bordered on infuriating. Carrying nothing, she seemed more cheerful than ever.

"No one asked you to carry our bags," I reminded him, keeping my tone soft. It had taken a minor miracle to get Arnie to agree to this plan, and I wasn't about to jeopardize the fragile goodwill between us. "But thank you for doing it."

"You're welcome," he replied, a faint smile tugging at his lips.

Without the burden of luggage, I could take in the scene around us. The market buzzed with life as we walked through it, humming in a way that Facehaven hadn't managed to be. Where the city had felt all shine and glamour, the empath caravan was brimming with earthy, natural beauty. Crystals, talismans, pendulums, and oddities spilled from carts repurposed into storefronts. The air smelled of roasting chestnuts and meat cooked over open flames. Some boys played rhythmic music near the dock, their feet dangling above the water, while a group of girls swayed to the melody.

I had never been to an empath market before. As a child, I had begged Irenee to let me visit when the caravans passed through the Orchard, but she had refused every time. Irenee despised empaths, their rootless lifestyle an affront to her rigid sense of structure. She dismissed them as frivolous, their joy something incomprehensible and, perhaps to her, threatening.

Watching the lively scene encircle us as we entered, I could easily imagine what Irenee would have made of it—she would have absolutely hated it. I laughed to myself as two dreamy-eyed girls darted up to us, placing daisy chains around our necks. "Go in love," one of them said warmly before disappearing into the crowd.

Copper led the way to a cart without a line, stopping before an older woman dressed in flowing silks and adorned with jingling silver necklaces. Her wares, a few humble rows of smooth river stones, stood in stark contrast to the intricate, fanciful displays at the stalls surrounding her. But there was something about her quiet presence that commanded attention.

Though Copper had led us there, she slowed to a stop, now looking intimidated. We were all uncertain what exactly we were walking into. I decided to take the lead. "Excuse us, ma'am?"

"Sibella," she corrected, straightening her posture on the stool she perched upon, her voice sharp and precise.

"Sibella," I said, starting again. "We were wondering if you could point us to the caravan leader."

"The barker?" she snapped. "You've already passed him. He would have been the one shouting at you when you came in."

I thought back to the round man standing on a box at the entrance, loudly advertising the caravan's services and wares in a booming voice. He hardly seemed like a leader tasked with organizing travel and collecting fares, but maybe caravans didn't operate in ways we would find familiar.

"Okay. Thank you for your time," I said with a slight bow of my head, eager to move on. Something about her presence left me nervous and jittery.

"Pick a stone," Sibella ordered, motioning to the smooth objects arranged on the table in front of her. We exchanged uneasy glances. None of us wanted to be rude, but this wasn't why we'd come.

"That's all right," Arnie said, failing to hide the annoyance in his voice as he shifted the suitcases in his arms yet again. He'd refused to put them down in the mud the entire walk. "We're not looking to buy anything."

"Who said buy?" Sibella growled, looking offended. She motioned to the stones again. "Choose."

The authoritative anger in her tone startled me into action. Without thinking, I snatched up a plain gray stone, then held it up to her with both hands, as if offering it as an apology.

"Why that one?" she asked, one impossibly thin eyebrow arching as she studied me.

"It was right in front of me," I admitted, somehow knowing she would see through any attempts to lie.

Sibella said nothing at first, her keen eyes scrutinizing me as though I were a piece of fruit at a market. She extended her hand, and I dropped the stone into her palm. She brought it close, examining it with what felt like unnecessary intensity.

"You are not a risk-taker in nature," she declared without lifting her eyes from the stone. "You settle." The words stung more than I expected, and I let out an involuntary huff. Her eyes snapped up and pinned me in place. I immediately regretted expressing my indignation.

"But this stone is rough and chipped," she continued, her gaze continuing to bore into me. "You could have chosen a smooth stone to keep in your pocket, but you took a stone that held some unpleasantness, some danger. You have a hidden potential for greatness," she said, her voice softer, "but so long as you keep reaching for the closest stone, you'll never achieve it. You will settle like a heavy stone into the soil and gather moss until you cease to be noticeable."

She ended her lecture by tossing the stone back at me. I caught it awkwardly, pressing it to my chest as I fought the heat rising to my cheeks. I thought of the way I had spoken to Arnie the night before and felt a pang of regret. Is this how he'd felt under my scrutiny?

"I'll try it," Copper said, breaking the tension. I noticed her voice was less confident than usual.

She stepped forward, carefully scanning the stones before selecting a square one with a subtle sparkle. Holding it up, she displayed it with a bit more poise than I had. Sibella took the stone and inspected it with the same intense focus.

"People like you," she began. Copper smiled bashfully, and the praise made me bristle, still reeling from my own reading. "You have the outward appearance of confidence and sincerity," Sibella continued, her voice measured. Copper's smile became stiff, looking like she was bracing herself for the incoming negative statement. "But that is a mask." The words hit hard, and I saw the girl falter for the first time. "You use your wit and kindly demeanor to conceal what lies beneath. You fear you are plain and uninteresting. But that is not true." Copper's eyes flickered with hope, Sibella sounding like she was going to deliver soft praise. Instead, the woman's voice remained steady. "The truth is that you do not know who you are, and until you do, you will never know what you want."

Copper plastered on a smile, though it lacked her usual spark, and reached to reclaim the stone. "Thank you for the reading," she said with a feigned sweetness. "And thank you for the stone. I actually like the sparkle, superficial as it may be." Her final words were clipped, a small but deliberate act of defiance. I reached out to give her hand a quick squeeze.

"Young man," Sibella called to Arnie, gesturing to the stones still scattered on the table.

"Absolutely not," he said, not even sparing her a glance. He turned to us instead, his face twisted in aggravation. "I'm not letting some kook humiliate me for her own amusement. You've gotten your stones, and she's had her fun. Let's talk to the barker before my arms fall off."

"You wish to book passage?" Sibella asked, completely unfazed.

"We do," I blurted, trying to steer the conversation back on track. "How did you know?"

"People ask to see Bernard for one of two reasons," she said matter-of-factly. "To lodge a complaint or to ask for a ride. Typically, the complaints come from uptight, angry housewives, and the requests for passage are from wayward youths with bags." I glanced at our pieces of luggage, feeling foolish. We were pretty obvious.

"Bernard is the barker?" Copper clarified.

"Yes," Sibella replied. "And my husband will say no unless your friend picks a stone." She gave our group a wide smirk, her tone daring Arnie to challenge her.

He sighed, muttering under his breath as he passed the luggage to us. He stared down at the stones, clearly waffling between choosing something or walking away. Twice, he reached for one before pulling back. Finally, his hand hovered over a smooth black stone with white lines etched across its surface, perfectly symmetrical and polished by time. He pointed to it instead of lifting it, refusing to meet Sibella's gaze.

"That is the most beautiful stone in the bunch," she said with a nod, though her tone was flat. "Every swaggering young man chooses it. They think it shows their superiority, but really, it reveals their predictability." Her words cut, but like with my and Copper's reading, there was no malice—only harsh truth.

"Boys like you bore me," she added after a moment, her tone a little less neutral.

But then her demeanor shifted. She placed her hand gently over his, and her voice softened. "You are capable of originality, but you've smothered it. You've tricked yourself into believing that makes you more of a man. But we need you to be better—you can be better, Arnold."

He finally looked up to meet her gaze. "How do you know my name?" he asked, his voice a bit faint.

She gestured to his luggage with a grin. "It's written on your suitcase." Copper let out a quiet snort beside me. Arnie shook off his daze and reached for the stone, but Sibella swatted his hand away.

"Don't I get to keep it?" he asked, his tone defensive as he glared at Sibella.

"Did you not hear a word I just said?" Her expression was heavy with disapproval, her voice sharp enough to make him flinch.

"What about booking passage?" Copper interjected, stopping Arnie from arguing further. "Will you talk to your husband for us?"

"There's no need," Sibella replied as she began gathering her laid-out stones into a neat pile. "There are three cots open in Rainer's cart. You can take those."

Relief washed over me, and I let out a breath I hadn't realized I was holding. "Thank you, Sibella," I said, stepping forward to offer her my hand. She ignored it entirely, sweeping the stones into a velvet drawstring bag with practiced precision. I awkwardly lowered my hand, feeling the sting of rejection.

"How do we pay you?" I asked, determined to end the interaction on a respectful note. She paused her task, then let out a single, loud laugh that caught all of us off guard. She looked at me, her face alight with amusement, and spoke through a smile so knowing it sent a chill up my spine.

"Oh, you sweet things," she said, "you just did."

Chapter Ten: The Witch's Wagon

I couldn't sleep. The wagon jolted and swayed, tossing me around on the narrow bunk. Just when I felt myself drifting off, we'd hit another bump in the road, or Arnie would snore loud enough to rattle the boards. I rolled onto my side, sighing in frustration, and glanced at the stranger lying across from me in the low light.

Sibella had said we would be staying with the caravan's hired illusionist, but that was all she'd shared. He hadn't even introduced himself. He'd stumbled in just as the caravan lurched into motion, swung up to his bunk in one fluid movement, and promptly closed his eyes, muddy shoes still on.

I couldn't imagine how he found that position comfortable. He lay with one knee bent, foot flat on the bed, his cap pulled down over his entire face. Relaxed, sure, but not a good position to sleep—or so I would have thought.

Rainer, as I later learned his name, looked nothing like the other caravan members. Most others

I'd seen had an easy, unkempt grace to their appearance—long hair, loose-fitting clothing, and soft fabrics colored like autumn. But not him. He wore black trousers that fit snugly, a thin sweater stretching up his long neck, and a pressed blazer, all flawlessly black. Even his mud-smeared shoes had an air of elegance, crafted from black and white leather with intricate detailing. He looked like he'd stepped out of some polished city square and wandered into this muddy caravan. I couldn't help but wonder where he'd bought his clothes, or if I could ever afford them.

"Care for a drink?" he suddenly asked, his mouth moving but the rest of his body remaining as it was. I flinched, unsure if he was actually awake. Maybe he was talking in his sleep like Copper sometimes did.

"I…" I whispered, not wanting to wake Arnie or Copper. "Are you awake?" Rainer pulled his cap from his face and turned toward me, and my breath caught. His features were sharp, almost foxlike, and his eyes, golden and warm, glinted in the dim lamplight. I suddenly felt all too aware of my tangled hair and oily skin. He didn't linger on me long before hopping down from his bunk as effortlessly as he'd climbed up. Without a sound, he crossed the small cabin to a metal shelf, grabbed a green bottle and two glasses, and disappeared out the door. A gust of icy air swept through, flickering the lamplight. Copper and Arnie slept on, oblivious.

I hesitated. He'd taken two glasses; it would be rude not to follow. Wrapping my blanket around me, I clumsily climbed down from my bunk, misjudged the distance, and landed in a heap on the floor. I scrambled up, hoping no one had seen my ridiculous dismount, and shuffled toward the door, my blanket trailing underfoot.

Stepping outside onto the small deck, I was immediately grateful for the blanket, even if it made me look a little childish. The cold bit into my skin, and the wind whipped my hair across my face. The stars above were brilliant—a shimmering expanse of light against the dark void. Rainer leaned casually against the railing, utterly at ease. I, on the other hand, gripped it tightly, convinced the next jolt would send me plunging into the black forested abyss around us.

"You'll be fine," he said with a chuckle, handing me a glass. I managed a shaky smile, feeling absurdly small next to him. He poured out an amber liquid into both glasses, filling my glass with a measured amount and then his own nearly to the brim.

"What is this?" I asked, hesitating to drink something unknown, even if it was from a charming stranger.

"Do you really want to know?" he asked, his voice low and teasing. After a moment long enough to make my heart start beating nervously, he smiled softly and said, "We call it mole. It's molasses liquor."

I took a tentative sip. The sweetness hit first, followed by the sharp burn of harsh alcohol. My reaction must have been obvious because Rainer's grin spread wide, a flash of white teeth in the starlight.

"I'm Hildegarde," I blurted, then quickly added, "Hildegarde Fern," deciding a fake surname might be wise.

"Rainer Kitz," he replied, dipping his head in place of a handshake. His name intrigued me—it didn't follow the naming conventions of the Green Veil. Names usually came from family territories—mine was from Thorough Woods. Raemond's came from Valour Loch.

"Kitz is unusual," I said, curiosity getting the better of me.

"It's old language for fox," he replied, offering me the bottle to hold while he adjusted his cap. His hair was a pale platinum that could only have been achieved by dye or being born during a lightning storm—according to the old wives' tale. However, lightning storms were especially rare these days, with the government-employed weather evokers who monitored and suppressed extreme weather.

I clutched the bottle and my blanket tighter against the chill, captivated and wary in equal measure. Rainer seemed too polished, too peculiar for the muddy life of a caravan. Yet here he was, offering me molasses liquor under a sky full of stars.

"How do you like it?" Rainer asked, holding out his hand for the bottle. Grateful for the chance to free one hand, I passed it to him and pulled my blanket tighter around my shoulders.

"It's nice," I said, though my face betrayed me as I took another cautious sip. The drink was far too sweet and sharp all at once, but I didn't want to seem ungrateful.

"It's an acquired taste," Rainer said with a knowing smirk. "Some of us find it helps us sleep."

"That makes sense," I replied, forcing myself to take a slightly larger swig. The cart lurched just then, one wheel hitting a steep dip in the road. I staggered and threw my weight against the wall to steady myself while Rainer barely swayed, moving in perfect rhythm with the motion.

"Does that serving size guarantee some rest?" I asked, gesturing to his glass, which was already nearly empty.

"I don't sleep," he said simply, his eyes shifting upward to the stars. He didn't seem the least bit bothered by the admission.

"Not at all?" I asked, trying to keep my tone neutral, though my mind buzzed with health lectures from my childhood. I could still hear my primary teacher's squeaky voice warning, *"Sleep is a safe haven for budding wizards and witches."* She'd always enforced daily naptime with that motto.

"Not for the past few years," he replied, still gazing at the sky. "Hasn't seemed to slow me down." I had to admit, he didn't look like someone who lacked rest. His smooth complexion and alert demeanor suggested more the opposite.

"What do you do at night then?" I asked, only realizing a second later how intrusive the question sounded. But Rainer didn't seem offended.

"I entertain young ladies like yourself," he said, raising his glass to me with a mischievous glint in his eye. Before I could react, he shrugged off the comment with a chuckle and his tone shifted to something more casual. "Mostly, I read. I've got a collection of rare books in a hatch under the floor. You can borrow one if you'd like."

He stepped toward me, closing the distance in a single, graceful stride. His height was suddenly imposing, and his voice dropped into a light warning. "Just be sure to return what you take. I'll know if you don't."

"Oh okay," I mumbled, retreating a step without intending to. My awkwardness was painfully obvious, but Rainer only continued to look amused. I held up my glass, feeling the warmth of the drink settle in my chest. "I think this is starting to do its job," I said, tapping the rim with my fingernail before downing the rest in one go. It burned all the way down, and I winced, taking a moment to recover. "Ahem. Off to bed with me," I concluded, sounding like a much too old version of myself.

"Sleep well, Hildegarde Fern," Rainer said, leaning back against the wall of the wagon with a smile that could have melted ice. I nodded in return, fumbling my way back through the cabin door.

The cart jolted again as I stepped inside, and I heard the faint clink of glass from outside as Rainer remained alone in the cold night. I couldn't help glancing back once before climbing back into my bunk, his silhouette still and composed against the endless black.

Sibella had tasked us with husking corn for the crawfish boil that would feed the caravan tonight. The three of us—Copper, Arnie, and I—had been hunched over our buckets for two hours, and the pile before us still looked insurmountable. I didn't mind the work as much as the others seemed to. As an herbalist, I was used to spending hours on tedious tasks. If anything, the repetitive motion felt grounding.

To my left, a group of merry boys lounged on the deck of a motionless cart, strumming their guitars. For three days, I'd watched them do little else. They stopped only to eat and drink whatever the dancing girls brought them and passed out only when they'd had too much to drink. I couldn't help but wonder if this was their typical job.

"Do you think we'll have time to go to the beach once we get to Inntinn Bay?" Copper asked, aggressively tearing a stubborn chunk of husk from her cob.

"We're not on vacation," Arnie muttered. His pile was noticeably smaller than ours, and I couldn't tell if it was out of spite or lack of skill. "We need to stay focused on our goal. Besides, it's too cold to swim."

"I know," she said with a disappointed sigh that made her sound like a child. "It's just… we haven't been to the beach since we were kids."

"Me neither," I admitted, catching the scent of crawfish from downwind where a group of children were peeling them. "Not since Uncle Maxx died." The mention of Maxx brought a brief silence, broken only by the strumming nearby.

"Did you ever eat at that little soup shop in Juniper Bay?" Arnie asked after a moment, a rare note of humor in his voice.

"Oh, yeah," Copper said, her face lighting up. "They had that chowder we loved. Why'd we stop going?"

"Because the chef was a total quack," Arnie replied, incredulous at her lack of memory. "He'd throw people out if they complained— flip tables even."

Copper burst into laughter. "That's right! Dad would just stare at his lap while Mom yelled right back."

"Didn't he have a funny voice?" I asked, trying to picture the scene.

"Yes!" Arnie pointed a cob of corn at me, excitement sparking in his eyes. "He had this weird accent no one could place."

"Dis soup iz my master-piece!" Copper cried, throwing her hands up in an exaggerated impression. The memory was so vivid—and her delivery so spot-on—that all three of us dissolved into laughter.

Our laughter must have carried because a warm, familiar voice called out from behind me. "You three seem to be having more fun than anyone else here." I turned, wiping tears of laughter from my eyes. Bernard stood with his hands on his hips, his ample gut jiggling slightly as he chuckled beneath his thick gray mustache.

"We're sorry, sir," Arnie managed through giggles.

"Don't apologize," Bernard said, lowering himself into our circle. "Anyone who can find joy in a simple task is fine by me." Over the past three days, I'd grown to appreciate Bernard's warmth and generosity. He also never pressed us about our travels, offering kindness and support without prying. Irenee's advice to accept help when it came to me echoed in my mind, and I silently thanked her for it.

"You kids have been a real help," Bernard said, clapping a hand on Arnie's shoulder. "I'll hate to lose you in Inntinn Bay."

"Speak for yourself," Rainer's voice cut in as he appeared from behind a nearby cart, three goose carcasses draped over his shoulder.

Bernard clicked his tongue in disapproval. "You know I hate hunting."

"And you know I hate shellfish," Rainer shot back. "A man's gotta eat." He lowered the geese until their limp heads dangled directly in front of me.

"May I help you, Mr. Kitz?" I asked, glaring up at him.

"Pluck these when you get a chance," he said with a devilish grin.

"And why would I do that?" I countered. Three nights of sharing drinks and books had dulled the hypnotic effect of his charm.

"You won't finish *The Decline of Necromancy* before we reach Inntinn Bay. Defeather my geese and it's yours," he said silkily, driving an excellent bargain. Copper giggled at the phrase "defeather my geese," but I ignored her.

"Deal," I said, grabbing the carcasses by their feet. I had a feeling Rainer's reading literature wasn't the kind I'd find in a common book shop, and studying outlawed magic was starting to give me quite a thrill.

"Always a pleasure, Hildegarde," Rainer said with a small bow before striding away.

"I'm not done with you, young man," Bernard barked, standing up to hurry after him.

"He's an ass," Arnie grumbled as I began plucking feathers.

"He's gorgeous," Copper said, staring after him.

"He's not so bad," I admitted, though my attention was drawn to puncture wounds I'd just uncovered on the goose's neck. Four sharp, clean marks—not the kind an arrow or blade would leave. I kept my suspicions to myself, focusing on my work.

The camp buzzed around us as preparations for the feast continued. Lanterns strung between wagons bathed the grounds in warm colors, and children squealed as they collected kindling for the bonfires. The caravan's icebox was hauled out to chill casks of ale and wine, and a band launched into a lively tune. Copper tied a bright scarf into her hair, the colors complementing her cropped locks. Next to her, I felt plain in my sweater and slacks.

"I'm going to change," I announced, brushing feathers from my lap. "If you see Rainer, give him the geese."

Back at the wagon, the familiar warmth inside welcomed me. I swapped my sweater for a flowing blue blouse with gold buttons and draped my green cape over my shoulders. Satisfied with the way the blouse fit, I reached for the lamp. A quick pull of the chain, and the room filled with the soft glow of red light.

"Hildegarde."

The sound of my name made me lurch backward, my shoulder slamming into the wall. The voice had come from above. For a moment, fear stole the air from my lungs, but as my heartbeat settled, I forced myself to look up.

"Rainer," I exhaled, pressing a hand over my racing heart. "What are you doing in the dark?" Embarrassment shot through me as I realized he must have been there the whole time. "I was changing!"

His expression was unreadable—eerily blank. Without a word, he swung down from the top bunk, landing with practiced ease.

Ignoring my comment, he answered, "I was doing a bit of light reading." His voice was flat and unnerving. Leaning against the bed frame, he added, "Some books are better read in darkness."

A shiver prickled down my spine. His tone, his demeanor, everything about him felt off, colder than I'd ever seen him. Something in my gut screamed at me to leave the room as quickly as possible.

"Right," I said, forcing a shaky laugh as I edged toward the door. "Well, I'll see you out there. Don't let those geese go to waste."

"Hildegarde Fern." His commanding voice stopped me in my tracks. I could feel him close behind me now. "Don't you want your book? We had a deal."

"I'll get it later," I said, carefully turning just enough to meet his eyes over my shoulder. My mind raced, reminding me that no matter how much time we'd spent together, Rainer was still a stranger.

"Makes sense," he said, a grim smirk on his lips. "You've got plenty to read already."

Before I could decipher his meaning, he lifted a hand to the bed and retrieved something from it. My breath caught when I saw what he was holding—*the* book.

"Anything you want to tell me, Hildegarde?"

My blood ran cold as the silver insignia of high sorcery glinted in the dim light.

How had he found it? How long had he known?

The book dangled from his fingers, swaying slightly as though mocking me. I couldn't move, couldn't speak. The room seemed to shrink, the walls pressing in closer with each passing second.

Chapter Eleven: The Witch's Chase

My throat tightened as I tried to find the words to explain myself. I could feel the weight of Rainer's presence as he stood before me, the heavy spellbook hanging ominously between us.

"That's—" My voice finally came out, raw and unsteady. "You had no right to root around my things." My voice hardened as the words came out. I hoped an offensive stance might mask my panic.

Rainer raised an eyebrow. "I was under the impression we were sharing books on this trip." He lowered his arm to let the book drop to his side, the dull thud of its weight against his leg sending a jolt through me.

"Not books in locked bags," I shot back, though the words felt flimsy as they left my mouth.

"A kiss-clasp is barely a lock," he replied, his tone dripping with condescension. "Certainly not enough of one to protect something like this." He lifted the book up to eye level, its silver emblem catching the light again, flickering as if it were alive. "A bit of harmless curiosity should *not* have led me to this." His face, sharp and angular, was etched with an anger that I think expressed concern, and perhaps reprimand.

I held his gaze, unsure whether I should speak or bolt. Finally, I managed to relax my throat and find my natural voice, softer but still pointed. "Can I trust you with this?"

"No!" The shout erupted from him, startling me. "You can't trust anyone with this." His hand clamped onto my shoulder, firm and unyielding. With each word, he shook the book inches from my face. "You can't trust me, your friends, your boyfriend, or even your diary! Do you understand me?" I nodded quickly, his sudden intensity leaving me shaken.

"I need you to say the words, Hildegarde!" His grip tightened, his tone brooking no argument.

"I understand," I snapped, a defensive anger rising in me. I slapped his hand away with a crack that surprised even me. "I am not a child." I stepped forward, my anger lending strength to a new resolve. "I also am not a fool. I know exactly what this is and what it can do. I'll admit I hid it poorly, but I will not be threatened by some cheap carnival illusionist." I yanked the book from his grasp, clutching it tightly with both hands. "If you ever touch me or this book against my will again, I won't think twice about flattening you where you stand."

Rainer's shoulders tensed, his neck rigid, but his expression betrayed no surprise. Instead, he gave me a solemn nod, accepting the weight of my words.

I took a breath, willing my anger to cool. "I have a large stock of powerful tonics," I said, my tone calmer, more reasoned. "Give me one reason to think you'll betray me, and you won't remember this year, let alone what you saw here today."

"You're understood, Hildegarde," Rainer said evenly. "I have no desire to harm you. I've been on the wrong side of the law more than once. That's why you were never here, I never met you, and I never saw this book. No memory tonic necessary." His voice carried the weight of sincerity. "I'll forget you ever existed by the time we reach Inntinn Bay in the morning."

I nodded, the heaviness of his promise settling over me. I hadn't intended to drag anyone into my mess, and I couldn't blame him for wanting no part of it.

He sighed in frustration then. "You must understand the danger you're in, though. There's a reason there are only two high sorcerers alive today. Mess with these magics, and they'll bury you faster than the watchmen ever could."

"I have no plans to cast the spells," I assured him. "My interest in high sorcery is purely academic."

"Keep it that way." He exhaled deeply, as though letting go of something long-held. "And tell Arnie to do the same."

"What?" I blinked, confusion flaring. "Arnie isn't—"

The bellow of an unknown, authoritative voice pierced the night, cutting me off. My stomach dropped as silence fell over the camp. Even the band's relentless music ceased, leaving only the low bark of a man shouting orders in the distance. Rainer and I locked eyes.

"Stay here," he whispered, barely audible as he slipped out the door and closed it behind him with practiced silence. Alone in the wagon, my pulse thundered in my ears. I strained to make sense of the individual's distant shouts, but I could only hear the anger in them. My panic started a rapid drumbeat in my chest.

Footsteps pounded up the steps outside, and I snapped into motion, frantically searching for a hiding place for the book. My hands fumbled at the heavy trapdoor where Rainer kept his rare books, but I'd only cracked it open when the door burst inward.

"Watchmen! Get your things," Arnie hissed, closing the door behind him with a forced quiet. His face was set, his movements brisk as he began shoving clothes and belongings into bags indiscriminately. I stood frozen now, the book still in my hands.

"Put that thing away," he snapped, tossing me my satchel.

I barely caught it, my mind spinning. "Are the watchmen here for us?" I whispered, shoving the book into its hiding place.

"Does it matter?" he shot back, stuffing the last of our things into his bag. "They said they got a tip about illegal goods. If they find that book, we're finished." I nodded, my hands shaking as I grabbed the last of my things. "Let's go," Arnie urged, cracking open the door. Copper's terrified face came into view as she slipped inside, panting.

"One second," I said, dropping to the floor.

"Hildegarde!" she snapped, her voice taut with fear. Ignoring her, I scanned the trap's contents. My fingers closed around *The Decline of Necromancy*. I slid it into my bag's side pocket, then hesitated and grabbed *The Tragedy of the Fae-folk* as well.

"Hildegarde!" Arnie growled.

"I'm coming." I shut the trapdoor, slung my bags over my shoulders, and moved quietly over to him.

Copper peeked through the window. "They're still searching Bernard's cart. If we stick to the edge of the camp, we can make it to the woods without being seen."

"How many?" I asked.

"Two," Arnie murmured, his voice just behind my ear. Without exchanging any more words, we all slunk out the door and back behind the wagon.

As we hurried over to the next cart, a voice that was now clear enough to hear boomed, "Now folks!" I whirled around to see who had caught us, but there was only night and trees over my shoulder. "There's no need to get yourself into a tizzy," the voice continued, giving methodical orders in a magically enhanced voice. Once my heart retreated back down from my throat, I could tell it was coming from my left. A few carts away, I spotted two watchmen clad in pristine black uniforms, standing in front of Bernard and Sibella's cart. I could barely make out Bernard's rotund form in the shadows, just outside the lamplight shining brightly at the foot of his wagon's door.

"I'll gladly step aside, Sergeant," Bernard said with performative gaiety, "just as soon as I see a warrant."

"Don't need one," the second watchman piped up in a gruff bark. "Not when there's been a report made."

"And who made this report?" Sibella said as she glided into the light, positioning herself between the men and her husband.

"An anonymous report, ma'am," the first watchman responded. "We received word of restricted materials being transported in this caravan. As I'm certain you would agree, a matter of kingdom security is a very urgent issue that requires immediate attention." His voice made the hairs on my arms stand up. Something about the drawl of his voice was sticky, like molasses stuck on the hem of my sleeve.

"We need to go," Arnie rasped into my ear. I shushed him with my hand. No attention was on us yet, and something in me needed to see how the watchmen were going to treat our hosts.

"This is outrageous," Sibella snapped as she crossed her arms. "Give me your names. I will report the both of you for unlawful seizure." It was at that moment I noticed something for the first time—or the lack of something. All the empaths of the caravan were silent. My eyes having adjusted to the darkness, I could see them cowering in the doorways of their carts. None of the young children were visible. I had come to know this community as raucous and honest to a fault, always poised to speak their minds. The sight of them in silent submission felt wrong.

"Sergeant Beauregarde Mason, at your service," the watchman answered, giving her a bow despite the dry sarcasm of those last words. "And this here is Dexter Wheeler, if you please."

The hunched man next to him growled, "That's Officer Dex."

"Sibella," Bernard said as he laid his hand on her shoulder, "Why don't we step aside and let the men do their jobs? We have nothing to hide." After a long backward glance at her husband, she did as he asked, and the watchman I now knew to be named Dex stepped into their caravan.

"It's time to go." This time, the whisper came from Copper. "While they're busy." She was right, and I felt confident that Bernard truly had nothing to hide. But Rainer was a different story. What would happen to him if they found the books beneath his floorboards?

Forcing my fearful thoughts away, I glanced around us. We couldn't just run for the trees from where we stood. There was a field of empty space before we reached the dense forest, and three figures running away from the caravan were the very definition of suspicious. I edged further away from our current hiding spot to peer around the caravan line, past Bernard's cart. I spotted a slightly better option. At the end of the camp circle, a copse of trees jutted out at an angle, extending the forest's edge by a decent amount. It was only a few feet from the last cart before we'd hit tree cover. I motioned forward and around the carts, trying to make my thinking known to Copper and Arnie.

Arnie nodded in agreement and whispered, "One cart at a time." Copper reached out and squeezed my hand, and then we were off. We made it to the next cart, a gaudy blue thing with windchimes hanging down low from its awning. I made sure to give the cart a wide berth so as not to jingle the metal ornaments. As we reached the second cart after that, Dex's voice cut the silence of the camp.

"Nothing of note," he reported as he walked out of the cart, banging the door shut behind him.

We couldn't have been more than two carts away from them now.

"Nothing's ever easy, is it?" Beauregarde drawled. Arnie put up a hand to stop our progress and pointed below the cart to our left. Two pairs of black boots. We couldn't risk crossing behind the cart with the watchmen standing right there. We would have to wait for them to move.

"You reckon the compass is all charged up?" Dex said in a quieter grumble.

"Should be by now, but you know how I feel about all these new enchanted objects," Beauregarde responded. Something metal clacked together as he shifted his stance. "Whatever happened to good old-fashioned investigative work?" he huffed.

Then he continued in a louder voice, "Now let it be known that I am nothing if not transparent. There has already been concern about a warrant, so I will explain what we're about now." Copper, Arnie, and I all exchanged glances. His words were reasonable, but his voice dripped with condescension. "This here compass detects concentrations of magic within short distances. This method of searching has been approved by the king and the Senate, so I don't want to hear any griping about unlawfulness."

The three of us didn't need to utter a word to know what each of us was thinking. Before I had even registered my own movement, I had darted forward two more carts and was now standing with my back to Sibella and Bernard's cart. I could only pray that the watchmen were too busy inspecting the dial of their compass to be scanning the ground.

"Well, now it's pointing back at the cart again," Dex exclaimed. I went pin straight, feeling as if ice had just been dropped down the back of my sweater.

"Let me search this time," Beauregarde offered. "This kind of searching isn't really your strong suit."

"This is ridiculous," Sibella cried, her voice as sharp as I'd ever heard it. "There is nothing illegal in our cart!"

"Then you won't mind me taking a closer look so we can get this all sorted out," Beauregarde's voice came, muffled as he stepped into the cart. It creaked and shifted as its weight changed suddenly.

"Run," Arnie mouthed to us as he took off for the trees. I broke into a sprint behind him, hopeful that the watchmen weren't peering out of any windows as they searched Sibella and Bernard's cart again. I felt I was being punched and kicked by a series of small limbs as my bags batted against me.

"Hey!" We had just reached the tree line when a voice cut through the air, chilling every drop of blood in my veins. It must have been Dex, judging by the roughness of the voice. "You three!" I spun around and finally got a good look at the watchmen as they approached from the edge of camp. Dexter

Wheeler was at least a head shorter than the Sergeant, and he led a large hound on a heavy leash, which I hadn't noticed before. Sergeant Beauregarde Mason was tall and thin, with jet-black hair combed back from an overly angular face. He was every bit as unsettling as his voice was, and he was now only a few paces away from us.

I ran out of thoughts as fear froze me to the spot. That compass must have been pointing right at me, at the bag hanging from my shoulder containing all of my mother's illicit secrets. It was like the weight of the bag had struck me in the face. It wouldn't matter that I hadn't written the book. It wouldn't matter that I was nothing more than a kitchen witch. They would condemn me just as harshly as they had her.

A hand gripped my shoulder with considerable force, but it didn't belong to the watchmen. I turned to look behind me, and I saw Arnie holding tight to me and Copper, his eyes squeezed shut.

"*Ser disparu!*" he bellowed, the magical language somehow making his voice bigger than what he possessed. I felt a tug at my waist, as if invisible hands had taken hold of me, and then the world went black.

For a horrifically long instant, I was nothing. I had no form, no thoughts, and no location. I tried to find something familiar to hold onto—a memory to contextualize this disembodied moment—and I found my sloshing mind settling on a feeling. I was eight years old, at the top of the spinning wheel at the Midsummer Festival, my stomach lurching as I reached the zenith. And then I was falling, falling through empty air.

My knees hit gravel, and I took in a desperate gulp of air. The sting of rocks against my flesh was a welcome relief to the nothingness that had surrounded me an instant before. As my vision returned, I heard the lapping of a distant wave and smelled sea brine in the air.

"Arnie!" The gravel scattered as Copper moved suddenly from close behind me. I turned around as the scene behind me came into focus. She was kneeling over her brother, who lay convulsing on the rocks lining the path. Under the thick cover of night, deep crimson shone in the moonlight.

Blood. Blood was spilling from his nostrils, ears, and mouth. As I scrambled forward, I saw that it was even dripping from the ducts of his wide-open eyes.

CHAPTER TWELVE: THE WITCH'S BREW

The bed sheets beneath Arnie were soaked through with cold sweat where he had been lying for hours, trembling as his body rebelled against the great magic he had performed. Copper sat at his side all the while, patting the sweat from his brow with a washcloth and watching the steady rise and fall of his chest. I had planted myself at the small writing desk in the corner of the drafty apartment, poring over every herbal healing book I had, searching for some root or flower that could return dear Arnie to his typical, ridiculous self. But after hours of searching, I'd found nothing to treat an ailment of this severity, and my eyesight was beginning to wane from exhaustion and the staggeringly low light emitted by the single oil lamp in the room.

My body ached from top to bottom. It had taken nearly an hour to carry Arnie along the road he had transported us to and into the sleeping town of Inntinn Bay. Even though

Copper and I shared his weight, it had felt like my arms were going to snap clean off as we lugged the limp boy plus our luggage through the town's streets.

As we struggled down a dark, empty road, we'd had a heated discussion about taking him to a proper healer. But we ultimately decided that would be a risk we couldn't afford. If the healer reported the cause of his condition to the watchmen, it wouldn't matter the quality of his care—he'd already be dead. We lucked out in finding some discrete lodging in a fortuneteller's basement room—it was in one of the few buildings with their lights still on. Copper had remained hidden with Arnie while I pled for a room, and the fortuneteller thankfully went upstairs as soon as I paid, allowing us to shuffle Arnie in unseen.

In the few hours since he had cast the transportation spell, his bleeding had slowed and eventually stopped, bringing us some hope. However, as one concern vanished, two more appeared. His heart rate slowed dramatically, and a powerful fever took hold of him. I tried brewing a few common teas used to treat flu symptoms and fatigue with the herbs I had on hand, but each attempt resulted in the liquid being violently and disgustingly rejected by Arnie. Glancing over at the poor boy as he labored over each crackling breath, Rainer's words of warning bounced around my mind: *'Mess with these magics, and they'll bury you faster than the watchmen ever could.'* By the grace of my chosen school of study, the burden of keeping my friend alive fell heavily upon my aching shoulders.

"Anything yet?" Copper queried from her perch at her brother's side.

"Not for this," I said, trying to mask my growing frustration for her sake. "I have nine ways to treat a burn, four ways to treat gout, and at least a dozen hangover cures, but nothing to jumpstart a heart or break a fever of this severity." As I spoke, I flipped through pages faster, tearing a few in my anxiousness to find anything useful.

"Didn't they teach you any advanced healing recipes in your senior herbalism course?" she asked desperately.

"I'm sure I'll learn some when I start school," I said with a sigh. I rested my head in my hands and looked down at the wood grain of the desk. "But for now, I'm as useless as a primary school kid with a brew kit."

"That can't be true," she urged, attempting to rouse me from my defeated attitude. "You were in the top five of our class. You must have read something *somewhere* that could be of use. I bet there wasn't an herbalism book in the library you didn't check out."

"They don't supply advanced healing books to general students not going off to an advanced academy," I snapped, unable to keep my voice even this time. I hadn't thought much of it before, but that limitation now seemed incredibly restrictive. "It's because most of the herbs you need for those brews are…" I trailed off as a thought hit me like a train.

"Are what?" Copper cried, standing up and scrutinizing my expression.

"Are poisonous!" I said, beaming as I flipped to the last chapter of my massive reference book. "Copper, you're a marvel."

"You lost me," she said, scrambling over to my station. "How is poison helping us?"

"Usually the most toxic plants contain the most powerful healing properties," I breathed, scanning the index with my pointer finger, looking for familiar names. "You just have to know where to look." I let out an exclamation of triumph as I found the names I was looking for. "Barberry! That can restore his energy… And foxglove! That'll bring his heart rate back up for sure." I clicked my pen and began scribbling notes in my dog-eared little brew book. "I can char some olive leaves to help with the fever, grind up some swallowwort for blood flow, and boil gentian liqueur to kickstart the whole brew." I furiously scribed each thought as it came to me, ensuring I remembered each piece.

"And this'll work?" Copper whispered, her voice tense as she clasped a hand on my shoulder. She looked at my wild scrawls as if they might hold the answer to the universe.

"Oh, it'll work," I said, nodding to myself as I leaned back in my chair and set my pen down. "As long as I dry the swallowwort completely, pluck healthy petals from the foxglove, make clean cuts on the barberry bark, and thoroughly burn the olive leaves."

"And… if you don't do all those things?" she asked, eyes wide and intent.

I took a deep breath and looked up at her. "It will kill him."

"Are you sure you can do this?" she questioned, holding my gaze.

"Top of my class," I said with a nervous grin, "remember?"

Copper gripped my shoulder painfully tight. "Right."

Of all the ingredients I planned to use in my brew for Arnie, I had only the olive leaves, those being the tamest of my chosen components. If consumed raw, they would induce vomiting, which *was* useful if someone had ingested something bad. However, when burned to a crisp, the ashy remains could be used in a tea to alleviate strong fevers. Since no apothecaries were open at this time of night, I brewed cup after cup of the burnt leaves, hoping to lessen his discomfort enough for him to get a few moments of much-needed sleep while we waited for dawn. Copper, too, drifted in and out of slumber, periodically laying her head down beside him on the mattress while still half-sitting in her chair. I stayed awake, using the small hours of the morning to perfect my timings and measurements for the most powerful brew I had ever attempted. By the time the sun rose, I was content with the specifics of my recipe. The only thing left unchosen was the ingredient of intention.

Every potion of note required an intention to activate the dormant power within the raw ingredients. In the past, I had used things like a sigh, a tear, even a whispered name to finish off brews—but those had come from prewritten recipes. I had never had to think one up on my own before.

The sound of footsteps crunching on loose pebbles pulled me from my concentration. Through the squat window above my head, I could see a few pairs of boots and loafers shuffling by on the gravel street. The town of Inntinn Bay was finally stirring.

"Copper," I hissed.

She gave a sharp, snorting inhale and sat up from her partially reposed position. "I'm up," she insisted, rubbing her cloudy eyes.

"It's morning." I kept my voice low, not wanting to wake Arnie, whose skin glowed a sickly gray in the dim light. "I'm going to find an herb shop down at the harbor. There's still plenty of olive ash. If I'm not back in an hour, stir a spoonful into a cup of hot water for him."

"Do you need money?" she asked, still sounding foggy.

"I'll make do with what I have," I replied, not wanting to dwell on our draining budget. I pulled my cloak around myself and hitched my satchel onto my least sore shoulder.

"You can leave that here, you know," Copper said as she motioned to the bag. "I'm not going anywhere."

"Right…" I said flatly, "Because you're both in a state to deal with any trouble that might come from it being here."

"Fair point," she conceded. She was trying to be strong, but I could see she was off-kilter. Her eyes had lost their usual sparkle. I could only hope she would be restored when Arnie was, but a cold fear started to crystallize in my gut, telling me something had broken beyond repair.

The cool ocean breeze stroked my cheeks as soon as I stepped onto the street. Instinctively, I pulled my cloak tighter across my chest. From outside our cellar apartment, no trace of the water could be seen through the row of gray-paneled houses standing stories above me—no doubt built that way to secure coveted ocean views. But the scent was unmistakable: salt and recently deceased fish, oddly pleasant in the crisp morning air. My boots crunched on loose gravel as I followed the working-class crowd down toward the harbor, their blue jumpsuits and thick woolen sweaters hazy in the dawn light.

As I rounded a corner with the others onto a wide lane, the vast expanse of water finally came into view—gray and dark in the early morning mist, with choppy waves crashing along the rocky beachfront. Tethered to the outstretched docks, vessels of all sizes rocked in the unsettled waters. The crew members aboard paid no mind to the motion as they hauled cargo off the boats by the boxful.

"Oysters!" an older woman called from a stand to my right. "Oysters and prawns!"

The street was filling quickly with carts and vendors, though this market bore no resemblance to the caravan. The caravan merchants boasted brightly colored signs and velvet tongues while these sellers called out their wares without frills or charm. I watched sales happen with barely a word exchanged—most were just a few counting hand gestures and two nods.

I scanned the street for an herbalism shop or cart but found only fishmongers and the occasional fortune teller. Of course, the proper storefronts were likely on the hill near the academy. After several minutes of peering and pacing, I resigned myself to asking for directions.

"Excuse me," I said, approaching a fish cart during a brief lull in customers.

"Yeah?" the scruffy young man grunted, wiping his wet hands across a heavily stained apron. "Whattaya need?"

"Do you know where I could find a medicinal herb dispensary?" I asked, my voice unnaturally high-pitched.

"A wha'?" he responded, leaning forward.

"An herbalism store," I repeated louder.

He ran a calloused hand through his short beard. "Don't know if we got a steady-going one." That possibility hadn't occurred to me, but it made sense. Few herbs thrived in this climate, and with the kingdom's trade routes, ready-made brews were easy to ship in.

"Oy, Dave! We still got an herb store?" he barked across the lane.

"A what?"

"A potions shop!"

"Oh, right. Isn't there one down on Bleak Street? By the post office?

"Nah, they just sell cooking oils." Their voices were curt and forceful, but neither looked as if they thought it rude.

"Doesn't that northern fella got some sorta chemist shop?" said a large woman who had just come up to stand in line behind me.

"Yeah, with all them animal parts and whatnot," a new member of the growing line added.

"That's on Drewy," the large woman affirmed.

"Thank you so much," I said, turning to face her. "And Drewy is…"

"Down on the right," she signaled, pointing down the road. "Just past the war memorial."

"Thank you all!" I called as I scurried away. No one responded—they were already back to business.

The crowd thinned as I turned onto Drewy Street. It was a cramped alley, one side lined with a gray wall marked by graffiti and the other with three storefronts bearing boarded-up windows and faded signs. Doubt gnawed at me, but I carried on. At the dead end, a warm light caught my eye—an illuminated lamp above a narrow stairwell leading down. I descended the few feet of stairs cautiously, peering through the condensation-fogged window before opening the door to the gentle jingle of a bell.

A long counter stretched across the small store, shelves behind it lined with neatly labeled jars. Some contained dried herbs; others housed preserved animal parts suspended in foggy alcohol. No one stood behind the counter. The only signs of life were a swanky record humming from a gramophone and the thick scent of cinnamon from burning candles. I struck the bell left at the center of the counter.

"Was that the bell?" a shaky male voice called from the back room.

"Yes!" I responded, keeping my voice cheerful.

"Brilliant!" A slight man in a blue sweater-vest emerged, peering at me through horn-rimmed glasses with a warm gaze. "What can I do for you, miss?"

I steadied my breath. "I'm an herbalism student," I said carefully, "working on a thesis about the healing properties of poisonous plants." The lie felt heavy on my tongue.

His brow lifted. "Your instructor approved this thesis?"

"Well…" I began while leaning in, "I thought I might ask for forgiveness instead of permission," I said with a weak mischievous grin, hoping to appeal to his curiosity.

He studied me for a panicked heartbeat before cracking a smile. "Understood. What exactly are you looking for?" I pulled my recipe from my cloak pocket and smoothed the wrinkles out over the counter.

"A cup of swallowwort," I began.

"Dried?" he asked with a hint of suspicion.

"If you have it."

"I wouldn't sell it any other way." He turned as he spoke and pulled a footstool to the middle of the large shelf behind him and stepped up to remove a tall, thin jar from a high shelf. "Next," he asked, setting the jar down on the counter.

"A foxglove stalk," I continued.

"Make sure you avoid—"

"The stems and leaves," I interrupted, wanting to prove my knowledge. "Yes, I plan to."

He nodded, giving me a more generous smile now. Reaching below the counter and pulling out a jar of preserved stalks, he said, "Of course you know this—it's your thesis." He shook his head and blushed a bit. "Carry on."

"Three barberry sticks, each at least three inches." I watched as he resisted offering further wisdom and instead scanned the shelf on the left for the ingredient. He found it and placed it quickly beside the other waiting jars.

"And lastly, a bottle of gentian liqueur," I concluded.

"Funny," he said as he cocked his head. "That isn't a toxic one."

"No, but it can quicken the metabolism when boiled, lessening the chance of negative reactions from the other ingredients."

"Huh." He ran a hand through the scruff on his chin. "Well, the gentian is over with the other alcohols to the left of the door." I looked where he had prompted and crossed to get a better look.

"So you'll boil the brew in the gentian for how long?" he asked, grabbing a scrap of paper. I felt a little flutter in my stomach as I realized he wanted to note the idea for himself, but I did my best not to show too much excitement.

"Just until the first bubbles," I explained as I found the bottle and pulled it from the shelf. "The other ingredients should already be in the liqueur as it heats." He scribbled down my instructions as I spoke. The flutter changed to a swell of pride.

As he weighed and packaged all the ingredients, he smiled and said with a chuckle, "And here I've only ever used gentian for a good time." He sealed each ingredient into its own paper bag before consolidating the haul into one bundle. He informed me the price altogether was fourteen gold and twenty-six silver. It was far more than I had hoped to spend, but I'd never been skilled at haggling. The register dinged and opened on its own as soon as the total was spoken. It was a simple enchantment, but it worked well in adding a lot more pressure. I parted painfully with my coins and took my change with a small, polite smile before securing the parcel under my arm and turning for the door.

"May I just ask," the shopkeeper started before I could leave, "what is this brew going to do?"

"I'll know soon enough," I said with a grim smile. Then I exited the store, the gentle jingle of the bell sounding behind me as I practically fled up the stairs.

CHAPTER THIRTEEN: THE WITCH'S WORK

The merciless scent of sweat and blood wafted through the door as I entered our basement apartment. Deep, pitiful moans suddenly sounded with such volume that I slammed the door instinctively behind me to contain the cries. I ran down to see Arnie thrashing on the bed and Copper using her full body weight to hold him still.

"Hildy!" she cried breathlessly. "Thank the stars you're back."

"What happened?" I asked as I dropped my bag and parcel to the floor with a thud and sprinted to my friend's side.

"It just started," Copper panted as she held his convulsing body down by both shoulders. "I was bringing him more ash tea, and he just started having this fit." As she spoke, Arnie began producing a wet choking sound, and then a dark spray of blood spluttered from his mouth.

"Hildy," she whimpered, her eyes growing wide with terror as she watched her brother. "What do we do?"

My mind went to a thousand places all at once. I saw Arnie as a boy darting through the trees, felt Copper's hand clasp mine as it had done so many times in our growing friendship, heard the sound of Rae and Arnie's laughter carry across the waters of Crystal Lake, watched the blood pool around the naked woman in my dream, smelled the burning of my many failed brews. And all the while, Rainer's words of warning seeped through: *"Mess with these magics, and they'll bury you faster than the watchmen ever could."*

"Keep holding him down," I instructed, determination snapping my mind into place. "Make sure he doesn't hurt himself. I'll work as quickly as I can."

Copper nodded, helpless tears streaking her cheeks. I knew I needed to work both swiftly and accurately in my brewing—any misstep in the preparation would kill Arnie faster than the blood-fever. I attempted to still my shaking hands as I emptied the bottle of gentian into a pot on the small stove and set it to a low flame. I hadn't intended to start heating the liqueur so early, but our limited time forced improvisation.

First in the pot were the olive leaves, which I charred in the flames from another burner, burning the tips of my fingers as I lit each and dropped them directly into the pot. There was a short burst of flames each time a burning leaf met the simmering alcohol. No matter how poorly my fingers had fared, this was the easiest step by far. I drew in a shaky breath as I moved on to the toxic ingredients.

Luckily, the swallowwort petals had come already dried, but I still had to dust each for any remaining pollen, which was as lethal as arsenic if ingested. I would have liked to dust each petal twice for safety, but Arnie's desperate cries urged me on. Next, I plucked the foxglove flowers from their stalk and used a scalpel from my brew box to slice the green pedicel off each before rolling them in my palms and tossing them into the pot.

With each ingredient, the brew's scent grew stronger. Though floral in nature, the plants were bitter herbs, creating an odor not unlike rust. The smell choked me as steam began to rise from the pot, nearing a boil. I only had moments before the first bubbles surfaced, and I had to be sure to get in my barberry bark. With no time to do things properly, I improvised by slicing the sticks directly above the pot with the same scalpel I had used for the foxglove. My fingers suffered yet again as I caught my skin under the knife several times. The last scrap of bark fell into the pot just before the contents began to boil.

I realized with a jolt that I had yet to add an ingredient of intention. I hadn't even decided on one. As the bubbles rattled the ingredients, panic filled my chest. I had mere moments to make a choice, and if it was the wrong one, all this would be for nothing.

The bead of scarlet blood forming on my injured finger drew my focus. Blood? I allowed myself a brief moment to consider it. Arnie's pain had begun with blood—perhaps that was what was necessary to end it. Without further hesitation, I held my finger above the pot and squeezed it with my other hand until a round drop fell into the brew. The liquid instantly began to sizzle as if sound waves were running across its surface, every ounce of it turning the same deep red as the blood. Without pausing to consider what I had just made, I emptied the pot into a ceramic mug waiting beside the stove.

"It's finished," I proclaimed, carrying the smoldering cup to the bed, careful not to spill a drop. "Hold his shoulders and keep his head propped up so he doesn't choke."

Copper did as she was told, peering at the cup's scarlet contents with an equally fearful and hopeful look.

"Arnie…" I said, catching my friend's frantic and far-away gaze, "This is not going to be pleasant."

No sooner had I given the warning than I clasped his chin in my hand, smearing blood and spittle on it as I forced his mouth open far enough to pour the boiling liquid down his throat. Arnie fought the two of us as the potion scorched its way through his body, but I leaned in to keep his mouth firmly shut, one hand still under his chin and the other on top of his head. Once I heard him take a shuddering inhale, I let go, and he violently swung himself forward to sit up, clawing at his throat as if it could alleviate the dry burning that ran down it.

Copper released him, looking expectant and horrified as his skin grew pink. I dropped the empty mug on the bedside table and climbed onto the pillows behind him. Wrapping my arms around his chest, I pulled him back against me, holding him tightly as the potion worked its way through his body.

"You're okay," I breathed against his ear. "You're okay." His guttural cries began to fade to quiet sobs as the fever broke in mere minutes, covering his skin in a cold sweat. The color returned to his face as his frantic breathing slowed. We all sat in silence, me holding Arnie while Copper mopped the sweat from his brow.

"I—" he croaked, words getting stuck in his dry throat.

"What, Arnie?" Copper clasped his hands in hers.

"I am such an idiot." A small and pained smile twitched at the corner of his mouth. Copper and I looked at each other, and at last, I let myself breathe a sigh of relief. Copper was the first to laugh, and I joined soon after. Arnie could only manage a few amused exhales, but it was enough to banish the dread that had been building in all of us.

"Yes, you are," she and I responded together. I let Copper take my place supporting Arnie, and I went to get him a well-deserved glass of water, adding a bit of burn balm from my brew box to soothe his throat. I returned to find the two moments from sleep, huddled together on the narrow bed. They looked so alike side-by-side—the same soft chins, cheeks dappled with freckles, brilliant red hair, and an unnamable quality that made them seem well beyond their years and entirely innocent all at once.

"Thank you," Copper whispered without opening her eyes.

"You're welcome," I murmured as I set the glass of water on the bedside table. A gentle snore rumbled from Arnie's nose. I pulled a thin cushion from the seat of a chair and lay down on the floor beside my slumbering friends, pulling my cloak around me like a blanket. For the first time in what felt like ages, we all slept soundly as the daylight streamed in from the window above.

The chill struck my cheek like the choppy waves against the rocky cliffs of the bay. I gazed longingly at Copper's thick wool peacoat and wished I had packed more strategically. Of course, it was only wet ocean breeze that made the temperature so chilly down at the docks, but

I took it as a warning for what was to come, with winter sneaking around the seasonal corner. Arnie still looked a bit like a corpse as he spoke with a hairy captain a stone's throw away. Copper had let him take the lead on securing passage to the Citadel, knowing he was still feeling inadequate and emasculated from the events of the last few days. We also certainly would have drawn more attention as two young girls trying to lead that kind of negotiation. I looked down at my boots and hunched up my shoulders in an attempt to shield my face from the wind. Copper's shoes entered my limited field of vision, and I felt her forehead press against mine.

"It is freezing," she said as her breath steamed down between us. We huddled closer together. "I can't feel my fingers." She spread out her long fingers for me to look at, and I could see that they had gone a bit blue.

"You didn't bring gloves?" I asked, suddenly feeling less envious of her packing choices.

"I did," Copper replied indignantly, "But they're packed away under my bras and underwear, which I'd rather not show all of these sailors by digging through them."

"But you have nice underwear," I mused.

"Exactly," she said with a decisive nod. We both started giggling then. It was the kind of unearned laugh that can only result from exhaustion and absurdity, both of which were in good supply between us. I removed my leather-gloved hands from my cloak pockets and held her blue fingers between mine, rubbing back and forth to warm them. We caught the attention of a few passing sailors and dockworkers, laughing over seemingly nothing as we huddled together and held hands.

"What did I miss?" Arnie's voice prompted, causing us to look up from our hands. He looked pleased with himself, and some color had returned to his cheeks. Perhaps he was flushed from the cold, or maybe it was the pride of success after greasing the palms of a frightening captain.

"Just warming up," I said, sliding my hands back into my pockets. I had the feeling Arnie wouldn't find the discussion of his sister's underwear even half as amusing.

"You better get used to the cold," he grunted as he tightened his scarf. "It won't be any better on the boat."

"Did you find us something?" Copper asked, bouncing slightly from foot to foot, her hands now in her armpits. Arnie nodded.

"A small shipping freight," he said and pointed to a mid-sized steamboat bobbing in the waves a few vessels away. "They leave tonight for Tangere but are stopping off at southmost port at Camp Valiant to let their small hold of passengers off. From there, it will only be two or three days on foot, unless we can find a ride."

Camp Valiant. How was I going to explain all of this to Raemond? What would Irenee have told him in her letters? Surely she wouldn't send sensitive information through the king's postal service. That had been Lacey's mistake.

"Why couldn't they drop us off further north?" I countered. "It would bring them closer to Tangere and let their passengers off closer to the Citadel."

"All ports north of Camp Valiant have been closed to civilian use," Arnie reported. "It sounds like the border fighting is picking up a bit."

My heart jumped. Suddenly, explaining my predicament to Rae seemed like a gift; the alternative would mean he had left the camp and was stationed at the front. Copper squeezed my shoulder.

"Hey," she cooed, "this happens every few years. A few rogue factions from the Ridgebacks try at an invasion, and every time, they are stamped out like weeds. We haven't had major casualties at the border in years. He'd be in far more danger working law enforcement like his dad."

I nodded. Copper was right, but the uncertainty still filled me with cold dread. I could only pray Rae was at the camp when we arrived.

"How much did this set us back?" I asked, wanting to focus on more immediate concerns.

"Thirty-five silver—almost all we have left," Arnie admitted as he frowned. "But if we pull our weight on board, they said we could get some money back at the end. Hildy, I mentioned that you cook, and they seemed really pleased with that."

Copper and I both nodded, knowing that was a great arrangement.

"We at least have enough left for some soup and a few drinks," Arnie said as he smiled sweetly. "I say we get some food in us before we embark."

"Come on then." Copper looped her arm around her brother's neck. "I saw a nice-looking pub down the street with our name on it." I trotted along behind as she led us down the docks to a seaside tavern. Its little sign creaked in the wind, and it was a struggle to make out the name: Freddy's.

Freddy's was packed full of loud dockworkers, all clad in dark blue jumpsuits. The walls were covered in old photographs of ships, and large, wooden fish hung behind the bar. A raucous cry shook the frames as the workers reacted to an event in the game booming over a crackling receiver.

"It must be the Crusaders game," Copper called as we shoved through the crowd to an empty booth in the back. "They're playing the Leviathans in the moonbroch quarterfinals."

"I hate moonbroch," Arnie whined. "I can still hear the sound of bones cracking when Dad brought me to that Hemlocks game."

"Oh, grow up," Copper teased. "Broken bones are a part of life."

"I was six!" he snapped.

"I've never been to a game," I confessed. "Irenee isn't a fan."

"Your aunt? Not into all-male, state-sanctioned violence? I would have never guessed," Copper taunted as she slid along the torn leather lining the booth seats. I took the place next to her as Arnie settled in across the table.

"How're you feeling, Arnie?" I called over the noise. He leaned forward, facing his right ear toward me.

I repeated my question and he bellowed back, "I'm feeling pretty decent, actually. I won't be picking any fights anytime soon, and this still hurts a bit," he said, stroking the large scab that covered the bottom of his chin. "But you did really well with that brew."

"He's right, Hildy." Copper clasped my arm where it lay between us on the table and shook it lightly. "Anyone who claims that herbalists are soft hasn't met you."

"All right, you two," I grumbled, blushing. "Let's get some food in you both." I signaled to a waitress, and she made her way through the sea of tables and customers. All three of us ordered a bowl of chowder and a buttered roll. We didn't say much more as we ate. Copper started listening to the game and hollering along with the crowd. Arnie ate slowly and gratefully, closing his eyes from time to time to savor the soup. I mindlessly picked tufts from the inside of my roll and thought of Raemond. I couldn't decide what troubled me more—the thought of him fighting on the border or how little he had crossed my mind the past few weeks. I felt the cool touch of his ring against my chest and tried to remember how he smelled. Bonfire and evergreen. I could recall it intellectually, but I couldn't pull the memory of the sensation from its hiding place in my mind.

The sun hung low in the sky as we made our way back to the dock where the old steamboat waited to take us to the other side of their world. Streaks of deep red and amber lit the waters along the horizon in a two-toned kaleidoscope. Copper stopped at the lip of the dock and stood basking in the light. I watched the sunlight bathe her face as she took in a deep breath of sea air with closed eyes.

"Copper?" Arnie asked, uncertain what she was planning.

"How long until we disembark?" she asked in response, her eyes still closed.

"I don't know," he said, setting his suitcase on the dank wood and rolling up his jacket sleeve. "Maybe about ten minutes." No sooner had the words left his mouth than she started frantically stripping the laces from her boots. She kicked them off with a gleeful cackle. Once her feet were bare, she hopped down off the dock and landed on the sand below. She took off running, her long scarf billowing behind her.

"It's frigid out here!" I called after her. "I'm not making you a tonic when you catch your death." I gasped reflexively when her toes hit the water. Copper, on the other hand, let out a giddy yelp as the ocean water lapped up against her ankles.

"What's the hold-up, guys?" she called back, her voice having jumped several octaves. "Afraid of a little water?" I turned to Arnie to lament the absurdity of Copper's taunt, only to find him peeling off his loafers.

"Seriously, Arnie?" I pleaded, shivering as I thought of the sting of the frigid water.

"We haven't been to the beach since we were kids." A smile tugged at his thin lips, his face illuminated by the setting sun. "Could be fun." With that, he abandoned his luggage alongside his sister's and dashed down the sand to the waterline. Copper cheered at his approach, and he pumped his hands above his head like a champion fighter in response. Then he abruptly stopped at the edge of the sand to carefully roll up the cuffs of his slacks. He screeched as a wave broke at his feet and pooled around him.

I gave a bark of laughter, set my suitcase and brew box on the dock, then sauntered down onto the sand. My feet sank with each heavy step. The limited sunlight silhouetted the siblings as they clasped hands and spun in a circle, gradually building speed while kicking at the ocean spray. They separated moments before an impending fall, both laughing boisterously and doubling over. Copper shrieked when Arnie unexpectedly kicked a few drops of water in her face before returning the favor in an even greater splash.

I didn't take off my shoes nor join them at the waterline. Instead, I stood sinking in the sand, watching my friends enjoy a rare moment of escape, albeit a freezing one. I smiled as the sun tucked itself into the horizon behind them, forcing the fears of tomorrow far back in my mind. Dear Arnie had been moments from death that very morning, and now I was watching him cavort in the sea like a child. It was a rare victory to savor.

Chapter Fourteen: The Witch's Voyage

My boots slid on the slick deck as I boarded, but I caught myself with a clumsy next step. Night had begun to fall around the boat, now rocking with abandon as it stood tethered in the turbulent bay. In the flickering light of the oil lamps, bustling men swept around us, hauling cargo, sacks of potatoes, and growlers of dark ale in their thick arms.

"Passengers this way," a gruff, female voice called from somewhere on the other side of the deck. I squinted to identify the source of the command. "All passengers to starboard, if you please." I knew my nautical terms well enough to follow the shouted instructions, leading the other two like ducklings behind me to the right side of the ship. I spotted the group of our fellow travelers. Three young, colorfully dressed women stood huddled shoulder to shoulder as the ocean spray repeatedly misted them. Two men stood close enough to them that I thought they were all together at first, but then I noticed the women were decidedly huddling with their backs to them.

"Listen up, my doves!" I then located the husky woman who directed the group's attention. She stood a head above the tallest passenger and held an oil lamp that illuminated her square jaw, which sat atop several layers of a heavily wrapped flannel scarf. Her unbuttoned trench coat whipped about in the wind, revealing the same navy jumpsuit that the others wore.

"Welcome aboard the Rambler. We're glad to have ya with us on this lovely evening." She spoke with the commanding volume and subtle warmth of a strict mother. "I'm Mrs. Marin, and I am acting chief steward of this vessel. For those of you unfamiliar with seafaring rankings, that means I see to the kitchen, living quarters, and passenger arrangements. In simpler terms, you are my responsibility, and I will do my best to make this a painless journey for you folks. That being said, the Rambler's a bit long in the tooth, and your fares reflected that. This vessel is by no means a luxury liner. She clocks in at a whopping four knots in good conditions, so this hop across the pond will take us a little under a week if the wind stays on our side."

I gripped the iron railing along the edge of the hull as the boat took a sudden lurch. Unmoved Mrs. Marin continued, "She handles fine in open ocean, but if you find yourself feeling sick from the motion, focus on the horizon for a bit. If you do get sick, please try and vomit off the side. We have a strict rule that everyone cleans up their own sick, so you'll want to try and avoid that embarrassment. We're packed in tight here, so you eight will be sharing a bunk room." The young women to my right whispered nervously to each other at that. "Ladies, if you need a place to change in private, you'll have to do so in the commode. Room's a bit tight, but it's manageable with some flexibility. If you follow me, I'll show you down to your accommodations."

Mrs. Marin turned and led the way down a narrow flight of stairs just behind where she had been standing during her lecture. The light in the corridor was blinding as it reflected off the white metal walls. The clacking of heels on the iron stairs drowned out whatever the two men in front of me were chuckling about, but I thought it might have been in relation to the ladies trotting down the stairs before them. The bunk room was located a few steps from the bottom of the stairs and smelled heavily of cleaning fluid.

"As you lot can plainly see," Mrs. Marin began as she backed down the thin aisle that separated the two rows of bunks, "space is limited in the cabin. I recommend you spend most of your daylight hours above deck to ward off cabin fever." Copper dropped her suitcase on the bed to her left with a flat thud as it struck the metal frame through the thin mattress. Mrs. Marin continued, "We don't have much to offer you folks in regards to entertainment, so you'll have to make do with a bit of old-fashioned conversation or find some other ways of distracting each other." The two men sniggered at this, looking pointedly at the women. Mrs. Marin gave them a flat stare for a few seconds, then continued. "Of course, if idleness is unbearable, you can always pitch in around the ship for a chance at a small refund when we reach our destination. Any questions?" A small hand shot up from one of the bashful young ladies in the front. Mrs. Marin gestured for her to speak.

"Is there a room suitable for a bit of light sewing? We have a few alterations to make to our party dresses, and I'd hate to damage the fabric with sea-spray." She spoke in a sharp, high pitch with pursed lips. Her two companions nodded in solidarity. I noticed then that they all wore matching cape coats, pumps, and pill-box hats, differing only in color. The question-asker wore magenta while the other two had baby blue and lime green ensembles.

"Welcome to your studio, ladies," Mrs. Marin said as she outstretched her arms to indicate the cramped bunk room. Her eyes twinkled with amusement as the girls returned to their nervous chattering. Mrs. Marin pulled a crudely folded piece of paper from her coat pocket. "I suppose we should see that we've got the right folks. When I call your name, just go ahead and raise your hand. Daschel Brook?" The broader of the two men raised a hand. Mrs. Marin continued down the list. "Gary Strand?" Daschel's gangly companion half-raised his hand. Mrs. Marin squinted at her list, "Missy, Sissy, and Casandra Fairbanks?"

"I'm Missy," the girl in lime green squeaked.

"I'm Sissy," the blue one added in a similarly light voice.

"Casandra," the one in dark pink said, "But I go by Kissy." Copper stifled a laugh, and Arnie jabbed her with an elbow. The girls looked to be around my age, except for Kissy, who looked closer to being in her early twenties.

"We're sisters," all three spoke in unison. Mrs. Marin raised her eyebrows.

"You certainly are," she said as she scribbled something down on her list. "Helen Purslane?" I scanned the room for the missing passenger before hearing Arnie cough, "That's you," under his breath. Belatedly, I raised my hand. "And lastly, Lisel and Cormac Burnet?" Mrs. Marin concluded as Copper and Arnie raised their hands in unison. She crumpled the paper back into her pocket. "With that, I'll leave you folks to settle in for the night. Breakfast will be served at six." With a nod of her large head, Mrs. Marin shuffled out of the room, leaving the passengers to their own devices.

I surveyed the cramped room. Daschel and Gary had already claimed bunks in the back corner. Luckily, there were a few more beds than there were travelers, allowing for a bit of separation. Copper swung herself lithely onto the top bunk. Arnie settled in beneath her, and I set my things on the bottom bunk next to him.

"Thanks for the heads up with the names," I hissed at him as quietly as possible.

"Did you think I'd be stupid enough to give our real ones?" He hissed right back, hanging his coat over a ladder rung.

"No," I whispered, trying to fluff up the thin pillow provided, "But a warning would have been nice. Aliases are less convincing if you don't respond to them."

Copper popped her head down from the top bunk and said in a hushed tone, "I strongly doubt they've gone through the trouble of submitting the passenger names to any transit authorities. This all feels…" she paused to motion generally at the shabby bunk room, "very off the books."

"Something bothering you kids?" Daschel said suddenly from his bunk, his voice loud and heavy with a thick coastal accent. "All that whispering over there… Not the best time to be picking a fight."

"We're fine," Copper said, avoiding eye contact.

"Our mother says to never go to bed angry," Sissy added, neatly folding her blue coat over her arm. "It's terrible for your skin."

"Like fatty foods," Missy piped up, folding her green coat in the exact same way.

"And what's her name?" Arnie asked, tone innocent. "Prissy?"

"No!" Sissy said, looking greatly offended. "It's Elisa."

"But does she go by…" Copper began softly.

"Lissy?" Kissy finished for her, "Yes, she does, but only with close friends." Kissy held herself with a more regal, mature composure, contrasting the tittering, more precocious nature of her sisters. As she carefully removed hidden pins from her hair, she inspected Copper and I with a cat-like intensity. I began to fidget with discomfort. "What brings you north?" she asked in clipped tones.

"I'm visiting someone at Camp Valiant," I responded, trying to ignore her judgmental stare.

"Your boyfriend?" Missy chirped, perking up.

"My fiancé," I corrected, the word feeling foreign on my tongue. It was the first time I had called Raemond that out loud. Even though this was old news by now, and only for helping build our cover story, I still felt a jolt of electricity in my gut.

"You're engaged to a soldier?" Sissy gushed, "How completely romantic!" She placed a gloved hand over her heart.

"When's the wedding?" Missy asked as she perched on the edge of her bed, holding a goose-feather pillow that she had just pulled from her trunk. She clutched it like a little girl holding her favorite stuffed toy.

Inspired by the genuine interest, I gushed, "Next Harvest! We're having it on the banks of Crystal Lake where we got engaged."

"A Harvest wedding," Sissy proclaimed dreamily. "That's so rustic and cozy."

"You should wear lace," Missy announced fervently. "Lace will look gorgeous against the colors of the turning leaves." Sissy nodded emphatically.

"Lace is a floral pattern," Kissy interjected coolly. "A simple crepe dress would suit the season best. It'll be easy to accessorize with the gloves and cloak that you'll need for an outdoor wedding." She spoke as one who was an expert on the matter, and so I took a mental note. Kissy may have been condescending, but her advice felt founded in knowledge and experience.

"What color dress should I wear?" Copper interjected, rolling onto her stomach with her head propped up with a pillow. "I'm her maid of honor." I knew she was only asking for the sake of play, but after all this, she would be the obvious choice. My best friend was Raemond, but he had his own vital role to play in the ceremony. Irenee would be giving me away, and there was no other girl I felt as close to.

"Red would be too on the nose," Sissy said, "and a maroon is too close to your hair color." Sissy glanced at her elder sister to see if she was going to disagree, then inspected Copper with pursed lips. "Marigold could be quite striking with your complexion, and it would match the leaves." Sissy's pitch increased with excitement as she continued, "And your accent color *must* be gold, of course—you will have so many choices for the jewelry!" Sissy made eye contact with her sister again. "Is that right, Kissy?"

"It's exactly right, Sissy." She dolled out her approval like one would a treat to a dog in training. Sissy smiled from ear to ear with pride.

"As thrilling as late-night wedding planning with strangers is," Arnie said, unlacing his shoes as he spoke, "I think we should all get some shut-eye while we can." Daschel and Gary grunted in agreement, having already removed their shoes and over-shirts, emitting the pungent smell of their combined body odor. The Fairbanks sisters began a systematic bathroom routine, each taking over the cramped bathroom one at a time, coming out in silk nightgowns and hair curlers. I decided not to attempt changing into my pajamas and settled into my stiff bed in my sweater and slacks. Copper managed to change into a matching pajama set under her covers. She came to sit on the edge of my bed, tying a few cloth rollers in her hair.

"It's kind of weird, isn't it?" she whispered to me. "Talking about the wedding."

"A little," I conceded, equally quiet. "I mean, I've been dreaming of marrying Rae since I was little, but I've never *really* pictured it. The cake, the ceremony, me in a big white dress."

"A blushing bride," Copper said with a melodramatic sigh.

"More like a terrified one. What if all this changes things?" I hadn't spoken this fear out loud until now, and I felt the rush of nervous adrenaline spike my heartrate. "I've never kept a secret from him before. Not a real one."

"And you still haven't!" Copper leaned forward, her voice rising to just above a whisper. "You aren't lying—it's just not something you can put in a letter. Once you see him, you'll tell him everything. This weight on your shoulders will get lighter, I promise."

I frowned, fidgeting with the bed sheet. "But it isn't fair to involve him in this. He's working toward a military career, so he can't be a part of whatever this mess is."

"Hildy, I know things seem scary after what happened with Lacey and then Arnie getting hurt, but at the end of the day, we're just a few kids on a typical rebellious adventure. I don't think looking into your mother's secret club is going to affect the fate of the nation, much less your fiancé's job prospects." She reached out to still my restless fingers.

"I hope you're right, Copper. I would love to be overreacting. I just… I have this feeling that things are about to get…" I searched for the word, unable to pinpoint the premonition that was scratching at me like a rough clothing tag.

"Get what?" Copper asked, looking alarmed at the possibility of some ominous divination.

"Nothing," I exhaled. "I'm just tired."

Only once Kissy was fully satisfied with her full nighttime routine did the room go black. Copper climbed back down to her bunk, and within a matter of minutes, I was drifting off to sleep.

She stood on the peak of a gray cliff, looking out over the turbulent sea. The rocks beneath cut into her bare feet with their dull but jagged edges. Her matted, black hair clung to the wetness of her face despite the whipping wind. A repeating, hollow thud kept a persistent rhythm as fragments of a great vessel beat against the cliffs below. She looked straight down at the shoreline, her toes clutching the cliff's sharp edge. A wave crashed with a hiss onto the white sand. As it retreated back to the sea, it left a stream of crimson blood in its wake. There was another, and another, and another, until the shore glowed as red as the rising sun on the horizon. The scarlet canvas below displayed an array of shredded bodies, as scattered and irreparable as the ship itself. She did not attempt to count them. She didn't have the time.

"Is this what is to come?" she asked, barely a whisper.

"It will come and come. There will be no stopping it now," a voice answered behind her. She did not turn to look at the speaker.

"What gives us the right?" A torso washed ashore, ripped at the waist.

"We do."

Out in the distant water, white foam gathered around the disturbed surface as a great beast thrashed its limbs one last time, then retreated to the black fathoms below.

I woke to darkness. The room had grown sticky with the hot breath of my sleeping bedfellows.

Daschel and Gary traded rattling snores back and forth, denying me a moment of silence to drift back into sleep. Images from my dream flitted through my mind as I tried to piece the scene back together. I clicked a knob on Irenee's watch to illuminate its face: five o'clock. I checked the small countdown in the corner: *335 days*.

I swung my legs around and set my bare feet on the cold floor. In the darkness, I fumbled around for my boots and pulled them on. I pulled my cloak off the ladder rung and fastened it over my shoulders as I tiptoed to the cabin door. A beam of artificial light shone in from the hallway as I made my exit, eliciting a groan from a half-conscious Copper. That was the last sound from my bunkmates as I closed the hatch softly behind me. Light bounced off the corridor walls from the overhead lamp, as blinding as it had been before. I followed my memory up the flight of stairs and out onto the deck. It hummed with a quiet energy as a few tired but focused crew members went about their business in peace, only speaking to pass along reminders and procedures. The air was cold, wet, and had the melancholy glow of morning awaiting the sun.

"You looking for the kitchen?" a passing member of the crew asked as he wiped a sea-sprayed brow.

"I am, actually." I wondered if he'd asked because I was a woman or if that would be the only reason any passenger would rise this early.

"Down aft," he said, motioning with a straight hand to the stern of the boat, "and below deck." I graced him with a thankful nod before following his promptings. The scent was easy to follow once I descended the slatted steps—bacon and flapjacks. It was a smell that had pulled me from bed more than once. Of course, when Irenee was cooking breakfast, there was always the faint scent of burning to accompany the enticing aroma.

Behind the heavy metal door that separated the kitchen from the corridor, I found Mrs. Marin flipping perfectly round flapjacks on her own. Despite her solitude, a great deal of work was being accomplished. A suspended wooden spoon stirred a large bowl of batter without a hand to guide it, the pan containing the sizzling bacon strips shuddered back and forth to keep the meat from searing to the metal, and a solo knife flew over peaches with expert precision, pitting and slicing in perfect rhythm. There was even a compact gramophone playing unfamiliar music sung by a man with a low, gravelly voice in a minor key. As a flapjack landed with a sizzle, Mrs. Marin looked up from her stove.

"Are you one of the 'issy's'?" she asked through squinted eyes.

"Hil…en. Helen Purslane," I said, barely catching myself

"Ah, right," she said, snapping her fingers in self-frustration. "I *will* learn all your names. Of course, by then we'll be dropping you folks off."

"At least you get three for the price of one with the Fairbanks," I mused. "Just switch up the first letter of the pattern and you've got a good shot."

Mrs. Marin laughed, the sound low and raspy. She pointed to me with her spatula. "Are you the one who's supposed to be good with cooking?"

"I'm an herbalist," I started. "Or, I guess one in training," I said, correcting myself. "I like to cook."

"We aren't picky on the Rambler," Mrs. Marin said, speaking with the pride of the down-to-earth working class. "We don't take much to any fancy spices and whatnot, but bring whatever knowledge ya have."

"I don't know a lot of cooking techniques, but I know that in brews, a bit of aged ginger can help with motion sickness," I offered, wanting to be useful but not step on anyone's toes. "I also grew up with my aunt throwing mulberries into the flapjack batter, if you have any of those around."

"We do. Sounds worth a try," the imposing woman said, yielding her spot at the stove and sliding the thin distance between the counter and the island to the bowl of batter. A single touch stopped the circular stirring motion of the spoon, and it sank into the thick batter. She began grating a gnarled ginger root over the bowl and told me where to grab the box of mulberries from under the counter. I squeezed into the space and found the berries quickly. She took the container from me and tipped the entire contents in. They bounced with muffled thuds along the wooden slats as they cascaded into the waiting batter.

"Cook 'em up," Mrs. Marin commanded, slinging a loose rag over her shoulder. The first of my flapjacks burned black around the edge, but the following few improved, with the rest soon becoming cooked to perfection. They formed a picturesque stack on a green ceramic plate that Mrs. Marin put out for me.

After checking in a few times, she appeared satisfied with my work and left me unsupervised as she focused on frying up the bacon. Flapjacks had been the first dish I'd ever learned to cook, and Maude had been an excellent chef. She may not have looked like the housekeeping sort, but she had been a woman of staggering skill in the kitchen. I could still envision the perfectly ironed apron cinched tight around my mother's tiny waist, and I could easily recall the smell of cinnamon associated with almost all her baking.

"Get any sleep?" Mrs. Marin asked over the sound of sizzling fat.

"A bit," I answered as images of blood-stained sand and dark waves flashed unbidden through my mind.

"It gets easier," she offered. "I'm at the point where I can't sleep on solid ground anymore."

"How long have you been with the Rambler?"

"Going on twenty-six years now. It's no Royal Navy, but we think of it as home."

"Who's we?" I asked, flipping a doughy disc in a smooth, practiced motion.

"Who on this ship isn't related to me?" she said, chuckling as if an old friend were there to share in the joke. "First mate Lou, the bald one, that's my husband. Donnie's my oldest—he's down in the engines. Then there's Junior, who works cargo. Our other boy, Marty, is the first mate on a sister vessel. Lou's so proud of him. A few of my cousins are aboard doing some temp repair work this trip, so you'll see them mucking about too. And Captain Bobby is my husband's uncle."

"That's a long list," I said in awe, almost letting a pancake burn.

"Can't throw a dead fish on the Rambler without slapping a Marin. Only me to keep em all in line, though." She smiled with pride.

"And you're all enchanters?" I asked. Most transit workers trained in basic enchantment to keep the engines running.

"Nah," she rasped, scraping and flipping some of the glistening pork strips. "Just me and the handyman cousins. Of course, I didn't get any sort a formal education. Lou, Marty, and Bobby all got licensed in divination. That's why you don't see us slamming into many icebergs. Donnie and Junior are Camp Valiant rejects. They call themselves self-taught evokers, but I call them two dumbasses with big arms."

I choked back a laugh, not sure if that would be rude. "But the Rambler's engine is run on an enchantment, though, right?" I asked. It wasn't a fancy ship, but that was a reasonable expectation.

"On its good days." She pursed her lips. "Good enchantments are expensive. We make do with temporary spells and a bit of upkeep. That's why all the cousins are here. When they can't keep her stoked, we just throw some coal in there. That's where the big arms come in." The ship suddenly took a greater-than-average tilt to the left. "We've got our system down—it's all perfectly functional."

CHAPTER FIFTEEN: THE WITCH'S NEW RECIPE

By the third day of travel, I was baffled as to how the Rambler remained in one piece. The great beast stumbled over waves like a tipsy sailor finding his way home from the local bar. Twice, I had been thrown from my bunk by a great rock to the right, and Arnie had been sick at least three times a day, failing to make it over the edge on several occasions. Copper managed fine with the lurching, but she got more and more antsy being contained in such a tight space. The two guys in the group never got any more interesting, and in fact got lewder and more unpleasant every evening. It became a group effort to avoid interactions with them as much as possible.

As the days passed, the Fairbank sisters appeared less and less shiny. Their hair lost its volume, and their outfits lost coordination. I could hardly blame them, given the unfortunate lack of changing space in the cabin. I couldn't tell if it was their diminished glamour or their enthusiasm for wedding planning, but I found myself liking the sisters more and more each day. Sissy, in particular, had an unjaded sweetness that I found refreshing.

The two of us sat on wooden crates, enjoying a bit of sun and fresh sea air on the main deck. Sissy busied her dainty hands stitching a sailor's torn jacket while I scribbled down a few recipes I'd been dreaming up in my restless nights.

I decided to indulge some of my curiosity. "Sissy, I have to ask… Why are you on the Rambler? You and your sisters seem fairly well-off. Why not take a nicer boat north?"

"We *are* well-off," Sissy said, pausing in her stitching. "Or, we were… I mean, we are, we will be, soon…" she stammered. "Daddy's a very successful man. He's just hit a rough spot. He decided it wasn't prudent for us girls to do the season this year, but Mother wouldn't hear of it. So they compromised. We get to do the season, but we do it… on a budget." The last word seemed like raw garlic in her mouth.

"Do the season?" I needed clarification. She couldn't possibly be referring to big game hunting.

"The season," Sissy said, emphasizing the word as if that were all the explanation needed. I stared at her blankly. "The social season? Galas, parties, lunches in the park?"

"And during the season you go to them?" I guessed.

"Yes, exactly."

"And there's a name for that?"

"There are several."

"Huh." I looked at her, processing this new information. "You and I lead very different lives."

"Oh, Helen," Sissy said as she rested a hand on my knee, "I'm sorry you don't get to go to parties."

"Thank you, Sissy," I said, deciding to take the pity as the kindness it was intended to be. We smiled at each other and returned to our work.

The following two days carried on at the same drudging pace. Each morning, I woke before the others and helped Mrs. Marin in the kitchen. Missy continuously offered to join me but could never seem to rouse herself before the wake-up bell. After cleaning the breakfast dishes with Copper, I would read a few chapters of the books I'd taken from Rainer and try not to think too hard about the caravan and what might have happened to them.

Lunch took little preparation, but I always helped to set it out. Then there was laundry to be done and sewing to help with. The Fairbanks worked day and night on altering their collection of dresses. I wasn't great with a needle and thread, but I helped pin them when needed. Dinner was usually a stew or casserole of some kind, which made for simple preparation and heavy cleanup. By the time the dishes were done, the crew would have drunk themselves to bed. Most nights, Daschel and Gary would join them, making it even trickier for the ladies to dodge unpleasant interactions in the bunk room.

"We should say something," Copper said in a sharp whisper, three of us gathered in the bunk room alone. Sissy had stayed in bed much later than usual, so Copper and I had gone to check on her. She was sitting on my bunk in between the two of us, looking distraught.

"I don't want to make a big fuss," she whispered, pulling her robe tightly over her chest.

"What did he say to you?" I asked, not in a whisper.

"I couldn't repeat it," she said, looking over to the men's two bunks and frowning as if she'd just tasted something disgusting. Sissy sat up straighter and said, "I don't use language like that."

"Did they threaten you?" I pressed.

"No," Sissy answered quickly. "Not really."

"What does that mean?" Copper prodded.

"They didn't say they would. They just said… they wanted to." Sissy looked down at her pink slippers, shame creeping across her lovely face.

"Wanted to do what?" I asked, my face growing hot with anger.

"I'd… just put on my nighttime rose water. Gary said it smelled good, so I thanked him, and then Daschel asked if I smelled that good everywhere. I didn't know what he meant, but then he asked about my—" Sissy's cheeks went bright scarlet as she clamped her mouth shut.

"I'll kill them." Copper moved to stand, but I stopped her.

"Lisel, don't," I warned. "If you kill him, then I don't get to."

"Would you two cut it out?" Sissy hissed. "I'm a big girl—I can take it. Don't go making a scene. It will only make things worse." Copper and I exchanged pained looks. "Please," Sissy pleaded. We both sat back down beside her, and she squeezed each of our hands before getting up. "I'm feeling much better now, thanks to you two. I'm going to get ready and come up on deck with everyone."

When Sissy stepped into the bathroom, Copper snapped, "I hate this." Her leg bounced up and down with pent up anger.

"Me too," I replied through gritted teeth. That night, I did not dream of storms or women with long black hair. I dreamt of disembodied hands pinching and grabbing at me from all sides and leering red eyes peering out from every bush and windowsill.

Mrs. Marin was quiet as she stirred the porridge, her broad arms straining against the thick oats. There wasn't much left for me to help with this morning, so I stood over the sausage patties and watched them brown on the hot plate.

"Mrs. Marin?" I asked over the low sizzle, breaking the silence.

"Yeah?" She did not look up from her work in the pot.

"On the Rambler, has there ever been an issue with…" I searched for the right wording. "Have you ever experienced…"

"The boys getting a little rough?" Mrs. Marin said, finishing my question for me. "It happens. Not so much to me, but we've dealt with it in the past."

"And how do you…" I started slowly.

"Deal with it?" She swept in once more, "If one of the boys puts his hands on you, you come to me, and Lou will set that little rat straight."

"No one has put their hands on me," I clarified. "It's just that sometimes Daschel and Gary make comments that are… inappropriate." I didn't understand why this was so hard to talk about.

"Helen," Mrs. Marin said, stopping her stirring to look at me. "If I had a penny for every lewd comment a sailor threw my way, I'd have the fortune to fund a fleet." She gazed at me with soft eyes, "They're just words. They're as heavy as we make them."

"But it seems like…" I stumbled to find the right phrase, "There should be consequences."

"There will be," Mrs. Marin assured me. "In one way or another, things come back around." I nodded half-heartedly and turned to search the spice drawer for cinnamon. My skin still crawled from the memory of the disturbing gazes and unwanted touching from my dream. One row down from the cinnamon, my gaze danced over a jar of dried uragoga. A smile formed on my lips. I was familiar with the root, or, as it was more commonly known: ipecac.

Daschel and Gary had been sequestered to a private cabin to keep their mysterious stomach bug from spreading to the other passengers. This left the main bunk room quieter and with a far more pleasant aroma for the remaining couple nights of travel. Mrs. Marin placed me in charge of delivering the ailing men their bowls of broth and toasted bread, all seasoned with my new secret ingredient. Because they always seemed to feel worse after eating, Mrs. Marin concluded their bodies simply were not ready to digest food. I told her that I could try to make a brew to ease their discomfort, but that I was somewhat unskilled with healing brews. Whether she could see through the lie, I never knew, but she decided to err on the side of caution and allow them time to overcome the illness naturally.

In the now warm and comfortable cabin, I took diligent notes as Kissy listed overdone floral arrangements and the most effective methods to utilize when planning seating charts.

"You want to structure the hall in a circular layout so that no one table appears to sit in a back corner," she instructed as she pinned in the last of her curlers. "And be sure to distribute relatives and close friends throughout the tables. The easiest way to avoid offending guests is to leave it entirely unclear who is at the 'important table,' excepting the wedding party, of course." I nodded along like a student in an exclusive tutoring session.

"But we'll know which table is the lamest," Copper chimed in from her top bunk where she was bouncing a pair of rolled-up socks against the ceiling, "It'll be wherever you stick Cormac." She angled her arm to chuck the socks down and back, hitting Arnie on the upper arm.

"Speak for yourself, Lisel," Arnie retorted, dropping the book he'd had his nose in all night to throw the socks back up, but he missed her.

"How could I be at the loser's table?" Copper questioned. "I'm going to be Helen's maid of honor." Her voice dripped with pride at the self-bestowed title.

"Cormac may end up being the best man," I thought out loud. "For all intents and purposes, he is Rae's best friend."

"That's rich," Arnie laughed, his tone sardonic. "We haven't been close in years. I'd rather be at the loser's table."

"Just you wait," I said, giving in to the urge to tease him. "He's going to be so thrilled to see you when we get to Camp Valiant." My stomach dropped as it always did at the thought of seeing Raemond again. "It'll be like nothing ever

changed," I assured, half for his sake and half
for my own.

Sissy's yellow rain cloak billowed in the
wind, its vibrancy a stark contrast to the gray
skies that loomed around her. Throughout the
voyage, I'd noticed a pattern—whenever her
sisters made a game of pecking at her and all her
perceived faults, she'd end up out on the fore of
the ship, staring at the constant horizon.

"Cup of tea for your thoughts?" I said, sliding up beside her with a sturdy ceramic mug in
hand. Sissy took it gratefully, her fingers blue
and quivering. "Perfect weather for mermaid
watching, isn't it?" I said with a grin.

"Don't be silly, Helen," Sissy giggled, "Mermaids are just in storybooks."

"Right," I conceded, uninterested in explaining sarcasm in the moment. "I always thought
the whole idea was quite scary, don't you think?
Beautiful women lurking in the waters waiting
to drag you down into the depths."

"You've clearly never been to a cotillion before," Sissy said, her eyes full of bitterness as the
steam from the mug wafted up around her. It
was a sharp contrast to her usually sweet, lovely
face.

"Hey," I said, leaning my weight against the
rail, "I thought you were excited about the season."

"Leviathans," Sissy said, ignoring my comment. "I've always been terrified of those."

"Just another story," I said, pressing my shoulder to hers as we looked out past the prow to the choppy waves beyond.

"We hope," Sissy mumbled as she took a long sip of her tea.

On the eighth and final day of travel, the shores of the north country finally came into view. Though just a green line resting on the horizon, we passengers had all come up on deck to watch it grow.

"It's unseasonably warm," Kissy said as she shed her peacoat with a grimace.

"It's always warmer in the north," Sissy corrected, her face tilted up to enjoy the sun on her cheeks.

"I know that it's *warmer*," Kissy hissed defensively, "But it feels more so than usual." With that, she folded her gloved hands over her knee and sat unnaturally upright on her stool.

"It's the weather evokers," Arnie explained from his perch on one of the steps to the upper deck. "They always keep it comfortable near the Citadel."

"But we have weather evokers in the south," Missy said with a pinched brow, tilting her head at him.

"Less skilled and less of them," he said, "but you're not wrong."

"Not that I'm complaining," Copper started from her spot beside her brother, "but it doesn't really get you in the Yuletime spirit."

"I'm sure they'll roll out one night of powdery snow for the Yuletime festival and keep it just cold enough to prevent the snow from melting. Then it will be right back to mild and sunny," Arnie said with certainty.

"He just has an answer for everything," Missy remarked with a hand over her heart. He tried to stifle a smile as his cheeks lit up.

"You talk enough, you're bound to get some of it right," Copper interjected, followed by a snort of amusement from Sissy. The hue of Arnie's cheeks deepened. We settled back into our contented silence as the ship tossed itself along the blue waves below. Daschel and Gary had even regained a bit of color in the midday sun from where they had been propped up against the cabin wall. A day without my food deliveries had settled their stomachs tremendously, and they had almost returned to complete health; though, we were all thankful they were still lacking their usual exuberance and conversational proclivities.

The stretch of green earth grew before us throughout the afternoon, now displaying subtle hills and patches of trees. The crew called out commands while running in and out of doors, scaling the masts, and hauling cargo up from below. With the chaos building on deck, I wandered up to where Captain Bobby sat casually behind the wheel, holding steady course with one hand and a newspaper in the other. I had yet to speak with Captain Bobby and saw no reason to change that now, especially since he appeared so engrossed in his reading. I shuffled quietly past him to the railing and looked down, watching the hull slice through the water. Only then did I register the great speed at which we had been traveling all along. I took a daring step up to the first rung, balanced my weight against my thighs on the top rail, and grabbed hold of one of the taut wires that stretched from the hull to the mast. I must have looked like a triumphant voyager, with the wind at my back and adventure before me, but I did not feel triumphant. With every moment, my dread grew like the land on the horizon, my heart flooding with something colder and heavier than the Rambler itself: uncertainty.

CHAPTER SIXTEEN: THE WITCH'S RELIEF

"I will miss you every day," Sissy declared as she held me tight in her thin arms and laid a loud kiss on my cheek. "Promise me you'll write," she said, releasing me just enough to lock eyes.

"I promise," I answered. I was sorry to lie to my new friend, but I couldn't go on being Helen Purslane forever. Behind us, the cargo was being unloaded haphazardly onto the dock as a few members of the crew shook hands with Arnie and Copper. Kissy and Missy were already seated in the shiny automobile sent by their godfather.

"I wish we could take you on to the Citadel, but we really can't delay. If you have any spare time before your voyage home, you must come to call," Sissy insisted with an earnest smile.

"It will be a quick trip," I said, honestly this time. "I doubt there will be any spare time." She nodded in acceptance before taking me back into her embrace.

"You have been the most wonderful companion, Helen," she cooed in my ear.

"So have you," I declared before returning Sissy's kiss on the cheek. "Go on now." I shooed her off. "You have some very important parties to attend."

"Best of luck," Sissy cried, aiming an enthusiastic wave to Copper and Arnie as she scuttered off toward her ride. A driver clicked the door shut behind her as the engine rumbled to life. Sissy leaned out the window as the automobile began to pull away and cried, "Kiss your soldier for me!"

I smiled as I watched my friend fade away in the clouds of dust that trailed the glamorous car.

"No chance of us getting a ride to the Citadel in one of those?" Arnie asked, now at my side.

"I doubt it," Copper said as she emerged, completing our trio. "But we are leaving with a bit of money. Mrs. Marin gave our industrious Helen twenty silver for all the kitchen work." She presented the pile of well-worn coins to me with both hands. "Oh, and she wanted you to have this too…" Arnie took the coins so she could fish something small from her pocket and hand it to me. I held the small glass jar up to read its faint label, and a shameless smile rose on my lips.

"What is it?" Arnie asked, squinting in the sun.

"Consequences," I answered before tucking the uragoga root safely into my brew box.

✢ ✢ ✢ ✢ ✢ ✢

The Rambler had docked at the road furthest from Camp Valiant, but it was only a short walk before the clashing metal and calling of drills filled the air. The smattering of trees cleared to reveal a seemingly endless expanse of perfectly aligned canvas tents. Between these tents shuffled scruffy boys dressed in matching green uniforms, faces painted with dirt and glowing with adrenaline. In each of their eyes, I caught a glance of the adventurous twinkle Raemond had always possessed.

After being waved into the camp by a clearly overwhelmed recruit who never even took our names, let alone raised an eyebrow at two girls entering, we made our way through the narrow passages between the tents. We repeatedly bumped into the parade of boys, all eager to offer up an "apologies, ma'am" before bustling off to wherever they were going. With each encounter, my heart leaped, half expecting Raemond to be the next to offer an apology.

"Do we know where we're going?" Copper said, trotting to catch up to me as I plowed forward. "Is there a reference desk or something?"

"I don't really know," I admitted. "I guess I didn't expect the camp to be this big."

Further in, I spotted a larger, possibly official-looking tent, and we tentatively walked up. Just inside was a well-polished young man carving runes into an arrow. He looked up in surprise. "Ah, excuse me. Can I help you find something?" He stood, setting his task aside.

"We're fine—" I began.

"We're looking for Raemond Wimple," Copper interjected.

"Wimple…" the young man muttered, appearing to search through a mental catalog.

"Not too tall," Arnie clarified, "black hair, full of it." I shot him a withering look.

"Doesn't narrow it down much," the man said with a chuckle. "I'd check up at Information. They'll have a registry. Of course, you'll need to be family to visit."

"She is," Copper said, motioning to me. "As long as fiancées count."

"That should be fine," he assured. "The information tent is right at the center of camp. Just keep down the path you were on and you'll bump right into it. And if you do happen to lose your way, ask any of the boys for help. They'll set you on the right path."

"Thank you," I said in relief, and we started back on our way. Nearing the center of camp only further illuminated a fact that Copper had denied so passionately over Harvest dinner—there was not a witch in sight. I was hardly surprised, though.

Raemond had received an early acceptance due to his superior application, which was quite special. Boys who wished to join the military could always apply, but they weren't actually accepted until they started training—if they were not fit for the profession, it would become clear pretty quickly. But there were rumors that this was not the case for the witches who applied. People said that not a single witch from the Orchard who had sent applications to Camp Valiant had received any form of a response—not even a rejection letter. The rule was unspoken, but it demonstrated plainly that witches need not apply.

The center of the camp offered a reprieve from the perfectly aligned tents and instead boasted an array of open canopies offering various services. One desk read "Leaderboard and Rankings," another displayed bowls full of fruits, vegetables, and hunks of bread for the trainees to grab as they ran to what was likely class or training. My eyes landed on a large "I" painted on the canvas of one of the stations, and I started toward it.

A boy in a wrinkled uniform sat at the desk, hunched over a textbook of some kind.

"Excuse me," I said, hesitant to interrupt his focus.

"Oh! Can I help you?" He looked up from his book to reveal a pair of bloodshot eyes paired with dark circles underneath.

"We're looking for Raemond Wimple," Arnie informed the exhausted trainee, cutting to the chase.

"Relation?" he asked automatically.

"I'm his fiancée," I declared, ignoring my building sense of imposter syndrome.

"I can't give out a bunk number to anyone but family," he explained with a total lack of empathy, "but I can ring his tent, and we'll see what we get." Without another word, the boy spun around on his stool to a wall of tiny bells behind him and started to search the rows, his pointer finger floating along them. Once he found what he was looking for, he flicked a tiny brass bell. There was a little twinkle of sound, and then he spun back around. We looked at him expectantly, and he stared back at us.

Realizing we didn't understand what was going on, he stated, "And now we wait." His gaze returned to the textbook on the table. We stood uncomfortably in the shade of the canopy, not entirely sure what we were meant to be doing. Arnie tried to surreptitiously step closer to make out what the boy's textbook was about. Copper fiddled with a bracelet around her wrist and hummed quietly to herself. I tried to slow the relentless pounding of my heart. I could not imagine a more nerve-wracking way for this reunion to have unfolded. At any moment, Raemond could walk right up to me, and I had no way of knowing what direction he would approach from. I was left feeling dreadfully exposed.

The thought of seeing his gentle eyes again, being held in his arms, and unburdening myself to the person who knew me best in this world filled me with a warm joy. But the very same sentiment sent a chill down my spine. Did Raemond really know me now? Was I the same witch he had left on that train platform? Images of Rainer holding a spell book, Beauregarde's cold eyes, Arnie's blood, and men poisoned by my own hand flashed through my mind. But nothing weighed as heavily as the concealed book that hung across my shoulder.

"Hello!" a voice called from behind us, and for a moment, I forgot how to breathe. "Did y'all page my tent?" The voice continued, and I gave a deep exhale. It wasn't Raemond. Not unless he had developed a mountain accent in a single month. I turned to face the stranger.

He was tall and lean—too lean to be an effective soldier. His uniform shirt was unbuttoned and untucked, giving him an air of casual disregard.

"They're looking for Wimple," the unenthused information desk attendant informed him. The boy tousled his sandy blond hair and looked down at me.

"Oh, shoot," he said with a sympathetic smile. "Y'all just missed him. He left for the Citadel this morning." He studied me for a moment, then his face suddenly lit up. "You're Hildegarde!" Before I could react, he pulled me into a tight embrace, his enthusiasm overwhelming.

"Oh, right, sorry," he said as he released me just as quickly, stepping back. "Gotta do introductions. I'm Tucker Kindly, Rae's bunkmate." He extended a hand to me and continued, "But you can just call me Tuck."

"Well, you can just call me Hildy," I replied, shaking his hand as an unexpected sense of relief settled over me.

"I've heard so much about you," he said earnestly, laying a second hand over mine. After a lingering moment of heartwarming eye contact, he finally released me and turned to the others. "Pleased to make your acquaintance," he said, extending his hand to Copper.

"Copper," she replied, shaking his hand firmly. She had followed my lead in abandoning our false names.

"And Rae's told me about you too," Tuck said as he turned to Arnie, his face a study in concentration. "Don't tell me—Allen?"

"Close," Arnie said, looking slightly taken aback. "Arnold."

"I knew that," Tuck said with a tsk, scolding himself. "There is the funniest picture of you two and Rae in our tent," he added, looking at me. "Y'all wanna come see it? I don't have my earth manipulation training for another hour." His excitement was palpable.

"That'd be great, actually," I admitted. I wanted to see how Rae had been living these past few weeks.

"Well then, follow me," he said with a grand sweeping motion. "Thanks, Pete," he called back to the desk attendant, who didn't bother responding. Tucker led us south, back into the sea of tents.

"You said Rae was headed to the Citadel?" Arnie asked quickly. "What's he doing there?"

"He didn't tell ya?" Tuck turned to face us but kept walking backward. "I was sure he would've mentioned it in his last letter." Guilt twisted my stomach as I imagined the stack of unanswered letters piled up on my kitchen counter. Surely, Irenee would have sent him some word unless she felt it wasn't safe.

"He's getting a commendation from the General Major!" he proclaimed when we all shook our heads. "Only five recruits receive it each year. He's really something—not only is he good, but he's also a great teacher. He's the only reason I didn't wash out of the program in the first week. You must be mighty proud of him," he beamed, directing the last sentence to me.

I smiled at the thought of Rae tutoring the slower boys after a long day of his own studies. I could only imagine how thrilled he must have been to receive that commendation. It would only make his dream of becoming a King's Man more attainable. His life was going just as he'd planned. If only he knew how far mine had veered off course.

"Here it is," Tucker announced as he held open the front flap to a tent that looked identical to all the others, allowing us inside. It was small, with bunk beds on the right, a desk and chair on the left, a trunk, and a small stack of pillows on the floor.

"That was Rae's idea," he said as he pointed to the pillows. "We like to do our coursework together, but there's only one desk, so that's what I use. He uses the trunk as a table and sits on the pillows. Convinced a lady in housekeeping he needed them to elevate his leg after twisting an ankle in training." Tuck leaned in and whispered, "Only he never even twisted his ankle." He grinned mischievously.

"That sounds just like Rae," Arnie muttered, flipping through a book on the desk. "Getting what he wants no matter who he has to inconvenience."

"He said you were a prickly one," Tucker said with a nod. "Here's that picture I was talking about." He pointed to the right wall where a few photos were tacked to the canvas. The first one that caught my eye was from my front yard, taken before the academy's Beltane dance. I wore a pink dress and a chain of daisies in my hair. Rae, in his usual fashion, had refused a necktie but compromised by wearing a polka-dot shirt that matched my dress and tucking a daisy behind his ear. The most cherished photo from that day was the one where Rae had suddenly lifted me from behind, causing my legs to shoot straight out in front of me. My face was one of utter shock while Rae's was full of laughter. Of course, that was the one he had saved.

Below it was the picture Tuck had mentioned. Both Arnie and I smiled instantly.

"I took that!" Copper exclaimed, shoving in to get a better look. The memory of that day at the dock flooded back. Arnie had fallen asleep in the sun, forgetting to apply ointment, and we had taken the opportunity to write *I am an idiot* on his back with sunscreen. The resulting sunburn had been spectacular.

"Rae's got all kinds of photos up there," Tucker mused. "He was thinking ahead. I just brought the one of my girl back home."

I scanned the photos but found only ones of myself and the Wimples. "I don't see it up here," I said, turning to him.

Blushing, he reached into his pocket and pulled out a small snapshot. "Joy stays right next to my heart."

I gazed at the girl in the photo, her infectious smile and rosy cheeks radiant. "She's beautiful," I said.

"Where's home?" Arnie asked, uninterested in looking at the photo.

"Searchville," Tuck answered, briefly gazing at the photo before returning it to his breast pocket. "It's about fifteen miles west of the Mount Tempus city center. We're a small community of friends."

"You're from a Boon collective?" Copper asked in surprise, her eyes lighting up with curiosity. "I've always wanted to visit one. They sound like heaven."

"Maybe," Tuck said with a laugh as he tousled his hair again. "To me, it's just home." My curiosity was likewise piqued. The Boon religious group was often the subject of speculation and ridicule, as any fringe group is likely to be. The members lived in empath communes throughout the nation, practicing radical pacifism. The Boons believed the power of the living soul was the holiest thing on earth, and so they refused to eat meat, participate in any form of violence—avoiding harming even insects—and went to extremes by most social standards in order to uphold their beliefs.

"So why join the military?" Arnie asked bluntly, his eyebrows scrunched in confusion. Copper gave him a harsh scolding sound, but I was also interested in hearing his answer.

"Weeeell," he drawled, rocking back and forth on his heels, "The communities as of now are unprotected. Since we live outside of the main city centers, the response from law enforcement is notoriously slow, and all the while we're sitting there with our crops and crafts just waiting to be robbed. It's unsustainable. So I had this idea one day while watching a mama jay chase a crow away from her nest that maybe we could have our own kinda law in the communes. One that protects the people and their belongings without the use of lethal force. So I prayed on it for a good long while and talked to the elders. They told me to go get my license to serve, and we'd figure it out from there." He looked up from his feet with a bashful grin. "I don't wanna hurt nobody, but someone's gotta keep my family safe."

"Tucker Kindly," Copper said, her eyes wide, "I have always wanted to meet a Boon, and you did not disappoint. Joy is a lucky girl." His cheeks pinked up as his smile further animated his deep dimples.

"I'm the lucky one," he exclaimed. "Rae has been the best friend I've ever had, and now I get to meet all of his favorite people. Y'all most certainly did not disappoint either. It's just a shame you had to miss him. He'll kick himself when I tell him."

"Maybe we'll bump into him around the Citadel," Copper offered with her unending optimism. "We're heading that way, too."

"No kidding!" Tucker cried, looking delighted at the coincidence. "How are y'all getting there? I could see you to the train." Arnie glanced at me, a subtle reminder that documented travel was not an option. It was a necessity that had become more pressing after being forced to identify ourselves with our proper names.

Thinking fast, I managed to spit out, "We were thinking we'd hitch a ride where we could and just walk the rest of the way." I shrugged. "We're traveling on a tight budget."

"Well I can't let you do that!" Tucker proclaimed with wide eyes. "The road to the Citadel is crawling with highwaymen and nasty characters. I'd be a pretty lousy soldier to let two young ladies travel that way unprotected." He paused and looked at Arnie. "Er, no offense." Copper let out a soft giggle, but Arnie seemed uncharacteristically unfazed by the slight. "Allow me to act as your escort for the journey," he said to me, bowing unnecessarily. For a moment, his eyes sparkled with the protective kindness I saw so often in Rae.

"That's… really not necessary," I stuttered, worried that Tuck getting involved might be more of a hindrance than a help. "It would take you away from your studies for too many days."

"Not at all," he said, his excitement growing. "I could borrow a jalopy from Equipments. Not as fast as the newer models and a tad bumpy, but if we leave now, I could get you to the Citadel by tomorrow afternoon." Arnie, Copper, and I exchanged loaded glances as we considered his offer.

"And you'd be allowed to do that?" Copper clarified. "It wouldn't get you into trouble?"

"Not one ounce," Tuck assured. "The camp's rules of chivalry demand that we perform acts of public service when required. In fact, I could get into trouble for *failing* to offer myself."

"Fine by me," Arnie piped up. "I've still got sea-legs and wasn't too keen on a week-long hike." He clapped Tucker on the back, who beamed at him in response.

"I'll go check out the keys." He pulled a pre-packed rucksack off a hook and slung it over his shoulder.

"Tuck!" I called after him as he bounded out of the tent's flap, "Thank you. You're very kind."

"It's all in the name," he said with a wink, then disappeared. Copper guffawed.

"Well, that worked out nicely, didn't it?" she said, sitting down on the bottom bunk and letting herself relax. Arnie crossed slowly to my side, where I continued to look over Rae's photographs.

"Do you think that old dock's still there?" he asked behind my shoulder. "It was barely standing three years ago, and it's been ages since I've been back." I stared back at the familiar young folks in the photograph with the creeping feeling of tremendous loss. I didn't answer for a long moment.

"It's still there," I promised, more to myself than him. "Things don't just go away. Not when they've lasted so long." I continued to look over the images until the subtle warmth of Arnie's body heat disappeared from my shoulder. Lower in the array was an aged photograph, older than the others by at least a decade. It was faded a bit, but the figures were still recognizable under close inspection. The photo was posed and contained a great many smiling people.

"Hildegarde! Arnold! Raemond!" The sound of Mrs. Penning's voice echoed in my mind. She was calling out for us missing children while scanning the Wimple's front yard. She held a red-headed girl in her arms who was whimpering into her shoulder. Arnie had not allowed Copper to climb the tree with us. He'd said she was too small and would only hurt herself, and then the three of us would get in trouble.

Above Mrs. Penning, Arnie, Rae, and I giggled in the branches of the great oak, all dressed in once crisp, white garments that had become stained with grass and dirt throughout the day.

We covered our mouths to mask our hiding spot and shot each other grins of chaos.

"All right, boys and little lady," Mrs. Penning called, *"Mr. Wimple would like to take a photo on the front steps."* We did not respond, but we descended further into giggles, unable to contain ourselves. I remembered hearing Mrs. Penning speak softly to someone before a sudden gust of wind blew the oak leaves, revealing our hiding spot in the tree. At the base, Mrs. Penning was now looking up at us with Copper in her arms, Maude Birch at her side.

Maude stood with crossed arms and pursed lips. I thought she was glaring up at me, taking in the utter mess of the May Day dress she had sewn from scratch, but when I met her gaze, her eyes did not burn with fury but rather gleamed with pride. Her face kept that proud glow as the group photo was taken on the Wimple's front steps only moments later. She had wrapped her long, beautiful arms around my waist to mask the large smudge of dirt that stained the front of my dress.

"You all right, Hildy?" Copper's voice snapped me back to the present moment.

"Fine," I replied as a single, hot tear traveled down my cheek. I thought about taking one of the photos, tucking it into my pocket and carrying it with me, but I did not. I left the memories tacked to the side of the tent and turned away, pockets empty.

CHAPTER SEVENTEEN: THE WITCH'S ROAD

Drip, drip, drip. The drops came in a slow rhythm, echoing across the hollow walls. The cramped space was enveloped in near-total darkness save for the light from a single flame tucked into the corner of the cave. A haunting melody bounced all around the stones.

"Whistle, whistle..." The source sat hunched in limited light, their pale skin bare against the cold stones.

"Whistle you gales. Whistle from south to north." Matted black hair hung about their face and most of their body, shielding it from view.

"Blow strong, blow fast, and blow true." The figure shuddered after their last lyric and released a small yelp of pain. The hair moved slightly then, revealing a glimpse of a bare woman's breast.

"Set the child's course." Her song was finished, but it echoed off the stones for many moments after.

A small glimmer of light reflected off some sort of scaly creature resting in her lap as it shifted in the shadows. It had been coiled against the thighs of the songstress, but now it was unraveling itself to reposition within her lap, and more light danced off the creature's back as it shifted. The woman answered in kind, resting a hand on the serpent-like creature and lovingly stroking its black scales. Another small yelp, and the woman began her song once more.

"Whistle, whistle..." The dripping of the cave beat on.

"Whistle, you gales. Whistle from south to north." The creature's scales slipped across her legs as it continued to move about.

"Blow strong, blow fast, and blow true." Her breathing grew labored, perhaps even painful.

"Set the child's course," she cried, arching her back to cradle the creature as she held it to her breast. Its reptilian face glinted in the light as it suckled.

I woke to Tuck's singing. "I'll marry you at harvest, and stay warm all winter long." The song crackled over the old radio as we bobbed along down the dusty road, the twang of the vocals buzzing in the fragile speakers.

As I shifted and sat up in the front passenger seat, Tucker gave me a small salute without taking his eyes off the road. "Afternoon, Hildegarde." His rosy cheeks warmed in the soft light of the setting sun, and the whole automobile cabin seemed coated in gold. "You've got a powerful snore on you," he added, sounding impressed.

"Sorry about that," I grunted as I stretched my back from the twisted contortion I had fallen asleep in. In the flashing reflection of the window, I saw the imprint of the seam of the leather seat stamped perfectly across my face.

"No bother," Tuck assured. "Rae's the same way. You're going to make a noisy pair. Wouldn't want to share a wall with you folks when you hitch up."

His grip on the wheel was light, his fingers resting calmly at the bottom of the circle. He lounged in his driver's seat with complete confidence in his control of the vehicle. I had never driven a motorcar; they weren't too common in the Orchard. The expense was too lofty for a territory where most everything was within walking distance.

Once, however, my father had borrowed one for a business trip from a wealthy colleague. I could still envision the way it had sparkled in the midday sun when he drove it up to our front gate, red and opulent. The roof had been stowed away, and Dad had looked as giddy as his dignified face would allow as he stopped the car before the front garden. I, no older than six, had screamed and bounced in excitement at the surprise, unable to properly express my elation, but Maude had hardly looked up from her iced tea. She'd stayed hidden away under her wide-brimmed sun hat. She was in a state he often described as "one of her moods," and he called for me to join him in the shining motor-marvel. I had climbed into the passenger seat, hot from the glaring sunshine, and we took off to race and scatter dust across the Orchard roads. Maude had called out just before the engine's roar covered all sounds, *"You bring my baby back in one piece."* I didn't remember her ever looking out from under the comfort of her great hat.

Tucker went back to his crooning as I rested my cheek against the cool window, watching my breath fog the glass, then disappear. Rolling along beyond the glass was a repetitive stream of trees, still boasting a few green leaves despite the season at hand. By now, the Orchard would be blanketed with fresh snow, the sun bouncing off every inch of it, blinding folks out on midday walks. Irenee would be shut up in our little cottage, draped in a well-tailored house cloak, likely hunched over some technical journal. Maegon would be left without her sledding chaperones this year while Raemond and I languished in the perpetually mild north.

"So Tuck," Copper began, popping her head through the gap between the front seats, startling the two of us. We both had thought the other two passengers were sleeping. "What's training been like? Is it as regimented and grueling as they say?" Her hair was matted up on the right side of her head from her own odd snoozing position.

"I don't know if I'd call it grueling," Tuck began, adjusting his sitting position slightly. "Otherwise, I probably wouldn't have made it this long." He chortled at his own self-deprecation, then continued, "But it is plenty rigid. Lots of rules and regulations. They're always getting on my case for looking sloppy. But you learn a lot in a real short time. You have to, I guess. They're working you from dawn till dusk." I could see how Raemond could succeed in a structure like that. He liked to be kept busy. I could never get him to sit still and enjoy the quiet. A temperament like that was wasted in the peace of the Orchard.

"What have you been studying?" I followed, wanting to get a better picture of Rae's day-to-day lifestyle.

"Well, they split the elemental studies up into different subjects. Stone work is pretty simple since you can picture the intention real clear in your head, like 'move that rock,' but wind work is tricky 'cause you can't really picture it. You've gotta, well, just sorta *feel* it. Not everyone can do that. That's why you see most evokers slinging around rocks on the moonbroch courts. Not much to it. Water work ain't as hard as air, but it's still tricky. They won't let me touch weather work until I shape up with air, which I get."

"Is Rae working with weather yet?" Copper asked, knowing I'd want to know.

"You betcha," Tuck replied without a beat. "They let Rae work with everything."

We pulled into a small clearing to make camp for the night. With no one else on the trip knowing how to drive, Tucker had come prepared for the detour. He set up a small canvas tent for the three of us, planning to sleep in the backseat himself. He had the structure secured in record time, and then he even began laying out three sleeping mats, pillows, and quilts for us. Watching Tuck labor away at our accommodations, I decided to set about starting up a campfire since he had proclaimed himself to be "dangerously inept at fire working." Copper perched against the vehicle's bumper and started telling the preoccupied Tucker a story that made him laugh every few seconds from inside the tent. I struck a match and held the flame to the small pile of kindling I'd collected.

"Need any help?" Arnie asked, standing on the other side of the woodpile. I could only see his shoes in the small patch of light, but once the flame took, I could meet his eyes in the dim evening glow. I didn't need help, but it was clear he was restless and needed to feel useful.

"Yeah," I nodded. "Get down here and help me stoke the flames. Blow on it, but not too hard." Arnie followed his instructions, and we spent a few silent moments building the small tendrils into a respectable blaze. I settled into a seated position by the fire with my legs crossed, and he laid out his jacket before sitting beside me. One of Tuck's laughs echoed from the tent as Copper launched into another tale. "You doing all right?" I asked, looking over at him from the corner of my eye.

"I'm fine," he said too quickly. He nodded to himself and repeated, "I'm fine."

"You don't have to be fine," I prompted. "I'm not fine. Everything that's happened… The watchmen and the caravan, Lacey… we have no idea what horrible things might have happened to them all." I twisted to look him straight in the eye. "Arnie, you almost died."

"I know that," he said, continuing his nodding as he looked deep into the flames. "That's the point—I'm fine." He spoke in an even tone, never breaking his focus on the growing fire. "I should have died. I'm not a high sorcerer, Hildegarde. All these years of study and rejection letters. I was so sure they were wrong. That they just couldn't see my potential. But they were right. I'm not extraordinary—I'm fine." He took a moment to take a shaky breath before continuing, "That spell tore through me like a pair of scissors. I never had a chance. If it wasn't for you," he finally turned his neck to meet my gaze, "it would have killed me."

"You can't fail once and give up on your dream," I said after a long pause, scrambling for the right thing to say to Arnie's sudden sincerity. "That spell was advanced. It would have been a struggle for anyone."

He shook his head. "That spell… I stole it. Every day we traveled with the caravan, I'd find a quiet moment to pilfer through it. It wasn't easy, you know. You didn't sleep much. But even just reading it felt unnatural. I could feel the power, but it was like it was squirming, trying to get away from me. Those magics aren't mine to attempt—they're yours."

"No," I said slowly, my brow furrowed in confusion and discomfort. "It's a bargaining tool, proof of her story, maybe even currency. She didn't mean for me to use it. I'm not a powerful witch. If anyone knew that, it was my mother." It was easy to recall the cold stares and effortless dismissals my mother had given so freely.

"Can I show you something?" Arnie asked, nodding toward my shoulder bag. I instinctively clutched the strap and looked about. Both Copper and Tuck had disappeared into the tent now, their enthusiastic storytelling continuing. I brought my lips to the clasp. It popped open in an instant, and I pulled the book from its concealment. As always, it buzzed in my hands. "How much have you looked through this?" he said, reaching for it.

"Not much," I answered honestly. "There's nothing in there that I want to know." I handed the book off to Arnie's waiting grasp, and he began to flip through its pages.

"Maude disagreed." He stopped on a page, having found what he was looking for. "See this?" He scooted his body up close to mine to show me his findings. I had to bring my face close to make out the small text he was pointing to. In the flickering firelight, the only thing I knew for sure was that it was Maude's graceful penmanship. "They're notes," Arnie explained as I continued to squint. "She wrote little notes in the margins in red ink—

instructions and warnings for *you*. She even addresses some of them to you specifically." He went back to flipping through. "Here, like this one: *Hildy, confidence is as important as strength. Be sure of your convictions.* She wanted to teach you."

I began to scan the pages, my mouth agape, looking for red ink. Each scribble was a note of encouragement or concern from another time. It was a time when Maude was making plans for the worst and writing letters of desperation to her confidants. How had she hidden all of this from her family? How had she put on her lipstick and baked pies knowing that disaster stood at arm's length? Had she really believed *I* could cast her spells? The thought chaffed my mind like coarse wool.

"All right!" Tucker announced as he began to emerge through the tent flap. I snapped the book shut and jammed it back into its confinement. The duo entered the glow of the now roaring fire; Tucker carried a brown paper parcel perched on a cast iron pan in one hand and a set of metal skewers in the other. "Who wants some weenies?"

Tuck had led an interesting life, to say the least. Around the fire, he caught us up on his whole story. We were cautious not to share too much of our own travels, so we instead encouraged him to dive deep into his unique upbringing. He was the oldest of nine siblings, had raised sheep and chickens on the community farm, participated in weekly barn dances, and had promised to marry his neighbor, Joy, at the age of ten—and he had so far remained true to that vow.

"Does she mind much?" I inquired. "You being here?" I could hardly imagine that his pacifist fiancée would be excited about him being in rigorous military training.

"She worries," Tuck conceded, "and complains. But she knows I wouldn't betray my faith or do anything too stupid. At least, I hope she does." He took an impressive bite of his sausage.

"I know how she feels," I admitted, sipping on a mug of warm ale.

"You shouldn't worry," Tuck insisted, mouth full. "Rae's aces. Ask anyone."

"I'm sure he is," Arnie grumbled to himself. We sat in silence for a moment, with only the crackle of flames for entertainment. I saw Copper begin to open her mouth, likely about to cut the tension with a joke, when the sudden sound of tires rolling slowly over gravel crawled through the campsite. Arnie was the first on his feet, and he was instantly lit by the glow of headlights only a short distance away. The rest of us stood to watch the truck veer into the pull-off, parking behind Tucker's vehicle. Three silhouettes emerged as the engine sputtered off.

"Evening," Tucker called, stepping in front of our group. "How can we help you, folks?" The three figures stepped forward into the light. They were all men, none looking much older than thirty, dressed somewhat shabbily.

"Don't need much help," the man on the left answered, chuckling as if Tucker had just made a joke. "Unless you want to help us aim." The others laughed.

"We just stopped to take a leak," another clarified. Their faces were lit ominously from below, casting shadows over their eyes and obscuring their facial features. He went on, "But it smells like you're cooking up something good over that fire." The other two mumbled in agreement.

"We'd be happy to give you a few sausages for the road," Tuck replied coolly. "We're just about to turn in for the night." I could see the military training apparent in all Tucker's actions, each of them calm and deliberate.

"We'll take you up on that," the man in the center said. He gave a slight smile that failed to put me at any ease. I noticed Arnie take the slightest step forward to put himself between the strange men and me. Indignation prickled me for a small moment, but gratitude quickly took its place.

"If y'all don't mind," Tuck said, turning to look at all of us behind him, "Could you roast a few up for these folks?" Copper nodded with a false smile and distributed the skewers. The men disappeared behind the tree line to attend to their business while we got to silently roasting the sausages, exchanging anxious glances. Tucker remained standing, holding his focus on the tree line. After a few moments, he turned to us, smiled reassuringly, and mouthed, "It's fine."

Cool metal kissed the soft of my neck. Before I had time to react, a hand grabbed hold of my hair and pulled me to a standing position without dropping the blade from its place at my throat. My body went stiff with white shock as I took a shaky breath in through my open mouth. Copper spun around, dropping her skewer into the fire as she stood. Arnie sprang to his feet, his face turning a sickly pale. Tucker stepped toward me and my assailant, his hands raised in surrender. His mouth moved like he was speaking, but I could not hear the words. The only sounds I could register were the ragged breath against my ear and the hollow thud of my heartbeat. In the shadows of my peripheral vision, I could tell the other two men stood on either side of me and my sudden captor.

"We ain't here to hurt nobody." The wet voice was hot against my ear as the man spoke. "Just trying to make us a living." Bounty hunters. The thought sped through my mind. Men hired by the watchmen to track us down.

"There's something in this camp worth a whole lot more than that old jalopy over there," the man to my right growled. "Hand it on over, and we'll be on our way." Not bounty hunters, then. My brain sluggishly caught up to Copper and Arnie's realizations as their eyes flitted over the shoulder bag now wedged between me and the thigh of the man pressed against me.

"We don't want any trouble, boys," Tucker spoke in a calm tenor with both hands still raised.

"You're welcome to whatever you like, but I doubt any of our supplies will fetch you too large a sum." His assurances carried full confidence, entirely unaware of the precious cargo we carried.

"Now I don't think that's truthful," the same man said. "See, we picked up a reading of some very potent magic coming from these coordinates just about an hour ago, and from the looks of your setup, you've been here for at least that long. So, you'll give us whatever it was that made our signal spike like Mt. Tempus if you want the little lady here to keep this pretty head."

They were relic hunters. I had heard of these gangs from Raemond. Mainly low-level enchanters and empaths, these men made their living stealing and trading highly regulated magical artifacts. They must have tracked the book to our campsite. But how could it now hang mere inches from them without their detection?

I tried to look out of the corners of my eyes to get a better picture of the two men off to the sides, but the man had a painfully tight grip on my hair. All I could see were Copper and Arnie, who were clearly panicking based on the sizable circumferences of their eyes.

"I don't know nothing about what you mean," Tucker said, though more hesitantly now as he noted that the three of us looked much more afraid than confused. "But feel free to look through our belongings for the item. We won't try to stop you." He took a step back and held his hands wide to reinforce his openness.

My heart quickened as the two lumbering men began to root through the campsite. One went to search the jalopy, throwing Arnie's suitcase to the ground, which opened and scattered its contents across the gravel. The other disappeared into the tent. In that same instant, the man with his blade to my throat took notice of the shoulder bag, and Copper sprang into action.

"*Rubair iann,*" she cried, her hand outstretched to point at the knife. Though I couldn't see the blade below my chin, I could feel the metal soften unnaturally, turning to what felt like limp rubber against my skin. Before he could call out a counter-spell, I seized the chance at freeing myself from his grasp. In an unusual burst of courage, I snapped my head forward before slamming it back with great force against the man's nose. The crunch of the brittle bone crackled at the back of my skull, followed by bellowing cries of pain. The rough hands released me, and I scrambled away to Copper's waiting arms, my head pounding in agony. Hearing the chaos around the fire, the other two men came running from their search posts, weapons drawn. Tucker was quick to intercept the larger of the two, who was made all the more menacing by the hatchet he wielded above his head.

"*Terra voler,*" Tuck shouted, sending a well-aimed stone from the firepit at the hatchet, knocking it out of the man's hands with impressive force. The crack of a whip rang through the night air as the man who had come from searching the tent rasped, "*Afferrare.*" The end of the whip snapped around Arnie's ankle and, just as quickly, the man yanked the rope back, pulling Arnie off his feet. He hit the ground with a painful smack, but he managed to scramble back immediately and cry "*Fumo!*"

The incantation was a simple suggestion spell designed to disorient the subject, but in his panic, Arnie had failed to identify a target. I blinked and nearly tripped over my own feet as a cloud of thick, gray smoke blanketed the campsite. I could still make out Copper, though, who remained right beside me, and I grabbed hold of her shoulder to steady myself. She called for her brother, who had disappeared in the imagined haze that surrounded us as we heard blows landing on bodies and Tucker grunting as he continued struggling with the other man.

A pair of broad hands took hold of my shoulders, spinning me around to face the bloody features of the knife-wielding rogue who now held his shattered nose inches from my own. "Listen, you little brat," as he spat, droplets of spit and blood flinging from his lips and onto my flushed cheeks. "We're gonna take what we came for, even if it means we have to flay the lot of you."

"Hildegarde, duck!" Copper's command came right on the coattails of the assailant's threat. Without hesitation, I dropped to my knees, which stung at my fear-driven impact with the rough ground. Above me, I watched as a sizzling pan swept through the cloudy haze and strike something solid with enough force to clang like a bell summoning children in for dinner time. I dared a glance upward, and for a fleeting moment, the right side of the attacker's face was lit up by the embers from the pan that now scalded his flesh. A blood-curdling scream cut through the dark. With the smell of burning hair and roasted skin thick in the air, bile rose to my throat. Another massive clang echoed through the camp, and the screaming came to an abrupt stop. From behind us, I heard gravel crunch loudly from tires pealing out.

"*Fumo arett,*" Arnie's voice called tremulously from across the fire, and the smoke vanished. In the dim light, I saw my attacker slumped on the ground, knocked out cold and face horribly burned from the blow of Copper's pan.

I scanned the radius of the firelight for Arnie's assailant but saw no movement. It seemed he had abandoned his two partners and left with their vehicle. My attention was pulled back to Arnie, who had surged to his feet and was dashing toward Tuck. The brave boy was locked in close combat with the man who seemed to have forgotten about his lost hatchet and was simply focused on the fight at hand.

The two rolled across the campground, the man fighting for dominance with swings of his fists while Tuck tried to grab his arms to restrain him. A punch landed on Tuck's temple, and we all heard the impact. His head snapped to the side, and he was out like a light, but the attacker didn't let up, delivering another blow to Tuck's ribs. Arnie reached the one-sided brawl and seized the stranger's shoulders, only to be thrown back by an elbow to the gut. Neat, red words appeared in my mind. Warnings. Urgings. *Be sure of your convictions.*

With a steady hand, I reached out to the stranger as he dealt another blow to the unconscious Tucker, behaving like a mindless animal of rage and adrenaline. With a voice that was not entirely my own, I whispered, *"Finnir anois,"* before cracking my dry fingers in a clear, solitary snap. The man went pale and fell into an instant slumber. His body sprawled out in the dirt, sleeping peacefully.

My mind buzzed with incredulity as no repercussions happened to my body. Had I just cast that? What were those words? Where did that energy come from? How…

Taking a deep breath, I forced myself to return to the present moment. The camp was silent, and Copper and Arnie gaped at me. I realized that my hand remained outstretched, frozen in its post-snap position. I quickly dropped it and ran to Tuck, yanking him out from beneath his attacker's limp legs.

"Is he all right?" Copper asked, beside me in an instant.

"He's breathing fine," I said as I watched Tuck's chest rise and fall. I felt his wrist. "His pulse also seems okay. I have plenty of healing brews for the bruises and concussion."

"Where did the third one go?" she said suddenly, straightening up and turning in circles like a dog chasing its tail. She raised the pan up to her shoulder, menacing and ready.

"He took off running," Arnie clarified, still catching his breath. "Fled with their truck."

I scanned over the two unconscious bandits, clutching my shoulder bag like a lifeline. "They were here for the book," I said, knowing I was stating the obvious.

"Did anyone take it out of the bag tonight?" Copper asked. Arnie and I exchanged a guilty look. "Seriously?" she yelled, uncommonly angry.

"It was stupid," I admitted. "We're going to have to be more careful from now on."

"You think?!" She threw her hands up, one still holding the pan, as she scowled at both of us. This kind of fury didn't suit her well, though I knew it was well justified.

"You can yell at us later," Arnie said, waving her down. "We need to get out of here before these two wake up."

"Too bad our chauffeur is out cold," I muttered, lightly tapping Tuck's face for any signs of awakening. Copper leaned down and started rifling through his pockets, emerging with a set of jiggling keys. I looked up to her, frowning.

"How hard can it be?" she said, her face returning to its usual mischievous grin.

CHAPTER EIGHTEEN: THE WITCH'S CITY

The vehicle lurched and sputtered as Copper repeatedly failed to switch gears gracefully. She told us she understood the basics, but aside from getting the thing started and moving in a straight line, I wasn't confident she knew even the basics.

"So…" Tuck droned from the back seat, "remind me what happened to the third guy?" He had asked this twice before, but I indulged him again. It was going to take a little while for the medicine to fully heal his concussion and bruising, but his face looked better already.

We had been on the road for several hours now, and Tucker had come to after the first hour, to our endless relief. He seemed very impressed with how we had handled the bandits, and he insisted that he would take out a patrol of volunteers to secure the road upon returning to Camp Valiant. Selfishly, I hoped he wouldn't cross paths with any of the thieves again. I could only hope Tucker's attacker hadn't been aware enough to understand what I had done to him.

Honestly, I hardly understood what I had done to him. Copper and Arnie had tried to get me talking while Tucker was knocked out, but I had no answers for them. Logically, I could understand that I had performed high sorcery, and I was sure that if I looked back through the book, I would find that spell in my mother's perfect handwriting. But I hadn't learned it, hadn't committed it to memory, and yet it had come to me as easily as breathing.

Copper suddenly gave a squeal and reached back to whack my leg with her palm. "Look!" We all gazed out the dust-streaked front window. Silhouetted by the rising sun stood the grand city skyline of the Citadel. Steeples and towers cut into the brilliant orange sky at severe angles, and the polished stone of the luxurious rooftops reflected the sun's fresh light like a beacon calling wayward travelers to the city's open gates. The undisturbed waters of Lake Abraham sparkled like glass, dividing the great walled city from the royal compound that was barely visible in the morning mist.

In the hours we spent approaching the city, we rode past patches of farmland and their accompanying villages, each a bit more sophisticated and well-appointed than the last. Along the road, there were scattered estates with sprawling gardens and adorned gates, retreats for the city's oldest and wealthiest families, according to Tucker. Each grand property had been decked with Yule decorations that were equal parts luxurious and gaudy. Branches of holly and evergreen brushed the windowpanes, framed with delicate white flowers and red berries. Intermixed with the greenery were ceramic stars and paper suns glowing from within to remind passersby that while the holiday may be marked with a shower of material goods and general merrymaking, what we were really celebrating was the life-giving power of the sun. I could only imagine the kind of gifts the children who resided within those homes would be receiving on the twelve days of Yule. It was always Irenee's custom to bestow upon me some tailored garment that was far too formal for my day-to-day life. The gifts included things like a silk blouse embroidered in a gold-dipped thread—which I had worn only once to a celebration of the Lunar New Year—a velvet cap that looked as if it had been stolen from a great lady by her petulant servant girl when it sat on my unkempt hair, and the one gift that had proved regularly useful to me: my sturdy, green cape.

The walls that encased the Citadel were made of shining stone; it was marble, if Arnie's deductions were to be believed. As we approached the large gates, joining in the line of much finer automobiles, Tuck regaled us with trivia about the city's defenses and history. We rolled along at a snail's crawl with all of the other tourists as we passed beneath the ornate archway that marked the entrance into a world of wealth beyond any of our wildest dreams. The first thing I noted about the city was the perfect cleanliness of its surfaces. It looked as if each building, bench, and sidewalk had been scrubbed until it shone only moments ago. Next, I noticed the smiles. Each well-dressed pedestrian had a palpable demeanor of joy spread across their face, as if war and want had never touched them. Rosy-cheeked children flew brilliant, detailed kites within the lush green park that spread through the city's center, lovers strolled arm-in-arm, and even the old women perched on benches seemed to beam with a quiet contentment.

On every corner, the glimmer of gold was present, whether it be on a lady's broach, the decorated facade of a bank, or adorning the rims of passing automobiles. Between the gold accents were shades of white and delicate pastels. Even the men in dapper suits wore them in shapes of blush and periwinkle. The only brown to be found within the walls of the Citadel was in the soil beneath the tulip displays and painted across the hood of the beat-up old jalopy we had brought in to contaminate this perfect place.

I was so taken in by the luxurious scenery and people that I had hardly noticed Tucker and Copper's efforts to navigate through the city traffic to a boarding house that we had marked on our map. The robin's egg-colored building stood across from the park, sandwiched between a law firm and a three-story department store. The facade featured delicately carved white details and window boxes boasting an assortment of peonies and hydrangeas. Above the double-doored entryway hung a sign that read "Madame Margot's Home of Hospitality" in sweeping cursive. Copper parked the truck with a violent lurch. I hopped out in an instant, grateful for solid ground and to take the weight off my sore backside.

Tucker got out with us, his faculties and appearance now fully recovered. He leaned against the side of the truck and extended his hand to Copper for his keys. "Well, this is where I leave ya folks," he drawled.

"We just got here," Arnie said, looking perplexed as he hauled our luggage out of the truck bed.

"I'm not here for sightseeing. I was doing a service, and now I'm needed back at camp." He seemed chipper for a man about to drive another full day on his own, though I saw reluctance in his eyes as he looked at the three of us.

"Are you sure you're feeling good enough to drive?" I asked, spotting a nearly imperceptible trace of bruising near his eye.

"I've been right as rain for the last hour. You're a miracle worker, Hildegarde." I flushed at his compliment as I went digging in my brew box, pulling out the last of the healing brew I had been giving him. I had made a large stock of generic healing potions after the disaster in Inntinn Bay.

"Take this with you," I commanded, handing the green vial to him. "Take a sip every hour until it runs out."

"Always the fretting," Arnie tutted before offering a hand to him. "Thank you for your help, Tucker." They shook in a stiff, manly sort of way.

"Safe travels!" Copper said, and she threw her arms around him and planted a kiss on his cheek. With a few more heartfelt goodbyes, we all waved as Tucker Kindly rumbled off in a puff of exhaust.

We entered the lobby of the hotel, which was swarming with primped and adorned young ladies, all perched throughout the room and chatting excitedly around us. From the conversations, I realized the giddiness was all about the cotillion season at hand. The women who sat in the lobby furniture and those taking their tea by the windows were practically copies of the Fairbanks sisters, each dressed in immaculately tailored ensembles without a hair out of place. They were also demonstrating excellent posture and elegant gestures, as if they were being watched by pageant judges.

"Doesn't this seem a bit outside of our price range?" Arnie asked in a hushed voice. The instant he asked, several young women trotted by us with a fleet of shopping bags hanging off their arms.

"Tuck said it's the best price we're gonna get within the city walls," Copper said, marveling at the ornate ceiling above us. I wouldn't have believed it either if I hadn't witnessed the all-encompassing opulence of the city on the drive in. We waited in a short line to speak to the woman behind the check-in desk, dressed to match all the other employees—the same pastel blue as the decor.

"Good morning," she beamed with perfectly white teeth. "Welcome to Madame Margot's. What can I help you folks with today?" She made a point to make deliberate eye contact with each of us as she spoke.

"Hello," I said cheerily. "We'd love to rent a room for at least one night. Two queens, please." I forced a smile that hopefully mirrored hers.

"Let's see…" she trilled, pursing her lips as she scanned the check-in book before her. "Goody! We have one double room left. Aren't you all the lucky ones? That will be ten silver a night, though we do have a two-night minimum."

"We'll take it," Arnie responded without so much as a glance of general agreement from us. I understood that our options were limited, but still, it pained me to part with all of my earnings from the voyage on the Rambler.

"Great!" She continued, smiling as if her face was frozen. "And which of you is married to the gentleman?" She looked at Copper and me expectantly.

"What does that matter?" Copper responded with a tilt of her head, brow furrowed.

"The laws of Public Decency dictate that all instances of cohabitation between the genders exist only between immediate family members and spouses within city limits," she intoned, as if this was common knowledge.

"He's my brother," Copper answered, looking a bit rattled as she jabbed her thumb at Arnie.

"Then you are the wife?" the receptionist asked, making pointed eye contact with me.

"Yup!" I replied, seeing no other option. I linked my arm in Arnie's and gave an unconvincing giggle. "It's just so new, it's hard to remember."

"Congratulations!" she cried, perking up at the mention of a wedding. "When did you two get married?"

"Yesterday," Arnie and I responded in near-perfect unison. My grin came more naturally after that, and I continued, "This is a honeymoon of sorts for us—Yuletime in the Citadel. What could be more beautiful?" I leaned uncomfortably into Arnie and rested my head on him. He stiffly wrapped an arm around my shoulder, his face going bright red.

"And you… brought his sister?" she said, her smile never wavering, though her voice slowed at this.

"We're all very close," Copper responded with a forced smile of her own.

Copper and I shared a bed, as always, while Arnie got to spread out across his own queen-size. The room was drenched in a pale pink, and the white duvets that we crawled under lay on top of the most comfortable beds we'd slept in so far. Or perhaps it was our shared exhaustion that enhanced the comfort of the most-welcome mattresses. With the soft sound of Copper's breathing setting a soothing rhythm, I quickly fell into a deep sleep with the mid-morning light glowing against the lace curtains.

The stars twinkled in a deep blue sky. Across the grass, the heels of ladies' shoes sank into the soil as couples danced an intimate pattern. A small band stood below a string of bulbs, playing a melancholy tune with lyrics about a young man in a bloody war writing home to his love. The call of the fiddle filled the make-shift dance floor that gradually faded out into the tree line.

A few raindrops landed on the bare shoulders of the girls dancing in the glen. They looked up at the sky in annoyance as the rain started to pick up; it was soon drenching their satin and lace frocks. In a mad dash accompanied by giggles and shrieks, the couples darted off to escape beneath the cover of trees. All save for one couple, who remained swaying to the soulful rhythm at the center of the field, blissfully in-different to the downpour.

The woman buried her face into her partner's broad shoulder, loose black curls cascading down her back. The man wore a simple suit in a hue so dark that the water stains failed to appear. His face was likewise indistinguishable, it being pressed against his partner, cheek resting atop the woman's head. They danced like two faceless phantoms, completely entwined in the other's arms.

The man lowered his head to whisper something tender in the woman's ear. Her shoulders rose and fell with her own gentle laughter in response. They returned to their wordless dance as the band slowed its rhythm—the last breath before the song's end. The final chord hung in the air, thunder cracked, and a brilliant streak of lightning erupted across the night sky. In the flash of light, something glimmered on the small of the woman's back. In the same hand that was leading her in the dance, the man was holding a knife. Only he did not clutch or grip it as one might before they were about to strike. He held it loosely, as one might hold a pen between thoughts, idle and relaxed until the moment when it would be of use again.

Chapter Nineteen: The Witch's Gloves

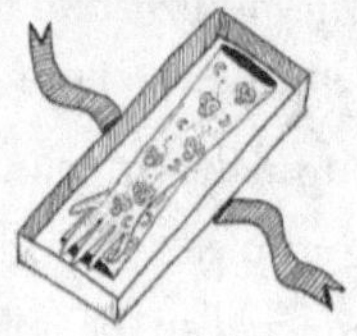

The streets of the garment district were packed shoulder to shoulder: holiday shoppers made their last-minute purchases and debutantes searched for the finishing touches to ensure their ensembles were unforgettable. The map provided by the hotel had outlined this as the most direct path to the Capitol building, but now I wondered if the roads through the financial district might be faster simply because of the lighter foot traffic.

I was awestruck by the mania that surrounded the holiday shopping in the city. In the Orchard, gifts were often made by hand, aside from the festive trinkets purchased at the Frost Festival. I typically crafted unique recipes for each of my friends and family. One year, my gift to Arnie had been a little velvet sack of toffee that had been infused with a hyper-concentration concoction. He had always claimed them to be the sole reason he had been able to read the entirety of *The Complete History of the Green Veil Senate* in a single evening. But here, shoppers seemed less inclined to personalize their gifts and instead flocked to whichever shop window dazzled the brightest.

I couldn't blame them, though. Even Arnie could not keep himself from being taken in by the ornate window displays, especially those that featured playful illusions of the legendary frost faeries flitting about, sprinkling glittering snow on the garments for sale.

"Can't we stop in just one of the shops?" Copper asked, pleading with the enthusiasm of a young child in a candy store. "We don't need to buy anything, but who knows when we'll find ourselves in the Citadel again?" The long rest we had taken that morning, coupled with the brilliant display of enchantment surrounding us, had clearly renewed Copper's spirits. I looked to Arnie to see how he felt, and he returned the look with an indifferent shrug.

"I'd like to," I responded, curiosity plenty high enough to give in to temptation. "Auntie Irenee always gets me such beautiful clothes for Yuletime. It would be nice to return the favor for once." I stepped out of the way to let a glamorous older woman pass with an arsenal of hat boxes. "That is, if there's anything in there that I could remotely afford."

Copper beamed as we scooted through the crowd to the nearest open entrance. The store matched its name, *Gilded Age*, with a spectacular display of gold scattered throughout the show-room inside. However, golden trinkets were not all the establishment had to offer. The room was an open space, with most of the offerings tucked neatly against the walls. Scattered throughout the center of the shop were ornate displays highlighting the favorites of the season, plus several glass counters where polished young women pulled perfumes and bracelets from velvet trays for the wide-eyed shoppers to better look at.

The first items to catch my eye were a pair of elbow-length velvet gloves, lit up in a tall glass case near the center of the room. Scattered across the purple sleeves were delicately embroidered storm clouds that produced streaks of silver lightning every few seconds.

"Those are Irenee gloves if I've ever seen some," Arnie remarked from over my shoulder. Copper had already wandered off to inspect some gowns on rotating mannequins.

"I can't imagine that I'd be able to afford them after paying for our room," I replied, recalling our remaining money with a twinge of sadness. Arnie was right, though—they would be the perfect gift.

"Well, let's find out," he suggested in an uncharacteristically optimistic demeanor. "Excuse me," he called to the worker behind the counter, who had just finished up with a sale of two clutch purses. The man approached with a hospitable smile. "How much for these gloves?"

Arnie asked, pointing them out amidst the sea of other animated accessories.

"A fine choice," the man said with a flourish as he removed the gloves from the case. He checked the price on a small paper tag concealed within the glove's interior and said, "These are four silver and eight copper after city taxes." I pursed my lips and looked at Arnie.

"I don't think I can justify that," I conceded, half to him and half to myself. The salesman nodded and went to return the gloves to their display, but Arnie raised a hand to stop him.

"We can swing that." He nodded to the employee as he riffled through his pockets for the coins.

"No," I insisted, "you don't need to do that." I put a hand on his arm to stop him, but he continued to pull out coins.

"Don't be silly," he said as he finished counting and gathered them into his palm. "A husband should treat his newly wedded wife," he said with a big wink, using a doting tone that didn't suit him at all. He punctuated his statement by dumping the coins into the waiting palm of the salesman.

"Very good, sir," the salesman said, recounting the payment with practiced ease, then nodding with satisfaction. "Would you like these gift-wrapped?"

"That would be great," Arnie responded without hesitation, and the man went behind the counter to set about his task. Arnie turned to me with a smile. "Irenee has always been very kind to me," he explained, stopping me before I could challenge him. "Plus, it's been a few years since I gave you a Yule present."

"The same could be said for me," I grumbled, completely caught by surprise by his actions.

"Not true at all," he said with a scoff. "You don't think I realized it was you leaving the little cakes on my doorstep each year?" My cheeks flushed. "Who else do I know who would endow a lemon cake with pleasant memories?" He grinned at me, the warmth in his eyes taking me back to our childhood years of close friendship.

"Thank you, Arnie," I said, squeezing his arm.

"You are very welcome." We watched the salesman make his way back to us with the finished product. The gloves had been placed in a rectangular box, wrapped in silver paper with little golden suns and adorned with a green satin bow. Just as I was about to thank the man, his attention was pulled to another customer.

"Excuse me," a familiar voice beckoned from behind the grand floral arrangement that divided the counter. "I would like to see these snowflake hairpins." The girly voice rang with the sing-songy pitch of a slight coastal accent.

I craned my head around the flowers and called, "Sissy?" just loud enough to be heard across the minimal distance. The blonde-haired girl looked up from the hairpins she had been inspecting, and her face contorted through the rapid expressions of confusion, recognition, and then joy.

"Helen?!" Her high-pitched cry pulled the attention of all surrounding shoppers as she abandoned the hairpins and scampered down the counter to me. Sissy threw her arms around me, and the force of the impact sent my body into Arnie's. The result was some sort of awkwardly coordinated group hug. An onlooker would not have expected it to have only been two days since our last meeting—it was more like we had just returned from a year in the border war. "Helen Purslane, you little devil, you!" she squealed.

She released me to look me over, which allowed Arnie to create a more comfortable distance between himself and us. Sissy continued in amazement, "You said you wouldn't have time for a visit, and here you are doing a bit of shopping!" The accusation in her voice was rich with teasing, easing my building fear.

It turned out that Sissy's coordinated ensembles during the sea voyage had been her equivalent of dressing casually. She currently wore pastel blue from head to toe. The coat she wore over her A-line dress had been embroidered with silver thread and pearls to match the jewelry set on her ears, neck, and wrists. Her perfectly white gloves matched her pumps and stockings. It also looked as though she'd had her hair lightened to an icier blonde to complement the wintery atmosphere.

"It's so great to see you," I said, clutching her gloved hands in mine. "You look so beautiful."

"Well, I'd better," she responded. "I make my debut at Yule's Eve tomorrow at the king's Gala!" She actually jumped with giddiness as she spoke.

"Now that sounds like an actually important party," I said with a sly grin.

"Oh, Helen—they're *all* important," Sissy answered with a smile.

"Hello, Cormac," she said quickly, realizing just then that Arnie was standing next to us. He responded with a small wave; those formalities dealt with, Sissy returned her attention to me. "But what are you doing here so soon? Where's your soldier?"

"There was a change of plans," I began, figuring the near-truth would be sufficient enough. "It turns out he's receiving a commendation here, so the surprise didn't quite work out."

"Well, then you must come to see us," Sissy erupted with enthusiasm. "Now that you have the time, you *must*. It would give my sisters such a treat to see you all, and heaven knows they need it now." She dropped my hands and immediately went to straighten her pinned curls.

"What's wrong with Kissy and Prissy?" Arnie asked from the sidelines.

"Missy," I corrected him speedily.

"Bless you," he quipped.

"They're terribly ill," Sissy said airily, either choosing to ignore his comments or having missed them altogether. "We think they may have caught whatever it was Daschel and Gary had on the ship." She reported the news like a gossip columnist might report a grim scandal.

I wished I had a way to convey to Sissy that it was impossible for her sisters' illness to have been contracted from those two brutes, but I didn't feel like outing myself as a poisoner.

"It's so very tragic," she continued with wide eyes, "to travel all this way and miss the first gala of the season." She shook her head so somberly it was as if she were reporting a death in the family.

"Guys, you have to see this amazing pair of shoes—oh!" Copper began, bounding up to us but then realizing who our companion was with a look of bewilderment. "Hi, Sissy!" She scooted in for a quick hug.

"Don't let me stop you, Lisel," Sissy beamed. "I want to hear more about these shoes." Copper grinned and looked Sissy up and down, taking in her ensemble just as I had.

"You're a vision, Sissy," she breathed, thrown equally by the chance encounter and the outfit itself. After a brief round of catching up, focused mainly on Sissy's busy schedule of garden parties and dress fittings, Sissy glanced down to check the small watch face that had been skillfully masked beneath pearls and gems.

"Oh foot," Sissy lamented. "I have to scurry. I have dinner with the Mammons in an hour, and I still have to change. Helen, here's a card with my godfather's address. Please come for a visit. I'll be free tomorrow, any time before noon." With a few

goodbye kisses on the cheek, Sissy Fairbanks
was off in a flash of silver and blue.

"Remind me exactly how the two of you became friends," Arnie asked, expression dead-
pan.

"She has a good heart," I shot back, looking
him right in the eye. "Sometimes that's not always clear on the surface."

The Capitol building did not bustle with holiday shoppers, but rather the well-dressed pa-
per-pushers who sauntered from office to office, holding the closed-door meetings that
would set new laws and referendums into motion. The grand lobby was open to the public,
so in addition to the senators and their staff, visitors and tour groups wandered about, gawking
at the great brass sculptures of the kings that
lined the walls. In a city renowned for its beauty
and opulence, the Capitol building was as impressive as would be expected, but it had a
greater, more refined dignity than the rest of the
glittering city. Devoid of pastel colors and
flower arrangements, this building was crafted
from polished marble and boasted shining
metal fixtures. Presumably, we were seeing the
city at its most beautiful and ornate—adorned
with extensive Yule decorations—and the Capitol building was no exception. At the lobby's
center, a great evergreen had been erected and

decked in glittering stars. An illusion had been cast over the tree to simulate crimson robins flitting about the branches, filling the echoing room with their simple song.

The wait at the information office had been longer than I'd expected, which allotted us only a short time before the end of the workday. The perfunctory older lady who had given us Haute Brood's office number had duly informed us that the councilman would halt all meetings with constituents promptly at five o'clock. It was from her that we also learned Haute's formal title: Chair of the Council of Transparency. The council's function seemed purposefully vague. Councilman Brood's office was on the fifth floor. As we entered the lift and gave the attendant our desired floor, two uniformed watchmen suddenly called for the doors to be held. The attendant obliged, and the two broad men squeezed in. My heart thundered in my chest.

"My apologies," the watchman closest to me offered when he accidentally brushed against me in the cramped space. "We're only going up to three. Should be out of your hair in two shakes," he informed me with a smile. I returned the gesture with a small smile and nod. To my dismay, the watchman did not remove his eyes from me, and instead, his gaze traveled to my hand, then the leather strap on my shoulder, and then my shoulder bag.

"That is…" he began, and I suddenly felt unable to breathe. "…a gorgeous timepiece," he finished, nodding approvingly. I exhaled in relief and thanked him for the compliment as the lift came to a stop on the third floor. "You folks have a nice day," he said and tipped his hat before both of them left, taking the tension with him.

There was a cheerful ding as we reached the fifth floor. I was glad to see that the halls remained somewhat empty, with only a few secretaries and aides passing through on errands. Knowing Arnie would remember, I turned and asked him, "What was the number again?"

"Sixteen," he replied without hesitation. His impressively accurate memory often came in handy, but it could also be immensely annoying. We continued down the hall for a short distance before reaching our destination. The door was cracked open a few inches, but it still seemed presumptuous to enter without knocking first, so I rapped my knuckles three times on the doorframe.

"Come in," a melodious voice beckoned. I pushed open the thick mahogany door to reveal a small office. The decor was sparse yet tasteful, with no reference to the holiday season. Behind a dark wood desk sat a spindly, middle-aged man. He sat very still, his eyes completely closed, while holding a steady hand above a single sheet of paper. "Just a moment," he said without opening his eyes. "Just checking for authentication."

He was very thin, almost as thin as Maude had been, and boasted every bit of her glamour. He wore a plum suit that was double-breasted with golden buttons and floral embroidery. There were few signs of his age across his olive skin. The only feature that gave him away as an older gentleman was his head of sleek white hair, which had been slicked back with gel.

"Legitimate," he announced. He opened a pair of deep brown eyes, stamped the letter with blue ink, and looked us over. "What can I do for you today?" He adjusted his tortoiseshell glasses, rattling the thin golden chain that secured them around his neck.

"You're Haute Brood?" Copper asked skeptically. None of us had known quite what to expect, but he still managed to defy some sort of expectation.

"Indeed. Nameplate hasn't been swiped," he said as he motioned to the small sign on the front of his desk that verified his claim. "I will ask again: What can I do for you?" There was a hint of annoyance in his tone now.

"I think you knew my mother," I began, unsure of how much to divulge. "I was looking for information on an organization you two may have been involved in." I attempted to hit close enough to the truth to clue him in without revealing anything that could come back to bite us.

"I've served on many a committee in my time," Haute answered coolly. "With many colleagues and fellow citizens. Could you be a bit more specific?" I couldn't help but feel as though I was being toyed with. The notion buzzed in the pit of my empty stomach.

"It would have been a *special* group," I pushed, attempting to hit the keywords hard enough to get my point across. "A very close group. One could even call it a sisterhood." All amusement fled from Haute's auburn eyes.

"I'm afraid my office can't give you the answers you require," he snapped, the corners of his mouth curving downward in tension. "Not without further inquiry and formal paperwork. Unfortunately, I won't be back in the building until the holiday has passed. Perhaps I could pencil you in for a later date?" His expression and tone were at odds with each other, and the duality put me even further on edge.

"We really need the information sooner than that," Arnie pressed as he stepped forward, eager to try his hand at persuading the tight-lipped councilman.

"I'm afraid my hands are tied in regards to scheduling. Aside from making an appearance at the Yuletime Gala, I'll be spending the rest of my holiday fishing on Lake Abraham, not taking meetings." Haute held pointed eye contact with me as he spoke. In a moment of subtle, hopeful confidence, I responded with a small nod of affirmation. I could only hope I had correctly picked up on his meaning. "Is there anything else you need?" Haute concluded.

"But we didn't get the first thing we needed—" Copper began to protest, but I put my hand on her shoulder to stop her.

"That was all, thank you." I gently directed Copper toward the door, motioning for Arnie to follow. "I appreciate your time."

"Have a most pleasant holiday," Haute called, his voice warm and friendly again.

"You too." I shut the door behind us.

I led the two of them out of the building in tense silence. Luckily, the calls that the building was closing justified the quickened pace I set for us. Twice, Copper tried to whisper a question in my ear, but I shot wide-eyed stares at her both times and she shut her mouth. It was not until we had descended each of the steps leading away from the Capitol building that I uttered a word, my heartbeat still practically in my mouth.

"Well, that was exciting," I said as I let out the deep breath I'd been holding and beamed, feeling somewhat unbalanced after the adrenaline rush.

"What exactly happened in there?" Copper asked, looking exasperated and confused.

"Yeah, Hildy," Arnie grumbled, joining his sister's bewilderment. "What did you get out of that interaction that we didn't?" I first felt a rush of pride, but then a wave of concern in deducing something they had not. No—I knew what I had heard. For the first time, I felt I was finally speaking the same language as my mother: the language of deception.

"He wants to talk to us, but he couldn't speak openly in the building," I said, waving animatedly at the Capitol.

"How did you figure that out?" Copper asked.

"He all but said it," I explained breathlessly. "He said, 'My office can't give you the answers.' Not *him*—his office." I waited for comprehension to dawn on their faces, but I was disappointed. "He was saying he couldn't give us answers in his *office*." They began to nod slowly.

"So… where are we meant to get the answers then?" Arnie asked, frowning.

"We need to make a visit to the Fairbanks," I said as I fished around my bag for the card Sissy had given me. "We're going to need three invitations to that gala." I found it sandwiched between my wallet and a tin of breath mints.

"The king's Yuletime Gala?" Copper asked, eyes going wide.

"Turns out Sissy was right. Parties can be *very* important."

Chapter Twenty: The Witch's Dressing Room

Rolph Haypenny was the sort of fellow who chose to fill his home with impressive things: paintings from renowned artists, a dagger from the Tri-Generation War housed in a glass box, and even an expensive, white, long-haired cat who wore a jeweled collar about her neck. He had more money than he needed. With no immediate family of his own to spend it on, it was clear that he poured his wealth into items that might properly convey his station.

Mr. Haypenny had made his bones in the shipping industry, moving enchanted garments and accessories from the factories of Facehaven to the storefronts of the Citadel. In recent years, Rolph had been of some assistance in the transport of various weaponry to the troops stationed at the border, and that relationship had yielded him an invitation to the king's Yuletime Gala—an honor he had been lucky enough to be able to extend to his three beloved goddaughters. Or at least, that was how he explained it to Copper and me as we sipped the afternoon tea he had prepared for us.

"Uncle Rolph has always spoiled us girls," Sissy piped up as an end punctuation his tale, directing a warm smile at the plump man. We had not expected Mr. Haypenny to be home, thinking that most businessmen would be occupied at their offices at this time of the day, but Haypenny, as we had just learned, often had the luxury of working from home.

"That must be such an interesting profession," Copper said, her tone overly polite. "Working with enchanted garments, that is— seeing all the spells and, um, things that make them… enchanted." She shifted in her chair, trying and failing to gracefully cross her legs.

"I seldom interact with the clothing items," Mr. Haypenny rumbled in a warm but gravelly voice, squashing the conversation topic. "A group of young ladies designs them, and another set of women make them and add the suitable enchantments. I'm the one who actually crunches the figures and ensures all operations run smoothly."

"He was kind enough to offer us girls our pick of his winter collection to wear to the gala," Sissy chimed in, adding a bit of life to the dying discussion. "You saw how pathetic the dresses we were tailoring on the boat were."

I recalled the brightly colored, ruffled dresses that had been laid out and modeled constantly on our journey, and I would have hardly called them pathetic. However, seeing the baseline opulence the sisters seemed accustomed to, I could understand their differing perspective. The stark contrast of Mr. Haypenny's parlor versus the dingy quarters of the Rambler further highlighted the Fairbanks family's financial troubles.

Inspiration dawning on me as to how to abandon our watchful host, I feigned a spike of girlish enthusiasm and declared, "Sissy, we would just *love* to see your dress for the gala! Wouldn't you, Lisel?" I nudged.

"Absolutely!" Copper hardly had to feign excitement at the mention of high fashion embellished with enchantments. "Knowing your taste, I'm sure the ensemble is a thing of beauty." Sissy beamed with pride.

"Will you excuse us, Uncle Rolph?" she asked with all the refinement of a member of the royal court. He responded with a dignified nod.

"Who am I to keep young girls from their games of dress-up?" He chuckled and settled back into his chair to finish his slice of orange cake in solitude. Sissy led us up the foyer steps at a trotting pace.

Copper grabbed my elbow to slow me down a few steps. "Make sure it's easy to access," she whispered in my ear.

"It is—it's right here," I whispered back, tapping my skirt pocket to indicate the hiding place of the suggestibility potion I had brewed using my

Fast-Friends candies. I had wanted to solicit Sissy's help without compulsion, but Arnie had convinced us that deception was the better approach. In a way, we were fugitives from the law with two watchmen on our tail, so if Sissy were ever to be questioned for her involvement in the plot, she would have to be able to state that it was against her will while she was under the influence of the truth-detecting magics they used in the court system. None of us were anxious to put her in harm's way. In this particular instance, deception genuinely seemed the most ethical solution.

"Come along, slowpokes," Sissy beckoned, sticking her head back out from her dressing room at the end of the hall. We did as we were told, scurrying into the sun-soaked room. Her dress had been draped over a cloth mannequin that stood in a more shadowed corner of the room, but even so, it caught the light spectacularly.

"Isn't it perfect?" Sissy sighed, beaming with pride. "Mother says that my complexion is too pink for a white dress, and Uncle Rolph's stylist was able to craft this in an icy blue instead, to match the season." The bodice was constructed out of shimmering blue silk with expertly draped off-the-shoulder straps. However, the garment's impressive splendor came from the ruffled full skirt that had been covered in thousands of sparkling crystals.

"It's stunning, Sissy," Copper said as she leaned in for a closer look at the stones, "but I'm surprised you didn't choose one with an enchantment." I was curious about that as well, since debutantes were hardly known for their subtlety.

"But I did," Sissy insisted. With a twirl of her skirt, she turned to the large window and drew the curtains. Even with the sunlight dulled by the heavy drapes, the dress continued to sparkle as if it stood in an open field at midday.

"Oh wow, that's lovely work," Copper said in awe. She circled to admire the dress from several angles, looking at it with the critical eye of an enchanter. "Was the enchantment endowed, or are there runes stitched within?"

"I haven't the faintest idea," Sissy said with a dismissive wave. She clearly wasn't interested in the workings of enchantments. It suddenly occurred to me that I had never seen her perform any magics.

"Sissy, what is your field of study?" I inquired, thinking perhaps she'd done something like light empath work. But Sissy looked at me as though I'd just asked her how she might most like to die.

"I don't have one," she answered, as if it had been painfully obvious. "The only academy in Inntinn Bay is for divination, and I certainly won't be studying a second-tier magic." She reopened the curtains in a smooth flourish.

"I had you pegged for an empath," Copper remarked, settling onto a velvet settee. She began sorting through the bowl of hard candies that sat beside it.

"Study in Tangere? No, thank you." Sissy seemed to find this line of questioning somewhat amusing. "As if anyone could find a suitable husband on that desert island." She giggled at her own joke. "I just don't see the point of it. If you're going to become a wife, why study at all? Two years of work to surround yourself with girls and men who are willing to settle for a second-tier career? It never made any sense to me."

She perched herself on the cushioned bench of her vanity before continuing her sermon. "I suppose it makes sense if you're from the Orchard or Facehaven—your academy is just down the road. You can be home to get dinner on the table with plenty of time, and then you have a hobby to fill the rest of your day once you're done with school. Of course, if you're planning to have children in the first years of your marriage, then it is truly impractical." She paused to look at both my and Copper's mixed expressions. "Don't get me wrong. I *do* appreciate the extension of magic rights to include married women. I just can't envision it fitting into my own life," she said with a delicate shrug of her shoulders.

I was awestruck. It had never occurred to me to forgo an education, even once I became Raemond's wife. Sissy's rationale made me deeply uncomfortable, as if she had just finished reasoning out something offensive. Only she hadn't. She'd expressed a commonly held view in the community of wives and mothers; a community I planned to enter soon. Why did her words feel like a dirty betrayal?

"Well, I'm never getting married," Copper said flatly, not looking inclined to elaborate. "But more power to you both." She popped a golden caramel in her mouth and settled back into the settee.

"Champagne?" Sissy offered cheerily, appearing oblivious to the discomfort in the room.

"Yes, please," Copper said, perking up and raising her eyebrows at me. I wrapped my fingers around the potion vial in my pocket.

"Where are Kissy and Missy?" I asked. Our plan would only work if we remained uninterrupted; trying to sneak something into a drink while avoiding three pairs of eyes instead of one would have been impossible. Our relocation to the dressing room ensured that Rolph would not interrupt us. We also had expected the privacy of a girl's room would be ideal, hence why Arnie was not included in this task. The sisters, however, were not barred by the same rules of convention.

"They were just too sick to pull themselves out of bed, I'm afraid," Sissy said, her lips pursed in pity as she removed the chilled beverage from its ice bucket. "Such a shame. They had really been looking forward to a visit." She inserted the bottle into a brass contraption that looked sort of like a brew stand for holding beakers in place, but with a funny top that the bottle squeezed into. With a turn of a crank that stuck out at the side, the cork of the bottle popped, causing Copper to jump at the sound.

"Oh well," Sissy said as she pulled the uncorked bottle from the contraption. "More for us." There was a notable hint of glee in her voice as she spoke of her sisters' internment. I thought of all the less-than-subtle jabs the sisters had made at her expense on our journey and wondered if she might actually be enjoying her solitude.

Sissy brought a flute of frothy champagne to Copper first, then handed me the other as I sat down in an armchair that was conveniently close to the vanity. She fetched her own glass, but she did not come sit down next to me, as I had hoped. Instead, she floated about the room, glass in hand, and rambled on about something to do with the difficulty of sitting down while wearing a crinoline.

"Sissy—" Copper interjected, cutting her off mid-sentence. "Would you mind if I were to look at the seams of your dress? I haven't been able to get the question of runes or endowment out of my head." Sissy looked perplexed at the sudden interruption but softened at the continued interest in her dress.

"Sure, Lisel." She nodded diplomatically, and Copper made her way toward the dress stand without setting down her flute. "Oh, let me hold that," Sissy said in a rushed breath as she reached for Copper's glass, which had come within spilling distance. Copper relinquished the refreshment before bending to lift the hem of the skirt. "Please be careful," Sissy pleaded, attempting to mask her terror as the dress's crystals clacked against each other.

"Would you mind holding the skirt up?" Copper said as she popped her head back out to peer up at the anxious girl. "So I could get a better look at the stitching?" She shot another glance my way, and I finally caught on to her plan. I set my drink down carefully and jumped up.

"I'll take the drinks." I reached out and gingerly grabbed the two flutes without any affirmation. Now empty-handed, Sissy breathed a sigh of relief as she took hold of the hem so that Copper could crane her neck to peer within the dress's interior. In that instant, I realized there was no way I could grab and pour the vial while holding both glasses.

"Wow, would you look at that," Copper exclaimed from beneath the fabric.

"What is it?" Sissy crouched to duck under the hem to inspect whatever it was that was of interest, and I seized the opening. I stepped back to the vanity and quickly set both glasses down on the table beside mine. I shoved a hand in my pocket, fumbled with the vial for a few heartbeats, then frantically dosed Sissy's with a few drops from the vial. "I can't see a thing," Sissy grumbled, her voice muffled by the wall of silk and crystal.

"That's because there is nothing to see," Copper explained from their fashion tent. I went to reseal the vial and then had a startling realization: I had no idea which glass had just received the potion. "There are no runes in the stitching," she continued. The fabric rustled with the worrisome warning that the two were returning to the light. Without another thought, I divided the remaining contents of the vial equally between all three glasses and stuffed the empty bottle back into my pocket. I grabbed two glasses at random before spinning around and tiptoeing back to the dress stand, though still keeping outside the invisible spill zone. "Turns out the enchantment *was* endowed," Copper concluded, and the both of them brought their heads back out, Copper's hair a bit mussed and static-y while Sissy somehow remained pristine.

"That is fascinating," I remarked with an exaggerated nod, then handed one of the laced flutes back to Sissy. While returning a glass to Copper, I widened my eyes to a comical size and gave the slightest shake of my head. She furrowed her brow at me, looking like she hadn't the foggiest idea what I meant. Before I could try my hand at a second gesture, Sissy raised her glass.

"To good friends," she announced. I had no choice but to follow suit, turning quickly to grab my own drink off the vanity. "May we never lose touch." She smiled warmly and raised the glass to her lips. Painfully oblivious to my promptings, Copper did the same.

"Lisel, don't!" My outburst startled them both. Sissy spat out a bit of her drink in surprise, and Copper nearly dropped her own glass, causing a fourth of the contents to slosh out and land on the carpeting. Both of them stared at me, concerned and looking for an explanation.

"There… was…" I began haltingly. "There was a bug!" I spat out. "In your glass, Lisel," I continued, nodding at her drink while looking at her with wide eyes again. "I didn't want you to accidentally drink… something bad." Copper nodded then, recognition growing in her eyes.

"I don't see a bug," Sissy said with a frown as she leaned in close over Copper's glass.

"I think it fell out with some of her spilled drink," I clarified.

"Well let's get you another glass then," Sissy insisted. "Who knows what that bug had stepped in." She shook her head in revulsion before taking a hearty swig from her own glass. I exhaled and sat down while Copper went to the wet bar to help herself to an untainted flute. I watched Sissy closely as she took Copper's place on the settee, not realizing the extended, absolute silence of the moment.

"What?" Sissy finally asked, shuffling uncomfortably under my stare.

"How are you feeling?" I asked, figuring that made the most sense to start with.

"Fine," Sissy she said, raising a shaped eyebrow. "How should I feel?" I had never administered a compulsion or suggestion brew, so I had no idea how long before it took effect.

"I would imagine you're feeling nervous," I said cautiously, testing the waters.

"Nervous?" Her head floated up to look at me, and I noticed her eyes looked somewhat glassy and vacant. Apparently the effect was fast, which was lucky for us.

"Nervous about the gala," I pressed. "It must be nerve-wracking to make your debut all alone." Sissy cocked her head a bit as her body relaxed.

"It is nerve-wracking to make my debut all alone," she said as she nodded, repeating the sentiment as if she was now beginning to think that.

"It might be nice to have some friends there." I continued, planting the seeds as Copper took a seat beside her.

"You're right—it would be nice to have some friends there," Sissy said, looking like that was a brilliant suggestion. "You two should join me!" she cried, perking up in her seat as if she'd just experienced an epiphany.

"Why, what an excellent idea," Copper declared, feigning big surprise and nodding too enthusiastically.

"There are *two* of us," I reasoned, "and you have two invitations that your sisters won't be able to use. It really would be a shame if those went to waste."

"I would give them to you in a heartbeat," Sissy said in a dreamy voice. "But they aren't transferable. You'd have to be my sisters to use them."

We had anticipated this, knowing how exclusive this gala was. "Why, I have a crazy idea!" Once again, Copper's acting skills left something to be desired. "What if Helen and I were made to *look* like your sisters. That way, we would be able to be there and support you." Sissy looked back at her, blinking several times.

"But you don't look like my sisters…" Even for someone under a compulsion spell, Sissy was slow on the draw.

"Lisel is a great enchanter," I explained. "She could place a glamour on the dresses that made us look like Kissy and Missy." Sissy's face lit up with a broad smile.

"How wonderful," she said, beaming. "It wouldn't be half as scary debuting when I had such good friends at my side!"

I was proud of how effective the brew was proving to be, though I still felt ashamed at manipulating someone with such a kind heart. I wondered if Sissy would have been equally as accommodating if we had asked her in earnest.

Perhaps I viewed our recent friendship with rose-colored glasses, but something told me she would not have shied away from a bit of adventure. But, if the potion worked as we intended, then Sissy would never realize that she had been manipulated at all. The events would turn into fond, if not somewhat foggy, memories, and she could never claim to be a willing accomplice. However, that did not bring me comfort.

Chapter Twenty-One: The Witch's Dance

I had not worn a girdle since graduation, and I certainly hadn't missed them. However, to fit into a dress tailored to fit Kissy's slim frame, I was currently wearing two: one to cinch my waist and another to tighten my rear and thighs—a much more complicated laced contraption. Copper had attempted to enchant the dress to let it out a bit, but she could only manage to lengthen the hem, which hardly helped, seeing as I already stood half a foot below the statuesque Kissy Fairbanks.

After several hours of tinkering with alterations and enchantments, we'd crafted two serviceable dresses. Endowing the dresses with a permanent enchantment had proved too difficult for Copper's level of skill, so we'd resorted to the simpler approach of stitching runes into the fabric. The addition of Missy's and Kissy's strands of hair, however, pilfered from their brushes by Sissy, had ensured the glamours on our dresses would be a perfect likeness, however temporary.

Though the fit was somewhat questionable, the designs remained stunning. Kissy's dress, now mine, was made of the white fabric Sissy's mother had insisted did not suit her. Instead of sparkling crystal details, this dress was decorated with golden beads that had been arranged in geometric patterns across the bodice and then in clean lines along the mermaid-style skirt. It was clear this design was intended for the eldest sister, as it left the wearer's shoulders and arms completely bare, which was considered a more mature style.

Copper's dress, being Missy's, was a bit more on the modest side. It was constructed entirely of green velvet and covered her arms with tight sleeves. Across the fabric was an array of delicately embroidered golden suns. Like Sissy's dress, the skirt sat atop a boisterous crinoline. However, unlike the other two full-length gowns, this one's hem fell just below the midpoint of Copper's calves, giving her the opportunity to showcase her favorite snake-skin boots. The choice of accessory was much to Sissy's distaste, but none of the Fairbanks' dainty heels had fit Copper's feet.

Neither of these two dresses had been endowed with any decorative enchantment, which Sissy reported to have been her mother's command. Since Sissy was the one making her debut, the Fairbanks matriarch had demanded that she be the one to sparkle. Their stylist had taken the request quite literally. I saw this as a happy coincidence, since I did not want to stand out more than we had to.

As the oldest, Kissy had been the only one of the sisters given the choice to invite an escort, which gave us a lucky break. Arnie now had a part to play. Lucas MaGraith was meant to travel in from his family's estate outside of Mt. Tempus, but when the sisters had fallen ill, he'd canceled his trip. Sissy was doubtful that anyone in attendance would know what Lucas looked like, and without access to any strands of his hair, Copper could not create an authentic glamour. She'd had to settle on a simple set of runes to alter his hair color to brown and sharpen his jawline a bit, as those were the only two physical characteristics Sissy had been able to recall clearly about the boy. So, with Arnie's rented suit and tails properly glamoured, our sleepless night of preparations came to an end, each of us no longer resembling our true selves.

The three of us, now adapted young social-ites, stood waiting at the front gates of the Royal History Museum, the domed building at the center of the city's largest park. A parade of shiny young women and dignified older couples strode past us, the sound of clacking heels against cobblestone unending. Polished black automobiles with tinted windows came and went from the paved loop that brought their passengers directly to the grand entrance. Arnie had been right about the decorative snow. Fluffy, white flakes speckled the darkening sky, even while the temperature remained perfectly mild. I had only a thin, cashmere shawl to drape over my arms, but I felt entirely comfortable.

"It's such a gorgeous night," Copper said, bobbing with excitement, and Missy's blonde curls bounced on the shoulders of her velvet sleeves. It was odd to hear her voice coming from a girl who typically spoke two octaves above her.

"What did I tell you?" the slightly altered Arnie huffed as he raised his palms to the sky. "A perfect snowfall just for Yuletime." The flakes fell into his dark brown hair before melting away.

"Well, I'm not complaining," I commented. I stretched out my palm to catch the snow, fixating on the peach-colored skin that now covered it. "It isn't even cold." I marveled as the flakes landed on my hand, soft and devoid of temperature.

"I am," the not-quite-Arnie grumbled. "It isn't natural. This is the frost season. Nature demands it to be cold." He seemed determined to be unmoved by the splendor and glamour that surrounded us.

"Arnold-Cormac-Lucas," Copper said with a sigh, "for one minute, can we just pretend that we're going to a royal gala for an exciting night out? No plots, no watchmen, no fear. Can we just walk through those doors, get a drink, eat some cake, maybe dance a little, and after that, *then* get to the doom and gloom?" She squared up to him, staring with her newly blue eyes. "When are we ever going to do something like this again?"

"Fine. One drink," he said, caving to his sister's powerful stare. "And then it's right back to business."

Copper threw her arms around him. "I knew my brother was still in there." She rocked him from left to right as he relented to it, albeit stiffly.

"Getting the party started without me?" Sissy's unforgettably precious voice emerged from a small crowd of passersby. As the pedestrians parted for her to walk through, I was filled with a strong feeling of pride for my friend. Sissy positively shone against the dark blue sky. Her curls had been pinned with the snowflake berets she'd been eying at Gilded Age, and her features were made all the more lovely by a touch of tasteful, light makeup.

"Sissy," I exhaled as I stepped in to get a closer look. "You look like a princess." She beamed and spun around, sending the large skirt of her dress billowing, streaking the darkness with bursts of light.

"I'm so unimaginably excited," she gushed, grabbing hold of my hands as she always did. "And I'm so glad you're all here with me!" She lowered her voice to a whisper and leaned in to say, "It's all so exhilarating… breaking the rules like this." A pang of guilt shot through my gut. As thrilling as Sissy believed this to be, it was all built on a lie—a planted idea that had been a violation of her own free will. Could a night of social revelry make up for that betrayal?

"You should have seen my driver's face when I told him to let me out on the corner," Sissy continued. "He must be thinking that I ran off to have a secret rendezvous beneath the moonlight." She chuckled at the idea of a scandal.

"Now, if I know my godfather," Sissy continued, speaking seriously, "he'll head straight to the back room to drink brandy with the other important men. He'll either stay back there all night or drink himself past any ability to recognize you before he comes out. If anyone asks about your illness, just tell them you made a speedy recovery."

"And if people start talking to us?" Arnie inquired, looking incredulous at such minimal instructions. "How do I be Lucas MaGraith?" He flourished his hand over his face to illustrate the point.

"No one in there knows Lucas," Sissy responded. "He was a last-minute get, a real bottom of the barrel escort. He's certainly no staple of society. If you want to fit in with the boys in there, just laugh at everything they say and be rude to the servers."

"They sound like a fun group of guys," Arnie commented dryly.

"As for you two…" she said, shifting the focus to her new imposter sisters. "If anyone talks to Kissy, say hello and then make a backhanded comment and walk away. Missy, just agree with everything she says and follow her when she leaves." Sissy noticed our amused smirks and shrugged. "They aren't complicated girls."

"We can do that," I said, giving Sissy a confident nod.

"All right then," she said, taking my hand in hers and looping her arm through Arnie's. She turned to the museum and smiled widely. "It's showtime."

When Sissy presented the invitations to the doorman, I felt the intoxicating effects of exclusivity wash over me. Even though I was under a glamour, being included in an event so elite felt like a delicacy. As the doorman ushered us in with a gloved hand, I silently reminded myself to savor the experience. Copper was right. For just one drink, I could simply be a girl wearing a beautiful dress at a dance. And what a dance it was.

As soon as we walked in, the glass dome was above our heads, and we could see visions of frost faeries dancing and flitting about. They were sprinkling snow onto the branches of the golden evergreen that stood proudly at the room's center, sitting on a richly colored, polished wood floor. Beautiful people floated between the tables; each setting was adorned with a towering centerpiece of white hydrangeas. All the servers wore black bowties and balanced silver trays piled high with mouthwatering displays of pastries and cheese on nimble fingers.

The crowd was at its densest around the bar, which spanned the entire length of the back wall. Crystal glasses had been arranged into a tower of sorts, and champagne trickled down them like waterfalls feeding hidden grottos. Guests gave gasps and coos of delight as each glass was removed. Those who did not choose champagne instead watched the graceful bartenders serve up flaming cocktails and glasses of vibrantly colored wine that glowed like stained glass.

Across the expansive room was a large stage with emerald and gold paneling along the front edge. On that stage, I could just see a well-dressed band, arranged with their shiny brass instruments over two sets of risers. In front of them was a large group of young couples dancing to the swinging music of the horns. The faint memory of a dancing couple in a dream darted through my mind like the frost faerie illusions above us.

"This ain't no Orchard party," Copper whispered at my side. She gawked at the room filled with magical splendor, eyes darting all over as she tried to take in everything.

"No, it is not," I responded emphatically. I was still feeling overwhelmed by the spectacle we'd just become immersed in. "It's missing the stale ale and manure."

"Don't knock a classic Orchard blowout," Arnie rebutted from the other side of Sissy. "We've had some pretty good ones."

"If you're telling me that you'd rather be throwing rings at the Flower Fair than drinking champagne from an actual tower, I don't think I can call you my brother anymore," Copper retorted without looking at him, too busy scanning the immense scene before her.

"Isn't it spectacular?" Sissy linked my arm in hers to match Arnie's. "Worth crossing the ocean for—even on a ship as decrepit as the Rambler." She squeezed us close as if we shared a decade of stories. "Drinks?"

We made our way through the flow of the crowd and to the bar. Sissy, Copper, and I all pulled a glass from the champagne tower, giggling as our hands were splashed by the cascading alcohol. We devolved into laughter even more when Copper shook off the liquid on her hand and accidentally sent the drops flying directly onto my face. Arnie puffed up his chest as he walked up to the bar and ordered something containing a foolish amount of whiskey. Once we each had a drink in hand, I raised my glass for a proper toast.

"To Sissy," I proclaimed.

"To sisterhood," Sissy corrected, giving us an innocent smile as the glasses clinked. Copper, Arnie, and I exchanged a look. This night was more about sisterhood than Sissy could ever know.

"Lucas and I," Copper began, failing to hide a smirk when using his new code name, "are going to go grab a few snacks. Which table did the doorman say we were at?" She looked at Sissy, knowing the girl would have ensured committing it to memory.

"Table eighteen," Sissy said without hesitation. "We'll meet you there in a few minutes."

"You two have fun," Copper said before leaning in to whisper, "But don't go too wild with the dancing. You rip the dress, that enchantment isn't worth a bag of hay." With a wink, the pair scurried off into the crowd. I took a moment to scan the nearby crowd, but I saw no sign of Haute.

"Cassandra Fairbanks?" came a shrill, overly enthusiastic voice from just a few people away. Sissy and I both spun around to locate the speaker as a buxom young lady approached us in an alluring but ostentatious red dress.

"Mimi Shilling," Sissy quickly whispered in my ear. "Went to charm school with you. Awful person." She had scarcely finished when Mimi reached us and leaned in to kiss me on Kissy's cheek.

"Mimi, it's been too long." I gave my best attempt to mimic Kissy's controlled, condescending tone, even remembering to purse my lips.

"Truly," Mimi responded with a wave of her adorned hand. "Sissy, congratulations on your debut," she declared in a voice one might use with an infant.

"Thank you, Mimi," Sissy responded cordially. "You look beautiful tonight."

"Thank you, dear. I swear, I spend half of my husband's take-home pay on these silly dresses." They both laughed insincerely. "I was so sorry to hear about your father's financial woes. Your dress is lovely, considering your budget."

"Thank you, Mimi," Sissy said with a small curtsy, maintaining her composure. "I will give your best to our father."

"Please do," Mimi said with grating emphasis as she draped her hand over her heart, hardly covering her cleavage. "I'll tell you, Kissy, I hardly recognized you. I remembered you being taller."

"Why, I had a similar problem," I declared, mimicking Mimi's hand gesture. "I hardly remembered you at all." The woman's performative smile fell for a moment before she recovered.

"We should be getting back to our group," I continued, not wanting to get any deeper into conversation. I gave her a quick kiss on the cheek. As I led Sissy away, I called back, "Don't be a stranger, Mini."

"Her name was Mimi," Sissy corrected, bringing a hand up to hide her smile.

"I know," I said, giving her a mischievous grin, and Sissy let out a snort in her attempt to stifle her laughter.

"That was a perfect Kissy impression," Sissy said after regaining her composure.

"You were right about these girls," I mused, thinking back to our conversations on the boat. "There are no mermaids here... They're more like sharks."

"Never enter the waters unarmed," Sissy said in partial jest as we arrived at table eighteen. Aside from the four name cards in front of the seats designated for our party, there were two other place settings, but they were currently vacant.

"So, Sissy," I began as I held out a chair for her, wanting to ease the difficulty of sitting in a crinoline, "what all do you do at these things?"

Sissy maneuvered her way into the seat with a grateful hand squeeze. "Well, you mingle, you drink, you sit, and you wait for someone to ask you to dance."

"What if no one asks you to dance?" I lowered myself into my own chair—the tightness of the dress around my legs and ankles made walking the greater challenge, not sitting.

"I don't really know," Sissy said as she shrugged, looking as if she'd never considered that possibility. "I guess then you drink more." We laughed and subsequently polished off our glasses of champagne. Before we could even consider returning to the bar for a refill, a server swept in with a bottle and topped them off. Another followed shortly after with an assortment of spiced cakes, of which I helped myself to three and Sissy one, saying she just wanted a bite. The song the band had been playing ended in a crescendo, and I joined the other guests in applauding them. As a handful of dancers returned to their tables, Sissy nearly choked on her champagne as she started frantically gesturing to the table now visible in through the parting crowd.

On a raised platform across the dance floor was a long, ornate table with a few unmistakable guests seated along it. Seated between the piles of cakes and towering candelabras was the Green Veil's royal family. On one end, I could clearly make out Princess Arabella, a stately looking woman in her late twenties. She had just leaned over to speak to her daughter, likely correcting her posture based on the young girl's reaction of sitting up straighter and dropping her elbow off the table. Princess Arabella's son, no older than five, sat on her other side and was throwing his food about while clapping and babbling. He received no criticism from his father, a handsome and bearded councilman whose name I could not recall, who had just signaled for a server to refill his wine glass. Everyone knew Arabella's face from her visage on postage stamps and advertisements—she'd been the royal family's poster child as long as I could remember. But she gave off a different energy in the flesh. She appeared colder and more coy than the welcoming, joyful images of her that we all saw.

"Just look at Abigail's gown," Sissy cooed with envy. "I would give anything to have an ounce of her grace." Seated beside her sharp sister, Princess Abigail was a breath of fresh air. She was the younger sister, only a few years older than me, and had the sort of glow to her skin that exuded health from every pore. The gown Sissy was ogling was a soft pink that looked to be the texture of a rose petal. It also gave off a soft, golden glow that infused a few inches of the air surrounding her. Her hair had the faintest pink undertone to complement its blonde base. A joyful toddler bounced on her lap, disregarding etiquette and ceremony altogether. Her young daughter was so beloved by the kingdom that soft baby dolls had been created in her likeness and were sold across the territories—a fitting tribute to the little girl named Dolley.

The two princes, Warren and Calvin, were much younger than their sisters and sat on the opposite end of the elegant table. I could see them whispering back and forth while gorging on the delicate cakes. Warren, a young teenager, pointed without subtlety at a pretty girl as she walked past, and Calvin nodded and grinned with him, but I suspected he may have been too young to fully appreciate his brother's remark. At the table's center, flanked by their four children, two sons-in-law, and three grandchildren, sat the king and queen. At first glance, they looked just like any other rich, middle-aged couple. Queen Eleanor had a pleasant smile, and her graying hair was pinned into a lovely updo with golden hair clips to match the thin crown that sat amongst her curls. King Andrew was a physically unimposing man, but he had a confident posture and a strong jaw. There was also something in his eyes that sent a chill down my spine, as if meeting his gaze were forbidden and dangerous. I could hardly imagine him bouncing a baby on his knee as Abigail did.

As I surveyed the king, two figures appeared at his side like chess pieces sliding in to defend him. For a moment, I figured they must be friends or council members since they interacted so casually with him, but as soon as I saw their uncanny resemblance to each other, I realized that these two must be the Mage twins, the Green Veil's only living high sorcerers. Dorthia held a smoking cocktail lazily in a gloved hand as she draped herself against the back of the king's chair. She laughed at something he said and touched his arm with her free hand, a gesture both familiar and oddly sensual. Her hair was as dark as my mother's, but she wore it freely, the long strands hanging down below the seam of her backless gown. Marcus, too, was smiling at whatever the king had said, but his amusement seemed a bit wilder and unchecked, reminding me of the sneers of trickster faeries from books of my childhood. He was excessively thin and spindly, and his movements were as jerky as a marionette puppet's. He looked like the sort of man I would find myself nervous to be left alone with.

I had become so transfixed by the royal family that I hardly noticed another song had come and gone, but I quickly joined in the applause of those around me when it ended. During the cheers, the band leader came over from his conducting stand and took a place at the microphone.

"Good evening, citizens of the Citadel, and a happy Yuletime to you all." He spoke the same way Bernard had gathered the attention of the guests at the caravan's festival. "Please join me in welcoming the musical stylings of your very own Cynthia Barden!" The crowd erupted in thunderous applause as a mature, statuesque redhead sauntered across the stage.

"I think we have her record at home," I said, trying to recall why that name sounded so familiar. Based on the crowd's fervor, she was certainly popular.

"You and everyone else," Sissy cried, clapping furiously as she surged to her feet. Once the cheers settled, Cynthia began to sing an upbeat love song with the band. For the first time since we had entered, the dance floor filled to capacity. As the sultry voice blanketed the great room, I finally placed the artist. My mother had played her records whenever she cooked. That same voice had carried through all the cozy chambers of our home.

"I love this song," Sissy said in delight, taking a long while to adjust her dress so she could sit back down beside me.

"My mother really liked her," I said, wanting to give Sissy something true about me but knowing it could not make up for the piles of lies I'd fed her.

"My mother doesn't like music very much," Sissy pouted. "She says it gives her a headache."

"But your sisters don't?" I meant it as a joke, but Sissy didn't laugh.

"No. They all get along well. They are so much alike." She glanced over at me with a half-smile. "I love my sisters, I really do. But it's just that, sometimes…" She trailed off quietly, and I could tell she wanted to share something serious, so I scooted over to lean in close.

"Do you ever get mad, Helen?" she asked, looking at me without breaking eye contact. "Like, properly, painfully, petrifyingly mad? But you can't say or do anything about it, and you just want to scream and pull your hair out or shove someone, but you can't do any of that either, so all you can do is go to some private place and cry? Cry those hot, angry tears that you can't tell anyone about?" Sissy's clear blue eyes grew shiny with emotion, but she took a few deep, slow breaths and dabbed under her bottom eyelashes to keep her makeup from getting ruined.

"Yes, Sissy, I do," I responded with equal seriousness. "I understand." Sissy nodded and bit her lip.

"I know they don't mean to be awful," Sissy continued. "They just don't know how to be anyone else based on who they interact with all the time." I set a hand on her knee. "I promise that I still love them," she whispered, speaking into her lap.

"I know you do," I said as I reached out to squeeze her hands. I knew what it was like to love someone despite every reason to hate them.

"People think that I'm dumb," Sissy went on, "I know they do, and maybe they're right."

"You are not—" I began.

"Let me finish," Sissy interrupted. Her tone was more determined than scolding. "Even if I am dumb, that doesn't mean that I miss everything. I didn't miss how Daschel and Gary got sick the morning after they harassed me, and I didn't miss how it always seemed to get worse after you, an herbalist, served them their meals."

"Sissy, I—" I tried, but she cut me off once more.

"Thank you, Helen." I looked at her in surprise. "I would have just retreated to some corner and cried angry tears, but you stepped up, you fixed the problem. I admire you so much for that. And I didn't think I would ever be capable of standing up for what I felt was fair… To be strong like you were. That is, until you showed me how."

A dreadful realization hit me then. "Sissy," I hissed, leaning ever closer, "did you poison your sisters?"

"Maybe a little," she admitted with a grimace.

"Sissy!"

"It wasn't supposed to last this long," she said as she twisted her hands in her lap. "It was the night we arrived at Uncle Rolph's. We went to try on dresses, and Kissy told me I looked like a poorly stuffed sausage. Missy agreed with her, as always, and then Kissy told me the heavy girls at school used to dose their tea with mandrake root to shed a few pounds quickly. I just wanted to give her a taste of her own medicine, but I must have given them too much." I shook my head in disbelief and started to say something stern, then recalled all the uragoga root I had ground into Daschel and Gary's food. I swallowed back my words and Sissy continued. "I was going to tell someone, but everyone assumed they got it on the boat, and then I was having the most wonderful time without them pecking at me every minute. I will tell them as soon as I get home tonight, though, I promise." She looked at me with shame-filled eyes.

"When you get home," I admonished, "make them a pot of peppermint tea—very strong peppermint tea. Add the juice of an entire lemon and a large pinch of shaved ginger. Once all the ingredients are mixed, whisper the word *leigheas* into the pot. Get them to drink every drop. They'll sleep for several hours, and when they wake up, they should be fine."

"Leihas?" Sissy repeated, and I nodded encouragingly.

"Close. Say the first part deeper, in the back of your throat, and soften the final vowel." She repeated the incantation a few times until I felt she had it down.

"Sissy, don't let anyone tell you who you are, ever." I held eye contact with her until she nodded. "And please don't poison any members of your family again."

"Never again," Sissy promised.

"Now go get yourself another drink," I said, smiling.

"But I haven't finished this one yet," she replied, giving me a small frown of confusion.

"No, but if you head that way, that boy who's been staring at you this whole conversation might just ask you to dance." I gave a nod toward the freckled boy who attempted, unsuccessfully, to avert his stare in time to go undetected by Sissy as she craned her neck around.

"Why, I think I'm feeling thirsty," Sissy announced, beaming at me as she gracefully rose from her chair.

"Go get him," I teased as she started to walk away.

"You know what?" She spun on her heel to face me. "This is a *great* night." With a small wave, she was then taken up by the current of milling guests. I chuckled as I returned to my spiced apple cake, tapping my foot to the schmaltzy ballad Cynthia had transitioned into. Out of the corner of my eye, I spotted the glamoured forms of Copper and Arnie hurrying to the table.

"Target located," Copper whispered with a heavy breath. "Second story balcony, six o'clock." She spoke like she was in one of her favorite murder mystery books. I looked back over my shoulder and up toward the open second-story walkway. A gaunt man stood in a white suit, surveying the party like the king he worked for.

Chapter Twenty-Two: The Witch's Confidant

Haute Brood had certainly dressed for the occasion. He sported an impeccable suit that had a matching white cape, plus gold rings that complemented the chain hanging from his glasses. He watched the graceful young dancers as they swayed to Cynthia Barden's music; he watched with such concentration that he hardly seemed to notice us as we walked hesitantly up behind him.

"Excuse me, sir?" I asked, my voice catching in my throat a little from nervousness.

"May I help you?" he asked as he peered over his shoulder, looking unperturbed. He must have somehow known we'd been walking up to him already.

"Yes, you said you could," Copper began as she stepped closer to the poised man. He looked her over, squinting through his pointed glasses.

"Who is it under there?" he asked, eyes narrowing. I recalled him scanning papers looking for forgeries. Clearly, his powers of perception could not be thwarted with a few simple glamours.

"We spoke yesterday," I interjected, wanting to cut to the point, "about the sisterhood." Haute's eyes grew wide with concern. He reached out to clutch my arm with the speed of a snake's strike and spun us toward a set of double doors without another word. I felt like a petulant child being dragged to their room. There was a small pause as he waved his hand over the door handle in front of us, and I heard a soft click. Without a second glance, he pulled us all into the room.

As the doors shut behind us, we found ourselves alone in a dimly lit exhibit room, the walls bare and pedestals empty.

"Are you out of your minds?" he hissed, still holding my arm. "What are you doing here?"

"We're here to see you," I retorted as I yanked my arm free. "You told us to meet you here tonight." I was baffled by Haute's outrage.

"I most certainly did not," he burst out, eyebrows scrunching together in equal bafflement.

"Yes, you did," Copper chimed in. "It was in the code."

Haute rolled his eyes and buried his head in his gloved hands. "The *code*, as you call it, clearly stated that you should meet me at the fishing dock on Lake Abraham tomorrow." My bewilderment spiked. "I told you that I spend the holiday break fishing. Do I look like a man who catches his own fish?" He gestured at his immaculate ensemble. Copper, Arnie, and I exchanged embarrassed glances as he pressed on. "So to clarify, you thought I was telling you to break into the most exclusive event of the year to share *state* secrets in a *state* building swarming with *state* officials?" He crossed his arms, glaring at the three of us.

When Haute put it that way, I felt exceedingly dull for misinterpreting the message. A lakeside would have been a far better location for a private conversation.

"Are we safe in here?" Arnie asked suddenly. "Is anyone *listening*?" He mouthed the final word as he gestured around the room.

"Always," Haute snapped, looking beyond exacerbated. "However, luckily for you fools, I helped design the museum security. There is no active surveillance in unused exhibit rooms." He strode over to the closed door and removed a set of keys with a flourish. "And I still have a key for this one." He turned the key, and a deadbolt clanked into place, signaling some sense of safety.

I cleared my throat. "All humiliations aside," I said, swallowing my stinging pride, "we're here now, and I'm really hoping it was worth the risk." I looked him in the eyes with as much earnestness and pleading as I could muster.

"You shouldn't be," Haute huffed, looking too angry to satisfy my request as he dropped a few rune-carved stones along the bottom of the door. I remembered enough from my enchantment class to know these were sound muffling runes. "The people out there are not your friends, and should they discover your true intentions of being here tonight, even I will be unable to shield you from the consequences."

"What consequences?" I asked, frustration rising. "We've been chasing rumors and whispers for weeks without one solid answer. What is so taboo about asking a question? What was my mother involved in?" I stepped toward Haute, determined to get something out of this interaction.

"You have a chance to leave this all be," he said, not answering me directly. "All you have to do is go home—go back to your lives." His expression softened as he gave me a more compassionate look. "This isn't your burden."

I hesitated, considering the easy out. Could I do that? Could I hop on the first train home and take the unanswered questions with me? Irenee would understand. If she knew how many people had warned me to turn back, and the dangers we'd brushed against, she'd drag me home kicking. Rae would return eventually, and our lives would go on as they were always meant to—in blissful simplicity. It could all end here.

But it didn't, because Arnie spoke up.

"Maude Birch." He presented her name like a master card player laying his hand on the table. Haute's head snapped to look at Arnie, who stood defiantly with his arms crossed. "She was her mother." He nodded toward me.

"Maude?" Haute exhaled the name, staring at me as his eyes filled with melancholy. "Maude Birch? I haven't…" He ran a hand across his sharp jaw and released a deep sigh of surrender. "You all should sit down."

He motioned to a wooden bench intended for those who wanted to take a good, long look at whatever paintings had once hung in this room. We did as they were told, arranging ourselves in a line and gazing up at him like expectant school children.

"You… knew her?" I asked, uncertain of Haute's role in my mother's story.

"Oh yes," he said, nodding several times. "Your mother was one of the best friends I ever had."

"I don't remember meeting you." I was certain I would have remembered Haute if he had sat in one of his brilliant suits in my drawing room.

"I never came to visit your home. In truth, Maude and I only met face-to-face once. At a party not unlike this one. Baldwin was receiving his new title, and there was a formal reception honoring him in the Capitol building. Well, not just him, but all the newly appointed department chairs. With Baldwin's charisma and Maude's grace, they were hard to miss." He paused and rubbed the back of his neck self-consciously. "I don't really fit in with the men at these events," he confessed. "I can only discuss automobiles and market prices for so long.

So I found myself falling into conversation with your mother. We seemed to be two cuts from the same cloth."

"That was the only time you two spoke in person?" I asked, logging away mental notes with as much detail as possible, unsure what would be important.

"It was," Haute confirmed, "But it was only the beginning of our friendship. After that, we wrote to one another. In the beginning, we exchanged little more than casual gossip and amusing anecdotes, but as the months went on, we became each other's confidants. The purest type of friendship is one where you have nothing to gain from it. As I revealed more about my private life, it became prudent to mask certain passages of our letters. It's no secret that our government has a fondness for rooting through the mail. I should know—it's half of my job description. So I began cloaking my letters with an inference charm." Noting our lack of reaction to the term, he explained, "It's a fairly complex practice of empathy." "If you know the reader well, you can focus an intention on your writing that transcends its actual meaning."

We blinked up at him. Even Arnie seemed uncertain what kind of spell he was talking about. Seeing that his phrasing did nothing to improve our comprehension, he sighed and said, "It's like writing in code, but the key is already in your reader's head. It's personal, which makes it unbreakable. It is also one of the most complex forms of empathy—you're essentially planting thoughts in someone else's head with nothing more than paper and ink. So, when Maude replied with an inference charm of her own, executed flawlessly, I knew she was not an average housewife."

"She was a high sorcerer," I blurted, wanting to speed the story along. "I already knew that, and it sounds like you did you too." Haute nodded soberly. "What *is* the Sisterhood?" I asked, my hands gripping my knees tightly.

"It's an organization like any other," Haute explained with a shrug. "It has leaders, members, and a mission statement."

"What's the mission?" Copper prodded, now on the edge of her seat. He took a deep breath before answering.

"To free the women of the Green Veil." The familiar words rang in my ears.

"That's what Lacey said," I mumbled, feeling transfixed on Haute's face. I could almost feel the intensity bouncing off the walls of the small room.

"You were the ones involved with Lacey Neddles about two weeks ago?" Haute clarified.

"Do you know what happened to her?" Copper gasped, almost in agony.

"Mrs. Neddles was taken in for questioning on charges related to an illegal bootlegging operation in Facehaven, or at least, that's what her public arrest record says. No one has seen or heard from her since." Haute removed his delicate glasses and cleaned them with a small piece of silk that he pulled from his pocket.

"What does that even mean?" Arnie huffed. "Brewing alcohol is legal in all nine territories."

"Not without a permit," Haute pointed out. "But that doesn't matter. It's a trumped-up charge. They can't charge her for being a member of the Sisterhood because that isn't illegal."

"Try telling that to the watchmen," Copper growled.

"It is perfectly legal under the constitution of the Green Veil to assemble, to speak your mind, and even to openly object to any and all laws. So, how would it look if some sweet older mother got locked up for exercising her constitutional rights?" Haute's eyes darted between each of us, making sure what he was saying was getting through. "They won't charge you with conspiracy or treason—they'll charge you with performing unlicensed magics or identity theft or bootlegging. Anything that will put you away without raising eyebrows or questions."

"Like illegal conjuring?" I asked, staring hard at nothing on the ground.

"Yes, exactly," Haute said, his voice growing gentler. "And once they've got you, they will throw you in a hole in the ground, seal it up tight, and then throw away the hole."

"How come this kind of stuff isn't getting reported? Why aren't we hearing about it?" I wanted to believe him, but my sense of logic was scraping against it. "If people were being detained for exercising their rights, wouldn't there be *some* rumblings out there? This isn't a nation of sheep."

"There are rumblings all over the place," Haute confirmed with pursed lips. "Student organizations, city organizers—people have noticed the pattern. But the territories are so spread out and disconnected that the movements can never travel far enough to unite and gain traction."

"And the Green Veil's main newspaper, *The National Observer…*" Copper said slowly, wheels turning in her head. "And also the national radio waves…" she trailed off, comprehension dawning on her face.

"Yes," Haute nodded, looking a little relieved that we were finally piecing things together. "They are both funded and run by the royal family."

"So nothing is going to be published or broadcast that would show them in a negative light," I said, catching up. Arnie gave a low whistle.

"But what is so harmful about this sisterhood? What does 'free the women of the Green Veil' mean?" I asked, still clinging to a hope that things couldn't be that bad.

"Look around you!" Haute erupted, swinging his hand toward the door. "Think about that meaningless display in the lobby—young girls are waltzing around in corsets, stilettos, and enchanted finery, being passed around for inspection like cuts of meat at a market. Take a walk through any academy of higher education—the men outnumber the women ten to one. Or, better yet, take another stroll around the Capitol building. The only women you're going to find are the secretaries of men like me, who sit behind their thick mahogany doors with their heads in the sand. We slam doors in the faces of every young girl in the kingdom and then thank them for a sacrifice we were never asked to make. The illusion of equality has been so skillfully applied that I have to stand here and explain it to two young witches who have been manipulated by it all their lives."

Copper and I glanced at each other with wide eyes; I wasn't sure who was more shocked.

Haute paused for a beat and then came to sit next to us on the bench. He made pointed eye contact with us two girls before saying, in a steadier voice, "They put a toy dust-pail in your hands as infants and bet on you to never ask for more. And if you do, you're punished for it. Sure, they'll give you permission to make your best attempt at an education, but you'll have to resign yourself to a loveless and companionless life. Make no mistake—it isn't a choice. It's an effective deterrent and masterful solution to weeding rebellion from the gene pool." He exhaled slowly and gathered himself again. "I understand the irony here—a man is sitting you ladies down to explain how your voices have been rendered obsolete. But, please understand that I am speaking as the product of four decades in government service and two in the service of women like your mother. There are countless women who looked at the unsolvable maze of their lives and demanded a new path. The repression isn't a side effect of some law passed with the best of intentions. It is a deliberate plot to diminish and disenfranchise witches from making any impact on the Green Veil or its people."

My head was reeling. Irenee had expressed similar views to me on occasion, though a bit watered down. I had always taken them as the embellished ramblings of a woman who had been dealt a bad hand in life. But if Haute was correct, and that hand had been dealt to every woman of the Green Veil, it wasn't a matter of luck. The deck itself was rigged. The thought could not find a place to settle within my mind. I had always believed myself to be the master of my own destiny, or at the very least the narrator of my own story, but the notion of an institutional puppet game shattered everything.

"But, why?" Arnie rasped, leaning forward to look at Haute, who sat on the other side of us. "What's the point?"

"I wish I had that answer," Haute said, sounding apologetic. "I have been seeking it out for twenty years, but with no success." As he spoke, he rose back up and began pacing in front of a wall with dust lines that indicated it had boasted several large plaques. "What I do know is that power is the most valuable thing in the Green Veil, and the men within it don't seem interested in sharing. The closer we get to the true answers, more of us disappear."

"How have you remained undetected this long if you're so closely involved?" I questioned, leaning forward to rest my arms on my knees.

"In the Department of Transparency, my job is split equally between bringing certain truths to light and making sure others stay in the dark. I'm very good at what I do." He spoke matter-of-factly, but his expression was haunted.

"My mother…" I said, beginning the question I had been dreading ever since Irenee had first sat me down. "What happened to her?"

"She was betrayed," Haute whispered, shaking his head. "Revealed as a high sorcerer to someone within the government. They don't want girls going to school, let alone achieving the greatest feat in the magical world, and most certainly not when she is a suspected member of a society of revolution-aries. I saw the warrant for her arrest as soon as it was drafted. *Illegal conjuring*."

Haute scoffed. "They would have never aimed so high if they were not intending to enact the death penalty. I knew her only option was to flee. There is a community of women deep in the Thor-ough Woods, run by widows who wish to master their magics away from the prying eyes of men. They live just beyond the border of the Green Veil. It's the only sanctuary women like your mother have. We made arrangements with our only other member in the Orchard to be a checkpoint for her.

Transportation spells are fairly easy to track, so we crafted an exit strategy that prevented that. Instead of directing the spell to the sanctuary, she transported herself to another nearby home and left from there. The witch in that home cast a powerful cloaking charm over your mother's landing point, which provided the cover she needed to fully escape the area undetected. I know she made it to the checkpoint, but that is all I know. There is no way to communicate with the women beyond the border because they take their security very seriously."

"So she's alive?" I said, my voice higher than normal. My heart was racing in my chest. "She made it out?" Haute gave me a small nod.

"To the best of my knowledge, yes." He spoke with trepidation, but the words still soothed my fears in a way that I hadn't known I needed.

"How do I get there?" I asked, compelled to reach the end of this. Unexpected tears welled up in my eyes, and I fidgeted with the hands that didn't look quite like mine.

"There's a house off the banks of Crescent Lake," Haute began, giving his instructions methodically. "On the southeast corner of the lake, below a lone pine tree. There is a witch there who could escort you if you choose to go. If you do, you will need one of these." He reached inside his cape and presented a silk coin purse. He opened the pouch with a small pop and dumped the contents into his hand. A few silver coins shone in the dim light. Haute offered one to me, and I turned it over in my palm, examining it.

"It's warm," I remarked as I tried to read the small inscription.

"They heat up in the presence of another coin," Haute explained. "It's how we identify ourselves without speaking." I finally was able to get enough light on the coin to read the small inscription.

"Sow?" I read aloud. "Like in a garden?"

"No," Haute corrected, "S-O-W. The Sisterhood of Whispers."

"I have another question," Copper interrupted. "Why help?" She looked confused and still a little suspicious. "If you aren't affected by this plot, why get involved at all?" Arnie's gaze darted nervously from his sister to Haute and back, bothered for once by the directness.

Haute gave her a pained smile, not looking offended. "Suffice to say, I know what it is like to live with limitations and shame. And to be rejected by my society for the regretful accident of my birth, with no way of altering the simple truth of my identity."

I stared at him, befuddled. I looked at Copper and Arnie, who both looked as confused as me.

Arnie started, taking on our mutual question. "I don't see what's so wrong with you."

Haute gave a wry chuckle. "Thank you. I'm glad to know that I've improved my ability to mask my *abnormality*." I scanned him again, but I still could not make out what he was referring to. "I'm embarrassed to say that getting involved wasn't even my idea. When you are born like me, the best defense is to fly under the radar. It was Philip who talked me into it." He savored the name like a precious fruit. "He said that I needed to use my position for good, and he was right. I had a debt to pay. My work had sent enough revolutionaries to prison—or worse. My Philip was right about most things."

"You loved him," I said, putting the pieces together with a click. There was something new in Haute's eyes in that moment. Was it gratitude?

"Yes, I loved him," he said. The words carried more weight than I had ever experienced in my life.

"You're…" Arnie began, but then trailed off, not knowing the appropriate word to use.

"Queer?" Haute finished for him. The word hung like a foul odor in the room. "It's a distasteful word, but we never set about picking a new one. I suppose the naming rights for my community fell to those who despise us."

Couples of the same gender weren't a mystery to me. I'd heard the concept whispered about in rumors and gossip throughout my childhood. But queer folk had only ever been the butt of the joke, like the boogeyman in the closet or a thinly veiled warning of having gone "astray."

As far as I knew, I had never met a queer person, but the idea of two men together had never seemed sinister to me. There was something arresting about meeting a type of person that you have only ever heard nefarious things about. Haute wasn't alien or wayward—he was just a man who loved.

"Where's Philip now?" I asked.

"He was arrested for trespassing six years ago," Haute said, his voice suddenly filled with a combination of rage and hollowness. "They never told me where." He took in a ragged breath, his lip quivering ever so slightly. "I never saw him again." A hearty tear rolled down his weathered cheek, and he swiftly wiped it away. "No one should have to choose between love and life. It is inhuman."

"I'm so sorry," Arnie breathed. "That's… That's awful." We sat in silence for a moment, collectively processing an invisible world of heartbreak and shame that had just been made visible to us.

"Did my mother know?" The question came out of me almost compulsively.

"Did she ever," Haute said, bringing a smile to his lips. "Maude was one of a small handful of people in the world whom I could talk to openly about him. She knew when his snoring was at its worst, and when we were at our best. I wrote to her about Philip constantly. The two of them would even ask after each other like old pals, even though they had never met. Your mother had a tremendous capacity for love."

I snorted at this. "My mother?"

"You don't need to be soft and maternal to be loving," Haute responded, his tone warm but reprimanding. "I'm sure you saw the side of her that I did."

Sarcasm aside, I thought back—I did remember that Maude. I remembered the back scratches, the hair smoothing, the sleeping in my twin bed to ward off nightmares. I was coming to understand that Maude was never just one thing. She was as intricate and intangible as a spiderweb.

"You said there was another member of the Sisterhood in the Orchard," I said, the words coming back to me suddenly. "The one who helped to conceal her transportation spell. Would they know if she made it to the sanctuary?" Hope swelled in my chest.

"I suppose Ruth would have known Maude's destination—" Haute began, but stopped abruptly as the Penning siblings viscerally reacted to the familiar name.

"Did you say Ruth?" Arnie said as he jumped to his feet, eyes wide and expectant.

"She's our other member in the Orchard," Haute said in confusion, glancing back and forth between us. "Or at least she was until—"

"She died two years ago?" Copper interrupted, her expression shifting to one of world-shattering dread. I could do nothing but watch as Haute nodded, still lost. And then I saw the wave of realization wash over him.

"Arnold and Copper? I should have known by your hair…" he breathed, the words heavy. They did not have to respond. The horrible truth filled the room like poisonous gas.

"Mrs. Penning was in the Sisterhood?" I asked, stunned.

"She was," Haute affirmed, "until her untimely demise." His gaze dropped to the floor.

"There is no way—" Arnie began to object, but Copper cut him off.

"Now just hold on," she said, waving her hands as if she could slow all this down. She stood with he brother to gape at Haute. "Are you saying her death may have been related to all of… *this*?" The words struggled to leave her mouth as if her own lips had forgotten how to work properly.

"I think it is possible," Haute replied cautiously.

"How?" Copper boiled over, "How would you know that?!" I could see that the only thing keeping her from tears was her bewilderment.

"There was a member of the Sisterhood in a small coastal town—Madame Chantilly. I was told your mother met with her on the same trip where it was suspected that she had contracted her sleeping sickness," Haute said, making a point to remain clear and calm as the two grew visibly more upset.

"And?" Arnie challenged, the two of them standing side-by-side.

"And…" Haute continued, "Chantilly was later revealed to be a government informant." A dull thud sounded as Arnie kicked the bench we had previously been sitting on. Copper covered her mouth with her hand and shook her head, still teetering between anger and despair. I racked my brain for some comforting words to say or things to do, but all I could think of was the tiny, sweet woman who had given me more motherly affection than anyone after Maude left. No words came.

"I don't know what force brought you three together," Haute said, cutting through the palpable agony, "but somehow the children of the only two Sisterhood members of the Orchard have become united. And then you found me, and you found answers. Now it is up to you to decide what to do with them." Haute outstretched his palm to the Pennings, in which he still held two coins.

Copper looked to her brother, who only then stopped pacing in a small circle. Arnie looked at me, blinking away tears as if that could hide them. In that moment, a lifetime of friendship flooded the space between us. In his eyes was both the man he had come to be and the boy I had always known. He looked at me with desperation, bereavement, and absolute trust—a trust that was sealed from our past and current friendship. He shut his eyes for a brief moment, and when he reopened them, he turned his gaze to his sister. He offered her a small yet confident nod, and they reached for the coins.

"I am sorry to have brought you this pain," Haute murmured as he looked at our shattered group. "Your mothers were brave, exceptional women, and I am proud to have worked beside them. What they were forced to endure was unimaginable and reprehensible. And, while I do not relish being the bearer of any more ill news, Hildegarde…" He paused to meet my gaze. "There is something you need to know. One more injustice to be repaid."

I looked at him, petrified by the idea of one more horrible truth. As if delivering some ancient prophecy, Haute closed his eyes before saying. "Your father, Baldwin, did not go searching for Maude to bring her home safely. He wanted to be the one to bring her in." My brow furrowed with disorientation. "Your father was the one who reported Maude to the authorities."

My ears burned hot, and I could taste the beads of sweat forming on my upper lip. I watched as the room darkened and fell out of focus, but I couldn't hear a thing—not the words of shock from my friends or the apology from Haute. In that dark, blurry, silent void, I doubled over and vomited the contents of my stomach. But the gnawing, painful truth in my stomach was not relieved. My reality—past, present, and future—was little more than a house of cards stacked by the hands of male strangers.

Chapter Twenty-Three: The Witch's Retreat

Before Haute could object, Copper ran out of the room to fetch a glass of seltzer for me from the bar. No one spoke after she left. Haute found a seat across the room where he sat and stared down at his polished shoes. Arnie sat beside me, moving a comforting hand in circles on the bare skin of my back. I felt foolish, receiving the pity of a friend who had just learned of the possibility of his mother's murder. I knew I should be the one stroking his back and cooing words of condolence in his ear, but I could not bring myself to move or even speak.

My father, Baldwin Birch, had remained an unmarred memory in my mind throughout this adventure. Even after Irenee's story, I had been unable to rationalize my father as any kind of villain. Maybe he had been misguided in a few of his actions, but who in this world could be called innocent of that? He had wanted a family and had believed Maude to have shared in that want. I had truly believed that he only ever wanted to protect her, to protect me. But what kind of protection was it to rob an eight-year-old girl of her mother? What kind of love was it to accuse your own wife of a crime punishable by death?

The week following Maude's disappearance was frozen in perfect condition in my memory; it was sealed away in what felt like a time capsule, as it seemed moments of great misery often are. Baldwin had been shattered by the news. I could never forget the image of him throwing a vase of flowers against a wall, an act of aggression that had seemed frighteningly at odds with his naturally soothing demeanor, especially to one so young. When he had left to search for Maude, he'd clutched me in a tight, constricting hug, whispered "I'll be back for my best girl," kissed me on the forehead, and had left.

Irenee had been the one to sit me down to tell me that my father, my safe harbor in a storm, was never coming back. I cried for five days, utterly confounded as to how I could have gone from the daughter of two parents to an orphan in a single week. Irenee and Maxx moved in to take care of me, Raemond and Arnie came by to try and cheer me up, teachers excused me from classes and wrote notes of condolence, but even with the showering of love and support, a small light inside me had been snuffed out, unable to burn again. And now here, at this moment, another spark within me had just been extinguished.

"Did anyone ever find out why?" I spoke at last, my eyes somehow feeling too heavy to look over at Haute. "Anyone in the Sisterhood?"

"No," Haute sighed. "Nothing concrete, though I do have my suspicions." His gaze turned thoughtful as he clasped his hands under his chin.

"Care to share with the group?" I snapped, anger flaring in me unexpectedly.

"Hildegarde, I didn't know Baldwin well," Haute began, looking unfazed by my tone. "All I knew of him came from your mother's and Ruth's reporting—he was prideful and ambitious. Those are traits that can serve a diviner well in their career. That is, of course, when you see success in your future. Unfortunately for Baldwin, a few years before your mother's disappearance, he reached a plateau. I was told that when he looked into his own future, he saw that he would never rise from his current station, instead slowly settling into mediocrity. And there your mother was, only beginning to stretch her muscles and already more powerful than he would ever be.

"According to your mother, he tried to mask his resentment with drinking and smiles, but in private moments when intoxicated, he made his true feelings perfectly clear. He wanted her to stop attempting to learn higher tiers. He wanted her to be a wife and mother, nothing more. That wasn't a role Maude was willing to play, and I believe he punished her for it."

The girdle was making it difficult for me to take deep, calming breaths. Arnie piped up instead, his voice filled with disbelief. "But she was his wife. He wouldn't have turned her in out of something as small as jealousy... Would he?"

Haute leaned forward and clicked his tongue in a scolding manner. "Jealousy wasn't the nail in the coffin. It was something far more potent—humiliation." Arnie gave a small "oh" of understanding, and Haute continued, "The humiliation of a proud man can start wars. It's certainly enough to write a damning letter."

At that moment, Missy aka Copper returned empty-handed, sliding through a crack in the door as if she were trying to keep a house cat from darting out.

"How were you not able to get a seltzer?" Arnie asked, motioning to her seltzer-less hands in exasperation. She ignored him and looked at me.

I saw that her face was flushed, and she was breathing heavily, as if she had sprinted up the stairs. "There's something that you *need* to see." I stood, sensing the urgency, and nearly stumbled in the leg-restricting dress, but Arnie caught my elbow as he also stood.

"I will give you all a slight head start." Haute motioned toward the door. "It's best if we aren't seen leaving together. Nor do I think it wise for us to have any further contact in the near future." He stood, smoothed the creases in his dress pants, then tugged at the corners of his jacket. "If you should ever require my assistance, send a letter directly to the mailroom of the Capitol building and address it to 'Finch Geheim.' And make sure the cloaking spell on it is absolutely foolproof."

I felt a sudden rush of gratitude to the man, realizing that this conversation had been a great risk to his personal safety. "Haute, I'm sorry to have asked so much of you tonight. Thank you for speaking to us." Arnie and Copper nodded in quiet agreement.

"You are members of the Sisterhood now," he replied. "My door is open to you if you ever should wish to use it." He gave us a soft smile, then gestured at the door. "Leave the Citadel as quickly as you can, and do not stop moving until you reach Crescent Lake. Trust no one but each other. In fact, don't fully trust each other, either…" He hesitated, then said, "Just be careful." We all nodded. "Now go." Copper pulled at my hand, guiding me back through the door.

I was grateful to be rid of the scent of my vomit as we slipped back onto the open balcony. The room had fallen ominously silent, though everyone seemed focused on the stage and didn't notice our appearance. Cynthia no longer stood on stage, and the band sat still, their instruments resting; the dancers had all returned to their seats. Everyone was listening closely to the stately, uniformed man speaking into the microphone. I focused on his words, picking up what I guessed was the middle of his speech.

"…now more than ever, our people can enjoy the dignity of a life without fear," the man boomed. "Our children can sleep soundly in their beds without the carnage of war intruding into their innocent dreams. This great land has seen the return of growth and development in our economy. And most importantly, our families are whole and stable once more, raising the future of the Green Veil in peace and prosperity. None of this would be possible without the sacrifice of the brave young men who protect our borders, guard our territories, and enforce law and order in our towns." A smattering of polite applause circulated. "That is why our king has chosen to show his gratitude to these noble young men on this Yule's Eve. This evening, we honor the sacrifice of our youth by honoring the youngest among them. Ladies and gentlemen, it is my honor to present the top-ranking recruits of Camp Valiant!"

The man stepped to the side and held out an arm to acknowledge the line of young soldiers that were filing onto the stage. The crowd showered them with generous applause until the last recruit took his place in line. The familiar, tall figure was dressed in a formal, deep green uniform and looked more dashing than ever—it was Rae.

Copper gave a muffled squeal in my ear. "I told you you'd want to see this!" I gaped from our view on high as the decorated officer read their names in alphabetical order. His lovely black curls had been cut down to the same neat, short style as that of the other boys in the line. He looked stronger, the angles of his jaw and cheekbones more pronounced than before, and his shoulders somehow seemed broader, but maybe that was just an illusion of the uniform. His face mimicked the stern nobility of his fellow soldiers, but there was a slight twitch of a smile at the corner of his mouth when his name was finally called. He walked forward in smart strides to receive a golden pin on his lapel. I practically melted where I stood. In that glimpse of a smirk, for a fleeting moment, I was not a revolutionary or a criminal, my mother was not in exile, and my father had betrayed no one. For just a breath, I was a girl in love with a boy, and my heart swelled with pride for him.

"Now we would like to honor the servicemen among us tonight." With all the pins distributed and names announced, the man at the microphone moved the ceremony along. "If you are currently, or have ever, served in the Green Veil military, we invite you to now stand and be acknowledged." A smattering of men rose from their seats as the crowd erupted in unsparing applause. I couldn't take my eyes from Raemond, who now clapped for his brothers in arms.

"Guys," Arnie hissed, "we need to go." He hooked his arm in mine to pull us away, but I resisted, staring at him in outrage.

"Rae is here! How can we just sneak away now, with him having absolutely no clue what's going on? We're engaged!"

"You seemed pretty hesitant to let him in on everything when we were on the Rambler," Copper pointed out. Missy's yellow curls shifted around her shoulders as she tilted her head at me.

"Things were different then," I insisted. "I was nervous and not sure what to tell him. Heck, I'm *still* not sure. But now he's here in the room, and I can't just walk away." My fears and concerns had fallen away at the sight of Raemond; all that was left was a burning need to be held by him.

"I didn't mean to hit a nerve—" Copper began, but Arnie cut her off.

"It's the watchman from the caravan," he whispered in a strangled voice. "He's here, and he just looked up at us." We froze and both followed his gaze into the crowd. An immediate chill ran down my spine when I spotted him—Lieutenant Beauregarde Mason. He was seated at the first table, close to the stage. I had barely laid eyes on him that night at the caravan, but his too-sharp features and oily black hair were unmistakable. Clearly off the clock, he wore a tailored suit and had his arm draped around a small blonde seated beside him.

"We have to leave *now*," Arnie pleaded, his eyes ablaze with anxiety.

"Let's just hold on a second," Copper countered, putting a hand on his arm. "Remember that we're wearing glamours, and they aren't actively looking for us here. This could be the last chance Hildy gets to see Rae in who knows how long."

"Did you listen to a thing Haute said in there?" Arnie growled, straining to regulate his volume. "It isn't worth the risk."

I closed my eyes and whispered, "Arnie's right." It hurt coming out, but I knew it was the truth. "Rae isn't involved, but the moment we speak to him, he is. We should go." My resolve did nothing to ease my pain, and I clenched my fists to stay focused.

"Are you sure, Hildy?" Copper asked, resisting Arnie's tugs as she looked at me. "It's Raemond." I looked back at the stage where the boys were now exiting into the wings.

"I'll see him again," I said, not really responding to her and more promising myself as he disappeared into the curtains. She gave my arm a small squeeze. Wordlessly, we turned to walk down the marble stairs, going as fast as we dared without attracting undue attention. I went straight to table eighteen where Sissy sat, having been returned by her dance partner. A flutter of relief lit up her face.

"There you are," she cried, a hint of annoyance in her tone, though her face showed only a smile. "I thought I'd all but lost you three." I took Sissy by surprise and enfolded her into a tight embrace. "Oh, goodness," she giggled, "is everything all right?"

"Thank you for everything you've done for us tonight," I said into her ear, not releasing her. "It meant more than you'll ever know." I slithered out of the hug to look Sissy in the eye. "We have to go now. Please have a wonderful evening, and a beautiful life." I spoke with the certainty that I would never see my new friend again, and she blinked back at me with pursed lips.

"What? But I—" She was still stumbling over her question by the time we'd gotten out of earshot. A few strides later, a crowd of forest green filled the dance floor. Raemond and his fellow recruits were reentering the room, now as guests. He stood only tables away, wearing a heart-melting grin as he shook the hand of an older gentleman who had stood to greet him. Now, much closer, I could catch all the changed details in Rae. His skin glowed with the memory of days spent under a warm sun, and a faint beard shadowed his jawline more visibly. He could have been the poster boy for a young, eager soldier if it had not been for the resilient twinkle of mischief still present in his eyes. I knew if I did not leave that instant, if I allowed myself to advance even a foot closer to the boy who carried my soul in his pocket, I would not have the strength to walk away. I directed all my willpower toward the exit and turned away.

A dry ripping sound came from the hem of my dress as a passing escort stepped on my train, tearing the fabric. Before I could even register what had happened, Arnie wrapped his arm around me, gripping my shoulder tightly.

"Put your head against my chest," he whispered into my ear while holding me firmly against his body, obscuring my face with his hand. I could hear the frantic thud of his heart as I obediently buried my head in his chest. It hit me then—my glamour had been stitched into the fabric of the dress by Copper's capable hands, and judging by Arnie's swift reaction, those runes had not survived the rip. We continued at a hasty but awkward pace until we reached the open doorway, Arnie trying to act as if he were comforting me, until we stumbled outside.

"You folks get home safe," called the front doorman as we passed his post.

"We will," I heard Copper answer in a forced, cheery tone. We swept past him, and I felt the crisp, open air of the street on my skin.

"Can we afford a taxicab?" Arnie asked in a hushed voice, only slightly loosening his grip around my shoulders. From under his elbow, I could see a few well-dressed boys huddled together not far from us, passing around what may have been a cigarette.

"We're going to have to," I mumbled into Arnie's shoulder. I could just make out a queue of parked cabs lining the street beyond the gates, waiting to shuttle the intoxicated, danced-out partygoers to their homes.

"Any of you kids got a light?" I heard a man call out to us from the shadow of the front gates. His gruff voice brought up my memory of his face immediately—it was Dex, the partner of Beauregarde Mason, and he was now walking right to us. All at once, Arnie took my face in both of his hands and brought his lips to mine with such force that I could feel the pressure of his teeth against my own. My face burned hot with an array of shock, embarrassment, and the natural rush that came with having any decently attractive man's breath hot against my face. I would have shoved him away, but his kiss and hands were the only thing between my true face and detection, not to mention Arnie's own minimal glamour. Over the intimate sounds of breathing that I was currently sharing with Arnie, I could hear Copper address Dex from the safety of her glamoured form.

"No, sorry," she said in a good imitation of Sissy's squeaky voice. "But it looks like those boys over there might." I could only guess that she was pointing to the huddled smokers near the entrance.

Arnie held the kiss while the whiskey-drenched smell of Dex wafted past us, and from our entwinement, I heard his suggestive chuckle at the spectacle. "Enjoy it while it lasts," he slurred. "When they get older, alcohol just makes 'em mean." I heard his heavy footsteps thump away through the snow, over to the group of boys.

"All clear," Copper prompted after what felt like an incredibly excessive waiting time. I recoiled from Arnie's embrace and shot him a look of disbelief.

"Was there no other way you could do that?" I demanded.

"I don't know," Arnie shot back, shrugging. "It's not like I had time to think about options."

I huffed and started for the nearest cab. "I'm practically a married woman, for heaven's sake," I grumbled as I whipped open the passenger door. Copper laughed as she hopped in on the other side, sounding much closer to her usual joyful self since meeting with Haute.

"Madame Margot's… please," I said, catching myself as I accidentally snapped at the driver.

Arnie slid into the front without a word. "I've always wanted a sister," Copper prodded from beside me in the backseat. All I could muster was a glare. I was in no mood to be teased about my fidelity, especially since I had just fled from the sight of my fiancé.

We didn't dare speak about the night's events at any point on our journey back to the room. We sat through the cab ride in perfect silence, the staticky music of Yuletime carols ringing out from the antique radio. We crossed quietly through the hotel lobby, blending in seamlessly with the tipsy debutantes who were arriving at about the same time. However, the moment the latch on our room door clicked, we erupted into a frenzy of activity. Without any discussion, we busied ourselves with packing. Articles of clothing, shoes, and toiletries flew about the room as we stuffed our bags full, abandoning any sense of organization.

"Hildy," Copper called as she shoved her floral coat down into her duffle, "is the book safe?" Having had the same thought in that moment, I dropped to the ground to retrieve the shoulder bag from its hiding place beneath the bed. A great sense of relief washed over me as I felt the cool leather against my hand, and an even greater wave followed as I felt the familiar shape and weight of its concealed cargo.

"All good," I reported with a sigh, dropping the bag onto the cushioned mattress. After all that we had been through, and the urgency we were now all under, I felt no qualms about changing in front of one another. "Will someone help me with this?" I asked, struggling as I reached for the fastenings on my intricate dress. Arnie was standing nearest and mindlessly took the job, undoing each delicate button with nimble fingers. Copper's dress was one that she could undo herself, and in a flurry of outfit changing, she returned to the lanky redhead I had been missing all night. Once my buttons had been attended to, Arnie changed into a pair of wool slacks and a red sweater, without a request for privacy, likewise restoring his former appearance.

Now free of the girdles and heels, I sighed in gratefulness as I slipped into pants and sensible shoes. Looking around the room, I was impressed with the packing we had done in such a short time. We were practically ready to hit the road—the only thing left to do was to discuss our destination.

"Where exactly are we heading?" Copper asked, as if reading my mind. "Obviously, we need to leave the city, but what is the plan? Should we lay low somewhere?"

"I need to go to the sanctuary in the Thorough Woods," I admitted, finally voicing what had been in my mind since our meeting with Haute. "If my mother is there, I need to see her. I need to know what happened. I have too many questions to go home and carry on. Maybe, when I have the answers…" I closed my eyes in a sort of prayer, "Maybe things can go back to how they were before." I opened my eyes and looked at my friends. They made no move to interrupt me. "I figure we should head to the train station. From there, I'll go as far east as I can in order to reach Crescent Lake, and you two can head home."

"Hildegarde," Arnie started, frowning at me, "we're coming with you to the sanctuary." He spoke with total resolve, almost as if he were offended at my assumption. I looked at Copper, who stood with her arms folded and her bag slung over her shoulder.

"You think we don't have questions, too?" Her mix of resolve and anger perfectly mirrored her brother's. "After what Haute said about Mom, do you seriously think that we can just go home and 'carry on'? I meant it when I took that coin. We're in this now as much as you are."

There was a moment when I considered arguing with the Pennings, but what right did I have to do that? Why shouldn't they get to chase their mother's ghost just like I had been doing for weeks? My love for them did not, and could not, outweigh my respect for their decision.

"Okay," I acceded, gathering up my own bags. Feeling like there was nothing more to be said around that, I pivoted and asked, "What are the odds that neither Beauregarde nor Dexter recognized me after my glamour broke?"

"How about we don't stick around to find out," Arnie retorted as he fastened the strap of his bag over his shoulder.

Suddenly, there was a hollow banging on the door. The three of us froze, not daring to breathe. The banging came again, louder and more insistent. We exchanged panicked glances, lost for a solution if watchmen were on the other side of that door. After a third round of pounding, Arnie quietly lowered his bags and raised a finger to his lips. He began to inch toward the door, unarmed. Copper and I stood helpless as Arnie glanced through the peephole. At once, his shoulders relaxed, and he swung the door open, pulling the intruder in by the shoulder before securing the lock once more. The boy stumbled in from the unexpected yank, regaining his footing at the center of the room.

"Hildegarde!"

"Raemond," I exhaled, my heart now pounding painfully in my chest.

Chapter Twenty-Four: The Witch's Confession

No one moved or spoke for an agonizing moment, tension filling the room like noxious gas. I looked at Raemond with longing eyes, now finally able to survey him up close. Rae's face tensed and relaxed as he cycled through shock, confusion, and eventually joy. With that shift, he bounded forward, closing the space between us, and took me in his arms. Regardless of my panic and amazement, we fit together as we always had—effortlessly. I wrapped my arms around his neck and breathed in his familiar, earthy scent for the first time in what felt like a lifetime.

"What are you doing here?" His hands found their way to my hair as he pulled my head back to look him in the eyes.

"I was just about to ask you the same thing, General," Arnie butted in, hijacking our reunion.

"Still just a private, Arnie, but it's good to see you too." Rae reluctantly released me to face interrogation. Copper advanced from the corner to insert herself as well.

"Don't think we aren't happy to see you, Rae," Copper began, "but it is of the highest level of importance that you explain *exactly* how you knew that we were here." Her face remained neutral, but I could see her fingers tapping against her thigh.

"I saw you at the gala," Rae explained, looking between us all for some clarity. "Or, I thought I did, so I followed your cab back here."

"You saw me?" I pressed. "As we were leaving?"

"Actually, no," Rae answered. "I saw Arnie when I stepped out for a smoke. He was getting into a cab, so I followed it here." All attempts to hide our panic vanished, and everyone spoke at once.

"What do you mean you saw Arnie?" I demanded.

"You saw Arnie? Like, actually *saw* him?" Copper asked, gesticulating wildly at her brother.

"It wasn't that I was a person who looked coincidentally similar to me?" Arnie asked hopefully.

"No, it was definitely you." Rae backed away from our barrage of questions, eyes wide. "What the hell is going on?"

I grabbed him by both shoulders to hold his focus. "Arnie was wearing a glamour, Rae," I said, seeing no point in hiding the information now. "How did you know it was him?"

"Why…" Rae started to ask, then paused, taking in our terrified faces. "We wear pins," he explained. "They disarm illusions like simple glamours." Copper slapped a palm to her forehead and slumped onto the end of the bed.

"You just had to save the time!" Arnie cried in exasperation, spinning to glare at her.

"Please shut up," she groaned, her face now buried in her hands.

"No point in giving Arnie a *full* glamour—not like anyone is looking at him," he said acidly. "Let's just slap a new hair color and jawline on him and call it a day. What could possibly go wrong?!" His frustration exploded with a dramatic wave of his arms.

"How was I supposed to know about the pins?" Copper snapped, now rising to face off with her brother.

"Why was anyone wearing a glamour?" Raemond interjected, moving to stand between the siblings.

"Everyone shut up!" I shouted, silencing the room with a sharp sweep of my arm. I looked at Rae, fear rising from the pit of my stomach. "Do you wear those pins even while off duty?"

Arnie and Copper's anger vanished like a pebble dropped into a thick brew. Their eyes widened as they caught on to my building horror.

"Yeah, we wear them everywhere."

The realization crashed over us like an ocean wave. Arnie hadn't been glamoured all night, not to the watchmen. The minute he'd walked into that gala, Dex and Beau would have seen him as the outlaw from the caravan.

"We have to leave now," Arnie commanded, throwing his bags back over his shoulders. Copper and I followed suit while Raemond watched in bewildered ignorance.

"We had to leave ten minutes ago," she corrected, throwing a pleading glance at me.

"I am really sorry," I said to Rae, the words thick and insufficient in my mouth. "We have to go, and there is no time to explain why." He started to interject, but I cut him off. "Not in a way you would understand or be satisfied with."

"Hildegarde—" he protested, but I stopped him again, this time without words. I threw my arms over his shoulders and gripped his hair in my hands, pulling his lips down close enough to kiss, though I had to stand on my toes to reach him. I kissed him with all the desperation and longing that I could not express in words. Then, as soon as it had begun, I pulled away. I pressed my forehead to his to allow for the intimacy of a whisper.

"I love you, Raemond Wimple," I said, blinking away tears as fast as I could. "And I always will. I know this isn't the end for us." I yearned to kiss him once more, but resisted; I somehow managed to tear myself away from him. He looked at me as if I had slapped him instead of kissing him, but I kept moving, gathering my bags. Before I could let the agony of his gaze paralyze me, I ran for the door, leaving him in my wake. Arnie and Copper were right behind me, restricted by urgency from showing any sympathy. We galloped down the stairs to the lobby, now jampacked with returning debutantes.

"Hildy, I am so sorry," Copper breathed as we waded through the crowd of crinolines, but I didn't speak. My willed stony resolve was the only thing preventing me from dissolving into tears. I dropped the keys to the room at the front desk without stopping or even acknowledging the cheery worker behind it.

"Thank you for staying with us," the receptionist called, her voice evaporating in the chatter of giddy socialites. Out on the street, the snow continued to fall in fluffy clumps, pricking the black sky with pinholes of white.

"Which way to the train station?" Arnie asked me.

"How would I know?" I huffed. It was becoming increasingly clear how unprepared, how entirely out of our depth, we all were.

"I'll go ask Smiles-McGee at the desk." Copper dropped her bags at our feet and shoved her way through two wide-skirted girls to get back through the lobby doors.

"We aren't cut out for this." Arnie ran his hands through his slicked-back hair.

"I know," I said, trying to take a deep breath through my nose. The doors opened wide behind us, and I turned, expecting Copper.

"You think you can just leave me in your hotel room like an idiot?" Rae's face was flushed with anger. It made total sense that he had followed us. Why wouldn't he? Just another tally in the growing list of things I'd done stupidly that night.

"Raemond!" Arnie's patience was wafer-thin. "For once in your whole damn life, this isn't about you."

"*What* isn't about me?" Rae's fuse was as short as Arnie's, and the two of them were starting to draw attention.

"The trains don't run on the first day of Yule—" Copper began as she darted back out the doors. "Oh, Rae's here. Excellent."

"Of course the trains aren't running today." I wanted to slap myself. So stupid.

"Rae," Arnie said, "how did you get here to-night?"

"Camp Valiant truck," he said with a shrug, mo-tioning to the beat-up clunker farther down the street. It was almost identical to the one we had driven with Tuck in. "It's how I got to the city."

"Sorry, Rae," Copper shouted as she shoved her hands in his coat pockets. He let out a startled cry of protest as she found what she was looking for. "We're robbing you." She jingled the keys at me and Arnie, and we bolted for the truck.

"I promise I'll explain when I can," I called back. "I love you!"

Copper unlocked the doors with a forceful turn of the key while Arnie and I tossed our bags into the open truck bed, save for my shoulder bag, which remained secured over my shoulder. Arnie hopped into the passenger seat.

"You aren't taking my truck! You aren't authorized!" Rae was right on our tail.

"File a report with the watchmen." We didn't have time for this. I slammed my door shut, and Copper started up the sputtering engine.

She started to adjust a mirror, then turned and looked behind us for cars. "For the love of all things good," I erupted, "drive, Copper!" The door across from me opened with a click.

"You heard her," Rae said as he slid into the back seat next to me. "Drive."

"Get out of this car right now!" I turned to him and smacked him on the arm.

"Not going to happen," he said as he slammed the door behind him.

"Get out or I will force you out," I yelled, shoving him with both hands and all the strength I could muster.

"I'd like to see you try," he challenged, not budging an inch.

"Copper…" Arnie pleaded, nearly whimpering.

She put the vehicle in reverse and stepped on the gas. "Sorry, Rae, but you're going on a road trip." With a violent lurch, she whipped out of the parking spot and veered into the city streets, clipping a curb with the back left tire.

"So, where are we going on this road trip?" Rae asked.

"Copper, pull over," I demanded, leaning forward in my seat.

"I can't do that, Hildy." She shook her head as she pushed the speed. "As far as I'm concerned, Rae is either going to have to perform a barrel roll out of a moving vehicle or he's coming with us to Crescent Lake because I am not stopping until we get there." I felt myself preparing to throttle every single one of my fellow passengers, but then realized that would hardly accomplish anything.

"Crescent Lake?" Raemond repeated, nodding thoughtfully. "That's what, six or seven hours away? That'll give us plenty of time to catch up, play some road games, and maybe explain just WHAT ON THIS GREEN EARTH IS GOING ON?!" His collected facade shattered like a window struck by a stray ball.

I knew I had to refuse his demand for answers, painfully aware of the dangerous position that would place him in. Maybe I could appeal to his reason instead. "Rae, this is deserting. You just received a commendation for your potential, and now you're going to throw it all away?" I gestured to his new pin to illustrate my point.

"How about you tell me what this is all about, and then I'll decide if it's worth throwing my career away." He took a deep breath to collect himself, then gave me a teasing smile, appearing determined to not take this too seriously.

Indignation flaring, I snapped, "Rae, this isn't funny. Under other circumstances, I'd find your disregard for your own safety and future sort of cute, but right now is not a time for jokes." I could hear the sharpness of my mother in my tone.

"Oh, calm down, Hildy," Rae leveled. He reached for my hand. "It's Yuletime—all the first-year recruits are given leave to go home for the holiday. I'm not deserting, and I'm not going to be kicked out of the service. Also, you would know all this if you had read any of the multitudes of letters I've sent you." I saw a glimmer of hurt flash across his face; a pile of letters was likely sitting in a neat stack on my desk back home.

"Didn't Irenee write to you once she had your bunk number?" I squeaked out. I'd assumed my aunt would have crafted some explanation as to my absence. She'd certainly implied as much in our conversations.

"Sure, once," Raemond replied bitterly. "I think it was all of three sentences: 'Dear Raemond, glad to hear you're doing well. Hildegarde has taken a short trip to Facehaven with the Pennings. I will convey your regards to her when she returns.' But that was weeks ago, Hildegarde. That's a long time to go without hearing from my girlfriend, even aside from the quick trip to Facehaven."

"Fiancée," Copper corrected from the front seat. "We all know you're engaged."

"Congrats, by the way," Arnie added with a sneer. "They say the key to marriage is communication. You two are off to a great start."

"You know what, Penning?" Raemond leaned forward to get into Arnie's field of view, his sharp face and short black hair lit up in fragments from the passing street lamps. "I don't think you have a leg to stand on when it comes to communication. You were the one to decide you were too good for us." Arnie scoffed and looked out the window.

"So, Hildy, when do you think he'll ask me to be his best man?" Arnie asked over his shoulder. "I hope he gets down on one knee."

"What's up with you two?" Copper said, looking at them out of the corner of her eye. "You've always been so close."

"We were until Hildegarde and I had the audacity to get our own lives," Rae snarled, prodding the volatile Arnie. "Go on, Arnold. Tell me I'm wrong."

"You know what, Raemond?" Arnie said, his voice constricted, "Why don't you try that barrel roll Copper was talking about?"

"How about you use all that advanced magic you've been learning to make me disappear?" Rae dug in. "Or are you still having issues with performance?"

"Tell him everything, Hildegarde!" Arnie erupted. "They can go ahead and execute him for all I care." I took a breath, preparing to intercede, when Copper suddenly spoke.

"Hildy's mother was a high sorcerer and member of a secret society with our mom until Baldwin turned her in for her magics. She had to flee, but she left behind her spell book for Hildegarde. We've been traveling across the country trying to follow different contacts and information, and we ended up embroiled in a silent war being waged between our government and rebel witches throughout the kingdom. A friend we met was arrested, or maybe worse, a caravan we were in was raided, Arnie almost bled out after performing a high sorcery spell, we broke into the gala to learn government secrets from a double agent, Arnie and I were told that our mother's death may have been a cover-up, and now we're headed to a sanctuary beyond the Thorough Woods because we're being hunted by two watchmen from that caravan who happened to be at the gala tonight where Arnie was wearing a useless glamour."

Copper had to draw in a deep breath after the rapid speech. That breath was the only sound within the cabin for a long moment. Arnie's eyebrows remained frozen high up on his forehead. Copper kept her eyes on the road, fingers clenching the wheel. I stared, analyzing every movement of Raemond's face as he processed. He sat completely still, mouth slightly ajar, and was blinking more rapidly than was natural.

"You know, sis," Arnie said, finally cutting the silence, "you picked one hell of a time to start taking me seriously."

"Well, you had a good idea for once," Copper retorted. She kept her gaze on the horizon, but I glimpsed a small smile at the corner of her mouth. The city gates pulled into view in front of us as she turned onto the exit street.

I continued my intense study of Rae's face, waiting, but then I became too anxious and whispered, "Rae?"

"I'm going to need to hear that again," he requested, voice small but still emotionless. The jalopy raced through the gates and away from the great walls of the Citadel.

The story was as hard to tell as I had expected, and I was glad to have the Penning siblings there to pick up the slack. Raemond played his part by being a focused listener, putting aside questions until the end, which was impressive considering how long and winding our explanations were. The questions he did ask us were things none of us had the answers to, like how the watchmen had found Lacey, or whether or not Rainer might have turned us in. I even learned a few things from Copper and Arnie that I hadn't gotten around to asking, mainly that Mr. Penning had been told that his children were attending a workshop in Facehaven for the break and would not be returning until the beginning of the academic year.

Over the first two hours, the story progressed relatively smoothly from our time in the Orchard, Facehaven, Inntinn Bay, and on the Rambler, but it stalled out when Tuck's name came up. Rae became immediately protective of his bunkmate, not wanting him to have gotten wrapped up in all this. When we got to the part about the attack on the road, Rae couldn't stop himself from interrupting.

"How did you manage to get the upper hand?" he asked me, eyebrows high on his forehead. "You know, after Tuck was knocked unconscious." He had been holding my hand for most of this, and his grip became almost painful. I took a steadying breath before I answered.

"I used one of my mother's spells to knock the bandit out. Somehow, I... was able to perform high sorcery." It was the first time I had spoken the words aloud, the first time I had admitted it to myself or anyone else. Saying it felt unnatural, like calling myself by the wrong name. Rae looked back at me with wide, fearful eyes, but he did not pull away. Instead, he placed his other hand over mine and squeezed it tight.

"Tell me the rest of the story," he said, visibly bracing himself.

When all was said and done, it had taken three hours to bring Raemond up to speed. The events at the Citadel were simpler to explain. Of course, we all silently agreed to leave my and Arnie's kiss out of the retelling. Justified or not, things were tense enough that I think we all wanted to avoid a second Raemond-Arnie faceoff.

We had not seen another vehicle on the road for over an hour, which was hardly surprising.

It was the dead of night as well as a major holiday. The faint silhouette of mountain peaks against the dark sky had grown closer with every mile; now they no longer stood on the horizon, but instead loomed beside us as we drove the winding roads around the foot of Mount Tempus. Copper had settled into her role as a driver, and the lurches between gear changes lessened notably over the course of the drive. So, it was jarring to all of us when the engine of the jalopy suddenly sputtered and hummed.

"What was that?" Arnie asked, happy to dodge Rae's most recent question, which circled back to Arnie pilfering spells from my book back in the caravan.

"Did we reactivate the runes before we left?" Rae asked, leaning over to peer at the dials on the dashboard.

Copper turned and frowned at him. "Gear-shifting runes don't need reactivating."

"They did fifty years ago," Rae corrected, "which was when this hunk of junk would have been manufactured."

"Are you telling me that our military has machinery over fifty years old?" she said, sounding offended. "Where are my tax dollars going then?"

With a small snort, Arnie answered, "Our dad's taxes go to schools, agriculture, and hospitals, mostly." He leaned his seat back, cutting noticeably into my space in the backseat as he stretched and rested a foot on the dashboard. "Besides, we've essentially stolen this military vehicle, so I think we've pretty much yielded the civic high ground on this one."

"Do you know how to reactivate the runes?" Rae asked Copper.

She frowned. "No—I was busy learning enchantments from this century."

"There was a sign a little while back that said we were nearing a town," I offered. "Umbra, I think. We could stop at a service station there." My panic from our hasty departure had eased considerably over the many miles we had covered, so it didn't feel like too risky a move.

"I don't like it," Arnie said immediately, turning to look at me. "We shouldn't make any stops."

I held eye contact with him and said, "Not really seeing another option, Arnie, unless you would like to get out and push us for the next three hours." Over the few weeks we had traveled together, I'd come to understand his irritability increased with his exhaustion, but that did not mean I had acquired any patience for it.

"I can see lights up ahead," Copper interrupted, pointing to a small jumble of buildings nestled into the mountain foothills. "Let's just hope the service station is open this late on a holiday."

I was once again reminded that it was the first night of Yule, my favorite holiday. But it didn't feel like Yuletime. It was supposed to be a time of hope—a celebration of the dawn of each new day to be spent with family. When the sun rose, children would awake to a lavish breakfast and a new toy, and when the night came again, they would sleep soundly with the comfort that eleven more days of celebrating awaited them. My only wish this holiday was for a soft place to land and renewed hope.

Umbra was a small town. It boasted no major academy or economic prospects. It was the sort of place that appealed only to those content in living a small, removed life. The decor and holiday energy felt especially warm and personal, despite the town being solidly asleep at this late hour. A wreath of holly hung on the door of every home, and twinkling candles sat in each window. Snow blanketed the front lawns. This was not the decorative snow of the Citadel, but honest, genuine snow that was thick enough to have been shaped into snowmen and forts across the small streets. Umbra's main street was equipped with a post office, an apothecary, a grocer, a few small storefronts, and—luckily—a service station with its lights glowing like a beacon. We released a collective sigh as we pulled in beneath the covered lot to see an open sign hanging mercifully in the window.

"I'll go speak to the serviceman," Rae said as he adjusted his blazer. "It's a military vehicle and I'm in uniform, so he should do it for free. You three, stay put." He spoke with an authority I had not seen in him before, and I wasn't sure I liked it. He got out and shut the door firmly behind him, then strode into the small building.

"How are you feeling, Hildy?" Copper asked, seizing on Rae's absence to check in. She twisted in the driver's seat to face me for the first time in hours.

"Honestly, I have no idea," I began, finding an odd comfort in it just being the three of us again. "I'm feeling so many things. I'm relieved that he knows everything, and that I can let go of all the guilt from keeping this from him, but…" I lowered my voice, despite the doors being closed and the windows rolled up, "so much has changed since he left. Now it's all catching up with us."

"Do you think your feelings for him have changed?" Copper asked softly, reaching out to hold my hand. I could feel Arnie shifting to look at me.

"No," I said without hesitation." I love Rae, maybe even more than before. I know I want to spend the rest of my life with him…"

"But?" she prodded.

"But he didn't sign on for this," I continued, appreciating her intuition. "Last month I was an aspiring herbalist whose greatest ambition was to have a greenhouse in her backyard. Now I'm an amateur high sorcerer who's joined a revolutionary society by accepting a coin from an old man. What if it's his feelings that change?"

Arnie cleared his throat. "Hildy, Raemond has been in love with you since before he could tie his own laces." His words were meant to be reassuring, but his delivery was more condescending than kind. "If he was going to fall out of love with you, he would have done so…" Arnie's stern pep-talk trailed off as his eyes focused on a beam of light that suddenly shone through our rear window.

I whipped my head around to watch a black automobile pull into the station lot, slowing to a stop mere feet behind us. The rumble of the engine ceased, and the headlights shut off. By the time our vision adjusted from the bright intrusion of light, the two front doors of the mystery vehicle had already swung open. Two men stepped out, and white hot fear flooded my heart as the driver made eye contact with me. His mouth formed a chilling smirk. A hearty bay echoed across the empty streets as their hound bounded out the open door, taking a seat beside Beauregarde Mason's shiny black boots.

CHAPTER TWENTY-FIVE: THE WITCH'S NAME

My hot breath fogged the rear window as I stared back into Beauregarde's stony eyes. Dex was a hulking figure in front of the passenger door, looking ready to lunge forward. Beau, however, leaned back against the hood, folding his arms across his chest. He was still dressed in his tailored three-piece, but he now wore a long leather coat to shelter him from the cold.

"Well, if it isn't my friends from the caravan." Beau's lips curled into a smile as he nodded at Arnie, his sharp voice clearly audible through the windows. "I thought I'd seen a red-haired boy at the king's gala, but I figured I had to be mistaken. Or that it was just a coincidence. But then Dex here said he saw you out on the street necking with some broad. It's the funniest thing—I had written off your little disappearing act back at the caravan as three kids hiding some naughty substances or something. You only came back into my mind when we questioned an artifact bandit who said three folks who looked just like you were carrying something mighty powerful on you. And then, to spot you lot poorly disguised at the gala? Now that's a coincidence I couldn't ignore."

None of us had so much as twitched since the automobile had pulled in behind us. We sat with wide eyes, each attempting to figure a way out of this. We could just drive away, but we wouldn't get very far, and I had to assume that the watchmen drove vehicles that didn't shut down after mere hours. We could flee on foot, but we weren't likely to outrun an automobile, not to mention the dog. We could put up a fight, but victory was highly unlikely.

"Why don't you three make things a little easier on yourselves and join us out here?" Beau pointed in front of himself like a stern father calling his children up. "It's a fine, crisp holiday evening. Just let me take a look at whatever spiked the interest of those bandits, and you can be headed back on home." I looked over my shoulder at Arnie and Copper in the frantic hope that they had come up with some sort of solution, but all I saw in their eyes was a mirror of my own fear. Drawing in a breath through my nose, I reached for the door handle and eased it open, stepping out into the frigid night air.

"There you are," Beauregarde declared, clapping his hands together as if rejoicing, though his face held no mirth. "You're a sight for sore eyes." The scattered sound of two doors opening and shutting echoed on the covered lot as Arnie and Copper joined me.

"And there's the boy who cast that teleportation spell," Beauregarde said, now applauding in Arnie's direction. "That was really something. I don't know if I've ever seen anything quite like it. Do you mind if I take a look at your license to perform…" He turned to Dex, "What would that even be? Conjuration?"

"It's packed away in my bags," Arnie gulped.

"By all means," Beau said, motioning toward our truck. He leaned against his car, arms crossed again, as he watched Arnie turn and rummage through his things for the license we all knew wasn't there.

As we stood there, Beau suddenly narrowed his eyes at me. "You're gonna need to hand over that shoulder bag, darlin'." I could have kicked myself. I shouldn't have been holding the strap so tightly—I'd basically been holding it above my head and begging him to search it.

"Can I see a warrant?" I asked, grasping at straws.

"You really don't want to make this any harder on yourself." He stepped toward me, and Dex mirrored him, so they now stood in front of their car. I drew back.

"*Tasrie alan!*" Copper cried without warning. Her hand was raised at the watchmen's black automobile, which instantly rumbled to life and accelerated forward. I felt the weighty force of

Arnie's body colliding with my own as he tackled me to the ground, landing just beyond the tire marks of the advancing vehicle. I heard several hollow thuds and looked up in time to pair them with the swift movement of Beau and Dex tumbling across the windshield, roof, and then trunk, eventually landing on the concrete with a few gruesome popping sounds.

The next thing I saw from the ground, just above Arnie's form, was a streak of bright red hair as Copper took off running down the road. I took hold of Arnie's shoulder and pulled him upright before I followed after her in the most powerful sprint my short legs could muster. An unintelligible, enraged incantation was bellowed from behind me a split second before a patch of slick ice slithered under my feet. The heel of my boot slid out with such speed that it sent both of my legs out in front of me. I came down fast and hard, landing first on my tailbone before rocking back from the force of impact, which whipped my head back into the solid ground, hitting with a wet, cracking sound.

A sharp ringing echoed through my mind as the sky spun above me. There were cries somewhere in the distance, but they sounded as if we were underwater. Time seemed to slow as the pain traveled out from the back of my skull with icy fingers. Against the frigid cold of the ice, there was warmth as well—a sticky, wet heat spreading through my loose hair. My eyelids hung heavily, and I allowed them to fall shut as the insistent urge to sleep took hold.

"God damn, that hurt."

I opened my eyes to the distorted voice above me. Beauregarde didn't quite come into focus, but his figure loomed before me, and I could tell he was bleeding from several places. Two powerful hands gripped me by my cloak and lifted me to my feet. I couldn't find my sense of balance as one of the hands clenched my jaw, forcing my spotty gaze up to meet his. Beauregarde's cool exterior had been replaced with an untethered rage, but he still held his menacing grin.

"That wasn't very neighborly. In fact—" His threat was cut short as a rock, no bigger than a robin's egg, struck him between his brow at an unnatural speed. His eyes rolled back in his head as he crumpled to the ground like a marionette whose strings had been severed. Without the aid of Beau's grip, I began to stumble backward into the snow, but instead of hitting the hard, icy ground again, I landed in a pair of warm arms.

"Hildegarde!" Rae's panic choked his voice as he stabilized me, wrapping me tight.

"Others... go..." I attempted to organize my thoughts as I tried to catch sight of Dex or the hound.

"Arnie and Copper were headed toward the town square when I came out," Rae began, half pulling and half pushing me to the jalopy at what felt like a horse's gallop; the bounding made my nausea almost unbearable. "The big guy and his dog were following them."

With a grunt, Rae unceremoniously swung me over the side of the truck, though taking care to cradle my head as he set me down in the bed, which had been badly dented by the impact of the watch-men's vehicle. As Rae started the nearly dead engine, I pulled myself up in time to see Beau shakily rouse himself. The jalopy lurched, sputtering and groaning as we pulled out and rolled toward town. I tried to get a hold of my senses as I looked around the luggage for anything of use. The shiny mahogany of my brew box gleamed in the light of a passing streetlamp, and I willed myself to a seated position to reach for it, pulling it in by the leather strap.

"Thish isa concussion…" I said to myself, fighting to center my thoughts around my slurred words. "Means my brain's hurt." I began rooting through the first aid section of the box. "Want… willow." I strained my eyes to read the label. It was an herb I used commonly to treat headaches, often adding a few drops to a cup of tea. "Close'nough." I shut my eyes as I proceeded to drain the contents of the sizable vial. The bitterness of the extract was staggering, and for a moment, it claimed all of my attention as I focused on keeping it in my stomach. After the unpleasant taste subsided, I watched as the scene around me became clearer. My thoughts started coming more easily. I then remembered that I had brewed a tincture made of yarrow after

Arnie's brush with death. "That'll do. Where are you?" I fumbled through my vials, glass clinking until I located the mixture.

I took a hearty swig—its effect was to stop the rush of blood from my wound—and the world came into perfect focus once again. By the time the jalopy lurched to a stop, I was able to clearly make out the white gazebo that sat in the Umbra town square, under which Dex held Copper's body against his own. Her back was pressed tight to him, with his arm held tight around her neck in a chokehold. Arnie stood at the gazebo's first step, holding Dex's bow at the ready.

"I will snap the girl's neck!" Dex bellowed, shaking Copper like a ragdoll in his anger. The arrow strung in the bow trembled in Arnie's hand.

"Watchmen bows don't miss," Arnie countered with a loud but shaky voice. Rae bolted out of the driver's seat but then paused, clearly debating whether inserting himself into the standoff would help or hurt Copper's chances.

"Not for you," Dex corrected. "In my hand, it forces the wind to do its bidding. In your hands, it's nothing but wood, and you've only got one shot."

Arnie glanced over his shoulder to where the jalopy had skidded to a halt and Rae was now standing, alert and focused. "You're right," he conceded with a nod. "I'm no evoker." He relaxed the tension in the bowstring. "But he is."

Arnie jerked his head in Rae's direction, then shouted, "*Teigh do!*" It was a conjuration spell I'd never seen him do before. In the blink of an eye, the bow vanished from his loose grip. Dex snapped his head around, looking for his prized weapon, and he soon located it in the capable hands of Rae, who was aiming the arrow right at him. Dex needed only a glance at Rae's uniform to know that Arnie's claim had merit, and in his moment of distraction, Copper bit deep into the meat of his forearm. Dex yelped in pain as she slithered from his grip and darted down the steps to Arnie. Dex pursued the pair as they fled in the opposite direction of the jalopy, spewing profanity.

"Rae!" I stood up in the truck bed. "Take the shot!" He did as he was told, loosing the arrow in the direction of Dex's back. It flew over his shoulder, landing in the soft snow. Rae looked back at me shamefully, and I blinked in confusion.

"I haven't learned wind spells yet," he cried. "It was just wood for me." He shook it off. "I'm going after them. You stay here," Rae barked, resuming his new, authoritative voice.

I vaulted over the edge of the truck bed and landed in the thick snow with shaky legs.

"There's no way—" I protested, but Rae interrupted, "Your skull was busted open like a walnut!" He used two hands to motion at me to stay put. "You aren't going to be able to help anyone in this state. If you love me at all, you'll lock yourself in that truck until I come back with our friends." He stared me down, waiting for me to cede, but when he saw no signs of that, he barked, "*Ardu oighir.*" The snow around my boots rose up and solidified to ice.

I bellowed in shock and outrage as he turned on his heel and ran off, following the tracks of the Pennings and their attacker.

"Raemond Wimple!" I screamed, calling at the boy in vain as he disappeared into the night. I sank down to the cold ground in a huff and began the maddening work of chipping away at my manacles of ice. The thought that my friends could be fighting for their lives while I sat making ice sculptures out of my ankles brought tears of rage to my eyes. My soul filled with a white hot indignation I'd not felt before. I had knocked out a bandit with a single word, poisoned two perverts without a second thought, infiltrated the government at a massive party, carried the world's most dangerous book across the country, and now had healed my own concussion in the back of a moving truck. And *Raemond*, my future partner, had the audacity to treat me like a damsel in distress.

Untethered anger boiled within me, and every part of my body felt like it was increasing in temperature. Beads of sweat rolled down my temples, and literal steam began to rise from the places where my skin made contact with the ice. I watched in frightened awe as the frozen surface around my ankles and the snow under my feet melted away like butter in a skillet, all without me uttering a word.

There was no time for me to consider how or why I had been able to perform a melting spell wordlessly. Focusing on following everyone else's tracks, I bounded across the square to the residential area where Copper and Arnie had disappeared. As I continued along the sidewalk, I passed several identical homes, each dark and silent with sleep. I listened closely for the sounds of a struggle, but the only noise floating through the night air was the blowing of wind through the pine trees and my feet crunching through the snow. And then a new sound arose—the growl of a dog.

The teeth ripped into my leg before I even saw the animal. I dropped into the snow, this time twisting to land in a seated position, and began kicking at the berserk hound. Not every snap the dog made landed on my skin; some merely grazed me or were thwarted by the thick fabric of my pants. Enough hit home, though, to cause me to cry out in pain.

"Down, boy," the unmistakable voice of Beauregarde commanded. The hound's aggression shut off like a faucet, and he sat down in the snow, the picture of obedience. Limping out of the shadows, Beau lowered himself into a crouch before me. He looked even worse than I did. The point of impact of Rae's stone had begun to swell and bruise, and the results of the crash were painted across his face in blood, staining his white shirt. Looking at the pair of us, it would have been hard to believe we had both been at a refined gala mere hours before.

"You kids got two hits in tonight," Beau said, simmering. "And you won't get another."

He unsheathed a hunting knife from his waistband and passed it back and forth between his hands. There was a feral, irrational gleam to his eyes that made me shudder. "You really don't know me very well," he said, gesticulating at me with his blade, smirking as he toyed with me. "We've shared some beautiful, fleeting moments. I've seen the look of pure fear in your eyes. We've bled together." He leaned in so close that our noses nearly touched. If my legs weren't screaming in pain, I'd have scrambled back faster than a water strider on a pond.

"We've breathed the same air." His breath smelled of liquor and meat. "And yet, you don't know me at all." The blade of his knife clanged against the concrete as he threw it into the street, descending on me with both hands. They wrapped around my throat as he pushed me against the cold ground, using his own weight to pin me down.

"You think the *sisters* can keep you safe from me? From us?" he demanded through gritted teeth, applying pressure to my larynx with his thumbs. I gasped for the little air I was able to draw. "You think your boyfriends are going to keep on saving you after they use you?" He breathed his taunts directly into my ear. "That's the thing they never tell you girls growing up. They tell you to stay home because it's better for the children. They tell you it's a noble sacrifice—it's your civic duty." He sneered. "None of that's the truth. The truth is that you're a *thing*." Spots started to dot my vision. "And things belong in homes, where they stay out of the way and under control. Tell that to your sisters." He released my neck from his merciless grip. I gasped for air, taking it in with deep gulps only to wheeze them back out.

"You see?" Beau raised his hands as if he had just proven a theory. "This is what happens when you insert yourself where you don't belong. You get damaged." I blinked away the tears from physical pain and emotional humiliation. "Now, because I'm kind and magnanimous, I'm going to give you the chance to go home, lesson learned. You just need to tell me one thing." He gripped the front of my sweater and pulled me to his eye level. "Who's the boy? Give me that high sorcerer's name."

The laughter erupted from me like a bucket that had sprung a leak. I instantly tried to repress it, but it sputtered back up, building upon itself in my bruised vocal cords. Beauregarde's face contorted in anger, and he struck me across the face with an open palm. But the laughter did not stop. If anything, it grew in intensity and raspiness, now bordering hysteria.

"You think this is a joke?" he screamed, droplets of spit pricking my face. "What's his damn name?" The laughter cascading out of me abruptly ceased, and I gave Beau a venomous grin.

"*Her name*," I began, baring my teeth as I growled at him, "is Hildegarde Birch." Confusion spread across Beau's twisted face like wildfire. I closed my eyes and let all thoughts fall away, seeking that state of perfect instinct that I had found only once before. "*Vola via*," I called, voice somehow clear despite the damage around my throat.

I opened my eyes just in time to see recognition dawn on Beau's face. Then a heartbeat later, he shot up into the air as if propelled by a catapult, arcing through the falling snowflakes before landing on the pavement below with the same wet crack I had made before. Only Beauregarde did not open his eyes, moan in pain, or attempt to return to his feet. The hound, having sat obediently this whole time, trotted over to its prostrate master and sniffed at the halo of red growing around his head. The dog looked up at me with dark, emotionless eyes before strolling away into the night, showing no interest in its broken master.

I hoisted myself upright with a great deal of difficulty, watching Beau carefully, half-expecting one last, defiant lunge, but it never came. Then I waited for disgust or regret to wash over me, but it never did. I looked down at his shell with an emotion that scared me: pride. But even as that swelled in me, I felt the adrenaline drain from my body. My vision began to narrow, and the throbbing at the back of my skull arose once more. The gruesome scene faded from view as I succumbed to exhaustion and blood loss.

I woke in my own bed, warm and drowsy. I blinked the world into focus, staring up at the tiny painted stars that had covered my bedroom ceiling since I was a child. *I can't be here,* I thought as I sat up. My floral duvet flopped down from my torso. The air in the room was cold, prickling against my neck and face. Someone had left the window open, and the winter air was pouring through it, along with an owl's distant call. I swung my legs out from the warm covers and placed my bare feet on the frigid wood floorboards. I looked down to see that I was wearing a set of red flannel pajamas, the kind my mother had always given me on Yule's Eve. I stood and shuffled toward my favorite plush robe, which hung from a hook on the back of the door. Wrapping it around me, I opened my door with a creak. A light shone at the end of the dark hallway, and I knew beyond that were some steps that ended at the kitchen. A melancholy record crooned from the gramophone below, a duet between a lush piano and the delicate rhythm of a snare drum.

I descended the stairs with ease. My head no longer throbbed, and my body seemed perfectly fine—all the events that had happened at Umbra seemed distant and dark. The kitchen area was even colder than my room had been. Wind jostled the pots that hung above the kitchen island, the windows behind them wide open. Seated below them was a woman draped in a silk nightgown, her bare arms glowing in the lamplight, and her loose black hair fluttering in the breeze. She turned her face to the light and looked upon me with amusement.

"Hildy." She shook her head. "You're supposed to be asleep." I surveyed my mother's pale face, as lovely and sharp as I remembered.

"I am asleep," I assured the phantom, knowing that at the present, I was unconscious in a random side street of snowy Umbra.

"That you are." Maude rose from her stool and glided across the floor toward me. She placed a freezing hand on my cheek, tracing my jawline with delicate fingers. "You look so much like your father." Her look was warm, but haunted. "I worried you would look more like me." She wrapped her spindly arms around me, cradling my head with her right hand.

When her hand touched my wound, she withdrew and made a concerned noise at the sight of my blood staining her white hand. "Oh, sweetheart, does it hurt?"

"It did before," I said, my hand floating up to touch the injury, my fingertips blotting the blood that had matted in my hair. "But it doesn't anymore." I absently rubbed the blood between my thumb and pointer finger.

"Come sit down." She ushered me to a stool and circled to inspect the gash. "You have to be more careful with yourself," she scolded. "Our bodies are breakable."

"I killed him, Mom," I said, voice hollow. "I killed that watchman."

"Shhh," she soothed, murmuring softly as she dabbed blood away with a cloth napkin. "It's over now."

"What's happening to me?" I asked, blinking as the orange light of the kitchen burned my eyes.

"You're growing up," Maude answered, "and I am so very proud of you." She began brushing my hair, though I didn't know where she got the brush from. Her humming filled the room along with the melody of the record.

"It's so cold." I pulled my robe tighter, hunching over to hide exposed skin.

"It gets that way sometimes," she cooed between melodic phrases.

"I'm bleeding," I reminded her.

"We do that sometimes." She set the brush down and laid her long fingers over the wound. With an odd pinching sensation, I felt the skin of my scalp tighten and reform. Suddenly, the pressure in my skull lifted. "All better." She concluded her work with a kiss on the top of my head.

"What do I do now?" I turned to face my ghostly mother, and she set a blood-soaked hand on my shoulder.

"It's nighttime." A sympathetic smile haunted her pale face. "It's time for you to come home."

CHAPTER TWENTY-SIX: THE WITCH'S SHACK

"It happened so fast," I heard Arnie explain, his voice tight with excitement. I began to stir, groggy from my stupor. "I didn't even really think about it." Gray light snuck in between the cracks of my eyelids.

"Let's just call it beginner's luck," Rae responded. The sound of his voice prompted me to open my eyes all the way and rejoin the world of the living. I let out a groan as I shifted my cramped legs.

"Hildy! Welcome back." Copper's relief was plastered across her face, which peered down at me from a close distance. Twisting my neck just enough to scan my surroundings, I saw that I was lying in the backseat of an automobile. My legs were a hair longer than the length of the seat, so they had been curled up somewhat unnaturally. My head was resting in Copper's warm lap, allowing for the pleasant view of her smile upon waking.

"Hildy's awake?" Rae asked anxiously, glancing over his shoulder from the driver's seat.

"How're you feeling, champ?" Arnie asked, his face coming into view as he craned his neck around the passenger's seat.

"Ouch," was all I could manage to croak, taking a full inventory of each unique ache across my body. There was a shower of relieved chuckles from the others. Copper leaned down and laid a kiss on my clammy forehead.

"You had us pretty terrified," she said with a soft sigh, stroking my hair like a concerned mother.

"We thought you were dead," Arnie said.

"For like two seconds," Copper defended, rushing to clarify, "just when we first found you."

"If I could make a request," Rae spoke up from the front seat, "I'd rather not have to find you unconscious in a pool of blood *ever* again. And also preferably not near any dead bodies. If that isn't too much to ask." His request was phrased lightly, but I could hear the deep trauma in his voice. I couldn't imagine the terror I would have felt if the roles had been reversed.

"Yup, I'll definitely work on that," I mumbled as I gripped the top of the backseat and tried to hoist myself up. Copper supported my back, guiding me to a seated position beside her. I reached for the throbbing spot on the back of my head and was surprised to feel only a sizable bump where the wound had been.

"Pretty freaky, right?" Copper asked, her brows raised high. "About an hour back, it just... healed up, all on its own." She raised her hands in the air as she shook her head, indicating she had nothing to do with it and had no answers to offer.

"I…" I tried to pull back my recent dream as it receded back into the subconscious void. "I dreamt about someone… Saying to come home…" I remembered a song playing, cold floors, and a brush running through my hair, followed by gentle fingers. She frowned, looking a little disappointed.

It hurt to concentrate on the vision, so I let the thought slide away as I scanned the exterior surroundings for context. "Where are we?"

"We're on the south side of Mount Tempus," Arnie said as he pointed out his window. "See?" I leaned over Copper to peer out. The sun had not yet risen in front of us, but a light gray glow illuminated the misty peaks of the mountains looming beyond. Snow-covered pine trees along the side of the road whipped past as we flew by. "We should be at Crescent Lake within the hour," he reported, as if this were the best news he'd heard that week.

"But who's—" I began, but Copper beat me to it.

"It's the watchmen's." She gave me one of her iconic grins. "The engine wasn't damaged in the crash, and our jalopy was fully out of commission."

"There also wasn't anyone in the service station," Rae added. "Just a jar and a sign that requested you pay for anything you took. There were parts and tools, but nothing I knew how to use. When the watchmen pulled in, I wasn't really sure what was going on, so I ducked down to wait and see the best way to intervene." He glanced at me through the rearview mirror, eyes apologetic.

"Couldn't have inserted yourself before Hildegarde cracked her head open?" Arnie asked snidely.

"Says the guy who was about to abandon me there," Raemond fired back.

"To be fair," Copper corrected with a raised finger, "we were all about to abandon you. Arnie wasn't alone in that." I tilted my head back to laugh, but then my head reminded me of the injury it had recently received, and so all I managed was a wince. The sun was rising over the horizon now, diffusing the gray with a soft yellow light. It was then that I saw the injuries all over Copper's face.

"What happened?" I grabbed her under the chin and turned her face to get the whole picture. Over her right eye, there was a thick gash cutting at an angle through her eyebrow. On the left side, her cheekbone was colored with a gruesome purple bruise.

"You should see the other guy," she responded with a defensive smile. I cocked my head in response, unsatisfied. Copper yielded. "Dex got a few good swings in is all."

"What happened to Dex?" I asked, straightening to look at each of them.

"Dex is dead," Rae answered without emotion, keeping his eyes fixed on the road. I inhaled with a small gasp and looked my friend.

"It was Arnie," she nodded, her eyes filled with something resembling pride. "He redirected one of Dex's arrows." I turned to gawk at him, but he offered nothing but a small shrug in return. "Turns out he can do a bit of decent evocation," Copper explained for him.

"I'd seen the spell in a book somewhere," he mumbled, looking uncomfortable at the praise. "It was a wild shot in the dark."

"Arnie, it takes an impressive amount of skill to enact that kind of spell," I said, voice full of awe. Raemond shifted uncomfortably in his seat, and I remembered the guilt on his face when he'd admitted to me his inability to perform wind manipulation.

"He did get a nosebleed from it," Raemond qualified, "but it *was* impressive. I arrived just in time to see it." He gave Arnie a small side smile.

"But right before you gave Dex his bow back," Copper needled, staring at the back of Rae's head.

"I didn't *give* Dex the bow," Rae snapped, the back of his ears turning pink.

"He took it pretty easily," Arnie said, joining in the teasing.

"The guy was built like a tree," Rae began to protest, but then he calmed himself with a deep breath. "Semantics aside, Arnie saved us all back there. He killed the guy."

"Are you… okay?" I asked softly, leaning forward to put a hand on Arnie's shoulder. My own memory of Beau slamming down onto the ground filled me with a hot and twisting sense of anxiety that I couldn't name.

"It was him or us," he answered simply. "It's funny, we learned all about our civil liberties and search and seizure rights in civics class, but those two barely seemed interested in bringing us in alive. I'm sure the reality of it all will hit me harder later, and I'll likely be reliving it for a while, but for now I feel okay." He looked back at me, nodding, and I gave his shoulder a squeeze before pulling my hand back.

There was a long minute of silence in the car. I couldn't help suddenly scoffing and said, "This is all just absurd. The three of us left home for a simple road trip less than a month ago, and now we each have a body count."

"I haven't killed anyone," Copper protested, almost disappointed.

"Gotta catch up," I chuckled.

"That's not funny," Rae said, looking concerned by our callousness.

I bit down on my lip, knowing I wasn't behaving like myself. "I think I'm still in shock."

"What happened with Beau?" Copper asked, meeting my gaze with concern.

I cast back to try and figure out where to start, and anger flared as I remembered. "You mean after Rae left me frozen to the ground?" Rae began to defend himself, but I cut him off to share the whole tale. I skimmed over my escaping the ice restraints, then explained all the details of Beauregarde's attack, taunts, and then his demise at my hands. The only things I excluded were how I had melted the ice without an incantation and the confession of my name to Beauregarde. Once the tale was done, Copper shook her head in amazement.

"I would have given so much money to see the look on Beau's face when you cast that spell," she said, beaming at me.

"That was pretty great," I agreed, remembering the fiery pride that had filled me in that moment. "The rest of it…" My voice caught as the wet cracking sound of Beau's body echoed through my mind.

"We're alive," Rae said, breaking the silence. "That's what matters now." Copper took my hand in hers and gave it a firm squeeze. Feeling overwhelmed with it all, I leaned over to rest my head on her waiting shoulder. Outside, the sun had now become visible above the eastern tree line. Its warm light speckled the tops of evergreens that spread across the distance as far as the eye could see. We all fell silent as Crescent Lake came into view, the hypnotic pattern of sparkling sunlight rippling over the dark reflections of the trees along the shoreline. We directed Rae per Haute's directions, and he soon turned off onto an unkempt road that followed the edge of the lake to its southern end.

After another hour or so of rocky travel, the trees along the shore turned from coniferous pines to deciduous oaks and walnuts. The snow thinned as the foliage grew lusher, indicating that we had entered a region back under weather control magic. The shore curved around a grassy bend, and a small shack came into view. It sat amidst a dense sea of tall, leafy trees, alone on what was nearly an island except for a thin strip of land cutting through the water. The mini peninsula was bare save for two things: the house itself and the solitary pine it sat underneath.

"That must be the place," I said as Rae brought the automobile to a stop in the tall grass. Around the lakeshore, there wasn't a single flake of snow. The thick display of leaves that each tree boasted defied the current season. It was common knowledge that the leaves of the Thorough Woods never fall. As I stepped from the vehicle and onto my sore and stiff legs, I noted the new weather; it was a chilly morning air, filled with a moisture that made it almost muggy, like after a rainfall in early spring. Robins and swallows chirped and sang in the tree branches around us, waking to the new day.

We traversed the pathway leading up to the homestead, which turned out to have paved stones leading to it. The tall grass growing along the sides brushed against my legs, leaving my pants damp. Near the end of the path, there was a crudely painted sign that had been stuck into the earth that read *Fresh Eggs for Sale*.

"Anyone fancy an omelet?" Arnie asked, grinning.

"Don't talk to me about food," I groaned, the empty pit of my stomach rumbling in protest. Rae reached for my hand and wrapped it in his. The house was a single story and a simple square design, boasting no wings or extensions. The wood paneling had been painted a deep red at some point, but it was now weathered and chipped from the wind and spray coming off the lake. The roof was missing a few of its dark shingles, and it sloped up at a steep incline, meeting at the peak to form an acute angle.

"Should we just knock?" Copper asked as we all crowded wearily on the small stoop.

"Is there a password or something?" Rae inquired, not having been filled in on Haute's instructions.

"No," Arnie said as he rolled his eyes. "This isn't some cheap mystery novel."

"Well, seeing as how this little ole trip became deadly, excuse me for thinking there might be some security at the safe house," Rae retorted.

"Oh for heaven's sake, you two." I dropped Raemond's hand and knocked on the door three times. A loud thump, and then a cacophony of metallic clangs sounded from within.

"Damnit," a muffled voice cried over the cascading metal. "Hold on!" The noises came to a stop, and wood creaked as a person made their way to the door. Suddenly, a little wooden hatch at eye level on the door slid open. "State your purpose." Two wild eyes peered out at us.

"Uh…" I wasn't certain how to proceed. This is where Haute's directions had ended.

"Are you here for eggs?" the voice asked hopefully, sounding female. I fished through the pocket of my shoulder bag.

"No," I responded as my fingers located the smooth metal object. "We're here for this." I brought the coin up for the disembodied eyes to see. The hatch slid shut, and several locks unclicked behind the door before it swung open to reveal an elderly witch. Her long, white hair was as wild as her wrinkled eyes.

"In with you then." She pulled the door open further and ushered us in with a frail little arm. We did as we were told and entered the shabby house. The home consisted of a single, incredibly messy room. Cluttered shelves and crates filled with dusty jars and salvaged trinkets jutted out from the peeling walls. A small kitchenette was situated in the back left corner with several piles of unwashed plates. A collection of gears and hinges had been spilled across the floor, spreading from an overturned box that lay beside an unmade bed.

However, most noticeable were the stacks and stacks of egg crates scattered about, sitting on almost every available surface. "I don't know how I am ever going to unload all of these damned eggs," the witch mumbled as she closed the door behind us. She secured the column of numerous locks and deadbolts with practiced ease. "No one ever comes to buy them."

"I didn't see any chickens outside," Copper remarked, inspecting the towers of packed egg crates.

"I didn't say they were chicken eggs," she snapped, then turned to walk farther into the house without further elaboration. She wore a faded housecoat that hung like a sack around her tiny frame. She could not have been more than five feet tall, even wearing her heavily padded slippers. Her face was small, all but lost in the folds of her deep wrinkles. A pair of thick, round glasses magnified her manic eyes. "Names," she demanded as she shuffled over to a desk concealed under a mountain of loose papers.

"I'm Hildegarde," I declared, relieved to take ownership of my name again. "This is Copper, Arnold, and Raemond." I motioned to each of them accordingly. The witch scribbled the names down on a clipboard she had excavated from the pile. "What's your name?" I asked politely.

"That's classified," she barked without looking up. "And you're seeking transport beyond the border, yes?" she asked as she continued to scribble.

"We are," Arnie answered, "To take shelter with the widows that live there," he clarified, looking at her disorganized desk dubiously.

"And so you're in some kind of trouble, then," she said, as if it were an already answered question. She peered over her glasses with accusing eyes.

"Yes, ma'am," he responded quietly.

"And what would that entail?" she inquired, not breaking eye contact. Arnie looked to Copper for guidance.

"Our mothers were members of the Sisterhood," Copper answered, motioning to the two of us. "We were trying to find some answers, and… we ended up involved in some violence," she said diplomatically.

"You're not getting arrested," the witch said, looking irritated by the vague answer. "I don't need names, but I need a clear list of offenses for our records." I looked at everyone in our group as I mentally tried to form an acceptable list.

Raemond spoke up this time. "To start, transporting magical contraband across territory lines." He began to tick things off his fingers. "Unlicensed use of evocation and conjuration, utilization of toxic substances for the purpose of bodily harm and coercion, the deployment of glamours to sneak into a government event, the solicitation and trade of classified information, two counts of murder, and three uses of unlicensed and unregulated high sorcery." That got the witch to pause, her hand frozen over her clipboard as she blinked at us in amazement.

"Oh," I added, "and two counts of stealing automobiles." The old woman stared us down for several seconds before checking several boxes on her form.

"Okay then." She set the clipboard back on the desk, clicking her pen shut with a flourish. "Let's get you folks out of the country before they hang you. I'll need to see each of your coins." Copper and Arnie fished theirs out of their pockets and presented them to the waiting witch. She then looked at Raemond expectantly. "And for the soldier?" she inquired.

"I don't have one," Rae admitted. "I joined up with them after they were given coins." The witch arched a single brow.

"But he can be trusted," Copper jumped in. "We're all together, *and* he's Hildegarde's fiancé." The witch didn't say anything, and Copper added, "Plus… you heard the list." The woman took in the sight of his blood-stained, formal uniform.

"I can send you through," she said, softening a bit, "but I can't promise they'll let him stay."

"That's fine with me," Rae replied in a rush, relief filling his voice. "We'll cross that bridge when we come to it." He reached once more for my hand, but I avoided it.

"Well, that's settled then." The witch clapped once as she moved to a small door on the eastern wall. "It's going to take a few minutes to get this thing fired up," she said, fondly smacking the aged wooden door, "so make yourselves comfortable."

"Is that…" Copper began as she came up to inspect the door, eyes wide.

"An untethered corridor?" the witch finished the question for her. "Yep! Built it myself," she declared, her wrinkled face shifting from irritability to pride.

"I've never seen one before." Arnie followed his sister, equally interested in the rare artifact.

"Not many have," the witch said as she busied herself with gathering materials that appeared to belong to a large, bizarre doorknob. "It's part conjuration, part horology, and entirely illegal. It takes a lot of energy to keep it running, so I disable it between uses. You can watch the process if you like or take a walk along the lakeside. Take a sip if you do—the water is pristine. And help yourselves to an egg if you want. There's a bowl of boiled ones in the icebox." She punctuated her suggestions with cranks of a wrench. Arnie turned to look for the icebox, but Copper reached out and pinched his arm, shaking her head adamantly. I recalled the witch's vague mention of them not belonging to chickens and wholeheartedly agreed with Copper's command.

Arnie sighed, looking defeated. "I'll go get our bags."

"Rae?" I touched his shoulder. "Will you come take a walk with me?" Rae looked at me and nodded, eyes filled with concern. He offered his hand once more, and I took it, leading him out the door and toward the lakefront.

"Worried about leaving, huh?" Rae nudged, looking confident in his ability to read me.

"Yes," I agreed. That was true, to some degree. I watched the pebbles crunch and shift below my feet as we walked.

"You don't need to be." Raemond stopped and took both of my hands in his, bending down to redirect my gaze. "I'm going to be with you every step of the way. For as long as we're alive." I could see the love and sincerity in them—it was the same look he'd had when we stood beside Crystal Lake and he asked for a lifetime by my side. The parallel between the two moments ripped at my heartstrings. I took a deep breath, hardening myself for what I was about to say.

"No, you won't," I whispered, forcing myself to maintain eye contact. I pushed through, making my voice louder and assured. "You can't come with us. You have to go back, and I need to go forward." The words seemed to ring in the silence as I watched the heart of the man I loved break before my eyes.

CHAPTER TWENTY-SEVEN: THE WITCH'S PARTING

"What are you talking about?" Rae stammered, his eyes filling with disbelief. "I'm not going anywhere."

"Yes, you are." I held my ground, finding resilience in the confidence that I was making the right choice. "You're going back to Camp Valiant and you're going to become the most honorable King's Man the Green Veil has ever seen." Despite my assuredness, tears began to well up in my eyes.

"No, I'm not," Rae insisted, squeezing my hands till they hurt. "You don't get to decide that for me." I could hear him trying to suppress his anger.

"Like how you decided for me when you froze me to the ground back there?" I pressed, pulling my hands out of his. The contact was sending cracks through my determination.

"That was wrong of me," Rae defended, his voice quavering. "I shouldn't have done it."

"You don't really think that," I countered. "I know you too well. You would have chained me to that jalopy and thrown away the key if that's what you thought would keep me safe." I stopped myself and took a breath before continuing. "I was angry when you did it, but now I understand, because I will drown myself in that lake before I let you follow us into a life of exile."

"I would follow you into any life," Rae cried, outrage leaking through. "I can't believe you think I wouldn't!"

"So you're allowed to protect me, but I'm not allowed to protect you?" I demanded, my own voice rising as I stepped back from our intimate stance.

"I'm already involved," Rae argued, switching tactics.

"Copper, Arnie, and I have been living and breathing this world for weeks, and you fell into this yesterday," I said in quick dismissal. Rae scoffed, running a trembling hand through his hair, but I pressed on. "There is no one living who saw you with us in Umbra. You can go back to Camp Valiant at the end of Yuletime like nothing ever happened."

"Like nothing ever happened?!" He gaped at my words. "You, my fiancée, are fleeing the country to escape this government, and yet you want me to go serve in the military that's hunting you?" I watched him clench and unclench his jaw.

"That's exactly what I want you to do," I said, my voice evening out. "You know what's really happening in the Green Veil. You can do more good from within than we'll ever do from without."

"*Without* is the keyword there," Rae said, coming to stand closer to me as he pleaded, "You're asking me to live a life without you." His anger softened. "I have no plans of doing that, not ever. That's why I asked you to be my wife."

"I can't be your wife!" I exclaimed, all the air rushing out of me. My tears began to fall the moment the words left my mouth. Rae looked at me as if I had sunk a knife in his chest. I forced myself onward, each word more excruciating than the last. "I can't go back to how things were before. I can't wish away what I know now. I can't be a wife to you, or to anyone." I closed my eyes and took a long, shaky breath in through my nose. When I opened them again, I saw that I wasn't the only one crying.

"Hildegarde," Rae breathed, "I love you." His voice caught in his throat. "I love you more than anyone or anything in my life." His eyes bore into mine. A lifetime of love and friendship flooded my chest, and I had to fight back a sob.

"My father loved my mother," I whispered, spilling what had been haunting me ever since we left Haute. "Everyone said so. Even when Irenee spoke of all his faults, even when Haute told me what he did, no one has ever denied that he loved her. And she loved him. So they bet on a life together, and they failed. Love failed, because it wasn't really there. It was an illusion, just like the controlling duty of family and child-rearing and any of the other lies they've been telling us so that we remain under the heel of their boots. The Green Veil took love, real love, away from girls like me when they convinced us we were inferior. My father's life was smaller than my mother's, and it tortured him. She had talent and potential and all he had was an illusion of superiority. That false belief was like a weapon, a dagger—he used it to maintain control because *he thought* that was right, in the end. He took my mother from me because he could. You can't love someone while keeping them in check with a blade to their back. And you can't love someone who is holding a knife against you."

I paused to wipe tears from my face, and Rae remained mercifully silent. "If I married you, no matter how happy we were, no matter how long we'd be together, I would spend my life waiting for you to pull that knife. So I have to go, and you have to stay. And that way we can both work toward a world where we can meet again as equals and share a life. A world we could give to our daughters without fear." Having finally unburdened the harrowing thoughts that had been weighing on my heart for some time, I gave myself over to sobbing. Raemond gathered me into his arms and pulled me to his chest. I buried myself in the comfort of his embrace, and the two of us stood that way for a good while, holding each other and mourning the loss of the life we'd both envisioned.

"Is there anything I can say?" Rae breathed into my ear. "Anything I can do to change this?" His voice was heavy with sorrow. I shook my head against his chest. He exhaled, and we stood there in silence longer, listening to the jarringly cheerful calls of morning birds all around us.

"Then what if we just stay here? At this spot, holding each other until we die of starvation?" he asked, attempting to inject some humor into his voice. I gave him a half-hearted chuckle before loosening my grip and stepping away. I reached below the neckline of my collar and pulled out my ring, still hanging safely on its delicate chain.

"I think I should give this back," I choked.

"Don't you dare," Rae said abruptly. "It's yours. I'd never use it for anyone else." He gathered my hand in his and closed it around the ring. "I want you to keep it as a promise—a promise that I will spend the rest of my life building that world. The one where you can live freely so that I can love you freely."

He lowered his head to press his lips against my curled hand. When he looked up, I gripped his face with both hands and pulled him in, bringing my lips to his in desperation. He entwined his fingers in my hair and held me against him as if the wind threatened to carry me away. Our tears mingled and blurred as we fought to freeze the moment in time, both actively and for memory. Then the time came, and Rae pulled away, but only far enough to speak.

"I meant what I said at graduation," he whispered. "I will come back to you. Every time." With that, he detached himself from me and turned on his heel, clenching both hands behind his head as he walked to the watchmen's automobile. The loss of his warmth was agonizing.

I watched as he slid into the driver's seat, my heart thumping in my ribcage. In a moment of weakness, I sprinted after him, trying to savor the last few moments when he was still in view. I had nearly reached him when the engine kicked on. Hearing the car, Arnie and Copper ran out of the house. I was standing only a few yards from the vehicle when Raemond turned to look at me. I racked my mind for something to say, some parting words that would convince us it wasn't the end, but nothing came. I raised a hand and did the only thing I could—I waved goodbye as the man I loved drove away.

"Where's he going?" Arnie demanded, running to my side. Copper reached us a second later and studied my tear-stained face.

"He's leaving," she concluded, watching for my response.

"He's dropping the knife," I gasped out as the tears continued to flow. Copper draped an arm around me, not asking for further explanation. I embraced the invitation to cry into her shoulder. Arnie stood in disbelief, watching the dust billow around the automobile until it vanished in the distance; for once, he had the sense not to say anything.

"Corridor's up and running!" the old witch called from the front step, either oblivious or apathetic to the moment. "Let's get a move on." She motioned for us to come in before retreating back into the shack.

Copper rubbed my back soothingly. "You ready for this?" she asked softly. I took a deep breath to collect myself, dried my eyes on the sleeve of my sweater, and looked back at her.

"I hope so," I answered. She linked arms with me, and Arnie walked over to stretch his arm awkwardly around both of us. Together, we started back for the house.

"I'm going to be the first person I know to leave the Green Veil," Arnie remarked, doing his best to bring some levity to the moment.

"Not if I go through first," I retorted, happy to take the bait. Copper half-pulled her arm out of mine to position herself so she could take off sprinting at any second.

Arnie waved her down and smiled at me. "You know what, Hildy? You deserve the honor." He offered his arm as if we were at a formal dance, and I accepted with gratitude.

A crystal-clear memory popped into my head. The three of us were all still in primary school, and it was one of those odd days when Raemond hadn't been allowed out to play due to bad behavior or poor grades, so we'd invited little Copper to join us. We were all playing pirates in the lake, to the point that our fingers were pruney and our teeth chattered. The memory brought a much-needed smile to my face as we arrived at the house arm-in-arm.

The magical door looked the same as when I had last seen it save for the ornate knob, which was pulsing with a faint yellow aura. In the silence of the room, I could hear a steady humming emanating from the doorway.

"Just step on through," the witch prompted without much gravitas. "It knows where you're going." We looked at each other nervously as we gathered our bags.

"What does it feel like?" I asked once my brew box was safely secured over my shoulder.

"Let me think," the witch said, pursing her lips as she stroked her chin. "It feels sort of like walking through a gap in the matter of the universe." Her voice dripped with annoyance, and she rolled her eyes. "Just go already."

"Thank you for your help," Copper offered as a way of an apology.

"Yeah, whatever. Send me a card from the sanctuary." She shuffled off to the kitchenette and began washing her dishes, making it clear that she would not be holding our hands any longer. We approached the doorway.

"After you," Arnie said, motioning to me. I reached for the knob, which buzzed with a static energy when I touched it. I turned it with conviction, opening the door to reveal a wall of the same yellow light that surrounded the knob. It was the color I imagined the sun would be if you could get a good look at it. I took a deep breath and stepped through the doorway, out of the Green Veil.

A warm, calming sensation rushed over me, feeling rather like I was slipping into a hot bath on a winter night. All I could see was the bright yellow light surrounding me as I took a few slow steps forward. My legs moved as if they were pushing through a pool of honey. With each step, my legs began to regain their former speed, and other blurry colors began to filter through the yellow light. Greens and blues circled above, and shades of brown appeared below. Walking faster now, the light receded quickly, and the colors started to take the form of sky, trees, and mossy ground. A gust of chilly air whipped through the warm stupor, and I shut my eyes to shield them from the sudden cold.

I opened them to the morning sun's light peeking through an ocean of big, beautiful trees with roots the width of grown men and trunks reaching up higher than the tallest tower of the Citadel. Bird song echoed through the perfect silence of the forest, which was only disturbed by the crunching of leaves as Arnie and Copper joined me in the grove. I turned to face my friends and was pleased to see their faces reflected precisely what I was feeling— unbridled bewilderment. Looking at each other, our shocked expressions collectively morphed into perplexed smiles, and then to flustered laughter.

"Quick, Hildegarde," Arnie exclaimed between giggles of relief, "do something illegal. Just for fun."

A branch cracked behind us, and we all whipped around to see who or what it was.

"Good morning," came an airy voice. A tall, natural-looking witch in a loose, linen dress stood at the mouth of the clearing, her hand raised in a friendly wave. I timidly raised a hand to wave back at the woman.

"Hello," I replied. "We just arrived. We came from the shack where the, um, classified witch lives…" I said, unsure how best to describe the grumpy old lady.

"Oh, Elsbeth?" the woman said, striding over to us. "She's no secret—just a pain." Looking entirely unfazed by our arrival, she was sipping a steaming liquid from the ceramic cup she was carrying with her. "I'm Lorna Beech." She extended her empty hand and shook each of ours in rapid succession. "You three look like you could use some breakfast."

Lorna led us along a gently worn path through the forest, asking light questions about the weather, what we'd brought with us, and where we were from. I was grateful not to have to answer any hard or complicated questions. I felt as if I had reached an emotional overload for the day, and the sun had barely risen.

"Our inventory may not be the most luxurious," Lorna continued, explaining what they had in the way of toiletries and other comforts, "but we have the necessities to get by with." She had a beautiful smile, warm and accessible, like you'd hope a mother to have. It was hard to tell her exact age; she had the subtle grace of an older woman but the spark and physical ease of a younger one. Her curly black hair had some gray in it, and yet her smooth, dark skin was hardly wrinkled at all. I could only guess she was somewhere in either her forties or fifties. She wore a pair of brown, practical trousers and a somewhat worn, double-breasted jacket in a faded green tartan. Atop her head of natural ringlets was a blue wool knit cap that squashed down her voluminous hair.

"Anyway, you'll have to judge our accommodations for yourself." She ducked under a low-hanging branch and led us to another clearing. "Welcome to the Willows."

The clearing opened on a wide stretch of grass with a single willow tree standing at its center. By normal standards, the willow tree was huge, but it was dwarfed by the other trees that surrounded the open area, not unlike the others we had seen since arriving. However, these trees held homes and decks built high up in their branches, connected by ladders and rope bridges. An entire community bustled above us, people just beginning their day. Women with hair hanging loose sat out on their porches, their figures outlined by the sky, sipping their morning coffees and calling greetings to each other from across the glen.

"How many of you are there?" I gaped, straining my neck to take it all in.

"In terms of actual widows?" Lorna asked. "Of the women who came here to study and live freely, there are about twenty of us. In terms of refugees like yourselves, that number is somewhere around a hundred now."

"One hundred?" Arnie responded in awe. "All here because of the Sisterhood?"

"Oh no," Lorna said, brushing off the assumption with a sip of her tea. "People come to us for all sorts of reasons. We have unwed mothers, whistleblowers, people who wish to be free to love whomever they choose, military deserters—really, anyone who was being failed by the laws and institutions of the Green Veil." The scale of this organization caught me completely off guard.

"I had no idea there were so many…" Copper searched for the right word.

"Outcasts?" Lorna filled in. "The Veil does an excellent job of hiding them, both from you and from each other." Lorna clasped her cup with both hands for a moment. "But not here." She held her chin up as she said, "Here we get to look each other in the eye."

She nodded for us to follow as she stepped on a wooden platform at the base of a thick tree trunk. Once we were all on board, she stomped her foot twice and the platform began to slowly rise up the side of the tree. As we neared the canopy, the staggering beauty of the great expanse of treetops came into view. There was no end in sight—just a sea of rustling, green foliage.

"How far out in the Thorough Woods are we?" I asked, gazing out into the leafy abyss.

"That I can't tell you," she responded apologetically. "We don't want anyone to be able to find us on foot. Elsbeth's is the only door—the only known way in or out. It's safest that way." The platform slowed as it reached its destination.

"Here we are!" She stepped expertly off the platform and onto the waiting veranda. "Your new home sweet home." She motioned to the snug little treehouse behind her. It was constructed only with natural wood, and it had not been painted. It was, however, colored in green from the moss and ivy that draped over its walls. "It may be a bit snug at first, but we'll get Hildegarde her own place soon enough. I do hope you Pennings are comfortable sharing a room." All three of us halted, picking up on the red flag immediately.

"We didn't tell you our names," I said, trepidation filling me. Lorna offered a bashful smile.

"You didn't have to. I actually met you all when you were no higher than my knee." She smiled as she recalled the memory. "I knew your mothers, both Maude and Ruth." My heart raced in my chest.

"Is she here?" I stepped toward her, now eager to move forward. "Do you know where I can find her?"

Lorna's smile faded. "Oh, honey…" She placed a soft hand on my cheek. "Your mother is dead."

Chapter Twenty-Eight: The Witch's Vow

The first couple days at the Willows were dark. Lorna's devastating news had rocked me to my core. This whole journey I had been piecing together all the missing information surrounding my mother, coming to understand and value who she was, and then, right as I thought I was going to fill the final hole, it was all obliterated.

As Copper and Arnie settled into our new home, I took to long walks in solitude and nights spent alone on the front deck. The two gave me plenty of space, interfering only to remind me to eat and sleep, both of which I was skipping.

That first day, Lorna had divulged everything she knew about the events leading to my mother's death. According to her, there was once a different sanctuary community across the northern border, inside the former country of the Ridgebacks. That information was a shock to me. From what we had all been taught, the ruins of the Ridgebacks were nearly uninhabitable, populated only with small factions of surviving radicals attempting to carry on with the war.

Lorna confessed that her knowledge of the region was sorely lacking, as she had never visited the other community, but she understood it to be much smaller than theirs and made up of less-than-reputable characters. Shortly after her arrival in the Willows, Maude had left for the northern sanctuary with a small band of military deserters who were convinced there were some powerful magical forces to be harnessed beyond the border. Lorna said she had begged Maude not to join them, fearful of the stories she'd heard about blood magic and necromancy being used by the people gathered there, but Maude dismissed her out of hand, vowing she would return after learning what existed out there.

But she never did return, and shortly thereafter, Lorna received word of what she had feared the most—a military strike on the Ridgeback community, no survivors.

As crestfallen as I was, I wasn't surprised. With all the stories I had learned since Irenee had sat me down, all the insights on my mother's pain and sacrifices I had gained on the journey, I had started to believe that Maude was more than my self-formed image of a selfish risk-taker who had abandoned her child all those years ago. But dying amongst a band of radicals in the search for greater power, without friends or family at her side, perfectly fit the updated picture of Maude that I had built: self-serving and reckless. I had the answers I'd set out to find, but the path before me had never been less clear.

Another sunset came as uneventfully as the others, the third sleepless night I had spent in this strange place. In the darkness of the forest, haunting and beautiful sounds echoed through the trees. I wondered absently whether the croaking came from tree frogs or restless spirits of the fae—in a place such as this, there was really no way of knowing. I sat on the wooden deck that held our adopted home aloft, my feet dangling off the edge and into the void of black below me.

"Hey stranger," Arnie called, lowering himself to sit at my side, straining to position his inflexible legs under the rail as I had.

"Hi Arnie." I stared forward. It had not been my intention to worry him or Copper these past few days, but I knew it had still resulted, and I didn't have the energy to fix it.

"Lorna wanted me to invite you to dinner tonight," he said, getting straight to the point. "She's having a few friends over to her place as a soft welcome for us."

"I think I'll sit this one out," I answered meekly, swinging my legs in the cool night air.

"Yeah." Arnie lounged back, balancing his weight on his hands. "When I lost my mom, I started sitting out a lot of things." He spoke with quiet honesty. "A world was busy happening without me while I stewed in it. Copper cried for a week, and then she made the brave choice to keep on living. You and Raemond grew up, started figuring out what your futures would be. You even went and got engaged. All the while, I sat in my room and watched. I thought I was grieving—that retreat was my way of coping—but I was wrong. I wasn't a man coming to terms with death. I was a boy hiding beneath the covers so I wouldn't have to face the monsters that lurked in the shadows. I didn't confront what had happened—I cowered." I looked at him for the first time since he had sat down.

"Are you saying I'm cowering?" I asked, a wave of indignation rising up and crashing into a wave of relief at being understood.

"You never cried," Arnie said instead of answering. "You were told that your mother has been dead for ten years, and you never shed a tear." He spoke without judgment; it was more like analytical interest.

"I did cry," I admitted. "Ten years ago, when she left. I cried for as long as my body would let me." I shook my head. "I haven't had a mother in ten years, so it hasn't been particularly instinctive to mourn someone I don't even miss anymore." The confession was uncomfortable and shameful. "I'm not grieving my mother anymore—I've already done that. I guess it's more that I'm grieving an idea. One that I had been foolish enough to construct over the course of our trip. I let myself get so fixated on an image of reuniting with this woman I'd hardly known and having her be proud of me. Of getting back the mother I'd been wishing for. One who would praise my accomplishments and weep for my sacrifices. But she isn't here. Not to be proud of me, or ridicule me, or even ignore me—she was never waiting since the beginning. I've been chasing a ghost, and it sent me running from the life I'd chosen. I'm not mourning her. I'm mourning… everything else." Arnie stared back at me with a softness and wisdom I'd never seen in him before.

"I'm not," he declared. "If someone had stopped me on that train platform in the Orchard and told me that we would end up here, in a treehouse, with our lives turned over and nothing to show for the trouble, I'd do it all again. Because they would also have told me that alongside all the tragedy and lies and humiliation, I would find my sister again, a person I've never known as well as I should, and someone that is well worth knowing. They'd tell me that I'd be tested and learn that I'm a better man than I thought I could be, one who can look at a world rigged in his favor and still want to fix it. They'd tell me that I'm no high sorcerer, but that I had promise as a conjurer or evoker."

He paused to look up at the twinkling sky, nothing inhibiting the expansive view. He continued, speaking up to the stars, "Any of those things would have made it worth the trouble. But if all they'd told me was that I'd get you back, the best friend I've ever had, one who I was dumb enough to push away, nothing else would have mattered. I would've gotten on that train without a second thought." He turned to glance at me as surprise filled my face along with a warm smile. He added, "I never told you how much I missed you, but I did."

"I missed you, too." I reached over and placed my hand over his. "And I'm sorry. I should've fought harder for you, instead of letting you wallow."

Arnie raised his brows, and his lips curled up into a sly smile. "You see what I did there?"

Realizing how well he'd drawn me back out of myself, I chuckled in defeat. "I hate you," I teased.

He laughed as he stood. "No you don't." He offered his hand out. "Now come on, let's go get some dinner."

With an exasperated sigh, I reached out and let him pull me onto my feet. He steered me to Lorna's with his arm wrapped around my shoulder. When we entered the cozy, crowded dining room, Copper's face lit up with relief. She rushed over to hug me tightly and gushed about how glad she would be to see me eat something.

There were eight dinner guests in total. I sat between Copper and a young woman named June, a shy redhead in a baby blue dress. She introduced herself with the story of how she recently came to the Willows; having become pregnant when she was only sixteen, she'd been faced with the horrific consequences of conceiving a child outside of wedlock. I hadn't been aware that the punishment in the Green Veil could range from imprisonment to the forceful surrender of your baby. Because she had been unwilling to marry the feckless boy who had fathered the child, June had sought aid from a local healer. The woman had been a member of the Tangere faction of the sisterhood and helped connect her to the sanctuary.

Seated beside June was a scrawny man, nearing middle age, with patchy facial hair and kind eyes. His name was Chip, and he told a tale of disobeying a command to fire on a smuggling ship during his time in the Royal Navy. The ship was reported to be transporting black magic spell books from the ruins of the Ridgebacks. However, Chip had heard from folks outside the military say that such ships were being used to carry refugees of war who wished to escape the carnage of their homeland. He'd refused the command from his leading officer to fire without confirmation that there were no travelers below deck. His team bombed the ship anyway, and the next day he deserted his posting.

At one head of the table was a quiet, impossibly old witch. Everyone called her Nana, but she never spoke. She merely gazed across the table with thoughtful eyes. She emanated warmth as she supervised everyone gathered there, periodically bringing a spoonful of pumpkin soup to her lips with a tremorous hand.

Lorna explained that Nana had been one of the founders of the Willows. She had lost her husband to the Tri-Generation War only three weeks after marrying; she'd only been seventeen. In her grief, she left her home in the Thorough Woods and just started walking, living off the land as she searched for the forest's end. She never found it—nor did she keep track of how long and far she'd traveled— but instead she found these houses in the trees, worn from years of abandonment. She made them her new home, and as things in the Green Veil began to worsen, she welcomed others to join her.

When Lorna finished sharing Nana's story with me, she tore a hunk out of her bread and chewed it happily for a moment. Then, before she'd entirely finished eating it, her eyes lit up as she said, "You know, the fae used to live in these forests." June chuckled at her certainty.

"It's true!" Lorna huffed. "Before the race of man declared dominance over the natural world, the people of the forest lived here, watching over the balance of nature."

"So what happened to them?" Copper asked, humoring her. It felt like most of us at the table believed the fae were just an old wives' tale.

"We violated the natural world," Lorna intoned. "We bent the climate to our will, did away with storms and excessive cold, forced crops to grow at unnatural rates, and wiped out any species that threatened us. We destroyed the balance, and the fae couldn't survive the fallout. Why do you think people of the Green Veil live in such a tiny corner of the world? We're never taught about the rest—it's all kept off the maps and out of sight. Why? Because it didn't survive the catastrophic events of early man and is now uninhabitable. The Ridgebacks are a barren wasteland. Keep walking through these forests, away from the magics we wreaked, and you'll see the wildlife grow more dangerous and hostile.

"Did you know that entire landmasses were swallowed by the sea when we shifted the tides? The Green Veil is sitting on the last patch of inhabitable earth and acting like that was the plan all along!" As Lorna poured out her spiel, her outrage grew to where it was almost comedic. The others laughed it off, clearly having heard all this before.

"She always gets this way around newcomers," said the one remaining member of the dinner party that I hadn't been introduced to. She patted Lorna's back, shaking her head with humor and affection. Patricia had short, mousebrown hair, a round face, and kind eyes. When I'd arrived at the party, I could tell that she lived here with Lorna. Patricia then explained to me that Lorna had been the reason she'd come to the Willows.

Before Lorna's marriage to her late husband, Richard, the two of them had been girlhood friends. After coming to the Willows to join the community of widows who were working on progressing in their powerful magics, Lorna sent for Patricia, who had never married. Lorna had told her it would be a place where they could live freely as they were, which Patricia joked was infuriatingly vague. When she'd arrived, the two of them danced around their growing relationship for some time before coming out officially as a couple, encouraged by the safeness of the community.

A month ago I had never met a queer person, and now I knew three. Legally, it was a punishable offense. The stated purpose of the laws introduced in the aftermath of the war was to repopulate a stunted country and return to a peaceful "family-centric" life. Couples like Lorna and Patricia, as well as Haute and Philip, could not conceive children nor "raise them in a balanced home," according to the king.

Why this dynamic was so punishable still confused me, but as far as I could see, the two witches loved each other just as well as anyone else I knew, maybe better. As I thought it over, watching the two of them interact with each other in such knowing confidence, I felt something akin to jealousy. They understood each other in a way Rae and I never could.

There was something magical about the evening. I hardly spoke a word, but I ate the simple meal and found great fulfillment listening to the other guests. For the first time, I listened to folks who were considered outcasts speak honestly and freely, unrestricted by convention or the threat of being overheard. I knew that if I had wanted to, I could have stood on the table and declared myself a high sorcerer for all to hear, and no one would have scoffed or come after me. No one here would be afraid of my power or want to snuff out my light.

Of course, I did not stand on the table, and I did not declare my great power. Instead, I listened to Chip and Lorna debate the morality of war in heated voices, only to change the subject to her soup recipe a moment later. For the first time since tripping over the rug in my attic, I felt like I was allowed to breathe fully, to take off an invisible girdle I hadn't realized I'd been wearing.

The night rolled to a close after we finished off Patricia's mulberry pie. June hurried off to relieve her friend, who had agreed to watch her son for the evening. Chip offered us a cordial tip of his cap as he passed through the doorway, Nana on his arm as he escorted her back to her home. Patricia wrapped the remainder of the bread in cloth and insisted we take it with us. Lorna took me in her arms, embracing me with an affectionate intensity.

"My girl," she breathed into my hair, "I am so glad to have you here." She released me after several seconds. "It is better to live a simple, free life than one in a cage, no matter how ornamented it may be." She held me in front of her to give me a long, assessing stare before bidding fond farewells to the three of us.

Back in our own home, Copper opened a bottle of cherry wine that Lorna had gifted her on their first night, pouring each of us a drink in the unadorned, ceramic cups our house had come equipped with. My cot was currently set up in the main room until Lorna could arrange other accommodations, but I intended to tell her not to bother. I had no desire to live in my own space; besides, I'd become so accustomed to the unique snores of the Penning siblings that I almost couldn't fall asleep without their background noise.

"What do you think Dad is doing right now?" Copper asked with a slight smile.

"What he's always doing after dinner," Arnie said, looking amused at the image he had conjured in his head. "Listening to moonbroch commentary in his underwear." I laughed along with him. If Mr. Penning was anything, it was predictable.

Arnie shook his head and took a drink. "What would he think of all of this?"

"He'd be proud," Copper said resolutely. "If he knew what we were doing, he would be cheering us on." Arnie didn't say anything, but he nodded. I couldn't help but think of Irenee hunched over some project at her desk. I didn't have to guess whether or not she was proud of me.

"I've been so caught up in the day-to-day changes of our lives," I said as I sat on my cot, sipping from my cup, "that I forget something important." I put the cup down to unclasp the leather band of my watch, tossing it to Copper, who was sitting beside Arnie at the kitchen table. "Irenee gave that to me before I left the Orchard. Read the dials at the bottom."

Copper had to squint to make them out in the low light. "Two hundred ninety-one days, six hours, and forty-two seconds?" She looked at me for further context. "Until what?"

"Until I see Irenee again," I explained. A look of understanding filled their faces, followed by surprise as they thought through the magical complexity of the watch, impressed by what Irenee had created.

"She could end up coming here," Arnie pointed out. "She is a widow."

"I don't think so," I mused as I shook my head. "I can't explain it, but I've had this feeling in my gut all night. It's telling me that we don't stay here—that we'll go back." I sat forward, leaning on my knees.

"We have to," Copper stated, putting her mug down with certainty. Both Arnie and I perked up at her conviction, startled. "Think of everyone we met tonight. All those stories where exile was the best option. We got here thinking it was all about wives who had been denied an education because of the misfortune of being born a girl, and it still is, but there's so much more to it now. It's like what Lorna said—they kept us from seeing each other. It wasn't until we got here that I even considered all the other people who have been beaten down and degraded by these laws that claim to protect us. How many invisible communities are there that aren't even talking to each other, much less looking for one another? I'd wager enough to make an impact on how our country decides things," Copper concluded as Arnie exhaled, taking it all in.

He took a hearty swig from his cup. "We aren't going to make much impact hiding up in the branches," he said. I nodded in silent agreement. After a moment, I stood and crossed to the table, taking my watch from Copper's hand and securing it back on my wrist. With it back where it belonged, I reached into my pocket and wrapped my fingers around something small and warm.

"I want to ask one more thing of you two," I said, feeling the gravity of all my thoughts and decisions in my mind. "Heaven knows I've already asked more than anyone should, but just the same..." I held the silver coin up for them to see. "I want us to promise that when the time comes—when it makes sense and we have a plan—that we'll go back and do something about it." I set the coin on the table with a clang beneath my palm. "Quiet oppression requires silence. I say we make some noise." I looked at them expectantly, waiting for their response. After a quiet heartbeat, Copper's face filled with her all-too-familiar troublemaking grin, and she laid her hand on top of mine.

"Let's make some noise," she affirmed, beaming. We both looked to Arnie, who was leaning back in his chair.

"What the hell?" he smirked as he brought the chair legs down with a thump. He slapped his hand down on Copper's, laughing. She jerked her hand out with a sharp cry, but she was still smiling.

We embraced the excitable frenzy of the evening as we polished off the rest of the cherry wine, swapping memories from the road and tormenting each other with childhood embarrassments. I knew the morning would only bring more questions that I did not have answers to, but for now, we clung to the ecstatic hope formed from youthfulness and friendship. We shared the blind determination of ones who knew they could change the world.

I had tasted what it was like to not be limited by others, and I wasn't going back. In that room, floating in the branches of uncharted wilderness, supported by companions bound in trauma and trust, I felt the beginnings of our new life, unbound and untethered.

Epilogue: The Witch's Willow

Having celebrated Nana's latest, unnumbered birthday, my head pounded with the memory of last night's wine. Yet I had still forced myself up, promising myself that today would be the day I visited the great willow at the center of our community.

The early morning sunlight lit the soft, dewy blooms around me in a warm light, and a gentle wind caused the branches to billow around me. It felt like another world under the willow, one where grace and beauty predominated. Lorna had told each of us to pay the great tree a visit once we settled in. She claimed it was the oldest in the forest and, as she had put it, it "had some stories to tell."

Standing under it, unable to see anything else outside the tree, I didn't hear any stories. There was only the warbling dawn chorus of birds as they woke and took to the sky. I could tell it was going to be a spectacular day. The air was misty and not uncomfortably chilly—it carried the pleasant foreboding of an early spring. I'd noticed that whether or not it had rained, the forest here always smelled of wet earth, a constant reminder that we were no longer bound to greater civilization.

With a nostalgic glance at my watch, I wondered what Irenee was doing at this moment. She was likely still asleep. With me no longer there to wake her with the smell of a hot breakfast, she was undoubtedly sleeping through the army of useless alarm clocks she had constructed. I let the thought of home slip away, being wary not to dwell on my homesickness; I wanted to greet the feeling but then let it pass through me without lingering. I was thinking about venturing over to Lorna and Patricia's to see if they could spare a cup of coffee when a voice spoke from behind me.

"I should have known that you'd end up here," the graceful, feminine voice said. "I was always losing you in the trees." My heart stopped beating as I questioned whether or not I was truly awake. With shaking hands, I turned slowly to confirm the impossible figure that was standing before me.

"Mother?"

Acknowledgments

I started writing *The Sisterhood of Whispers* six years ago in a studio apartment in Asheville, North Carolina. However, what started as an entirely solitary endeavor has become anything but. There are countless people that I want to thank for helping me make this book a reality. I will almost certainly forget someone. If that person is you, I love you and I'm sorry.

First and foremost, I need to thank my amazing editor, Heather Ryder. She took a chance on me and held my hand through the scary process of killing (or occasionally sparing) my darlings. Without her, I would never have truly found Hildy's voice.

I am lucky to share my life with the greatest man in the world—Matthew St. Lawrence. He gave me half of my name and a whole new world. He is my greatest motivator and has boundless enthusiasm and support for all of my creative endeavors, even when it cuts into Thursday Night Date Night.

My first three readers were Morgan Fuller, Chella Anderson, and Emma Siplon. They put the gas in my tank that I needed to keep pushing through rejection and doubt.

I have to thank my parents, Susan and Jim, for just everything. There's no other way to put it.

But more than anyone, I am grateful to you, beautiful stranger, for staying with me for over three hundred pages. I love you more than you know.